MAXIM JAKUBOWSKI ... e
was born in the UK ... r
in book publishing, he opened the world-famous Murder One
bookshop in 1988 and has since combined running it with his
writing and editing career. He has edited a series of 15 best-
selling erotic anthologies and two books of erotic photography,
as well as many acclaimed crime collections. His novels include
It's You That I Want To Kiss, *Because She Thought She Loved
Me* and *On Tenderness Express*, all three recently collected and
reprinted in the USA as *Skin In Darkness*. Other books include
Life In The World of Women, *The State of Montana*, *Kiss Me
Sadly* and *Confessions Of A Romantic Pornographer*. In 2006 he
published a major erotic novel which he directed and on which
15 of the top erotic writers in the world have collaborated,
American Casanova, and his collected erotic short stories as
Fools For Lust. He is a winner of the Anthony and the Karel
Awards, a frequent TV and radio broadcaster, crime columnist
for the *Guardian* newspaper and Literary Director of London's
Crime Scene Festival.

THE MAMMOTH BOOK OF

Best
New Erotica

Volume 8

Edited and with an Introduction
by Maxim Jakubowski

ROBINSON

RUNNING PRESS
PHILADELPHIA · LONDON

Constable & Robinson Ltd
3 The Lanchesters
162 Fulham Palace Road
London W6 9ER
www.constablerobinson.com

First published in the UK by Robinson,
an imprint of Constable & Robinson, 2009

A copy of the British Library Cataloguing in Publication
Data is available from the British Library

UK ISBN 978-1-84529-881-4

1 3 5 7 9 10 8 6 4 2

First published in the United States in 2009 by Running Press Book Publishers
All rights reserved under the Pan-American and International Copyright Conventions

9 8 7 6 5 4 3 2 1
Digit on the right indicates the number of this printing

US Library of Congress number: 2008936667
US ISBN 978-0-76243-633-0

Running Press Book Publishers
2300 Chestnut Street
Philadelphia, PA 19103-4371

Visit us on the web!
www.runningpress.com

Printed and bound in the EU

Contents

Acknowledgments and Copyright

Introduction

Maxim Jakubowski

Another year for the *Mammoth Book of Best New Erotica*, and another batch of wondrous thrills, both sexual and intellectual as our roster of authors trip the light fantastic with yet more fevered imagination than ever before.

I began editing this series of anthologies in 1994 and, year after year, I keep on being surprised and amazed at how erotic writers keep on challenging assumptions and conjuring up further scenarios full of lust, love, desire, feelings, fire and ice. And, more often than not, all at the same time.

I have always believed strongly that even though the border-line between erotica and pornography is a movable one, not unlike a fine line drawn in the sand that shifts imperceptibly following every repeated assault by the ebb and flow of the waves, in these pages we have always managed to avoid the vulgarity that sometimes glorifying the senses can lead to. And I think the many readers who have followed on this journey agree with me. For, most of all, these are stories not just about enjoyment of the flesh, but featuring characters, male and female, and sometimes in between, with personalities with a complex web of relationships, however bizarre they might often appear to the untrained eye. Sex is one thing, but the human factor is as important when it comes to the heartfelt provocation of good erotic writing.

Many names will be familiar to readers of past volumes, but I am particularly proud this year that eighteen writers appear in the series for the first time, and that a growing cohort of male authors also provides evidence that sexual sensibility is not just the domain of female writers. In fact, there are seventeen such men: lest the adventurous and inquisitive among you identify them behind occasional pseudonyms and sexless initials – it's a larger number than in the majority of previous volumes.

In addition, the geographical spread of the stories goes well beyond our customary British, American and Canadian contributors, with tales reaching us from Australia, New Zealand, Thailand, Vietnam and Italy. Had we chosen to translate stories from other languages, the book would prove even more international. For fans of alien forms of sexual expression, I can direct you to the *Mammoth Book of International Erotica*, which is still in print after a decade and more.

If you are new to our anthology series, I urge you to overlook any prejudices you have about erotica. Here, you will find more than crude sexual hydraulics and paper-thin characterization in the service of the sexual act; more than man meets woman and they fall into bed scenarios; there are also well-written, challenging and profoundly humane stories. Our lives are, whether we like it or not, dictated by our sexuality and the wonderful storytellers assembled between these pages will excite you, intrigue you, even make you laugh or, in some instances, cry. I hope you enjoy this latest adventure into the extreme depths of the human heart and body; this is erotica at its very best, culled from hundreds of magazines, books and publications, as well as from the Internet. Prepare for a festival of the senses!

Maxim Jakubowski

The Slave

Julia Morizawa

Scott ran his fingers through my hair and told me I was beautiful. When he said it, he looked me straight in the eyes. He wouldn't look away until I gave him a response. I knew this, so I stared right back. I took in every detail of his eyes so I would never forget the power behind them. The color, a blue so magical, as if the ocean and the sky had blended together after a storm. The shape, deep and wide, like the comforting shelter of a mother's womb. I took in his long, feminine lashes and his perfectly arched brows. I could see his honesty, his passion, and a mysterious history that held years of unrevealed struggle. When my observations caused an intense fluttering sensation in my stomach, I finally turned up the corners of my mouth, ever so slightly, and said, "Thank you."

I often wished that Scott and I were the type of people who could fall in love. The type of people who weren't afraid to do so. But to him, I was just a girl, and he was looking for a woman whom he could marry. And to me, he was just a home away from home. A comfortable set of arms that held me so much tighter than my boyfriend's. And both of us just wanted to hold on because it was a place of stability outside of our everyday hectic and unhappy lives.

My response made him blush. He gently pulled me toward him and kissed me on the forehead. The kind of kiss a father gives to his young daughter at bedtime. Scott was sitting in his thinking chair, an antique coated in burgundy velvet that could have easily belonged in a Charlotte Brontë novel. I'm sure the chair had experienced a lot of skin. A lot of body fluids and heavy breathing. That's why I liked it so much. It was a great piece of furniture to have sex on.

I was straddling him and my knees had begun to get sore. I adjusted my body so I was sitting in his lap, my legs dangling over one arm of the chair and my head resting against the other. I pressed my ass hard against his crotch before settling down.

"Where's your boyfriend?" he asked.

"I don't know."

"He sounds like an asshole."

I didn't reply. My boyfriend wasn't an asshole. In fact, no man had ever treated me better than he did. But we bored each other.

I focused my attention on a tall, thin bong centered on his dresser. It was a blood red color with Japanese letters made of silver etched in the side. I didn't know what it said, but probably something about peace or unity. It matched the fresh red paint on the walls. It matched the red silk pillows on his bed. It matched the red beads hanging from the door frame. Everything matched. It was almost suffocating.

"What are you thinking about?" Scott interrupted my silence.

"Nothing," I whispered.

"Don't lie."

I thought about it for a moment. I thought about the red, the suffocation, the way I felt with him.

"Life," I finally concluded.

"What about it?"

"I don't know."

He leaned into me as if he were going to whisper something in my ear. Instead, he kissed the top part of it, then slowly ran the tip of his tongue around the outside, and eventually bit the lobe around my earring. He leaned back. I could feel his stare, could sense he was about to say something else, so I turned to face him.

"I love the way you look when you're thinking hard about something."

Scott and I met at a Fourth of July barbeque. I went to see some acquaintances that I hadn't spoken to in a while. My acquaintances were Scott's closest friends. I immediately went to the bar and he was there pouring drinks for others. He was the type of man who looked best tired and messy. I watched his light curls brush the crease in his forehead every time he looked down. I watched his pink lips purse to the side every time he searched for a specific drink on the table. I was hypnotized by those lips. They looked as if they could never tell a lie. Or never tell a joke. He glanced up and caught me watching him. He offered to pour me a drink.

"What are you having?" I asked.

"Diet Coke," he replied. "I don't drink alcohol."

"Good for you. I could go for a screwdriver."

He smiled, made me the drink, and handed it to me. When our fingers touched in the passing of the glass, the area between my thighs began to throb. We didn't separate from each other the rest of the night. We talked about everything, from the weather, to the party, to our jobs, to politics, to God. We stood on the hillside together to watch the fireworks above the river. Once the show was over, most people left or went back down to the house for more drinks and small talk. We stayed. We lay down on an open patch of grass and shared a joint. We kept a look-out for shooting stars. The lights from the city illuminated the horizon. The shadowed blend and repetition of the trees around us faintly resembled a Warhol installment. Without the shimmering stars, the smooth, black sky could have easily been mistaken for water. Occasionally, the sound of a passing car below us or erupted laughter from the party echoed against the grass. But the sounds of our peaceful, steady breathing kept us oblivious to any disturbances. After a long, beautiful moment of silence, Scott said to me, "It was meant for us to meet here and be together tonight."

When he said that, I couldn't help but turn onto my side and face him. I couldn't help but feel a sudden rush of passion flow through my body. He turned toward me as well and wrapped his arm around my waist. He slowly rubbed his warm hand up and down my back, first over my shirt, then under it. When he kissed me, it was as if all the warmth in his body had been passed over into mine. I wrapped my palm around the back of his neck to pull him in closer, to kiss him harder. His tongue felt like warm silk in my mouth. When he moved it around and under mine, it was done perfectly, as if we had choreographed the movements ahead of time. He caressed my stomach with his hand, making my muscles tense up. When we kissed harder, he grabbed my skin tightly. He slid his hand under my bra and gently cupped my breast, then massaged it, moving it any way he wanted. I kept one hand on his neck and slipped the other underneath his shirt, feeling a thin trail of fuzz just below his navel. I pinched his nipples hard between my forefinger and thumb. I knew he liked it because of the soft, airy grunts escaping from the back of his throat. He slid his other hand up the back of my skirt and squeezed my thigh, then my ass. I moved my hand from his chest to his stomach to his crotch. I could feel him hard underneath his jeans. After undoing the button and zipper of his pants, I wrapped my fist around his cock, first over his boxers, then under. As I slowly slid my fist from tip to base and back to the tip again, his breathing became heavier, his vocalizations more difficult to control. He followed my lead and pulled my underwear to the side so I could feel a cool breeze pass through to my moist skin. He pushed his fingers inside of me, first one, then two, then three. I briefly pulled my hand away to spit in my palm and used it to moisturize his cock. I began to move my wrist and arm faster and he did the same with his fingers. I could feel his pre-cum dripping into my hand, helping me keep him lubricated. Our hips danced with our hands, synchronized in motion together. Suddenly, he pulled himself out of my grasp.

"Stop, stop," he whispered.

"Why, what happened?" I asked.

"Nothing. I just want you to come first."

He sat up, grabbed my ankles and pulled them toward him. He lifted my skirt and slipped my underwear off and let them hang on his wrist. He spread my legs open and held onto the insides of my thighs. I closed my eyes and rested my head against the dry grass. I felt his warm, wet tongue tease my groin, then the lips of my pussy, then my clit. He started slow and gentle. My breathing became heavy and a soft moan escaped my mouth. As he began to pick up speed, he slipped his fingers back inside of me and used his other hand to pinch my nipples. As soon as I came, he reached for his wallet and found a condom. He quickly opened the packaging and slipped the rubber around his hard cock. He leaned into me but stopped and asked, "Is this what you want?" I simply nodded. I watched him penetrate me for the first time. I squeezed myself tight around him and I could tell that he liked it. He felt so good inside of me.

We spent the rest of the night on that hill together. At one point a couple of men walked by. When they spotted us they quickly mumbled an apology and left. By the time the sun was rising, we were alone. Only a few others had crashed at the party, but they were all indoors. From then on, I spent at least three nights a week with him. We never got bored.

"There's so much going on inside of you," he continued. "It only makes me want to know you better."

I smiled and pressed my lips against his. "Do you have to work in the morning?" I asked.

"No, do you?"

"Yes, but I never sleep anyway."

He reached around me to grab his pipe and stash off the window sill. I watched him carefully pack the bowl and take a hit. He gestured for me to come closer. So I did. He wrapped his mouth around mine and exhaled the smoke into my throat. I took it in and slowly released it into the room. I couldn't help but cough a little. I watched the lines around his mouth curl as he took another hit. Sometimes he looked old. Times like these when I could tell he was tired and distracted. I was nineteen at the time. He was twelve years my senior. He still looked young and healthy, but sometimes I could see the age in him sneak to the surface. I caught a glimpse of us in the mirror and we looked beautiful together. I started to suck on his neck, but not too hard, so I wouldn't leave marks. I pushed my tongue inside his ear and rotated it in circles. He groaned. He always loved that.

"Careful," he warned, not meaning it.

"Why?" I tease.

"Because. You'll make me do bad things to you."

"That's what I want."

"I know it is."

I bit his earlobe nice and hard. Hard enough to almost break skin. In retaliation, he grabbed me by the waist, lifted me off of him, and threw me back in the chair. Then he was on top. He ripped off my shirt and my pants and kissed every part of my body. He unclipped my bra and pulled it away so he could suck on my erect nipples. He pushed his fingers inside of me, but only for a moment, just to make sure I was wet. Then he stopped. He stood up and just looked at me for a moment. I smiled. He smiled. We kept our eyes locked tight on each other as he slowly stripped himself naked. He removed his jeans and his cock emerged from within, already hard. He loved not wearing underwear. He loved letting his pants hang low so the top of his pubic hair was just barely peeking out. He slowly caressed himself, teasing me, letting me watch but not touch. Then he swaggered toward me, back into the chair. This time, he straddled me and pushed in close so the tip of his cock was level with my mouth. He wrapped his hand around my neck, just tight enough to turn me on but not hurt me. I teased him with my tongue. Just barely touching the head then pulling away. Kissing it but not opening my mouth. Licking it but not sucking. He became impatient and tightened his grip around my neck. I smirked then placed one hand around his cock and the other on his ass. I pulled him in closer, letting him slide to the back of my throat. I held him in my mouth for a moment, pursing my lips tight around the base, pushing my tongue hard against the underside. Then finally, I sucked. I sucked hard, using every muscle in my mouth to tickle his nerves. He released his grip around my neck and transferred it to the back of my head, helping me make the complete movements at the desired speed. He let his head fall back, his eyes closed, and released a moan of complete satisfaction.

We liked to play games with each other. Our favorite was when he played the Master and I was his Slave. He'd call me up in the middle of the night and demand a full-body massage. If I was in the mood, which I often was, I'd make the short drive to his apartment, struggle to find parking, and enter his room at his complete service. When I'd arrive, I'd find him already in bed, lying on his stomach, completely naked. I could see the stiffness in his toned, hairless back. The relaxed muscles in his ass. The blonde hair coating the skin on his legs. I often wanted to climb on top of him right then and there. But I knew I had to be a good girl and be patient, giving him what he had called me over for first. I'd slowly climb on the foot of the bed, lightly dragging my fingernails up the backs of his calves, then his thighs. I'd let one finger gently slip between his ass and tease his hole just for a moment. Then I'd straddle his thighs and get comfortable for the work to come. We kept a bottle of vanilla body oil on the bed stand. I'd grab it and pour a perfect circle of the thick liquid in the palm of my hand. I could feel the coolness travel through my wrist and into my body, creating a tingling sensation that moistened my pussy. Then I'd rub the lotion between my hands, letting the silk sink into my pores. I could hear Scott's breaths become shorter as he grew impatient. I'd use all my weight to dig into the dips just below his shoulder blades and rub the oil from my skin into his. I'd grab his body hard, holding as much as I could get. He was warm and soft, like clean laundry just removed from the dryer. Touching him felt like stepping into a hot tub after a long week of labor and overtime. The vanilla scent would creep into my nostrils, causing a feeling of floatation. I'd move my hands from the back of his neck down to his ass and eventually to his toes. Sometimes the massage would last for as long as half an hour, but usually, he'd want to take it elsewhere after several minutes. He'd flip over, interrupting my work.

"Get off of me! Lay down on the bed," he'd demand.

I'd do as I was told, knowing what would be coming. He kept a line of rope wrapped loosely around one of the bed posts. He'd use it to tie my wrists together above my head and secure me to the bed. I wasn't allowed to talk unless he gave me permission or wanted an answer to a question. I'd have to finish everything I said with, "Master." He always removed my clothing in the same order. My socks, then my pants or skirt, followed by my shirt, which he'd leave dangling around my elbows. He'd slap his cock hard against my body – my legs, my stomach, my face. He'd remove my bra and underwear. Then he'd stand back and just look at me. I could sense him observing the wetness between my legs while he jerked off. Then he'd return to me and rub his pre-come on my nipples and my clit. He'd tease me, let me lick the tip just so I could get a taste. Then he'd begin pushing the underside of his cock against my clit. Rubbing it, massaging my pussy, but not entering me. He'd ask rhetorical questions or demand details on how much I wanted him.

"Where do you want it?" he'd ask.

"Inside of me, Master."

"What part of you?"

"Anywhere you want to put it, Master."

He'd ask me if he was better than other men. If he had more stamina. If he made me come faster and better. He'd demand I talk dirty to him. He'd demand I describe how I wanted him to fuck me and where. And who would be watching. Eventually, I'd say something that didn't satisfy him.

"That's not what I wanted to fucking hear!" he'd scream. Then he'd flip me over, my wrists still attached to the bed post. He'd grab me by the waist and force me onto my knees. He'd pull his arm back and slap my ass. He'd slap me so hard I could feel the heat soar up into my arms. And he wouldn't stop until I apologized. I'd hold out until the pain was too much to take.

"I'm sorry, Master," I'd cry out. "Please forgive me, I'll do what ever you want, Master."

"Do you promise?"

"I promise, Master."

He'd stop the hits, but keep his hands tight around my ass, pulling my cheeks wide apart.

"I believe you," he'd respond. "But this will teach you to be more careful next time."

Then I could feel the head of his cock massage my asshole. He'd lubricate it first with the juices from my pussy. Then he'd slowly push inside. I'd squeeze my ass tight around it until he'd groan. Then he'd push in further, and further, and further. Until he was completely inside of me. He'd get comfortable with the motions before picking up pace. I could feel a tight, sudden pain when he'd push in too far. As his hips moved faster, I could feel his balls slapping against my ass. I braced myself against the pillow, pushing my head against the back board of the bed, grasping tightly to the rope around my wrists. Sweat would begin dripping into my eyes. My hair would cling to my neck. As he'd become rougher, I truly felt like he owned me. I truly wanted him to do anything to me. To abuse me. To use me. To hurt me. My grunts and groans would become louder and faster as the pain became harder to bear.

"Are you going to be more careful next time?" he'd ask through short breaths and erotic grunts of his own.

"Yes, Master," would barely escape from my lips.

"What was that?"

"Yes, Master," I'd repeat a little louder.

"I can't hear you."

"Yes, Master!"

"I still can't hear you!"

"Yes! I promise to be more careful next time, Master." Then I'd begin begging. "Please believe me, Master! Please, I beg you, please believe me!"

When my cries and pleas finally became forceful enough and honest enough for his satisfaction, he'd lean forward on top of me. He'd squeeze my tits with one hand and finger my clit with the other. Then he'd press his face against my neck, his chest against my back. I could feel his heart pounding. It beat in sync with mine. We would become one in those moments. In those moments of undeniable passion and intensity. Sometimes he would come inside of me, inside of my ass. Other times, he'd pull out at the last minute and come on my lower back. Sometimes it would spray on my neck and into my hair. When he'd finish, he'd massage his cum into my skin with his hand or cock. Then he'd lay on top of me, holding me, our breathing as one. Our bodies as one. Our spirits as one.

Scott pulled himself out of my mouth and slid his cock down my body, from my chin to my thighs. He left a thin trail of liquid on my chest, which quickly became cool once it touched the air. I was still leaning back in the chair, comfortable and secure. He gently parted my legs. I rested my heels on the edge of the cushion, knees bent, so my pussy was wide open to him. He gently massaged the insides of my thighs, then moved to my groin, then to the tiny hairs that had begun growing again on my bikini line. I felt a swarm of butterflies emerge in my stomach as he leaned in to kiss my navel. I felt energy flowing from the tips of my fingers and toes as he began to circle my clit with his thumb. My pussy tightened and I was about to lean my head back and close my eyes when I caught him staring at me. The look on his face was completely subdued, honest and reflective. Neither of us said anything. I analysed the shape of his jaw. His chin, which was perfectly smooth but pink from a recent shave. And his lips. The lips that I could not help but be attracted to since the first time I saw them.

"I love you," he whispered.

I couldn't help but laugh. Soft, but unexpected and rude.

"No, I mean it," he retaliated, "I really love you."

I smiled. He leaned in for a quick kiss. A peck, the kind a boyfriend gives his girlfriend when they're surrounded by family. Then he removed his thumb and replaced it with his warm tongue. He played with my clit, just barely touching it. Then wrapped his lips around it, sucking, kissing, nibbling. I could feel my wetness dripping onto the chair as he began to work faster. The gentle tickle created a magnificent warmth through my body. After only a few minutes, I knew I could come, but prevented myself from doing so because I didn't want him to stop. He knew how I liked it. He knew the best places, the best technique. He knew the right speed and the right pressure. He knew how to make me want to fuck him.

"Scott," I mumbled through heavy breaths, "I want you inside me."

I could hear him fumbling for a condom while he continued going down on me. I could hear him tear the wrapper with one hand and unroll it onto his cock. I could hear him moan as he pushed inside of me. My wetness lubricated his cock more than the condom. It allowed him to move inside of me smoothly, efficiently, perfectly. I pressed the heel of my left foot hard into his ass. I used the toes of my right foot to grip the skin on his side. He reached for my ankles and swung my legs over his shoulders. He never ceased the grinding of his hips. I lifted my head so I could watch us. So I could watch him fuck me. It was beautiful. He flipped me over, slowly so he wouldn't exit my body while doing so. He bent me over the back of the chair and climbed onto it behind me. He continued thrusting and grinding. I had to brace myself against the wall. This was always my favorite position because it allowed him to enter me completely. Because I couldn't see his face and his emotions remained a mystery to me. He fucked me harder and faster so my head repeatedly bumped into the wall. The chair against my stomach was making it more difficult to breathe. My knees began to burn and my thighs began to cramp. His grunts and gasps told me he was about to come. I waited, wondering where he would do it. Would he come into the condom and remain inside of me even after he finished? Or would he quickly pull out, rip the condom off, and come on my back? That night, I was hoping he would do the latter. But instead, he slowed down. He stopped. He pulled out. I turned my head to him.

"Did you come?" I asked.

He shook his head. Then he scooped me up in his arms and stood, holding me tightly. He carried me to the bed, as if we were newlyweds entering the hotel room we had reserved for the first night of our honeymoon. He gently laid me down on the fresh sheets. I could smell the spring scent of detergent on the pillow cases. The sheets felt cool under my body. Soft and clean, like grass after the morning dew has evaporated but the sun hasn't yet emerged. I kept my legs spread, ready to continue. Scott re-entered my body. He lay on top of me, but held himself up so I wouldn't be uncomfortable. He kissed my forehead, my cheeks, my chin, then eventually my lips. Even as his hips fell back into the repetitive motions of sex, he continued kissing me. We never kissed during sex. We'd bite, lick and suck, but never kiss. He didn't pick up speed the way he normally did either. He didn't push himself all the way in. He just continued at this comfortable, gentle pace. Then he held my hand. He locked his fingers between mine. Our sweaty palms clung together. Suddenly, I felt like I was his girl. And he was my man. A tight, threatening knot developed in the pit of my stomach. I felt like the wind had been knocked out of me. It became difficult to breathe, as if I were trapped in a Manhattan subway station on a humid August afternoon. I became light-headed and the sounds of us, of the room, started to echo. I felt like I was drowning. Suddenly, I realized what it was. In that moment, Scott was not fucking me. He was not having sex with me. He was making love to me.

Scott and I never once went on a date. We never went out together in public. We were a secret. A private, passionate combination of loneliness and erotic desires. But he was more than a fuck-buddy. He was a good friend. We had conversations that I had only dreamed of starting with my boyfriend, but knew I couldn't. We could spend hours together in complete silence, just holding each other, and that was fine. And the sex was amazing. Physically, he satisfied me completely. He gave me what my boyfriend didn't. He made me feel beautiful.

In that moment, I felt like I loved him. I felt like I could love him forever. I wanted to run away with him and spend the rest of my life in his arms. And I suddenly believed him. I believed that he loved me. I believed that he loved me for who I was, not just for my tits and ass. I no longer felt like a possession, a piece of meat. I felt like his body inside of mine was a true connection, not just an orgasm. And this sudden realization sent a thousand knives through me. My eyes began to water and I allowed tears to slide down the side of my face onto the pillow beneath me. I was confused. I was uncomfortable. And for the first time ever, I wanted him to stop.

For a brief moment, Scott pulled his lips away from mine and lifted his head to get some air. And with a complete lack of control, I pulled my hand away from his and slapped him hard across the face. He stopped, shocked, still inside of me. A look of utter confusion in his eyes. He couldn't tell if I was just playing or not.

"What was that for?" he asked.

"You're being too gentle . . . Master."

"Maybe that's how I want it right now." His voice was serious. Not pretend-serious, not sexy-serious. But downright, honest-to-God serious.

"Bullshit," I challenged. Then I slapped him again. Harder. Time stopped. I saw an infinite number of thoughts and feelings pass behind his eyes. Hurt, fear, confusion, disbelief, love, hate, passion, lust. Then anger. With a sudden force that I had never experienced before, he wrapped one hand tight around my neck and used the other to cover my mouth. He pressed down on me with the full weight of his body and pinned my thighs open with his knees. Then he fucked me. He fucked me so hard it felt like a metal baseball bat was breaking me from the inside out. He fucked me so fast that I could no longer feel the motions. All I could feel was my insides being torn, my organs being smashed, the skin lining my pussy ripping from rawness. Keeping one hand over my mouth at all times, he grabbed the hair on the top of my head and yanked so my chin hit my chest. Then he threw me back into the headboard. He leaned in to bite my neck. The pain from his teeth was unbearable. It shot through me, paralyzing, almost knocking me unconscious. I imagined Jesus being nailed to the cross. I tried to pull away but had no strength compared to his. When he leaned back again, I saw a small drop of blood on his bottom lip. I knew it was mine. Every time he banged into me, an unfamiliar and torturous cramp swallowed every nerve of my body. Never ceasing the thrusts of his hips, he let go of my hair and slapped me hard across the face. Then again, only harder. So hard that I felt a sudden pain in my eye and I realized he had knocked my contact lens out of its proper place. He was giving me what I gave him. Letting me know how it felt. Then he grabbed my neck again. My mouth was still covered, but he adjusted the positioning of his hand so it blocked my nasal passages as well. I couldn't breathe. That's all I could think about in that moment. I was not receiving any air. My lungs were swelling. I was crying. I was bleeding. I was bruising. I felt myself scream, but no sound escaped my throat. I thought I was going to die.

"Is this better?" he growled.

I couldn't respond. I had no way to.

"Is it!"

I blinked my eyes rapidly, as a substitution for the nod I couldn't give. My lungs were begging for the air they were no longer receiving. Blood was frantically pumping into my brain.

"Now listen to me closely," he instructed in a low, threatening tone. "I'm going to come. And when I do, I'm going to release my hands, and you're going to tell me that you love me. Do you understand?"

I blinked again. He continued ramming into me, merciless. Then his voice turned into loud moans of pleasure and excitement. His muscles tensed, his jaw clenched, as his fluids begged to be released. He quickly removed his hands from my neck and mouth and placed them on my breasts, squeezing them both roughly in his fists.

"Tell me that you love me," he demanded through his orgasmic moans.

"I love you," my voice was barely audible, not even a whisper.

"Louder!"

"I love you."

"Say it again!"

"I love you!"

"Say it again!"

"I love you!" I cried out in desperation, tears streaking down my face, praying to a God I didn't believe in to make him stop.

And he finished. He collapsed but stayed inside of me. Our bodies pulsated from the event, throbbing around each other. He cradled my head in his arms and pressed it against his own. He buried his face between the sheets and my ear. He saw my tears and gently wiped them away with his fingers. He held me like I was his child.

"I'm sorry," he whispered into my ear.

I wanted to say "Don't be," or "It's okay," but I remained silent.

"You bring out the worst in me," he continued.

I felt his warm body against mine. His gentle hands caressing my skin. His honesty. His pain. His love.

"I know," I answered, "I know."

I didn't hear from him for a week. I expected that though. I wanted to give him some time. I wanted to give myself some time. I had spent that week contemplating the experience. Wondering why I preferred for him to hurt and violate me than to hold and love me. Why it felt so wrong for a man to be gentle. Why I couldn't get turned on unless it was rough. I didn't see my boyfriend at all during that week either because the bruises on my neck and between my thighs needed time to fade away in order to avoid an interrogation. So I could avoid telling the truth.

Scott finally called me on a Thursday, about 3 a.m.

"Hey, baby." He always began our phone conversations the same way.

"Hey," I replied.

"Did I wake you?"

"No, I was just getting ready for bed."

After some general small talk and the sharing of our past week, he said, "We can't do this anymore."

"I know."

And I did. I understood. I agreed. I had come to the realization that two negatives don't make a positive. That it was a bad idea to have two fucked-up people taking their issues out on one another in bed.

"You don't know the power you have over me," he stated. Honest. Sincere.

The silence over the phone was long. But not uncomfortable. That's how it was with us. Finally, I told him the truth.

"I love you."

"I love you, too."

Silence again. Neither of us wanted to hang up. We kept assuming the other would have the balls to do it first. And he was the one that did.

"Good night," he said.

"Good night."

I waited to hear the click on his end. Even then, I didn't remove the phone from my ear until the dial tone began to beep.

Murder Intermezzo

O'Neil De Noux

While the orchestra is warming up, Germaine LeFebvre strolls into the Saenger Theatre like she's Aphrodite, some goddess of beauty, her latest lover in tow. I feel that familiar stab in my heart. Former Miss University of New Orleans, former Miss Louisiana, first runner-up to Miss U.S.A., Germaine is also the former occupant of my bed.

Her face is striking to behold, her lips a fiery crimson, her long red hair hanging in curls. Her form-fitting, blue velvet gown, with a generous slit up the front, reveals her sleek legs as she walks languidly, like a cat. She acts as if she doesn't notice the people staring at her, but I know her. She notices.

In her spiked high-heels, Germaine is as tall as her escort – another of her linebacker-types with broad shoulders, thick hair and a square jaw. He's young too, probably in his twenties. Germaine is thirty-one, a good two years older than me, although she works hard to look younger. How many nights did I watch her paint up that gorgeous face until it was – angelic?

I finally exhale when she sits, three rows down, directly in front of my date. Alma Burke looks mousy in comparison, with her short brown hair and small brown eyes. She squeezes my hand as I glance at her beige outfit with its full skirt and high-neck matching blouse.

I try to keep my breathing normal but I feel the sharp pain growing in my chest again, perspiration working its way down my temples, my mouth as dry as the Sahara. It's Germaine's touch, that lingering agony that sweeps through me every time I see her, which happens often, too often.

New Orleans is nothing but a big small town. Everybody knows everybody. And I know Germaine, the memory of her velvety skin haunts me. Closing my eyes, I can almost feel the touch of her lips, the firmness of her body beneath me.

She wants me to forget we ever kissed.

She wants me to pretend we never met.

She rips me to pieces every time I see her, a little at a time, shredding me, digging her way to my heart to tear it out and stomp it with her high heels as she walks away.

"Are you all right?" Alma leans close to my ear.

I nod and struggle to get my breathing back to normal . . . only the sledgehammer starts pounding my brain.

Thankfully the lights dim and the mellow cords of Tchaikovsky's *Romeo and Juliet Overture* swells. I blink the wetness from my eyes in time to spot Germaine turning to her date and I see her face in profile, the perky nose, the full, sensuous lips. The shooting pain in my chest grows.

Am I having a cardiac?

I struggle to my feet, the sledgehammer in my head pounding away, and stumble up the aisle to the rear of the theatre, shoving the doors, stepping into the lobby. No one at the refreshment counter pays any attention as I stagger to the men's room. Splashing water on my face doesn't stop the hammer or alleviate the pain in my chest, but cools me down a little. I hold on to the wash basin for support.

Slowly, the pain eases, the hammering stops and my breathing isn't as labored.

I dry my face, straighten my tie and go back in.

Alma grabs my arm. "Are you sure you're OK?"

I nod and pat her hand reassuringly. She squeezes my hand with both of hers as the orchestra moves through Tchaikovsky's *Capriccio Italien Opus 45*. I close my eyes and try to ride the music, try to keep from thinking of Germaine's lips, the curves of her body, the warmth of her skin. A vision of Germaine standing naked next to my bed flashes in my mind – the full breasts, light areolae, the flat stomach and neatly trimmed bush between those long legs – and my eyes snap open.

I force a smile at Alma and make myself think of the good times *we've* had recently, movies at the Palace Theatre with its stadium seating, the ballet, dinners at Commander's Palace and Arnaud's. Only my mind returns to Germaine, to those sensuous lips, to those legs wrapped around me like a spider and I can almost feel the soft folds of her pussy as I plunge in her, in and out, seeing fire in those cobalt blue eyes. She called out "God" when we made love and told me she loved me.

She told me that a lot, even when it was falling apart, when that far-away look came to her eyes and I could feel her drifting on a tide of boredom. The tedium of seeing me all the time was too much, she told me. She actually told me that. Those ardent blue eyes weren't meant for the domestic life. She was a tigress, after all, and needed to hunt the jungle of New Orleans night life, instead of spending her evenings in my apartment.

Now the anger grows in my chest as I sit here, orchestra playing more Tchaikovsky – *Waltz and Polonaise from Eugene Onegin*. Alma continues to hold my hand as I simmer. There is only one way out of this pain. I dream of strangling Germaine, of twisting that beautiful neck, crushing her lovely larynx, wiping that look from her eyes – the look of pity she gave me when she walked out for the last time – the look she gives me whenever she sees me now, when she even bothers to see me.

Slowly, as the orchestra slides through the quiet strains of the opening of the *1812 Overture*, I let my rage grow with the music, riding up and down the notes. The overture rises and plunges over the waves pulling my rage along, until the crashing cymbals echoes with the music's climax and I'm ready. My simmering is at its boiling point.

Intermission brings up the house lights. I fight to keep my rage in check, not to show it in my eyes. I ask Alma if she'd like a refreshment.

"A glass of champagne would be nice." She sits back with a smile.

Germaine and her lover stand and I move quickly up the aisle, ahead of them. She'll head for the ladies room. I move that way, along the tile floor to a large marble column just beyond the ladies room. Built in the 1920s, the Saenger has nooks and crannies and all kinds of hiding places.

If I can snatch her, I'll pull her behind this column and throttle her, end it all right here. The sweat is back, dripping down the sides of my face. A line forms outside the ladies room, snaking away from me and my pillar. Germaine, glass of champagne in hand, steps into the line and talks with a blonde woman.

It's too damn crowded.

I'll never snatch her like this.

I wipe the sweat from my face with the sleeve of my jacket. My heart thunders in my ears as I wait. The line moves slowly and Germaine's lover steps next to her and she takes his arm and they turn away from the line. I move out and spot them going back into the theatre. She'll have to come back. The line's too long now. And it hits me. The program. She hates Bizet. A cold smile comes to my lips. She'll wait for *Carmen* and go to the bathroom when it's empty. Perfect.

I grab a glass of champagne for Alma and reach my seat just as the lights go down. The driving notes of *Carmen Suite No. 1* begin, through the *Interlude* and I watch Germaine. When will she make her move? The *Interlude* rises, dancing through the score, but she doesn't move.

She suddenly likes Bizet? All the mood swings in the music?

No. It comes to me now. She's waiting for the *Intermezzo*. The infuriating *Intermezzo*, that brief entr'acte between the successive acts of *Carmen Suite No. 1*.

I lean to Alma and tell her I have to go to the men's room as the sickly, soft music of the *Intermezzo* begins. I reach the aisle just as Germaine rises. I hurry, feeling the power return to my arms.

Intermezzo – a short movement separating the major sections of a musical composition. *Intermezzo* – a short movement separating the halves of my life. The Germaine part and the post-Germaine part.

I reach the column outside the ladies room as an elderly woman enters. Can't go inside. Germaine won't be alone. I peek from behind the column and she approaches, digging in her purse as she walks, her high heels tapping the tile floor.

Timing it perfectly, I come around the column, not giving her time to look at me in pity. I grab her hair, shove my hand across her mouth and pull her back around the column. She's so light, she dangles in my arms. I feel her fists pound me as I shove her against the wall and work my hands to her throat. Those cold blue eyes are saucered in fear.

She does something I don't expect. She smiles, then purses those perfect lips. I have her throat and she's gasping but *purses those perfect lips* that glisten red, shimmering, velveteen. I lean close and our lips touch, softly, gently, my heart stammering now. And I lose the strength in my hands and let her go as I fall into the kiss, as our tongues entwine and our bodies press against one another.

Germaine pushes me until my back is against the pillar, then pulls her mouth away. We both gasp for oxygen. She looks into my eyes and opens her mouth as it moves to mine and we're back at it, French kissing, my hands rising to her breasts to knead them, her right leg wrapping around me as I work her around to put her back to the pillar.

I grind against her, pushing my swollen cock against her, feeling her pelvis move with me. I look in her eyes again and there's something else there, something cold and distant and she presses something hard against my chest. There's a sudden burning in my chest. Then another sudden burn and I hear it now, a popping. She yanks away and shoves me and I can't keep my balance. I stumble and see the silver pistol in her hand.

I look down at the burn marks on my chest and the blood seeping out. Still stumbling, I fall straight back, the back of my head bouncing on the floor. I can taste the gunpowder in my mouth now, can smell the coppery scent of blood.

A man stands with Germaine now, supporting her. He takes the pistol from her hand and I realize he's in a light blue uniform. N.O.P.D. He's supposed to be outside.

"His name is Roger Dalby." Germaine gasps to the cop. "He's been stalking me!"

The driving beat of Bizet's *Les Toréadors* reverberates through the theatre. The burning in my chest ebbs and I'm filled with a coldness. My heart, like thunderclaps, like cymbals, clashes over the music and I feel that incredible heartache again and Germaine's blurry face fades behind my tears.

I can't focus.

The music is gone now.

I'm falling, slipping into a silence so complete I can no longer hear my heartbeat, no longer hear my labored breathing.

I keep falling.

Are my eyes open?

It's so black.

I try to force my eyes open.

Where is the bright light you're supposed to see when you're dying?

There's nothing.

But wait, there is something.

It *is* a light.

Am I floating towards it or is it moving to me?

Yes, it's a light far away and getting closer.

Yes, yes, I'm moving toward the light.

Is it heaven?

Suddenly that familiar Catholic fear grips me.

Is it hell? Is it Purgatory? Will I roast for years in Purgatory?

Will I relive the evils I have done over and over again until my sins are paid for?

Or is it another *Intermezzo* in my life?

There's a sudden warmth and—

While the orchestra is warming up, Germaine LeFebvre strolls into the Saenger Theatre like she's Aphrodite, some goddess of beauty, her latest lover in tow. I feel that familiar stab in my heart . . .

The Shoot

D. L. King

"Do you mind if I touch him?"

I was working on a new body of images illustrating male submission. Yes, I know, it's a recurring theme with me, but I do so like the appearance of the male form restrained and straining. I was looking for subjects between the ages of twenty-one and forty-five with specific characteristics and so I'd sent out a call to dominants in the international community. I explained the project and invited them to send photos if they were interested and willing to come to New York for shooting sessions.

Evidently, my reputation is such that the offer of a free print will coax people from across the globe to travel to my studio. The farthest reply was from a woman in Japan. She was planning a trip and sent the most delightful photo. Language barriers often cease to be a problem when sex and art take over. Kazuhiro was transformed by Tatsumi's intricate rope bondage, and he will be a lovely addition to the show.

The woman, standing in my studio, shrugged her shoulders. "You have carte blanche. I've seen your work, that's why we're here."

I ran a fingernail over his nipple and watched it react. "What's his name?"

"Jordan."

Jordan's mistress was getting a signed print of her choice, in payment for today's session. That, and first refusal of the finished prints of her boy before the show opened to the public.

"Very nice, Jordan," I purred. Turning to his mistress, I asked if she'd brought his shaving things. She said she had and I told her to set them up on the table by the reclining barber chair. While she got everything ready, I directed Jordan to take off his sweat pants and climb into the chair. After fastening his wrists and ankles, I raised the chair to a comfortable height for his mistress.

The sweats were loose on him but there was still a mark that would show on film so I had a bit of time to kill. All in all, it wasn't too bad; it would have been a much bigger time-waster if he'd worn jeans. Of course, I prefer to have boys arrive naked to my studio, but that can only occur in winter. Boots and a coat somehow seem out of place in the summer. I took my time, setting up the lighting.

A half hour later, we were ready to begin. "Okay," I said. "When we communicated, you indicated you preferred to shave him dry, with talc, but I'd like you to use shaving cream today. The contrast pops so nicely in black and white, especially with the steel and mother of pearl of the straight razor."

As she began to shave Jordan, I started shooting; close-ups of her black-gloved hand pressing down on the base of his erection and the razor flashing in the lights, medium shots of his crotch, half-shaved with her black silk-clad torso as the background, a long shot, including his face; head back, eyes closed and mouth open. I shot from a slight angle, just beyond his feet, taking in the whole scene along with the edges of the black seamless paper roll, the light stand in the corner behind his head, and black electrical cords snaking around the floor. The industrial look can sometimes be the most intimate and voyeuristic.

I could imagine the finished prints on the gallery wall. Yes, these pictures would go well with last week's. Jordan, pale and russet, juxtaposed with the obsidian and pink of Geoffrey, I would hang them as diptychs. The two would pair so nicely for the shaving pictures.

I shot fast, as I always do. "All right, if you're finished with the front of him, let's have him on all fours on the table."

His mistress released him from the chair and walked him over to the low massage table. His cock stood proud and swung from side to side as he walked. Once she had him positioned, I walked over and gently ran my hand down his back and cupped his perfectly rounded ass. Although his breathing sped a bit, to his credit, Jordan hadn't made a sound since he'd entered my studio.

"Very nice, Jordan, arms in front of you now, on the table," I said as I patted his bottom, giving him the clue to raise it. "That's it, now open your legs for me," I said, gently pushing and prodding him into the position I wanted. I ran my finger up his hard cock and pulled and stretched his balls down in back. An involuntary shudder coursed through his muscles.

"Very good, Jordan. Later, Mistress will give you a nice reward," I whispered, as I smoothed my hands down the backs of his thighs. "Won't that be something to look forward to?" I detected a small tensing of his muscles and a drop of pre-come slipped from the tip of his cock and splashed onto the table, between his legs.

I fastened him to the table with black leather straps just below his knees and elbows, and at his ankles and wrists. It was all about the contrast. With Geoffrey, I'd used white leather straps. What a lovely pair they'd make.

Satisfied, I asked his mistress to complete the shave with his balls and anus. Using the bristles of the shaving brush to apply the creamy soap, she swirled it again and again over his pulsing opening. Helpless to fight it any longer, he treated us to the music of his lovely, deep moan.

I finished these first shots, impressed with Jordan's composure, and curious to see how he'd do during the strap-on shots. I always like to think ahead during a shoot. My thoughts kept bringing me back to Geoffrey.

Geoffrey's master kept him in excellent shape, as fit as Jordan's mistress kept him. Perhaps I'd ask to have them brought in together for one more shoot. I could see the close-up of Geoffrey's cock entering Jordan's delicious ass. As I said, it really is all about the contrast.

Tropical Temptress

Sage Vivant

The caldera of Pacaya Volcano seethed and smoldered under Leeanna's gaze. Transfixed, she stood as close to its very edge as her acrophobia would allow.

"There she is, living on the edge again," Leo chided affectionately. He stood closer to the tour group, several feet away from her.

"You have to see this," she said over her shoulder. She heard him approach and turned to him. "Isn't it incredible?" she whispered.

And, of course, it was more than incredible. Brilliant streaks of pumpkin, rose and gold provided the breathtaking backdrop for the volcano's giant caldron. It was nature flaunting its powerful beauty, defying words and surpassing human imagination.

"This view makes the sissy walk up here worth it," she concluded, wrapping her arms around him. Surveying the tour group, she noted the outright exhaustion that permeated them. What was wrong with these people? It was a beginners' hike, for God's sake! Most of the travelers weren't any older than she and Leo, so their lack of stamina seemed all the more confounding. She was the only one in the group with the energy and curiosity to peer into the caldera.

"It's funny," she said, half into his chest. "They'll go home and tell people they were here, but really, they're barely aware of what's around them."

"You'd climb in there if you thought you could, wouldn't you?" Leo chuckled.

"Hell, yes!" She pulled away from him and searched his face. "Doesn't the air here make you restless? Don't you want to just drink everything in? Swallow it whole?"

Leo was wonderfully indulgent. She could tell he liked Guatemala so far but she also saw bewilderment in his eyes when she'd asked her semi-rhetorical question. He was always supportive of her need for adventure. He often accompanied her on treks where she knew he wasn't fully at ease with the idea. Never stodgy but always her rock. She tilted her head to kiss him.

It was only their second day in Guatemala but some nameless hunger had snuck under her skin and into her blood immediately upon their arrival. She felt like she had a low grade fever. Her body was one big itch dying to be scratched.

"It's stunning but you seem to need something a little more physically challenging. What do you say to a long bike ride tomorrow?" he suggested, holding her tightly in his strong arms. "And maybe some snorkeling, if there's time?"

A noisy bus pulled up just down the road from the clearing where the travelers clustered. Expressions ranging from relief to delight lit up faces as bodies heaved themselves off the ground to head for air-conditioned comfort.

"Oh, no! Not a bus!" Leeanna groaned. "You mean, we don't get to walk back down?" The two of them stepped away from the volcano's rim and toward the beleaguered tour guide.

"May we walk back?" Leeanna asked.

"It will be dark very soon and the path may not be visible," the pretty Guatemalan woman replied in finely accented English.

"I always carry a flashlight," Leeanna said, patting her backpack.

"You'll need to sign a form then," the woman replied, "to release the tour company from responsibility."

"Is the path dangerous at night?" Leo asked.

"Oh, no. Just very dark," the woman said over her shoulder as she walked toward the waiting bus. "Please follow and I will give you the form."

"Leeanna, why don't we take the bus? There's no sense risking a walk in complete darkness. What if one of us breaks a leg or something? The idea of spending our vacation in a Guatemalan hospital isn't what I had in mind."

"I wasn't planning on walking," she grinned and dug into her backpack. "I'm going to run!" She pulled out her flashlight triumphantly.

"It's OK, Leo. I don't expect you to come along. But I've got to do something with all this energy and I think a two-mile downhill run in this clean night air will be perfect. You can take the bus and meet me at the hotel."

She knew he didn't like the idea. She knew they'd battle about it a few minutes longer. But she knew she'd be running down that hill soon.

She signed the form for the guide and stretched her calves as the bus revved its engine. She and Leo exchanged waves, and she let the bus get a head start.

Twilight beckoned with a mysterious urgency. She waited until she could no longer hear the bus and then closed her eyes. The air, thin but substantial, caressed her like a playful lover. The volcano hissed softly, a ceaseless reminder of its mercurial nature. She threaded her flexi-flashlight through her belt and set off on a sprint down the sloping path.

Her tight, compact body commanded that she run to unleash the tension, throw off this vaguely irritable mood that brewed inside her. But her soul demanded that she savor the restless stillness and give her surroundings her full attention. The two urges struggled for dominance, resulting in a jog that did not challenge her and forced her to experience her milieu as fleeting blurs. As she moved down the mountain, the air grew hotter and thicker, drawing sweat through her pores.

The path was certainly wide enough to present no obstacles. Darkness had suddenly descended and she felt for the button to turn on her flashlight. All was silent save for her breathing and the steady rhythm of her feet on the sandy road.

Ten minutes later, when she estimated she was halfway down the hill, she noticed what appeared to be a small fire some yards from the path. She stopped jogging immediately. The fire, mostly conspicuous for its smoke, seemed small and confined. Was it a campfire? she wondered.

And then she heard a soft cacophony of human voices. A man's voice quietly droned one chant repeatedly in a language that did not sound like Spanish. A female voice (or was it two?) hummed and moaned in a strange, lilting harmony with the man's chant. Leeanna moved toward the sounds.

The scent of burning wood mixed with a sweeter, spicier one that she couldn't identify. It was some sort of herb but with a heady, hypnotic quality. None of the human sounds stopped as she ventured closer.

Finally, she was close enough to see over the lush foliage and rocks. She remembered her flashlight and shut it off quickly to avoid being noticed. The fire provided all the light she needed.

Near the fire, a tall, muscular, dark man lay on his back, wearing nothing but a modest headdress of some beads and a few small feathers. His eyes were closed as he chanted, trancelike in his concentration.

Straddling him was a buxom woman, also naked except for the same kind of headdress. She, too, was dark but not as dark as the man. Both of them were covered with a thin film of some kind of oil, which made the formidable muscles on their bodies glisten by the firelight.

The woman turned away to reach something by her side. When she faced forward again, she raised her hands to the sky and Leeanna watched thick rivulets of oil run down her forearms and trickle to her shoulders. The chanting man took hold of her breasts and massaged them with oil previously spread on their bodies. She hummed louder as he kneaded her full mammaries.

The woman brought her arms down and placed her hands on his chest. But rather than rub the oil on them into his chest, she buried them between her legs briefly, then slid her pelvis to his shiny chest, illuminated magnificently by the small, raging fire.

The woman rubbed her sex over the length and breadth of the man's chest, sliding smoothly with the oil's help. Still he massaged her breasts. She reached behind her and took hold of his long, thick member, curved upward in the tropical night air like a fleshy sickle.

As soon as she touched it, both of them turned to Leeanna

and smiled with such an alarming mix of invitation and mischief that she froze. The woman rubbed her sex around the man's torso with wild abandon. The look she delivered to Leeanna had a preternatural quality and Leeanna instantly felt it was her own throbbing clitoris, her own creamy labia, sliding over the muscled man's chest.

Leeanna stumbled in her panic to flee the scene. The couple continued to stare, virtually penetrating her with their own sexual aura. She clutched her flashlight, turned it on, spun on her heel and sprinted toward the relative safety of the path.

She ran now. Enjoying her surroundings had proven an ill-fated venture and her body now screamed for release. Her legs jettisoned her forward without a trace of restraint. She was at the bottom of the hill in what seemed like seconds.

She could not halt her own crazed propulsion. She flew through the colorful streets of Guatemala City with frenzied purpose. Finally, her adrenaline dipped and she realized she needed directions. She leaned against a whitewashed building, panting and looking about like a fugitive. Around her, the city teemed with life. Her head span with it all as her labored breathing eventually returned to normal.

She made her way down the busy street, keeping her eyes open for an available taxi.

"Senorita!"

She turned toward the whiskey-voice to see a wizened Guatemalan street vendor siting behind his small table of trinkets tucked in an alcove between two buildings. There were many senoritas he might have addressed, but she knew it was she he intended to call. She walked toward him without fear, which she found curious.

He clutched some item of decoration in his hand and when she got close enough to see it, he opened his hand to display the item. She gasped in recognition. It was a headdress of beads and small feathers, like that of the oiled, copulating couple she'd seen on the path.

"You like?" He pulled the headdress across his palm, allowing it to stroke him seductively. "A woman with your power should have one of these." He smiled knowingly at her puzzled face.

She wanted to run. Instead, she asked why she needed the beaded item.

"You have the fire! The fire men worship!" His hands trembled as he spoke. "Can you not feel it?" he asked, suddenly somber and serious. She could only stare at him mutely.

From the array of baubles spread before him, he chose one and lifted it toward her face. It was a small pendant shaped exactly like the shimmering phallus she'd seen on the chanting man. Paranoia and fear gripped her, sending a chill through her otherwise humid body. The man ran his finger up and down the miniature penis, never taking his eyes off her. Her pulse raced.

"This is your kingdom, fine lady. The hard, thick gifts of many men, each one inside you, feeding your fire—"

She fled without hearing more. She ran wildly into the middle of the street, where a taxi slammed on its brakes to avoid contact with her. After reprimanding her in Spanish, the driver agreed to take her to her hotel, which was closer than she'd hoped.

"My God! Are you all right?" Leo exclaimed upon opening the door to their bungalow.

She probably looked frightful, she realized as she fell into his protective embrace.

"What happened? Are you hurt? Did somebody attack you?" He was visibly shaken by her outburst. He's probably blaming himself for letting me get home by myself, she thought.

A warm breeze moved about the room with a wicked sensuality. She separated herself from Leo, an action that did not feel as if she alone willed it. The windows and glass doors were wide open, curtains billowing, giving the impression that the insistent, swirling air had been impertinent enough to let itself in. It danced about the room, licking the contents, circling objects coyly before slipping on to the next. Thick, lush foliage rustled just outside, seeming to tremble in the wake of this invisible, elusive presence.

The couple stood in the doorway, immobile. She braced herself for the approach of warm air, for she instinctively knew it was headed toward her. It slithered over her body, through her clothes, caressing with feathery strokes. Her skin tingled and flushed and her knees weakened.

She was suddenly very aware of her own pussy. It twitched and pulsated, as if to remind her of something. The lips between her legs grew moist and full. Her clitoris ached to be touched. She felt her own juices threaten to run down the inside of her thighs.

She stood with her eyes closed, allowing this arousal, submitting to whatever it was that induced it.

Hot, fleshy lips brushed hers and her eyes sprang open. Leo stood before her, naked, with his clothes in a heap where he'd stood only moments before. He faced her, leaving just enough space between them to permit his lush body hair to tickle her electrified skin.

He pressed his enormous erection into her furry little mound and kissed her passionately. She was vaguely aware that he undressed her as his tongue probed the inside of her mouth.

The stealth wind did not leave the room as the couple came together. Its warmth simultaneously cooled their overheated bodies and fueled their most primal urges.

His hands covered every inch of her exposed skin in gentle, continuous strokes, over her back, arms, breasts, stomach, ass. Every new patch of skin he caressed burned hotter until she felt she might ignite like a human torch.

In all the years they had been together, she had never been so driven to have him. Their tongues wrapped and slithered around each other and she could think only of his bigness, his bountiful maleness. She wanted to consume him.

When he slipped his fingers between her legs, she called out with pleasure, throwing her head back involuntarily. His gentle and rhythmic caressing around her swollen wet clit went to her very core. Her arousal seemed to feed his; the wetter she got, the more purposeful his movements became. The sensation of her juices spreading over his busy fingers made her dizzy with lust.

She creamed into his hand, almost willing herself to deposit her gratitude there. He stroked her slowly, escalating her fever to thrilling, uncertain heights.

She moaned uncontrollably from the depths of her vocal chords as her body erupted into convulsions of ecstasy. He continued to stroke her as she came, and he held her trembling but powerful little body.

As the orgasm shook her, she realized this was only a partial release of her sexual tension. In her receptive state, something entered her, as well. Some unseen presence seeped through her skin, penetrating her mind and her spasming pussy. She welcomed it and felt a renewed hunger, an increased strength.

She looked at him like a starved animal looks at prey and pulled him toward the low, wide bed in the middle of the room. He paused at the small duffel bag he'd carried with him throughout the trip, kneeled at it to unzip it and reached inside.

She reclined on the bed as he tended to his bag. A forceful calm blended with her fiery passion and she ran her hands over her breasts and torso with sublime intent. She felt unimaginably delicious! She turned her head and noticed an unmarked bottle with a thick, golden liquid inside. Neither one of them had brought the bottle from home but she grinned as if she expected to find it there. She poured some of the oil into her palms, raised her hands to the ceiling and let it inch its way past her forearms, over her biceps. The pungent scent of sweet and spicy herbs filled the room. Where the oil touched her, she could feel the blood moving through her veins.

Leo approached, carrying a large jelly dildo with the familiar curved angle she'd seen so many times that evening. She'd known the moment she saw the man's cock by the fire that that particular penile shape was destined to fill her, sometime, somewhere. It seemed perfectly natural for Leo to know this, too.

"Oh, *yessss*," she cooed, spreading her legs to accept it.

As the dildo plunged deeply into her dripping snatch, it affected her entire pubis like the oil on her skin. Every artery, every blood vessel, every nerve ending sprang to life with an intensity she could barely withstand.

With every slippery entry, the dildo fed her its mysterious power. She threw her body toward it, wildly absorbing every shred of energy it transferred. It fired her deep pink mons and made her crave his mouth at the steamy center between her legs. He continued to pump her with the magical dildo and she concentrated on drawing his lips to her sex.

In seconds, his tongue lapped ravenously at her hot, velvet flesh, savoring the thick cream from her pussy and licking it off the dildo as he slid it in and out of her. His tongue circled her clit mercilessly, leaving her to writhe on the bed in mounting ecstasy.

When he flicked her clit so rapidly it vibrated, she exploded again, this time with long, drawn-out moans and tremors in her sex. Tiny sparks and bubbles sizzled throughout her mons area and her pussy continued to gush uncontrollably.

Leo stared at her with an awe she'd never witnessed before. His cock was nearly purple and hard as stone.

"Lay down," she urged. "I want to make you as happy as you've made me."

He complied instantly. His cock stuck up like a flagpole. She stuffed it into her mouth, gorging herself. She sucked, licked, and teased the head of it – all with an enthusiasm that bordered on manic. He was too close to his own release for her to continue. She wanted his precious jizz in her hot pussy, not her mouth.

She mounted him and began to spread the heady, scented oil over his chest. She slid her pert breasts over his chest, then followed with her labia. A hot, vibrant energy surrounded them.

Finally, she inserted his thick meat into her juicy opening. Her pussy squeezed and clutched at his cock, ravenous for him. In moments, his rod shot liquid fire into her. His cum, effusive and urgent, felt complete, like some kind of punctuation to a long, exclamatory sentence.

As they curled up in each other's arms, reveling in release, he whispered to her.

"I bought you something else, too."

"What is it?"

He reached toward the nightstand and returned with a small headband of beads and feathers, placing it on her head.

"This old geyser on the street told me I had to buy this for you. I wasn't sure you'd like it."

"Oh, no," she purred. "It's perfect," she smiled and fell asleep wearing it.

Matching Skirt and Kneepads

Thomas Roche

The sun cast skyscraper shadows across the leather fair, broken at each block by great gleaming shafts of molten light. Though it wouldn't be dark for hours, the settling sun meant that it had started to cool off a little bit, which everyone was thankful for.

Madame Iris threaded her way through the crowd leading Tess on a leash. She was taller than Tess, five-eight in bare feet and something terrifyingly greater in heels. The low heels of Tess' combat boots left her feeling like a pet heeled in Madame Iris's path, which she liked almost as much as the feeling of swelling, aching pain between her legs.

"Rolf! Bear! Look, Tess! It's Rolf and Bear!" Tess didn't remember meeting them, but then, she was very often blind-folded. Iris hugged a pair of hunky leather men, booted and jockstrapped and shirtless, one smooth and the other hairy. The contrast helped Tess understand that Rolf and Bear were, in fact, names. *Probably some hippy Burner fags*, Tess thought to herself with an internal eye-roll. Iris hugged them both and kissed Rolf, the smooth one (duh) on the lips, then the four of them edged into the shadow cast by a photography booth, which was not that easy. The crush of the crowd was still oppressive.

"How have you boys been? Good, I hope, all things considered?" Madame I's lilting voice went in and out of Tess's perception; the babble of the crowd still made it difficult to hear. Tess stood respectfully with her leash rattling softly between her tits as Madame Iris spoke with her hands. If they had been somewhere other than the street, or if Tess had been wearing her kneepads, she would have respectfully knelt at Madame Iris's side, perhaps even cast her eyes up to her Mistress as she spoke.

As it was, though, the red mesh kneepads had simply not gone with the plaid skirt, and a fashion queen like Madame I was not about to let her slave's outfit clash.

Tess twisted and squirmed slightly, acutely aware of the sharp pain as her clit alternately swelled and stung, deflated, swelled, hurt like hell. In an instinctive attempt to brace herself against the pain, Tess kept cinching her internal muscles, which didn't help at all.

Rolf and Bear were huddled close to the Mistress, laughing and talking as if Tess wasn't there, which either offended her or turned her on, depending on whether her clit was more in a swelling-with-pleasure moment or more on an ow-that-hurts moment.

Tess tried to let her mind wander; Rolf certainly had awfully nice pectorals, and that was a hell of a piercing. What the fuck did that tattoo on his left tit say? Was that . . . "Bitch Slut?"

". . . that's what I was telling my slave Tess just now," said Madame Iris, her voice raising as she glanced back at Tess. "Her snatch is off limits, so she's just going to have to lick more pussy!" The three shared a beer-and-a-half laugh, from which came a tittering "She doesn't already?" which might have been amusing except that all Tess could think was: "Snatch?!?"

Surely this was the influence of the two male homosexuals, she mused to herself. "Actually, she's been telling me she might want to do the other thing," said Madame Iris.

Rolf and Bear both feigned shock and dismay. Rolf, whom Tess had already decided was impossibly cute, almost lost her when he laughed: "Tell me she's not bisexual – those people are fucking crazy!" which caused Madame Iris to punch him very, very hard on the arm and damn, that lady could punch.

Rolf put up his hands in defense and said wryly, "Speaking for my tribe here!" which made awful things happen under Tess' skirt while she chewed on that one.

By the time the three had put their heads together and were whispering, Tess was in extreme pain and amazingly hot. Before she knew it, Madame Iris had handed her leash to Rolf, who gave her the kind of bedroom eyes that only a gay man could get away with, which didn't help the sharp swelling sensation in her skirt. Madame I disappeared into the long slit between the curtains at the back of the tent.

"Hello, Tess," said Rolf in a lascivious purr. "I don't believe we've been properly introduced."

Tess curtseyed, something she still did with phenomenal awkwardness despite hours of training at Madame I's hands. The combat boots didn't help. "Pleased to meet you, sir."

Madame Iris poked her head out and hissed: "Psst! Arty's done for the day. He says we can use it. Twenty minutes, OK?"

"Oh, honey, give me ten," said Rolf, his eyes lingering over Tess just long enough to make her shiver before he turned and kissed Bear deeply.

"Come on!" hissed Madame Iris. "We're on the clock, bitch!"

The leashed Tess obediently followed Rolf into the tent, not that she had much choice. Bear brought up the rear, and Tess was surprised to feel a firm pinch on her ass. Two things happened: first she felt a surge of outrage in her chest; an instant later, it turned warm and went dribbling down into her aching sex, as she understood, as she always did an instant after her outrage, that she no longer got to decide if her ass got pinched, or for that matter fucked. Or, perhaps even more to the point, if her sex got pierced.

Which made her remember even more acutely that she no longer had that authority, as her clit swelled rapidly and the dull ache turned sharp, midway between the very edge of pleasure and way more than she could stand.

Tess found herself in a white-draped chamber built out of translucent fabric, the shadows of partiers milling about just beyond still as visible as the sounds of their mostly obscene conversations were audible, as the mingled scent of their bodies was smellable. Punishingly hot, the fabric room was lined with ticking, cooling photofloods and had a camera tripod without a camera. The fabric that formed the sides was tied very tight. There was a small garbage can stuffed to overflowing with crumpled paper towels. Some friend of Madame Iris' had been shooting *extremely* naughty pictures in here.

The fabric chamber was furnished with a makeshift couch, foam rubber, Ikea-style, the kind that wasn't very comfortable but could still hold three people, especially if one of them was willing to sit in the big hairy one's lap, as Madame Iris did now while she accepted the leash back from Rolf.

"Well?" she asked, green eyes bright as she looked up at the faintly trembling Tess. "Show them."

Tess took a deep breath.

She obediently brought her slim hands to the hem of her skirt and gathered it, planting her feet just far enough apart that she could lean back and expose her sex.

A wicked smile on his face, Rolf leaned forward, close enough that she could feel his warm breath on her shaved sex.

"My, my, my," he said. "That *is* fresh." He reached out as if to touch her pussy, but instead petting her thighs gently. A hot wave went through her, and her clit really began to hurt for a second; then the sharp hurt went away and all she could feel was the surrender of letting it feel good despite everything. She closed her eyes, breathing slowly. Rolf slipped his hand between her legs and tenderly petted her cheeks, her upper thighs. She gritted her teeth to suppress a moan when he began to caress her lips.

"Shouldn't it be bandaged?"

"Not any more," said Madame Iris. "They came off this morning. See the tape marks?"

"Ooooh, I hate that," sighed Rolf, leaning very close, so close Tess thought he was going to lick her pussy. She had already begun to moisten to the idea when Madame Iris said, "Tess, give me your backpack."

The swaying Tess shrugged off her leather backpack, in which she'd been carting around the Madame's makeup and secret purchases all day. She knew the secrets were probably nasty little toys with which Madame would make her plaything's life very, very interesting in the days and weeks to come. She was right, but her timeline was a little off.

As she perched there in Bear's lap, Madame Iris unzipped the bag and pulled out an immaculate pair of tartan kneepads. The cool smirk Madame Iris gave her was coupled with the

smoldering stare, because both Mistress and toy knew that Tess
no longer needed to clash to be a dirty little cocksucker. Had she
lucked into an exact match, or was this a custom job she just
happened to be picking up at the fair? Either way, it was an
impressive bit of fashion manipulation.

"A gift for my plaything," said Madame Iris, her smile
broadening. "Who, Rolf, is your own personal Hoover for the
next—" she glanced at the elegant silver watch on her slim
wrist "—seventeen minutes. Go!"

She handed the kneepads to Rolf. He accepted them gratefully and broke the plastic thingie that fastened them together;
he selected one, stretched it and leaned forward again, his
breath warm on Tess.

"May I, sir?" said Tess, gesturing toward his shoulder.

"Please," he murmured, and she steadied herself with her
hand on Rolf's big brawny shoulder as she lifted her booted foot
to his knee and let him slide the kneepad over it. As he slid it up
past the top of her boots and then over her pink seamed
stockings, almost to the little plaid bows that matched her skirt
– and now her kneepads – so exactly, Rolf bent down and kissed
Tess's thigh, his skilled tongue swirling a circle that went from
gentle to insistent before he'd secured the kneepad around her
knee.

Tess swooned. He caressed the back of her calf a little
between combat boot and kneepad, then slapped it lightly.
Tess obediently lowered her foot and brought up the other
one. Her left thigh got the same treatment, but Rolf lingered a
bit more on her calf, bending to kiss that, which made her go all
liquid before he let her lower her foot. Tess was losing it; the
pain had started to go away, she suspected because her en-
dorphins were soaring.

The second Tess' foot was down, Madame Iris pulled the
leash firmly, and Tess was down, too, legs spread and face
inches from Rolf's good-sized cock, which he'd slipped out of
his jock strap in the split second when Tess was between
standing and kneeling.

Madame Iris kept pulling steadily, gathering the leash around
her hand in the way one might for an errant dog, reeling Tess in

until the slut put her lips on the glistening head of Rolf's cock. He had been in the sun all day and the heady scent of it had been a bit much for her in the instant before she put his cock in her mouth. But in the instant after it, she let everything go away, and the smell of his cock became like an elixir, as the taste of his already leaking pre-come got her drunk faster than a concession booth packed with $8 beer. She began to suck his cock.

Rolf's fingers caressed Tess's face as she bobbed up and down on his cock, his shaft parting her lips wide, for it was a fatty. The feeling of cock laid fully against her tongue was something she had missed in recent months; Madame Iris' strap-on was a very satisfying alternative, but hazelnut and toasted almond, as Madame Iris often observed on related but different matters, were never quite the same.

Perhaps most thrillingly, Madame Iris had orally trained Tess the way she never would have let a boyfriend do it. This was evidenced by the fact that without being told, Tess took a deep breath and relaxed her throat on the downstroke until her lips curved deliciously around the base of Rolf's thick cock. She'd never been able to do that before, and the feeling of having him all the way down sent an involuntary tightening through her sex, which had stopped hurting even a little bit as her arousal mounted.

She was so excited to have done it that she stayed down for long, long time, long enough to realize that while she found it a hell of a lot easier to deep-throat a dildo than a cock, there was something uniquely satisfying about that long, low sigh of absolute pleasure that came from Rolf's lips as her own lips settled down at his base.

Having taken a deep, deep breath and being very well trained by Madame Iris, Tess didn't feel a need to come up for air right away, so after the long sigh there was a moan, an "Oh, yeah," a longer sigh, a laugh, three laughs, and a kind of whooping sound and the slap of a high-five between Rolf and Bear, which would have been fucking bizarre if they were two straight guys and really wasn't any less so since they were gay.

When she finally came up, gasping, Bear was the one who purred, "Iris, I thought you said she was bi – I'm sorry, that is a fag. That girl is a fag."

"At this rate," sighed Iris, "you're going to try to take her home."

"Yeah, bring the van around, will you?" sighed Rolf, which she responded to by surging back hungrily onto his cock, working her head around in a big circle and listening to Rolf moan as her tongue pumped against him. She took him again but couldn't stay down as long this time, her throat aching. It didn't matter; her agenda had been achieved, and everyone was most impressed.

The last time she had sucked cock Tess had been completely untrained; now, she instinctively took the position she imagined would be expected: hands soft on the recipient's thighs, legs spread, back arched, ass pushed up as high as it could possibly go, high enough in fact, that she could feel the stretch of the position in her swollen clit. Her knees settled deliciously into the firmness of the new pads; this was a premium pair, and it aroused Tess no end to have her Mistress spend so much to ensure her comfort while she was being a slutty little cock whore.

Her lips glided up and down over the shaft of Rolf's cock, leaving a faint foamy lipstick smear on his mocha-colored cock. She alternated deep thrusts to the back of her throat and deep throats into it with long sessions of stroking her lips and flickering tongue up the underside of Rolf's shaft. He seemed to like it all, but particularly the fact that Tess was doing it so eagerly, murmuring to her that she was a good little cock-sucker and that she obviously had professional training, by which he meant, she thought with pleasure, that she was a whore.

Tess was so lost in the pleasure of sucking Rolf's beautiful cock that for a few minutes she forgot entirely that Madame Iris was watching and, she hoped, getting off on it.

When she glanced up she saw that Madame Iris was indeed getting off on it; she was kissing Bear deeply, and his hand had found its way between her legs, tucked under her patent-leather skirt into her thong panties.

What was *that* about? Tess didn't have the faintest idea that Iris was into guys – but then, when she'd started the morning the last thing she figured was that she'd end the day by sucking cock.

Tess concentrated on sucking, knowing that they had limited time and fearing, deliciously, the wrath of her Mistress if she failed to satisfy Rolf fully. She could tell he was going hot and heavy; he'd probably been half-hard all day, from the liberal flood of pre-come that glided easily down Tess's open throat.

In between her up and down motions, Tess glimpsed Madame Iris reaching into her bag and coming out with a pink smoothie, which Tess didn't recognize but which clearly wasn't brand new, given the fact that it was not packaged and already had batteries.

"Do you know how to use one of these?" Madame Iris asked Bear breathily, grinding her ass up and down on his cock.

He grinned. "I can certainly give it a shot," he said, and clicked it deftly on with his thumb, at the same time working the settings dial with his index finger and pulling Madame Iris's thong to one side as he lowered the vibe.

Tess's mouth at that moment was suckling gently at Rolf's balls, mostly because she was afraid from the sound of his moans and the quantity of pre-come that he was about to shoot, and they still had, what, eleven minutes or something? Rolf seemed to like the sensation, but Tess had never really used her mouth on a guy's balls before, so she was so immensely enjoying her experimentation that she almost didn't realize it when Madame Iris said quickly: "Not me!" and let out a long, low, laughing sigh of pleasure as Bear chuckled and slipped out from under her.

It all came on her in a whirl as she licked her way back up to Rolf's cockhead, working her lips around the tip as Bear knelt down beside her and moved the buzzing vibe to her clit. She felt a wave of terror – ow, this was going to hurt – and then just let go as she sank into the pleasure of it.

The vibe touched her swollen, pierced clit with an impossibly gentle pressure. It didn't hurt at all, except that it felt so fucking good that she wanted to cry, and when in her sudden and powerful arousal she tried to deep-throat Rolf again, she choked, because she was sucking air in great gasping sobs while she mounted toward orgasm.

Tess always went off like a rocket when she'd been teased for so long, and she hadn't been allowed to get off since the piercing – partially it was piercer's orders, but mostly, she thought, because Madame Iris was anticipating this moment.

Climaxing, Tess had to take her mouth off of Rolf's cock, letting out great shuddering groans and not even caring that people on the other side of the fabric could assuredly hear her.

She came so hard she almost forgot she was sucking cock, but the snaking of her Mistress's hand through her hair reminded her, and Tess felt the fingers of the Lady's other hand gently curving around the base of Rolf's cock as she guided Tess's mouth onto the head. Tess began to suck again, and Madame Iris seized Rolf's prick with both hands so she could feel it pulsing as he came.

Tess went dizzy with the hot spurt of come onto the back of her tongue and down her throat; she didn't gag or choke, but took it all, or as much of it as she could, drooling the rest on Madame's slender fingers.

When she came up, breathing hard, her chin was drippy and her clit was hurting, overcome by the post-orgasm sensitivity that made that vibe the most awful thing in the world. Bear withdrew it and clicked it off; he leaned in close to kiss Rolf, then Iris.

"Very good, Rolf," purred Iris. "Nineteen minutes."

"I would have come sooner," sighed Rolf. "But the little slut seemed to be enjoying herself so much."

"Let's give Arty back his photo studio," said Madame. "Drinks at the Stallion?"

"But of course," said Rolf with a smile down at Tess. "Just one blowjob doesn't break in a pair of kneepads."

The trio laughed. Madame Iris and Bear high-fived each other, which was weird, but not really *that* weird, Tess decided – all things considered.

Mr Merridawn's Hum

Cervo

It was strange to many in Little Costerbane that Mr Merridawn – who only came to town once in every several years – could make his clients now and then smile on the occasion of his involving them in his sad labors. Mr Merridawn was the hangman of the county assizes, and many other counties as well, thus making him a busy and prosperous man. Wearing a very large tricorne hat and a great black coat at all times, he was easily distinguished, but impossible to see, and thus, to know. Few would have made the effort anyway. As soon as he meets you, the hangman is soon solitary again. He is no man's friend.

Pale and thick-bodied, Mr Merridawn sported long, reddish-brown hair that came well below his shoulders. What's more, he wore a most voluptuous full beard that covered most of his remaining face like moss on a gravestone. His eyebrows bristled forth like thorns of a hedgerow. He was seen only to read the Book of Common Prayer and the King James, and thus was warranted a man of sound purpose and intellect.

A thrifty man, Mr Merridawn would stay at Old Jack's Hostelry where he kept his wagon, the many tools of his grim trade and put up his horses. These digs were much cheaper than the inn, or even the alehouse nearby. Though he never said as much, he clearly deemed them more suited to his station and calling. The polite folk of the town took that not amiss. Old Jack himself was a parsimonious sort who often said, "What you can't see don't matter, given how little most things matter when you can see 'em." Hence few candles were put out of an evening. Those that were lit were made of tallow and stank horribly. The patrons were grateful that none were replaced once burnt. There by Old Jack's hearth, in the light of a few candles, he would drink his strong beer, hum to himself, and chat of an evening with any man who dared chat back.

Late bibbers were reduced to firelight, but that was quite enough to see Mr Merridawn's coiled companion. Thirty feet of the finest half-inch hemp rope nested by him and never left his side. He oiled and worked it, tied and retied it, until the line – wrapped thirteen times about itself – slipped smoothly and without a hitch or tangle. He was a gifted expert like none other at his trade, however ironically anonymous he was as a man.

Within hours of Merridawn's arrival in Little Costerbane, a carriage stopped at the town's inn, as it always did during his dour visits. From it stepped a lone, veiled young woman in the black weeds of mourning. She would glide with the dignity of the grave to the inn's finest room, and sequester herself until the day of public retribution, when her father went to work. She was Miranda, Mr Merridawn's daughter. She lifted her veil only to those few female servants permitted to be near her. At such moments, she disclosed the loveliest, palest, and sweetest face a virgin maid could offer. When the town turned out for the hangman's entertainments, she too would slip quietly in mufti from her aerie.

Miranda was soft-spoken and tenderhearted. She yearned always for a pet, but she would not scruple to allow a little dog or cat to suffer the rigors of travel at her side while she followed her father over the land from gibbet to gibbet. Wherever she went, her kindness and beauty were such that young men and women yearned to be near her and serve her. She indulged them now and then in this passion with light conversation, but her true heart was elsewhere. A more steadfast love held Miranda, and that was to practice the hanging arts. She was drawn to men of the law whether they were bailiff or judge, petty criminal or felon. Then too, she loved men of all sorts with a discreet, but burning fascination that had nothing to do with jurisprudence.

Miranda loved men, for the most part, in the purest Christian sense with no taint of lascivious appetite, and she was careful to tell herself that almost daily. She would gaze at men all day long in pensive wonder. Some, however, she knew she secretly loved in ways that plucked at the buds of her bosom, and the tiny swelling between her thighs. She would think constantly of the eyes of younger men, now sparkling and now thoughtful. She compared their noses from long patrician slopes to upturned vales of impudence. She studied the shorn locks of farm lads at the dock, noting their sun-touched curls, as they were led away for birching or flogging. Their broad backs and sturdy, rounded buttocks – encased in snug leather breeches – forever made her want to test their strength. She wept for them sincerely as they wept heartily under her father's lash. Most of all, however, she pondered their penises. Far from ashamed of her feelings, she took this to be her secret vocation.

Until her majority, she had never touched a penis or seen one close enough to truly inspect its dimensions and contours. She would have liked to measure them, testing them, both erect and still, to see how they might differ or accord. She could see that penises were forever wrestling for freedom from the front of their young masters' trousers, and clamored especially when such young men gazed and smiled at her. The penises of older men showed interest, but with more calm reserve. Those bouncing forth from the front of boys popped up and down with no rhyme or reason at all. She could readily imagine the shape of a penis rising swiftly in pursuit of its natural target. She felt certain she possessed fine and dainty ways to raise any sort of penis, if only by teasing their masters. In so doing she was sure that they should plainly be distracted from all concerns including their own safety. As she drifted off to sleep, penises in long rows would nightly dance across her thoughts like sheep. Her fingers often found ways to enhance these stiffening fantasies and thus, she was no stranger to her own body's fragrant tastes and yearnings. What's more she could fulfill them. Such is the burden of the father of a clever girl.

In her reveries, the flat bellies and deep chests of rustic men seemed a natural bed where she might rest herself in warm delight. Sadly, however, she never got to test her skill because those men who she found most appealing were forever swinging in her father's noose before she could dally with their hanging parts. She was most drawn to young and handsome felons. She felt a naughty kinship with them, cut off as she was in the prime of her appetites as they were in the prime of their lives. Most of all, she hated the thought that they should suffer one second longer than the majesty of England's law demanded. To be hanged until dead, in her view, was enough discomfort for any man, especially a pretty one. It should be shortly done.

She longed to hang these men well and kindly – in the way of her father – so that they might suffer no more than necessary. As a wee girl in London when her father was still an apprentice, she had watched bread-stealing street urchins and near-starved whores hanged at Tyburn Hill. Often the executioner's weight had to be added by gripping their feet to help them swing with more finality. It was an unskillful business for often the head departed from the body leaving the corpse and hangman to fall in the reeking muck below. Other days were devoted to horrid tricks like splitting noses and branding wrongdoers. Such sights and screams of agony broke her little heart. She foreswore herself to the virtuous, though difficult, ideal of perfection.

Of Merridawn himself, those who met his gaze would mutter, "He's more in the company of death than life, let him keep the company of the shroud about him." Those unseeing souls who saw him thus could not, or would not, look beyond him to the slender dark shadow of his daughter, our sweet Miranda. It was perhaps just as well, for she was got out of wedlock with a laundress who proved overfond of opium until her deathly lapse into the chilly Thames. It is assumed she was carried out with the tide along with the day's other refuse.

Thus Mr Merridawn determined that he and his daughter should ride the county circuits in the wake of the assizes to do their punitive chores. For if father and daughter had no home, at least their temporary dwellings bore not the rotting stink of London's prisons. She was the object of his total care and adoration, and his every effort was devoted to her pleasure and satisfaction. She in turn, showed strict obedience. That might have made for a stunted nature in a lesser woman, but Miranda was possessed of a fine and active mind for which rebellion was unnecessary. She did not repulse confinement; she simply found ways to do exactly as she wished. Merridawn had no sons nor would he ever, being now of too great an age, he felt, to take a wife. He would thus be the last Merridawn to hang.

His daughter's girlish tragedy need hardly be stated. No woman in England, then or now, could hold the scabrous post of hangman. What would such a woman be called, "hang-woman," a word absurdly far too long? Hangstresse then? Any judge would think such a merciless task unbefitting for the mothering heart of a woman. But Miranda had one aspect now and then seen in womenfolk. She was stubborn as well as clever. It was that silent, stone-hard, and unendingly persistent stubborn-ness that only females can muster. She did not beg but fumed like well-dried peat. Her father, who loved her beyond his own salvation, relented and allowed her to become his secret appren-tice to assuage her, knowing all the while she could never practice the trade. Discretion, timing, and a measure of disguise along with some sleight of hand, made this study surprisingly easy.

Our modern hangmen are in some sense stage magicians. In cruder days, the object was to watch the penitent gag, retch and twitch his last at rope's end. It was thought instruction from the damned, but as time went on the crimes for hanging increased in number many times over. The crowds grew restless as they looked upon the jigging sufferers.

Science came to the aid of justice and so the draped scaffold with its "long drop" hid all. Like the rabbit fetched forth by magic from the hat, the hangman pulled a lever and made the miscreant disappear. All that remained was silence, save for the creaking of the rope upon the gibbet's beam. Mr Merridawn always wrapped the shroud himself after taking down the corpse to check his work. So the shroud was indeed his close companion and, though no one knew it, he had family there – his daughter – to witness his success.

And why should this worthy man not be at home by the shroud? He was born to it. His father had been a hangman before him in the West Country. His father's father had hanged many low fellows and even a few fat merchants in the area near Dover. His family, due to an understandable lack of popularity, moved about a great deal, but they were faithful to the hang-man's trade even when in harsher times the work was meaner.

They shouldered nasty tasks like maiming, branding or splitting tongues and noses. What's more, back when the Roundheads and the Royals were at each other, the demand had been quite ceaseless.

They felt it was their destiny to hang. Indeed it might have been, for it was secretly believed that Clodrose Merridawn had been one of the two masked, wigged, and costumed hangmen who had clean struck off the head of Charles Stuart at White Hall Palace in 1649. It had been, after all, a top-notch job.

Mr Merridawn never let on to anyone that his first name was Prospero, save his daughter, for he thought it too flighty a name for a hangman. The name was a drunken fancy of his father who liked the theatre. Miranda thought it very grand though and often called him Wizard, when she wished, like any impish girl, to get her father's goat.

Otherwise, she attentively scoured the iron spikes and washed the baskets of the sticky residue that would harden and smell unpleasant if it was not quickly scrubbed off. She saw to it that the braziers were filled with hot coals and then emptied before they were put into his caravan, and she made sure all the blades were sharp and that there was a sufficiency of faggots to light the sundry fires and tubs of pitch.

Her greatest pleasure was ensuring that all of the strands of the various whips, especially the cats, were neatly untangled, oiled and polished so that the lead balls fastened at intervals along each strand glittered smartly at least for the start of each flogging. She was not a cruel girl, and saw the law as the savior of order and peace. That was so in her eyes because the terrible fate of those who were caught in the law's vengeance served to warn others to stay clear of its leonine jaws and claws.

She did, however, have a deep weakness for hanging owing to the fact that it so often befell the youngest and prettiest of men who were nimble enough to try – but not to succeed – at poaching, robbing the high roads, and sheep stealing. She would comfort them in the night by singing to them softly before they dropped away from the light at dawn. On more than one occasion she had noticed that despite all the unattractive results of hanging, many of these men were taken down with their cocks still hotly erect and they had clearly ejaculated at their final moment. This was for her a new discovery, and something to consider when thinking of a stiff prick.

Ever since she had reached her majority, she had been fascinated by this awesome tribute to love, that young and strapping men should in the instant of their passing, not think of salvation, but rather of the flesh. She was unaware that their ardor was involuntary, and so thought it a serious matter that showed either their courage or the peril of their souls, or both. As she lay in her bed night after night, her hands would glide over her body as she thought about these things, her fingers finally settling in such places producing more direct and verdant pleasures, made ever-more manifest as she thought about those handsome bodies in demise. And so it was with the heaviest of hearts that Miranda Merridawn had returned to Little Costerbane on the news that the assizes had left work again for the hangman. The convicted was a man of perhaps two and twenty years, and thus but a year or two older than she. She went to the jail, unable to make herself do otherwise, and asked boldly to see him. She was instantly refused, in the name of decency, despite the claim that she had come to measure his height and ask his weight as a service to her father, since she said, "He is down by gout." This was an outrageous and childish lie. She was rebuked and told she deserved an appointment with the birch rod. This was a sentence she knew her father would rather die than carry out, but her appetite was great to see the tall young man, and the turnkey's refusal only served to make it greater.

So with the help of a chambermaid at the inn she contrived to dress herself in rags that the maid brought from the back of a common peasant girl. Once thoroughly washed and draped in a cunning way, even the rags acquired a certain charm on the person of Miranda Merridawn. They revealed just enough of her golden hair, the swell of her young body and gave center place to the wonder of her large blue-violet eyes. Even so, she could pass through the market town streets attracting no more notice than any blood and dung-spattered farm girl.

After a stop at the herbalist, she bought meat, fresh bread and a small, warm pudding along with two large drafts of strong beer. These she took for the condemned man's dinner, for he was to hang upon the morrow at the usual hour of dawn. The squire of Little Costerbane set great store by hanging, and so it was the assize's first resort as punishment when they passed judgments. The judges knew that a contented gentry makes for a long and peaceful tenure on the bench.

She found the young man of her desires in the darkest cell of the jail. He was not in good fettle and he stank. He had been left there for a week or two and was now in need of bathing. Plus he had been fed the usual offal boiled in swill that jailers give out as it saves money that can fatten their own dinners with sausages and cheese.

Miranda was possessed of great charm, and now seeming a mere peasant slag, she could, in the name of Christian charity, persuade the turnkey to let the young man out of the jail in her charge as her brother to make his peace with God. The turnkey, fairly drunk already, downed one of her drafts of strong beer. The lad was freed on Miranda's solemn promise that she would return him by dawn to face the hangman. The turnkey smiled warmly, and fell face forward to the floor, as was his wont at that late hour of the day. Miranda had learned at her father's side that a mean man may well be stupid but that a stupid man need not be mean. She wisely took the turnkey for the latter and concluded that, in the unlikely event he awoke before dawn, he would not raise the alarm. Otherwise she would have bashed his skull with his beer tankard to guarantee his silence.

The young man was a stranger to the town and so he caused no stir in his sorry attire when led away by what appeared to be his peasant wife. He stank no more than a peasant on the road. They repaired to a barn on a farm that was the family digs of the inn's chambermaid. Once inside, they were served by the silver moonlight that poured in through the open door. No other light was needed on that warm and pleasant night.

Such was Miranda's charm that the country maid had agreed to this trespass even though its discovery would at the very least lead to being stripped and whipped raw by her father, and perhaps worse if this criminal harboring of felons was discovered by the bailiff. But Miranda's great blue eyes and gentle touch were not to be denied. Once nestled in the barn, she stripped her convict, fed him, bathed his every inch, and carefully shaved him by moonlight. She had expected him to be terribly thin, but instead she found he was a man of great muscular beauty and strength if a bit poor due to prison fare.

To her utter delight, she had a sterling penis to herself for close inspection and he was happy to oblige. How sweetly did her fingers glide along the velvet sides. How interesting were the fat and throbbing veins that wrapped about the silky shaft. How thick and fragrant was the plump mushroom that capped the feast before her eyes. She touched; she licked a little, nuzzled here and there, brushed it with all sorts of touches and watched it bounce in varying replies. Slowly she came to see that cocks were independent souls, much like herself, and with this one she took delight in thinking she found a like-minded friend of some considerable standing.

She turned him round and pressing her tiny hands upon his cheeks she spread him wide for her to see. There within was the dark little star much like her own, but bigger. This she pressed and wheedled with her finger and soon discovered that the cock rose in acknowledgement of her attentions. This new surprise was quite amazing to her. She probed the hole while she stroked his cock until the young man seemed close to fainting at her touch.

He hardly spoke in his amazement at his fortune in finding this beautiful woman tending every single inch of his body to make it clean and quite perked enough to dance. At last, when she was satisfied, he lifted her chin on his own initiative, and slowly pressed his lips to hers. They yielded with a happy acquiescence that neither lover could deny. But yet it was not so easy for them to part. It was as though some flow of power from his mouth to hers had welded them together. A more objective eye would have remarked that in truth, she could not move with his arms fully wrapped and closed around her. She broke free, however, and was soon shed of her clothes. In the light from the loft they fell to playing in the straw. They rolled and kissed, tickled and scratched, probed and fiddled, as lovers will. They found their voices in sighs and giggles, and just as soon lost all

capacity for words for their mouths seemed always full of some
delicious part of each other.

He took her wrists in one of his large hands and held her still
as he kissed and kissed every inch of her, worshipping her as his
prisoner. The fragrances of her body – now tangy, now buttery
and sweet – mixed with the scent of the straw and the beasts in
their stalls. Her fingers beat a light, brisk tattoo upon his
nipples, which she then kissed and tweaked while letting her
hands wander over his body through its soft and sparse blonde
hair. When she came once more to his root, clustered all round
with its own furry hedgerow, her advance slowed. She let her
nails trace lines along his belly slipping this way and then
lashing down harder in that direction until he winced.

"I see," she said with satisfaction, as though making note of
some scientific revelation.

Then she ambled along the bones of his hips and down his
thighs until she worked her way between his knees in a harmless
investigation of their bony hardness. All the while, her nipple
had come to rest just at the head of his cock where the cleft in
the mushroom cap closed at the back just below the tip. She
could see its livid color growing deeper, even to a deep violet,
but better still, she could feel its hot pulsation against her
breast. He seemed, in the turmoil this aroused, unable to relent
or rebel against her attentions. She found that to her liking.

Thus fired, the man seized her and pressed his hot member to
penetrate her at once, but she held it firmly squeezing it hard in
her little hand at the soft entry to her cunt.

"No, not yet," she said, "I want to look at it and taste it."

What young adventurer of substantial parts could deny this
simple and flattering request? He lay back in the hay, carefully
removing any rudely intrusive strands of straw, and settled
himself with his legs wide apart. She rose and let the rest of
her clothing fall away. Free now to move, she knelt between his
legs and first slipped her fingers under his balls. These she raised
as high as they would go, stretching the skin on them until he
moaned softly. She allowed her nails to graze the surface of the
skin as she slowly released it. Then she cupped his balls in her
little hand and was delighted to see that her palm was hardly large

enough to contain them. She gently massaged them until his cock began to bounce in a clear demand for more immediate attention.

This she provided by running her tongue slowly up its underside and down again until she let its firm tip burrow in the recess were his cock met his balls. His reaction was most satisfactory in that he arched his back and thrust his hips upward in a silent plea for more. Instead she found this a fine chance to cup the roundness of his bottom in her two hands and test its springy resilience, which was, in fact, quite excellent.

By sheer instinct she decided next to throw her leg over his face and settle her cunt on his mouth. It proved the right decision. His tongue dove and lapped in the moist sea of her pussy, reveling like a sea serpent as she wiggled her rump down firmly onto his face. His view was now entirely consumed by the perfect cleft of her bottom and it was a vista of pure delight to him. His senses filled with the warm, wet taste and smell of her body. Soon she was bucking and clamping her thighs to press herself more tightly down onto his mouth.

To her surprise, his hands reached up to pinch her nipples. A sharp but exquisite pain raced from them to her cunt until she could not help but grind her sopping pussy into his face with all her might until she squealed and bucked even harder at the pleasures of his mouth. He came like a bull let out to pasture for the first time since winter.

She collapsed in a dreamy fog only to find herself facing his cock once again. This she took into her mouth at once and commenced a fevered sucking as she drove her head up and down so that the head of it nearly went down her throat. Dissatisfied with this, she wheeled around and screwed herself furiously down onto the shaft of his fat, smooth cock. Some young ladies know how to do these things by instinct. She had mastered the idea through a combination of pleasuring herself and studying the lie of stiff cocks pressing against the pants that enclosed them.

What's more she was no longer a virgin as one might guess. Instead, she had been deflowered during a midnight tryst with a cucumber in a warm bath. She had accounted it no great loss and now found it a positive sign of good fortune.

She now fucked the young felon until at last an herbal draft that she had slipped into his ale took hold of him. He fell into a heavy torpor at which point the sullen chambermaid appeared as instructed in the barn. She and Miranda placed the young man in a dogcart, and hauled him back to his cell past the jailer who was still recumbent in his cups on the floor.

Shortly before dawn the young man awoke to find Mr Merridawn seated across from him in his cell. He was for once not carrying his rope, as that now swung from the gallows outside, which was soon to find employment. Mr Merridawn smiled and hummed, saying nothing. The young man made to rise but he was still somewhat affected by the night's amusements and in any case the parson, the bailiff and his two local louts arrived before any conversation could begin.

In this passive state, the young man was led to the scaffold. There he was placed on the trap and, after a few brief words from the local squire on the majesty of the law, felt the noose placed around his neck.

Mr Merridawn paused in his hum to lean close to the young man's ear and whisper, "I won't use the hood, son. For you've nothing to fear. My daughter's waiting for you below." Thinking this some hope of salvation, the young man smiled. Then the hangman took up his hum once again, stepped back to the lever and, satisfied that all was in order, pulled it.

From below Miranda looked up into the rising light of day to see her lover as he plummeted to his death. All the while she had her fingers firmly at play in her pussy. When the young man hit the end of the rope, being of a virile age, he exploded immediately, coming in his trousers, though he was soon quite dead. Miranda made sure, with her carefully honed skills of the gallows, to come at the same time, and of course to avoid being struck by his swinging, still jerking, corpse. Once sated, she would cut the rope, as any hangman's assistant should, and let the man fall to earth where the bailiff's lout would see to his burial. The only sound heard was Mr Merridawn's hum.

Incurable Romantic

Lisabet Sarai

She is, without a doubt, the perfect slave.

I should know. I've trained half a dozen slaves over the last twenty years, and played with perhaps half a hundred more.

In Minneapolis? you ask, incredulous. The law-abiding, church-going, vanilla-flavored heartland?

Why would I lie? I'm past the point where I have to prove myself. We have our own kinky little community here, invisible to those who don't want to see, obvious to the initiates who know the signs.

Like Ilsa's collar. If you weren't one of us, and you happened to notice it, you might think it's one of those choker necklaces so popular with the Britney Spears set. It's braided black leather, strung with tiny diamonds. You might expect a matching diamond stud piercing her navel.

If you truly paid attention, though, you might recognize something unusual in the way Ilsa wears it. She holds her head exceptionally high, her back straight, her graceful neck extended, showing the collar off like a badge of honor. Which of course it is, my gift to her upon her completion of one year in my service. In truth, though, wearing it is her gift to me, a tangible and public statement of her total devotion.

She never removes it. The candlelight makes it sparkle, now, as I gaze on her naked, bound beauty. Her wrists are roped together and fastened to the hook in the ceiling. A few red-gold locks have escaped from her barrette and trail down her back, contrasting with the darker red of the stripes my whip has carved in her tender flesh. Her creamy skin is flushed and damp with sweat. I kneel behind her and use my tongue to gather a salty drop that has run down her spine, just as it is about to disappear into the shadows between her swelling butt cheeks.

Ilsa shivers in delight at my touch. I reward her by pulling her open and lapping at her anus. She is still loose and slick with lube and my come. She cannot help responding, pushing her hips back to invite me deeper into her dark recess. I draw away and land a rousing slap on one buttock. "Didn't I tell you to be still?" I growl.

We both understand that my anger is feigned. "Yes, Master," she murmurs. "I'm sorry. When you touch me, it's so difficult."

"A well-trained slave knows how to control herself." I don't tell her, of course, that she is perfect. "Clearly, you need more punishment. Turn around."

On tiptoe, the spreader bar between her ankles making her awkward, she manages to maneuver her body to face me. Her eyes are cast down, those long sooty lashes of hers (so different from her spun-copper hair) making spiky shadows on her cheeks. Her lips are parted, her breath fast and shallow.

I intend to apply my whip to her luscious breasts, gleaming and still unmarked in the light of the candles. Instead, I find myself kissing her, sharing the funky flavors that I just sampled from her butthole. She opens to me, not only her mouth but her whole self, allowing me to feast upon her until I am sated. She keeps nothing back.

Candlelight and kisses. I may be a nasty old Dom, but I'm still an incurable romantic.

It's true that I've never known surrender as complete as what Ilsa offers. I find it a bit scary. She tells me that she will do anything for me, and I almost believe her. I'm sure that she has limits; everyone has limits, that's SM 101. But I haven't found them yet.

I've used paddles and floggers of every description, clamps and clothespins, electricity and chili oil. I've staked her out, naked and in full view of the world, on the balcony of my condo in January. This is in Minnesota, remember. After ten minutes, her ivory skin turned blue. She never complained, never used her safe word. I hastened to bring her inside, wrap her in blankets and feed her hot tea and brandy. The clear light of adoration in her eyes never wavered. I was the one who felt chastened.

I've shared her at play parties, watching as my friends buggered and beat her. Afterwards, she was more tender and attentive than ever. I'll never forget the night that I invited two rising stars in our community, Master Shark and Mistress Valentine, to come over and try her. They were far rougher on her than I could ever be. After an enema and a caning, being fisted by Shark and pissed on by Valentine, she was bruised and exhausted, but apparently in a state of bliss.

"You know you could always stop them, Ilsa," I told her later. "They know your safe word, and they would honor it."

"But Master," she murmured dreamily, on the edge of consciousness. "I wanted to please you."

She does please me, of course. Sometimes I can't believe my good fortune, to have won the devotion of this angel/slave when she could have chosen a younger, more handsome, more energetic Dom.

Often, though, I realize that there is something wrong in our relationship, something missing. Thinking about her brings on an unpleasant anxiety, vague but annoying.

I'm thinking about her now, as I sit sipping Starbucks cappuccino and trying to read Murakami. Could any person truly be so pliant and submissive? What kind of childhood did she have, to make her this way? When I asked, she told me that her upbringing had been "normal", unexceptional. Did I believe her? Why would she choose a master so much older than she? Old enough to be her father? There must be some secret here, some story she won't, or perhaps can't, share, even with me.

All at once, my thoughts are rudely interrupted. Something slams into my chair from behind. My coffee leaps out of the cup and onto my lap. My cock is scalded, even through my trousers and undershorts. Anger rises in me as I turn to confront the culprit.

"What do you think you're doing? You should be more careful!" I don't need to shout. My voice naturally carries the authority of long years of dominance.

"Oh, I'm so sorry!" My first impressions are youth, plumpness, a certain disheveled quality that is not entirely unappealing. "Are you hurt?" She notices the coffee stain spreading over my crotch. "Oh, dear! I am really such a klutz!"

Her eyes are a warm brown behind wire-rimmed glasses. As she gazes in dismay at the mess in my lap, I find, to my chagrin, that my half-boiled penis is hardening in response to her attention.

She doesn't miss this sign. There's still concern in her voice, but I catch a hint of laughter as well. "I really apologize. I'll pay for the dry-cleaning, of course."

"No need," I say, more gruffly than I intend. I pull my chair closer to the wrought-iron café table, trying to hide my erection. "My housekeeper will get the stain out."

An image flashes involuntarily through my mind: Ilsa on her knees, nude except for her collar, scrubbing at my pants on an old-fashioned washboard. Meanwhile I tower over her, jerking off into her hair. This picture does nothing to reduce my arousal. I think that's the key to being a great dominant: a kinky imagination that is always at work, even at the most inappropriate moments.

"Oh, please, let me do something to make it up to you! I'll buy you another coffee." Before I can stop her, she's at the counter conferring with the barrista. I pretend to read, but actually I'm surveying her, trying unsuccessfully for a dispassionate evaluation.

She carries more weight than is fashionable, but it's all curves. Her soft olive sweater and jeans emphasize this. She has straight brown hair that she has tried to confine in a ponytail; wisps escape all over to hang untidily around her face. She moves with a determined energy, solid and confident. I contrast her headlong progress as she stumbles among the tables balancing two cups, with Ilsa's fragile grace. There's no comparison. Still, I find, I want her.

She seats herself across from me. "Double cappuccino with skim milk, both cinnamon and chocolate, right?" She barely gives me the chance to nod my assent. "I guess you're a regular here, too. I'm surprised I haven't seen you before."

"I'm pretty inconspicuous," I comment lamely, knowing that with my height and dominant presence, this is not at all true.

"Hardly!" she says with a laugh. "Anyway, I'm glad to meet you now, though I'm sorry to have damaged you and your pants in the process." She tries to steal a glance under the table, to gauge my current state of tumescence. I have foiled her by transferring my book to my lap.

"I'm Kate," she says, holding out her hand. "And you are . . .?"

"Riordan," I say, finally, when it's clear that I can't avoid answering.

"What an unusual name!"

"It's Celtic," I say. "Traditional in my family."

"Well, it's very romantic." Her smile is infectious. "What do you do, Riordan?"

"Officially, I'm retired. Early retirement," I hasten to add. "I was CEO for an industrial equipment distributor. Now I do a bit of this and a bit of that. Play the stockmarket. Do guest lectures for MBA programs. Write." Train slaves, I think privately. I try to imagine Kate shackled and on her knees and fail utterly.

"I noticed you were reading Murakami and wondered if you were a writer. He's not exactly in the bestseller category." She sighs and stretches her arms over her head, causing her sweater to bulge delightfully, and my cock to follow suit. "I'm working on a novel, myself. In my spare time, of course. My day job is writing advertising copy."

"Well, at least it's writing," I say. This girl confuses me, with her aggressive friendliness.

"Yeah, well . . . it's not much fun, but it pays the rent." She has an idea; I can literally see it light up her face. "Speaking of apartments, why don't you come over to mine for dinner some time soon?" She places her hand casually on my thigh. "I'm an excellent cook; all my friends say so."

She can see my hesitation. She turns up the pressure. "Please, Riordan, let me make up for my clumsiness by cooking you a nice dinner. How about tomorrow night?"

It's strange to have a woman call me by name instead of "Master". Once again, I have a sense of disorientation. I know I should refuse, for my own sake as well as for Ilsa's. But somehow, I can't. Or at least, I don't.

"All right. What time?"

"How about seven?" She tears a sheet out of her notebook and scribbles something in a round, flowing script. "Here's my address and phone number."

"Uh, thanks." Where did my usual eloquence go?

Kate glances at her watch and stands up so suddenly that she nearly overturns her own coffee. "Oh, God, I've got to go! I'm really late. Is there anything you don't eat?"

I shake my head, speechless in the face of her energy.

"Great! Well, I'll see you tomorrow, then." She grabs my hand and squeezes it enthusiastically. "Thanks for being such a good sport, Riordan."

My hand and my cock are both throbbing in the wake of her whirlwind departure. I'm puzzled by my own reactions. My well-honed instincts tell me that Kate has no interest in kinky games. She's young, fresh, horny, and 100 per cent vanilla. Whereas I have had dominant fantasies since I was in grade school. I really can't understand why the prospect of ordinary, unadorned sex, without any paraphernalia or power exchange, suddenly seems so intoxicating.

Ilsa is waiting for me at the door when I return home. She is completely charming in her French maid costume: translucent black organdy top, frilly lace apron, and bare buttocks. And her collar, of course.

"Good evening, Master. Would you like a cocktail before dinner?"

"Scotch on the rocks. Please." I feel awkward with my sweet slave, in the aftermath of my encounter with Kate. "But I think we will go out for dinner tonight. Wear the green silk sheath. Without any underwear."

"Of course." Ilsa is trying to smother her smile and remain serious and respectful. She loves it when I take her out and show her off. She is already imagining the clinging softness of the silk against her bare skin.

The sting of my palm on her exposed behind brings her out of her reverie. "What about my drink, slave? Do I have to teach you how to provide such a simple service?"

"No, of course not, Master. Right away, sir."

She hurries off, swaying on her spike heels. I admire the reddening image of my hand on her white flesh as she disappears into the kitchen. Perfection indeed.

The next evening, I chain Ilsa to the foot of our bed. "I have to go out," I tell her, as I hand her the water bottle and the chamber pot. "I have some business. I may be quite late."

Why am I lying to her? We both know that I am the Master. I am free to do as I wish. She has chosen to accept that. If I want to see another woman, isn't that my prerogative?

I realize that if I were going to a play party tonight, or to help break in another Dom's slave, I'd be telling Ilsa the truth.

I have no illusions about tonight's dinner engagement. I can see very clearly what Kate wants, could see it long before she opens the door wearing a tight red jersey dress that showcases her ample cleavage and plump, freckled thighs.

We don't even get past the second glass of wine. With dizzying speed, Kate propels me into her bedroom and sucks me into a hot, wet kiss. She tears off my clothes with such abandon that I worry, briefly, about damage. Then she sits me on the bed and does a slow, delicious striptease in front of me.

She slips one strap off her shoulder and I catch a glimpse of the black lace cradling her lush breasts. The other strap slides down and they're revealed in all their glory. No padding needed here. In fact the lace is so delicate that her rigid nipples visibly distort it.

Next she gradually raises her hem to just below her pubis. "Want more?" she whispers. My swollen cock bobs in my lap. I suppress the urge to grab her, rip her dress open and ravage her, and simply nod.

She pulls the dress over her head, displaying her black satin thong. Her breasts rise and tighten at the motion. My cock aches. I can't take much more of this.

Kate seems be losing patience, too. She slips the thong down her thighs and kicks it away, then unhooks the brassiere in front. Twin globes of ripe flesh spill out. I lick my lips, my mouth suddenly flooded with saliva. With a half smile, Kate takes a step closer and feeds me her abundant tits, one at a time.

Before I can understand how it happens, I am on my back, with Kate astride me, riding me hard. She's wild, bucking and squirming, all her monumental energy focused on that spot where our bodies join. She rubs at her clit with one hand, pinches her nipple with the other. I grab her hips and arch up into her, trying to give her what she needs to push her over the edge.

I'm enjoying myself, of course, but I am somehow removed from the scene. I watch our bodies writhing with the same sense of detachment that I feel observing a couple fucking at a play party. I am simultaneously aroused and distant. I'm as hard as I have ever been, but it feels as though I am a long way from coming.

Her orgasm is a noisy cataclysm, that, to my surprise, sweeps me away with it.

Afterwards, Kate feeds me quiche and salad in bed, washed down with two bottles of white wine. Then she snuggles up to me, trapping me in her arms, feathering my cheeks with kisses. "Thank you, Riordan," she sighs, half-asleep already. "That was wonderful. You're a fabulous lover."

I don't respond. What can I say? If you think that was good, you should try me when I've got a flogger and some nipple clamps?

Kate sleeps. I don't. I'm turning the whole experience over in my head, wondering what I have done, and why. I think about Ilsa, waiting for me in chains, and tears prick my eyes.

Near dawn, Kate rolls over, releasing me from her embrace. I tiptoe around the bedroom, gathering and donning my scattered clothes. I notice my shirt is missing two buttons, and that Kate snores.

I should kiss her goodbye, I know, but I'm afraid that I'll wake her. So I sneak out of her apartment like a thief, ashamed and guilty that I am abandoning her.

I haven't smoked in fifteen years, but now I buy a pack of cigarettes at a 7–11 and prowl the empty sidewalks of the city, lighting one after another, shivering in the October chill.

I've already forgotten Kate; it's Ilsa that I'm worried about now. In some strange way, it seems, I've betrayed her trust. She asks nothing more from me than to be her Master, to train her and mold her, to guide her towards more complete submission. To perfect her.

And what do I do? I leave her alone while I chase some juicy vanilla morsel who just wants me for my hard and willing cock.

I'm lazy, that's the plain truth of it. But that's not all. I'm afraid. I tell myself that I can't fathom Ilsa's limits, but have I really tried? Have I accepted the fact that I might need to give her more, push her harder, go deeper with her than I've ever gone with a slave?

Perhaps it's really my limits that need to be expanded. There are things I could do, implements I could use, that I've never tried. To be honest, they make me uncomfortable. If this is what Ilsa requires, though, can I deny her? I understand, suddenly, that it is not only Ilsa who needs to be perfected.

She's asleep, curled up on the carpet, when I tiptoe into the bedroom. A stray beam of early morning sunlight filters through the drapes and gilds her coppery curls. She looks like an angel, but what angel ever displayed the fading pink marks of a caning on her unblemished skin?

A pang of guilt and regret lances through me, as excruciating as physical pain. I don't deserve her. I should set her free.

I am about to turn away and slink out of the room, when she stirs.

"Master," she says, not trying to hide her smile. "You're home." She raises herself onto her knees, thighs spread, wrists clasped at the small of her back, as I taught her. She dares to look up at me. "I missed you."

I need to be stern with her, I remind myself. I need to offer her extremes of pleasure and pain that far surpass anything we've yet experienced together. I must be willing to bring her to the point where she trusts me enough to utter her safe word, without fearing my displeasure. No matter what it takes.

I must be fierce and implacable, cruel and merciless, immune to any doubt or fear, in order to be the Dom that she needs.

Incurable romantic that I am, I can only kneel beside her and take her in my arms.

The Other Woman

Ed Aymar

Are you married? Lilac69 asked.

Thomas had met her late at night, playing, of all things, online Dominos. He won the first two games and she won the third before either of them wrote anything in the text box at the bottom of the screen, a shy "hi," submitted by her.

Hello, Thomas wrote back.

And so it began. Lilac69 told him that she had a husband who traveled often and three kids whom, she joked, she wished her husband would take on his trips. Thomas was surprised to learn that she lived in Baltimore; he was a mere forty minutes away, in Annapolis.

Are you married? she had asked.

Thomas knew that he had no reason to be truthful or, for that matter, to believe anything told to him. For all he knew, Lilac69 was a thirteen-year-old boy from Pennsylvania, a transvestite from Texas, or maybe a college student in Taiwan. Or she could be what she said she was: a thirty-nine-year-old Baltimore woman contemplating divorce from a man who had, she was relatively certain, spent the last year screwing one of their neighbors.

I'm divorced, Thomas lied.

I wish I was.

Their conversation continued. Thomas hadn't met anyone online with whom he shared as many similarities as Lilac69. Location and age, for starters, and he discovered even more: they had both moved, at young ages, to the east coast from the west; they listened to the same music (both had been introduced, by their children, to the White Stripes); they enjoyed the same food; they went to the same web sites. They were insomniacs. They were bored.

Do you ever come down to Baltimore? she asked.

But one of her children needed attention before he could respond. I'll be right back, she wrote. She wasn't.

Thomas waited, watching the Dominos blocks that hadn't fallen for hours until he began to suspect that she had logged off. He stayed online for another hour, idly looking at news web sites and checking his e-mail until he gave up, shut down his computer, gave sleeping Julia a guilty kiss good night and fell to sleep himself.

He had been spending a lot of time on the Internet recently, playing Dominos and writing to strangers. He was usually online both at home and at work; he had even started skipping lunches and eating at his desk just to stay on the computer even more. His new addiction was wearing; he woke up tired the day after his conversation with Lilac69, fixed breakfast and walked Julia out. His office, where he worked as a managing copywriter, was a short ride from his house and Thomas was the first one in. He immediately logged on to the Dominos web site and was delighted when, minutes later, Lilac69 again appeared.

Sorry about last night, she wrote. Family drama.

No problem, he wrote back.

She wanted to know more about him: where he worked and where in Annapolis he lived, but Thomas didn't feel comfortable revealing such personal information. Lilac69 didn't share his reservations. After a few of Thomas' vague responses, she freely began to discuss her frustrations with her marriage.

We barely even fuck anymore, Lilac69 wrote. Thomas stood from his desk, hurried to his office door and shut it.

That would depress me too, he replied, when he sat back down.

What's the longest you've gone without it?

Depends . . . how long was I a teenager?

lol

The turn in their conversation to sex didn't surprise him; most of Thomas' online conversations were sexual. At thirty-seven, he wasn't entirely clueless with what was happening in the world, but it did seem that he had missed a couple of years when women had grown more sexually reckless. I want you to fuck my ass, they wrote to him, or they asked him to cum on my face or in my mouth or on my tits or on my back or in my pussy or between my toes. They wanted to be spanked, fucked, smacked, slapped, strapped, licked, bit, they wanted every available opening filled and fucked soundly, this invisible land of anonymous women. Their sexual experiences ranged from risky to bizarre: I had sex in the back of a movie theater, one woman told him; I sucked off a horse once, wrote another.

Did sex have anything to do with your first wife leaving? Lilac69 asked.

Thomas considered her question.

No, the sex was always good.

Then why did she leave, if you don't mind me asking.

Thomas had only one memory of why she had left, one that replayed over and over in his mind, in his dreams, coming to him suddenly during the day at work or driving home; everything else from that night three years ago – the phone call, the rush to the hospital, the halting way he explained what happened to their daughter, the funeral – were single snapshots, empty of anything but the physical moment itself, an album of images he never opened.

She met someone, Thomas wrote.

Were you ever with anyone else? When you were with her.

Once, he lied. You?

Once.

Was it worth it?

Oh God yes.

Why'd it end?

Guilt.

Thomas remembered waiting for word on his wife as he tried not to think about the terrible phrase the doctor had used (". . . pried her body from the car . . ."), hoping to a God he had never much turned to before that she would be okay, worried more than he could have ever imagined being worried when a man had approached him, an older man with wet blue eyes, holding hands with a smaller elderly woman.

"Are you her husband?"

Thomas was confused; it was hard for him to focus. "What?"

"Are you her husband?" the old man asked again.

"Of the woman in the car accident?" the smaller woman added.

"Oh, yes."

"We're so sorry," the old man said, brokenly. "We didn't see her. We didn't even see the red light. It was our fault."

"We were driving the other car," the woman explained.

Thomas looked around. Everyone in the waiting room was watching their little drama.

He turned back to the old man, the woman leaning over his shoulder, whispering into his ear. And Thomas suddenly felt something he had rarely felt before. His pain wasn't gone, far from it, in fact, but he knew that he wouldn't want someone else to suffer the way he was, the way he would. It was as if a path had opened before him; inherently, he felt it was the correct path, and he leaned toward the old man and whispered, "I know; I forgive you."

I don't know if I could do it again, Lilac69 wrote. Maybe. I wouldn't want to have another affair, though. Did your wife find out what you did?

No.

Was it worth it?

Yes, Thomas wrote, and there was that guilt, floating around him like a fly. He wished that, like a fly, he could bat it away.

What would you want? he asked her. If not an affair?

I just want to get laid.

Thomas laughed, and he glanced at his office door and adjusted the computer monitor so that it faced him entirely.

Glad we have that in common, he wrote.

You too?

Well, I am a man. It's always a priority.

A sudden e-mail reminded him of his lunch plans.

Hey, he wrote to Lilac69, I've got to step out for a moment. Are you going to be around later today?

I'll be here, she replied.

He logged off.

A minute later he logged back on and returned to the Dominos web site.

I thought you had to go, Lilac69 wrote.

My plans changed, he answered. He couldn't leave her.

I've always had this fantasy, Lilac69 wrote, near the end of Thomas' work day. Want to hear it?

You have to ask?

lol . . . okay, I just meet someone somewhere, some stranger . . . I always imagined myself in a park, and I see myself waiting at the railing, wearing a short skirt, and a man would come behind me and slide my skirt up. I wouldn't even turn around, would never see his face . . . I might feel his arms around my waist, or his hands over mine, or him kissing my neck, but I would definitely feel his dick. Real fast, rough . . . you want to hear something?

Okay

I started fingering myself.

Thomas was already wiping cum off his keyboard and hoping that no one walked into his office. He crumpled up a wet paper towel and threw it into the trashcan next to his desk.

Same here, he typed.

You're fingering your penis?

Not exactly.

Look . . . do you want to continue this conversation later? Lilac69 asked.

Later tonight?

Later in person.

They planned that the sex would be anonymous. No real names, no conversation, no formalities; afterward, they would delete their IDs and they agreed to never look for each other. The hotel would be the Renaissance in Baltimore's inner harbor; the time of their rendezvous, one p.m. Thomas took off the entire next day before he left his office and, as he did every weekday afternoon, drove to the Wilsons' house.

"She'll be out soon, Tom," Karen Wilson told him, standing in the doorway. Thomas could hear Julia and Karen's daughter,

Rebecca, talking in high voices somewhere behind her. "They're washing off makeup."

"Makeup?"

"Is that okay?" Karen asked, suddenly alarmed. "They came home wanting to try some on, and I didn't think it'd be a problem."

"It's no problem," Thomas assured her, although the idea did make him uncomfortable. "Besides, it's probably better that you supervise something like that instead of me." He meant it; Thomas trusted Karen, and her husband Paul, a great deal. Friends of his wife before she had died, they insisted on doing whatever they could to help raise Julia, including watching her for these hours between the end of her school day and his work day.

Julia appeared at the door, her cheeks red from scrubbing, faded blue over her eyes.

"I'm ready," she announced.

"You're clearly not," Thomas replied, and Karen laughed.

He fixed her dinner when they arrived home, chicken and rice and a small bowl of vegetables, and then she did her homework while he logged back onto his computer and searched for Lilac69. He didn't find her, and Julia finished her homework early so he turned off the computer, reviewed his daughter's schoolwork and they watched television for a bit. She fell asleep next to him around nine, as she always did, and he carried her to bed, logged back on and was greeted with an IM.

Are you excited? Lilac69 asked.

I am beyond excited, Thomas pronounced.

I wish I was fucking you right now.

They masturbated together, and Thomas didn't fall asleep until five. The alarm woke him at six-thirty and he groggily climbed out of bed. He staggered down the hall to Julia's bedroom and knocked on her door.

"Honey?"

"Yeah, Dad?" Julia had turned twelve a month ago and he had witnessed, and been somewhat alarmed by, the changes in her behavior. A curt "Dad" had replaced her endearing "Daddy," and she had started demanding more privacy; Thomas no longer felt comfortable walking into her room unannounced. Their conversations had also changed; Julia used to talk with him about anything, even topics that he couldn't imagine she cared about, such as his job or childhood or favorite summer vacation. But now she was only interested when he asked her about the boys in her class, or her girlfriends . . . and he knew, ruefully, that those topics would soon become her private concerns as well.

Thomas walked to the kitchen, flicking on lights along the way, and remembered his secretive plans for the afternoon. He felt immensely happy at the thought, especially since he hadn't been with anyone since his wife had died . . . and then he grew a little worried. Disease, scam, lies; there were a number of things that could go wrong. For all he knew, he could end up in a bathtub with his better organs carved out. And he had a responsibility to Julia. These thoughts panicked him, and he did his best to ignore them.

He had finished making eggs and was setting down her glass of orange juice when Julia walked into the kitchen.

"Scrambled eggs?" his daughter asked. "What's the occasion?"

"No occasion," Thomas said, as she settled in her chair. "Just know you like them."

"Thanks," Julia said, her fork already in her mouth. Every day she looked more and more like her mother. Thomas had also been an only child and never privy to observing someone else change and grow, and it was remarkable for him to watch Julia mature; sometimes it seemed like the changes happened overnight, as if she shed a skin every dawn. She had always been thin, gaunt even, but her cheeks were getting rounder, and her stomach and breasts had begun to fill. It wasn't because of a lack of exercise; Thomas took her to soccer practice on Saturdays and, until she had expressed a recent desire to quit, tae-kwon-do on Sundays. It was her mother's inherited body. Thomas often wondered what traits, if any, Julia had taken from him.

She set her fork down. "What are you looking at?"

"What?"

"You're staring at me."

"I didn't realize I was."

"Well, stop it," she said, irritably.

Thomas hurried to the computer after Julia left for school. Lilac69 wasn't online, but she had sent him an e-mail. A sense of dread rushed over him; he hoped she wasn't going to cancel.

I can't stop thinking about this afternoon, she had written. Renaissance, 1:00.

Thomas logged off and promised himself that he wouldn't use the computer again; he didn't want to appear overeager if Lilac69 saw he was online. He spent his morning on the couch, comfortably rebelling against the notion of doing anything productive. He ate a lot of crappy food, he watched and enjoyed some terrible television and he fought the urge to masturbate.

At ten o'clock he took a leisurely long shower and headed to Baltimore. He parked at a shopping pavilion near the harbor and bought and wore a new outfit – slacks and a polo and brown shoes – and sat near the harbor, watching the water, until he remembered that this was a place his wife had enjoyed. He stood and left. It was almost one o'clock.

The hotel was a short sunny walk from the shopping center, and he asked the front desk clerk if a key had been left for a Mister Bottomley (not my real name, Lilac69 had assured him).

The clerk looked through the desk, and Thomas realized he was going to tell him no key had been left.

"Room 606," the man at the desk said, and handed him a small envelope.

A woman shared the elevator with him as it whirred up from the lobby. She wore shorts and sandals and had French-manicured toenails and was startlingly attractive. Thomas wondered if Lilac69 resembled her . . . or was her.

The doors opened to the sixth floor, and he stepped out alone. Room 606 was three doors down.

Thomas was nervous, nearly shaking, but he fumbled the key card into the lock. He pulled open the door when the lock light turned green.

"Lilac?" Thomas asked. He wasn't sure if he should add the sixty-nine.

"I'm here," she said, her voice high and timid. He was relieved that she sounded as nervous as he was.

Thomas stepped into the room. He could barely breathe.

"Should I turn on the lights?" he asked. He could see a small bathroom on his right, and the edge of the bed around the corner.

No deliberation in her answer. "No. But close the door."

Darkness enveloped him when he did. Thomas walked slowly toward her voice, his hand pressed against the wall, and lay next to her shadowed form. He tried not to sound clumsy as he settled on the bed. His hand accidentally brushed her body and he felt a coarse lace and realized she was wearing a negligee; given the novelty of the situation, he had imagined that, like him, she would be cautious. Her readiness surprised him. They lay side by side for a moment, not speaking, each looking up, and he was starting to think that nothing was going to happen when she turned to him, swung her leg over and mounted him.

Her body wasn't heavy but it pressed down on him and the rush of sensations – the feeling of her thighs over his, her pubic bone grinding down – excited him. He could see a little, only a little, of her in the dark: a small protruding stomach; short curly hair; the curving outline of a shoulder as she bent and kissed him; the smell of perfume on the side of her neck. Her lips were chapped as their mouths met.

His excitement was growing and her hips adjusted and pushed down even harder. She lifted the lingerie off her body and he took off his shirt. His fingers traced up her sides and she inhaled sharply and squirmed; she was ticklish. Her breasts were smaller than he had assumed; each felt in his hand like a soft small bun of warm bread. She leaned over and, again, they lay side to side, her legs now circling his waist, her nipple now between his lips. A moan escaped her mouth. She reached down and undid his slacks, roughly, and his dick spilled into her hands. He pushed his pants off and, both naked, she pulled him hard, too hard and too high, and he held her wrist and guided her hand slower and lower. He reached for her and his hand disappeared between her legs and he felt hair, and then wetness. She was so wet that his hand slipped and his finger pushed inside of her too quickly. Her back arched and she murmured "ow" and he responded with an "oops, sorry" and, simultaneously, they stopped and laughed.

They massaged each other more genuinely now, kissing deeply, and Thomas remembered a time, after he had been married almost a month, when he had thought, not unhappily, that he would never kiss a different woman again. He enjoyed kissing Lilac69, touching her, feeling her nipple expand under his hand, her pussy opening and closing over the tip of his finger, the way her hips started to swing back and forth . . .

"I know we said we wouldn't," she said, speaking softly, her lips an inch from his; he felt her breath. "But . . ." Her voice dragged.

"What?"

"Can I go down on you?"

He nodded, and their noses touched. "I'd be okay with that."

"Good," she said, and her body turned, curved, and she curled by his legs. Her hand wrapped around his penis again and she kissed and caressed the head. Her lips closed over it and he felt her suck, and he heard her lips softly smack when she released. Her tongue slid over the tip, thirstily. His rush was starting – a low sound left him, surprising him, and her lips wrapped around his shaft. He felt himself fill her mouth.

"I'm going to come," he told her, urgently.

She stopped and pulled back.

"Did you bring a condom?"

"Yeah," he said.

"Put it on." And she rolled away from him and off the bed.

Thomas waited a moment to let the rise settle, and then he fumbled around the sheets until he found his pants, took the condom out of the pocket, tore open the packet and pulled the slippery condom on. He saw her silhouette lean over the base of the bed.

"Get behind me," she said.

He did. She leaned over, her ass a dark heart in front of him and he slipped inside her easily, too easily . . . she's had kids, he thought. Thomas realized she was playing with herself while they fucked; he could see her arm draped on the bed and he felt her other hand, felt her fingers firmly rub her clit as he disappeared inside. Her moans were louder now, timed with his, turning into cries as his hips pushed against her ass. He was so close to coming that he nearly pulled out but, sensing his state, she bent her lower back and lifted her hips and pushed into him. "Come in me," she implored him, her voice high. His thoughts were everywhere, as uncontrollable as if they were slipping on ice . . . and then they were all wiped away by a moment of sudden surprising tenderness, as if he had found whatever had been missing in him, whatever had been lost, here in this dark room, in her. Thomas came like he was trying to drown her, and he leaned over her body and reached around her hips and squeezed her body closer to his. The intimacy of his arms seemed to surprise her, and she said a faint "oh" and her muscles relaxed, accepting him.

He pulled out of her and shuffled around the bed. They lay next to each other, breathing roughly, exhausted, holding hands. The room smelled of her sex. She squeezed his hand briefly, released it and stood. The woman dressed. He watched the shadow of her leg lift as she slipped on one shoe and then the other, slightly off balance, leaning on the bed for support.

"Can I see you?" he asked.

She hesitated. "I thought we said . . ."

"I mean now, with the lights on, before you go."

"Oh, no."

The door opened and the light from the hallway spilled in, but she ducked out so quickly that Thomas saw nothing but a moment of dark, curly hair.

And then she was gone. The condom was cold on him.

There was a parents-teachers conference later that week, and Thomas couldn't help but feel that he was the one in trouble as he talked to each of Julia's teachers. He wondered how they would react if they knew he had had sex with a stranger he met online – the idea seemed grossly irresponsible now that he had done it. But none of the teachers had anything negative to say about him or his daughter: "Julia is a good student but a little quiet, which is certainly understandable . . . given the circumstances."

He was surprised that they characterized her as quiet. Thomas had thought, from her excited conversations with her girlfriends and her seemingly endless list of boys, that Julia was chatty in class. To learn that the opposite was true, and probably because of the reason her teachers suspected, disturbed him. His idea of his daughter was wrong. He was even more distant from her than he had feared.

And, even worse, over the last week he had essentially ignored Julia because he was obsessed with Lilac69. He wanted to see her, or talk to her, but she was no longer online, and the e-mails he sent to her were returned as undeliverable. He had no street address to go by, no idea of where she lived other than the city of Baltimore. He called the hotel and made up an excuse to try and track down the person who had reserved the room, but they refused to give him any information. He even considered going from row house to row house, knocking on doors until hers opened. The more time passed during which he didn't hear from her, the more desperate he felt.

Thomas couldn't believe that she had abandoned him this easily.

He couldn't contact her again; he knew that, he knew that . . . but he was so goddamned lonely. He wasn't sure what he had expected – some sort of relationship or maybe just an occasional meeting – but he hadn't thought that it would end this quickly. He felt like he had been drinking from a fountain and the water had suddenly stopped. And he knew that he would never hear from Lilac69 again; she had too much to lose. He, on the other hand, had nothing.

His life was spiraling down. A daughter growing estranged from him; a job that he didn't care for and, at best, was adequate at; now, adulterous sex with a stranger. How different life turned, all because of one night.

"You okay?" Julia asked him, as they drove out of the school parking lot.

"Sure," he said.

"You don't seem okay."

"Why's that?"

"I can tell," she told him, as the car's headlights cut into the night. "I've been watching you."

"Have you?"

"Sure," Julia said, and she crossed her little legs and ran a hand through her hair the way her mother used to, and Thomas felt his heart fill and ache at the movement, like the moment when you think you see somebody you once loved, "You watch me, and I watch you. That's the deal."

"That's the deal," Thomas agreed, gratefully. His daughter leaned into the crook of his arm and they drove home.

The Lonely Onanista

EllaRegina

I am living inside the Washington Square Arch. There are no windows so it's a bit tomb-like and claustrophobic, although a rudimentary air circulation system is provided through the nostrils and buttonholes in the façade's marble statues. On the rare occasion that I need oxygen I seek the great outdoors – I egress and enter through a secret hatch in the left-hand pocket of George Washington's breeches, something not patently obvious to the unwitting onlooker.

I have been hired by the Department of Parks and Recreation to do an interior décor project that entails completely wall-papering the vertical surfaces in dollar bills and paving the entire floor with quarters, edge to edge. I lodge in a tiny spartan room at the top, reachable via a cast-iron spiral staircase, where I sleep beneath a pane of glass in the roof (the structure's only source of natural light) on a single-sized Army-style metal cot, under an itchy woollen blanket. Other accoutrements: a sink, toilet and a bidet. I've also been supplied with a hotplate and a small refrigerator but I don't do much cooking, preferring instead to rely on Balance Bars, Urban Park Rangers' semen and the occasional falafel take-out from my favourite place on MacDougal Street as sustenance.

My work is painstaking and requires many breaks. I fill this time by reading, writing, masturbating, and entertaining the various Park Rangers whose job details likewise necessitate frequent pauses. They all have keys and enter the Monument the conventional way, through a door on the Arch's western side, scaled for a child's playhouse. They must stoop while entering, an amusing picture, especially given those hats they wear. I never know who might show up or when and this unpredictability gives my long days some excitement. And while their visits are indeed fun I am tiring of the Park Rangers – they each would like to plant their seed and grow little trees inside my belly but I will have none of it. I have no time to tend nurseries and have told them so. I put in a request with Human Resources to be allowed outside "entertainment assistance" – beyond the roster of Park personnel – and it has been approved.

You will be sent a rudimentary map of Washington Square Park, where a red circle indicates the location of a certain elm tree with a knot containing a key to the Arch door, hidden for you in plain sight, Boo Radley-style. You will enter the Monument and climb the black staircase. You will find me in my little garret, on my stomach atop the narrow bed, naked except for a pair of black kitten-heeled boots that end at mid-calf. My legs are wide apart, spreading myself open – I've hooked the boots into the corners of the bed's metal footboard – except my knees are pointed slightly inwards like pigeon toes so you have a mostly unobstructed view of the goings-on, what little there is to see.

I am masturbating, both hands at the ready underneath me, arms akimbo. This is my preferred position. My ass is gently bobbing up and down at a quick even pace, somewhere between *allegro* and *presto*, if I were a metronome. My body is completely taut, like a rope in a tug-of-war game played by Marines, every sinewy muscle in my legs, arms, shoulders and back well defined and twitching as a result of my efforts. My buttocks clench, right and left, involuntarily, occasionally revealing a spasm; my molars grind and chatter as if I were shivering. An extremely sensitive clitoris dictates the need for a layer of material between fingers and body. Thin cotton handkerchiefs suffice and one is in place – I'm lucky to have found a vintage store nearby with a seemingly unending supply. My favourite Ranger, the one with the sense of humour, has already visited me today and before leaving has dropped a load of quarters, stacked within a tied condom, inside my rectum, as ballast. A very thoughtful gesture, considering the fact that my complex yet simple onanistic process involves using my body weight and gravity in combination with the pressure from my fingers beneath me to cause the pleasure I seek. It's basic physics, really. The *O* end of the coin-packed condom sloppily protrudes from my anus in a clown's grimace.

You approach the left side of the bed, the direction where my head is turned. My face is at its edge – I am in a somewhat diagonal pose – and I look up at you, my dark hair in disarray, fallen over my pale face, my bangs in choppy clumps across my forehead. You see one big brown eye following your gaze, half a nose, a portion of mouth, its carmine lips slightly parted. You are still fully clothed. You unbutton your coat and take it off along with your beret and scarf. I watch as you undo your trousers, slowly, button by button. I would reach out and admire the soft wide-wale fabric of the corduroy but my hands are totally occupied. You extract your prick from its hiding spot. It is fat and long and I can see that it is already slightly throbbing. Although it is not the optimum setup for such things, given your height and the relative counterpoint of my horizontal state, you introduce yourself, in lieu of a handshake – another formality not physically possible at the moment – by gently easing your warm erection into my eager mouth, the saliva there already welling, and yet despite the awkwardness of our respective postures it is a most pleasant how-do-you-do. But, oh, I would so very much like to be able to properly arrange myself around your sweet upright cock and give it the salutation it so richly deserves!

You take off your shirt, your undershirt. I ask you to keep your trousers on as well as your shoes. You get onto the bed, between my legs, move my knees apart and sample, with your fingers and mouth, the glistening egg-white substance emanating from my body. You lay yourself on top of me, face down, your body perfectly aligned with mine, like open scissors. Your corduroy on my nakedness, your shoes decisively holding my booted feet still, your heavy knockwurst – now steadily pulsating – in repose along the length of my ass crack, cradled as if in a warm bun. I am aware of your heart pounding, almost in unison with my metronome beat. I match my breathing to yours. You lightly bite the nape of my neck, tug my head by the hair, then release it. Your belt buckle presses into the small of my back, hurting me, and I suggest that you remove it. You pull the leather strap from your trouser loops in one motion, like an expert swordsman unsheathing his rapier from its scabbard, and throw it to the floor. My ass is tilted slightly upwards, giving the hands below me room for leverage. This stance offers you the perfect angle for your entrée. You guide your prick inside me, slowly but firmly, filling me up. You lie there for a few moments, not moving, keeping enough stress on my body to make me feel in your command yet allowing me space to freely continue pleasuring myself.

You begin to thrust, at first exactly corresponding to my speed but soon I find that I am following the tempo of your movements instead of leading with my own. The roll of coins imbedded in my ass puts some weight on your prick and this excites you. You grind into me, *con gusto*, gradually increasing the intensity of your delivery. At a certain point I use all the energy I can muster, untangle myself from your powerful restraint and draw my legs shut. I hold them rigidly, as if they were glued from cunt to heels, knees pressed immutably together. I like doing this. It makes your plunging more challenging yet you are of such sufficient length that you don't dislodge a millimetre – there is a sensation of unretractable tightness, as if you were fucking the virgin of all virgins. I squeeze my buttocks, amplifying the effect.

The original idea was that you would "assist" me. I am, in the end, an Onanista, generally used to pleasuring myself, thanks to the lonely confines of my profession. But you have other plans. You use the strength of your own muscular knees, thighs and feet to break open my tight wishbone of a leg grip. You get on your knees, encircle my small waist with your hands and draw me up to a kneeling position, ass in the air, head down. I look to the side and see dozens of George Washington's eyes staring back at me. You release your grasp of my midsection and grab my hands from under me. They were still in their repetitive fingertip-tapping, trying to get myself where I needed to go. But you will not let me. You announce that my training wheel days are over and that I have to learn how to ride without them now. You confiscate my handkerchief – the ultimate taunt – put it to your nose, inhaling its luscious scent, and then shove it into the pocket of your corduroys. Your trousers have been half-on and half-off until this point. Now you fiercely kick them down, but not off, exposing your nakedness. You take my arms by the wrists and hold them together against my back. You resume your activity, flesh to bare flesh this time. My face is no longer in view and has practically embossed its features onto the sheet like the Turin Shroud due to your force. All that can be seen of my body on the bed is a round mountain of ass – with its narrow peak of waist – atop a triangle of open legs, hip to knee, my arms held behind me, your prick a blur of motion going in and out of my pussy.

You know what you are doing. I can sense that the finish line is just around the bend – "Look, Ma, no hands!" – and I sense that you sense it too, and that you are neck and neck with me in the race. You push harder into me, with such vigour that my body actually moves to the head of the bed. Were it not for the wall to stop me I would be doing a full somersault onto the floor. You can hear my teeth knocking again – my lower jaw swinging uncontrollably from side to side – a sure signal that the end is near. You are encouraged by that, the fruit of your labour, tangible proof that you are having a major effect on me, and it propels you wildly and then, suddenly, it starts – convulsing together: pussy, ass, prick. Feral sounds are emitted. You feel the coins in my ass moving from side to side in my everything jiggle. If they weren't so tightly packed they would be ka-chinking a tune like a pocketful of loose change. You let yourself go and lay some nice hot eggs deep within me, not stopping until your balls are completely empty.

We rest, you slumped on top of me, moist with sweat, yours and mine; your trousers at your ankles, your arms around me, cupping my small breasts, one in each hand. Our heartbeats gradually return to somewhere between *larghetto* and *adagio* and slowly you begin to collect yourself and your belongings. I, too, have things to do and places to go. I throw on a long velvet dress and a black coat and see you down the staircase to the too-small door. We emerge from the Arch into the darkness of the park. The Rangers have gone home for the night, their empty Flintmobiles lined up in a silent row. I let you keep the key. We part. You walk eastward with a fragrant souvenir in your back trouser pocket. I walk in the opposite direction towards Sixth Avenue – your runny eggs making shiny lines down the insides of my thighs, knees, calves; the stack of coins a stiff reminder in my ass – and head off in search of more handkerchiefs, just in case you never return.

Deanna

Don Shea

Deanna Clayton was the pride of Gilmer County, West Virginia, a mountain girl hard and brilliant as a diamond, who eluded her Pappy when he was drunk, but just barely, and won a National Merit Scholarship because there wasn't much else to do with all that violent energy and talent in a place like Gilmer County.

The scholarship took her to Smith College in Northampton, Mass, where she lasted one semester before informing the Dean of Women that the place was full of pussies in plaid skirts. Even at seventeen Deanna talked that way, used words like that.

After Smith, Deanna came to New York where she found employment as a topless dancer and landed another scholarship, this one at NYU. Deanna was smart and competent to the point of intimidating most people. She could have had almost any job she asked for, but she felt safe in the topless bar. She said she knew exactly what the men wanted from her and exactly how to handle them.

Baja, Mexico

Outside Tijuana at Agua Caliente we buy some sweet-smelling green marijuana buds from a cheerful one-eyed hitchhiker and float down the coast toward Ensenada, where we check into a motel by the sea. Our cottage is covered with red bougainvillea. Inside the room, a basket of plastic flowers sits on a table by a window facing the Pacific. The late sun catches the soft tips of Deanna's breasts and paints bright highlights around the hollows of her flanks.

"Oh, please."

"Lean back a little more."
"Please. I can't. I just . . ."
"I know. Shut up, darling, and lean back."
"I hate it. I love it. I hate you. Oh God."
"That's right. Vaya con Dios."

New York

Deanna graduates from NYU one month from today, Phi Beta Kappa, with a graduate fellowship at UCLA in political science. She's been living at my place on East 9th Street for about two months now and we've been in a sexual frenzy most of the time that feels like it could blow apart any minute. There's something uncontainable about her, a dangerous unpredictability that fuels my obsession and my anxiety, which are, finally, the same.

It's not easy with Deanna and me. We fight a lot. But I've never seen her cry except sometimes after she comes. When that happens, I love her so much I want to soak up all her pain like a sponge. I felt that way after she told me about Pappy Clayton and what he put her through.

But that's not the way I feel this morning. This morning Deanna gets up wearing nothing but these tiny white bikini panties with a little pink bow at the side and the first thing she does is take half a dozen nude photos of herself out of her knapsack and start showing them to me. They're actually pictures of her most private girl part if you want to know the truth, shot from different angles with the rest of her serving more or less as a backdrop. The pictures are black and white, sharply focused and savage.

So I just woke up naked and she's sitting on the bed showing me these pictures and I'm getting turned on, I can't help it. I know she wants me to ask her about the guy who took the pictures, and what went on between them, so instead I reach for her hip to pull down those little panties through which her dark bush is clearly visible, and as my fingers touch her, she stands and steps away, five feet eight, slender, imperious.

"Don't. I'm late. I have an appointment with my faculty advisor."

"Teasing bitch!"

"Just hold on to it for a while, big boy."

Half-berserk with lust, I watch her root through her knapsack for clothes. She pulls on a black tank top that looks like it's been painted over her breasts.

"Are you wearing that to go see your faculty advisor?"

"I think he's attracted to me. I think he might make a pass at me today."

"What are you going to do if he does?"

"Anything he wants."

"Okay, that's it. You're outta here. Take your stuff and get out. Leave the key. I'm not kidding."

"I'll go back to my place if you like. But no way am I through with that purple throbber of yours. Just look at it. Say, maybe before I go, I could . . ."

"Out! Goddamn it, I'm not kidding! Get out now!"

Baja, Mexico

Just south of Ensenada, a rocky spine of land hooks out into the Pacific and back toward the town. Punta Banda. We swim naked and spawn like sea animals in the rocky tidal pools. We eat roasted conch and melon in a wood shack restaurant by the sea and the juices drip from our chins. Deanna's eyes are feral and deeply blooded. I am sun-baked and cunt-fucked insensible. I could happily die right now, or happily go on to live a very long life. Either would be just fine, thanks.

"Dos tequilas grandes, por favor."

"Si, senor."

"Give me your foot."

"What?"

Deanna takes my bare foot under the table and slides it between her legs under her loose skirt. She lifts her hips and buries three of my toes inside her. Her eyes close.

"Move your toes."

"Deanna, for Chrissake . . ."

"Move them!"

Helpless to deny her, I stir my darling slowly until she makes a low keening sound and bites her lip and writhes on my foot like an

animal impaled on a pike. Just as she opens her eyes again, the boy
arrives with the tequila. She drinks hers neat in one shuddering
swallow.

Los Angeles

Six months after Deanna leaves New York for UCLA, the
software company I work for decides to send me to an IBM
internals school in Los Angeles. I call Deanna in LA the week
before I fly out. I haven't spoken to her in a year but the talk
gets flowing pretty well and I start missing her and all that
wildness and I tell her so. She says she misses me too. Then she
says some very hot things to me over the phone, some of which
concern her recent discovery of women as occasional lovers.

The things Deanna says get me going which of course she
knows and asks about, which only makes it worse, which she
also knows. She says all this talk is getting her impossibly hot
and thus the two of us agree that I should tack two weeks
vacation on the end of the three-day IBM school, which I do.

Deanna greets me at LA airport astride an ancient Harley
Davidson, nut brown, dark hair whipping in the hot wind.
Her Phi Beta Kappa key is clipped to her jeans loop with a
heavy brass ring. I mount behind her and reach around
under her T-shirt to grip her smooth muscled stomach as
we blast down the Santa Monica Freeway toward Venice.

Deanna lives in the second-floor front apartment of an old
clapboard house half a block from the beach. It's full of pillows
and bare wood and smells of cat piss and sunshine. As soon as
we walk in, she starts with me.

"Will you please take off your pants and shorts and give me
the shorts?"

She takes my jockeys and buries her face in them. I can't
stand it. I carry her into the bedroom and do not stop till I'm
numb and dry and mindless. I never even get my shirt off.

Later, we walk the boulevard by Venice beach, enjoying the
freaks and roller skaters and palm trees glowing in th LA sunset.

"I can't concentrate at UCLA. I'm afraid of success, like all
women. In my mind, actually getting the Ph.D. is very threatening. It's like growing a penis."

"That wouldn't become you at all. Are you seriously thinking about quitting school?"

"I've cut back on classes. I've joined some women's support groups. I'm teaching a day a week in Watts."

"What about this fear of success? I mean, since when?"

"Since childhood. Men have been conditioning me to fail since childhood."

"Listen, if you don't want to get a Ph.D. that's your business, but I'm not sure you should blame men in general. Personally, I don't feel much responsibility."

"Come back to the house. You fuck better than you talk."

We pull the bed into the front room with the bay window from which we can look out on the beach and the ocean and the street scene below. Deanna stands before me and slowly lowers her panties.

"Do you like it shaved? I did it to accommodate a woman friend." She kneels.

"Yes, it's . . . oh Jesus. I like that too."

She raises her head from my lap. Her eyes are the color of the ocean behind her.

"Later on, when you're inside me, I want you to push an ice cube slowly up my ass. Will you do that?"

Her head dips between my thighs again. Finally, at last, but also too soon, I feel it begin to build to where, although it is still some seconds away, I concede the inevitability, my inability to control it, although Deanna still doesn't know yet (and I treasure this transient secret), doesn't and won't know until the involuntary spasms betray me and I let loose the scream I am sitting on because the game is up and she couldn't mistake the explosion taking place in her mouth for anything other than what it is, which is to say, my complete and utter capitulation.

Three full minutes pass before my breathing returns to normal. Finally, I can speak.

"That was heroic. Olympian."

"Do I get a medal?"

"I was watching the scores. Nine-eight, nine-eight, nine-five, nine-seven . . ."

"Nine-five?" she says, turning toward me and arching an eyebrow.

"French judge," I say.

The time in LA is good and I am beginning to love Deanna again. I love her high cheekbones and clean West Virginia beauty, her quick cutting intelligence, the loneliness at the core of her erotic quest. But the house in Venice eventually feels confining and an edge begins to build. We need new settings to frame our epic fornications and heighten their reflection in our own eyes.

Deanna and I rent a Toyota, find a sitter for the cats, and head south for Mexico and the Baja peninsula.

Baja, Mexico

Deanna finds Tomas on the beach, a thin boy with quick black eyes who rents us horses and provides information on restaurants and points of interest. We ride three miles through Yucca and Cottonwood to a local hot springs spa. A huge, steaming pool has been formed by damming the mouth of an arroyo below the springs. The pool is lined with smooth slabs of cut stone and filled with Mexican families poaching in the sun. We take one of the private cabaña de baños, *a small room with a wooden bench and large stone tub set in the ground. Above the tub on the wall is a single massive iron lever and spout to admit the hot springs water.*

Deanna's already a little crazy from riding the horse. We strip down and smoke a joint and then she lies in the tub on her back with her hips positioned under the huge spout.

"Turn it on."

I kneel beside the tub, one hand on the iron lever, tumescent, stoned, mesmerized by the visuals. A beam of sunlight from the one high window illumines the swirls of fragrant smoke in the air and the tops of Deanna's knees poking above the tub. I watch her rosy kneecaps slowly move together and then apart.

"Turn it on. Please."

"Maybe we should wait just one minute more."

Soon her whole body is in motion.

"Please. Enough. Turn it on."

I throw the lever and the steaming water thunders down, cleaving her body and mind, bringing a transient peace.

Deanna grows restive. She wants an erotic setting that involves genuine risk. We pack food and canteens, gasoline and compass, and head south from Ensenada. Below Rosario, it's all desert, a dusty trail through dead, sun-blasted landscapes, with occasional trash heaps and tin shacks to remind us of the planet we're actually on.

"Car's running hot. Water temperature is up."

"Let's stop and take a walk."

The horizon is featureless, a shimmering heat line broken by a dry arroyo dipping to the west.

"Let's walk to the arroyo, see what's on the bottom."

As we approach the arroyo lip I hear a sharp clacking whir, like castanets. Five feet to our left a large diamond-back rattler is poised to strike. The snake is absolutely riveting in the empty landscape, the golden diamonds on its coiled brown body in sharp contrast to the erect black and white tiered rattle. I jerk Deanna backward as a burst of adrenalin floods my body. She pulls away and begins to circle the snake, her chest heaving.

"Deanna, listen to me. Listen to me!"

"Look at it. Did you ever see anything so beautiful?"

"Deanna. Listen to me. This is not LA. There are no emergency rooms. The closest doctor is five hours away!"

Deanna is standing just beyond the snake's range, undoing her belt. She slides her shorts slowly down her hips and steps out of them.

"I want to do it right here, right now. I want to be on top so I can watch the snake."

"This isn't funny. This is sick shit."

"Pussy."

Deanna closes her eyes and slides her hand between her legs. The rattle shatters the air, a second warning. I leap forward and drag her back.

I am not gentle. When I release her, she is gasping.

"I thought you had erotic imagination! I thought you had cojones!"

She waits until we are in the car. When I reach for the key, she slaps my face, once, hard.

We've been eating and drinking whatever we wanted, without caution, and the food and water finally catches up and hands me a 103-degree fever and nonstop diarrhea. Deanna's been like a coiled spring since we returned from the desert and I don't expect her to be overly sympathetic but I'm not prepared for the anger my illness apparently unleashes. After one night and one day of it she is stomping around complaining that I'm exaggerating my symptoms.

"Everybody gets this. It's nothing. How long are you going to stay in bed?"

"Give me a break. Why don't you go somewhere?"

"Give me the car keys. I'll go to Tres Cabras. Maybe hear some music."

"Fine."

The opium in the Mexican paregoric hits and I drift into damp, fever twisted dreams. The fever breaks around 2 a.m. and I awake, lucid, thirsty, and restless. Deanna is still out. I drink a cold Carta Blanca and decide to take a walk on the beach.

The night is filled with banal beauty, white caps gleaming in three-quarter moonlight, dark shifting clouds and gently crashing surf. I feel lightheaded and detached as I walk, my mind empty, pleased to be rid of the virus. Down the beach I can just make out the corral where Tomas keeps the horses and the shack where he lives. As I approach, I see the Toyota parked behind the shack and a dim glow through the open front window. Then, by the light of a kerosene lamp, I see Deanna from the rear, naked, astride Tomas. I watch the supple twisting lines of her dancer's back as she grinds into Tomas. I feel like an actor in someone else's bad play, obliged by circumstance to act out my part and deliver my bad lines.

I rip open the flimsy front door. Deanna turns, dismounts, and stands, her body glistening with sex and sweat. Tomas, terrified, bolts out the back door, his slender cock flapping like a foolish afterthought.

"Nice. Really nice."

"Vacation's over in two days. What were you expecting, eternal vows? A picket fence and roses?"

"*I wasn't expecting you to molest third-world children.*"

"*He's a delicious little slut, if you want the truth. Quite innocent, but his instincts are filthy. Whimpers like a girl when I rim him.*"

Deanna's tone is bright and casual but I can see she is fighting for control, fighting tears, and I'm fighting too, inside myself, because I cannot see a way out of this.

"*Enjoy him. Can you find your way back to LA without me?*"

"*You still don't get it, do you? You're such a goddamn romantic. The fact is, I blow things apart first, before the men get a chance to. It's the only way I stay sane.*"

"*Do you need any money?*"

"*Fuck you and your money, Jack.*"

"*Jack. That's a good name. That's appropriate. If I ever run into you again, call me Jack.*"

New York

Yes, I saw her again, about a year later, but it was pretty edgy. Some of the old heat was there, but by then the diverging lines had hardened. I was a technology consultant to large corporations and she was a radical feminist.

Two more years passed and then a final message on my answering machine: Deanna had her Ph.D.

Pretty good for a hard scrabble-abused kid from Gilmer County. I tried to call and congratulate her but the last number I had didn't work and she wasn't listed.

Listen. I'm not sure I want to know what happened to Deanna. What if she turned out to have an ordinary life?

A life like mine?

Boot Camp

Kristina Lloyd

Five inmates are sitting on the lawn on wooden chairs, as nice as can be. It's sunny here, with shadows of skinny trees slanting across the grass and light burnishing the five pairs of army boots arrayed before me. Our counselor is wearing tennis shoes. It makes me suspicious. Punishment shouldn't feel this good.

I've been waiting awhile and my knees are starting to ache. I'm on all fours at the head of a horseshoe of feet. I know when they let me move, my knees will be red raw, cross-hatched with imprinted grass. Lots of little blades. I should have worn a longer dress. Or kneepads. Hell, I should've been born wearing kneepads.

Lee has the biggest boots and I can tell he's lived a full life already. Maybe he's seen active service. Maybe he's been talking about war for the last fifteen minutes and maybe I'm meant to be listening. But I'm not. Instead I'm counting the eyelets of his boots, over and over. It's the only way to stay sane. Three pairs of eyelets rising up to the metal loops of a speed-lacing system, black laces crisscrossing over leather tongues, as beautiful a corsetry. They are British Army assault boots, size 12, standard issue for Soldier 95. I know this without asking.

José, the pussy, is wearing German jump boots. The leather is extra supple, the ankles have padded collars, and there's no need to break them in. Before I realized this, I once tried hitting on a guy by admiring his jumps, and he said, "Yeah, they're awesome. Fit like a glove right away." I couldn't see the point after that. I'm not looking for Cinderella.

Lee had to break his boots in. His feet would have ached, skin chafing and blistering, open sores stuck with fuzzy bits of sock, wounds painted with liquid skin. Maybe he stuck moleskin on the hot spots, tried saltwater to toughen up his toes. Either way, he had to seduce his boots into submission. And he had to suffer to get there. Oh yes, sir, Lee earned those beauties, and for his pain and his patience, I would happily lick his molded, dual-density polyurethane soles.

I had them all to myself last night, the left foot and the right. Alone with Mr Moon, I pulled out the laces, got rid of the dirt in each tongue and stripped off the paint. I lit a candle and kneeled over them, warming a spoon of polish over the flame, a spitshine junkie at her army boot shrine. I gave them four good layers of polish and let them dry several hours. And here they are now, back on his feet, dulled and black, waiting for my magic.

"Spitshine," says our soft-voiced counselor because today that's the name I asked for. "What is it you want to do here?"

I'm so wet and loose. He knows exactly what I want to do. *Exactly* because I wrote him a twelve-thousand-word essay and he graded it B-minus. "The structure was a little off, Kelly, and you didn't come to any conclusions."

"You dumb fuck," I thought as he handed back the paper. "There *are* no conclusions. This is it. Don't you get it? There is no end in sight."

So here I am on my hands and knees, gazing at five pairs of army boots, all in need of some love and attention. I'm so horny I can barely kneel. The detention block's at the far end of the lawn, and every Tom, Dick and Harry in there has probably got binoculars on my butt. The guys, *my* guys, sit with their feet planted wide, pants tucked in or hitched up so I can see everything there is to see; every last eyelet and lolling tongue; every stitch, scuff and scratch; every line of dust and each grain of Iraqi sand lodged in the creases that are etched in the leather.

That's how it feels. It's hallucinogenically intense down here. It's the Van Gogh painting five times over. And I'm at the head of this horseshoe of booted feet, and next to me on the grass is my Tupperware box of kit – polishes, wax, a range of brushes, picks, water bottle, panty hose, old T-shirts cut into rags – and Mr Larry H. Condell is asking what I want?

Well, what the fuck do you think I want, Condi? The last waltz?

The set-up's almost too much. Five guys baring their boots, and it's all for me. Sure, they've got their problems too, but this week it's my turn. We're engaged in some kind of cooperative rehab therapy. We learn about our own problems through learning about each other's. It's meant to be helpful. And it is, totally. I've learned, for example, that Lee's problem is he can't stop thinking about pussy. He wants to eat it, touch it, taste it, lick it, smell it.

In our first group session he sat there, hands held in his lap, staring at the floor as we waited for him to speak. He's huge, well over six feet, shoulders wide as a door. Eventually he closed his eyes, knuckles turning white, clenching like a prayer as he confessed to the room. I watched as the words came out, saw the blush creep over his face, the slight quiver of his nostrils. His voice was sad and shameful, barely above a whisper, and he said, "I live and I breathe pussy."

I tell you, that is so helpful it's keeping me awake at nights.

But now it's my turn. Having to say it is so humiliating. My throat nearly seizes up and I don't know if I can. But I stare at Lee's feet, blades of grass fringing his thick soles, and every inch of my skin prickles with need. There is something much bigger than me and it forces me to speak. "Sir," I say quietly. "I want to polish these boots till I can see my reflection."

"Louder!" barks Steve, shuffling in his seat.

Steve wears French combats, size 9. They're classic and simple: six pairs of eyelets and a broad ankle cuff fastened by two black side-buckles. Bright sunlight rests like a small, still star on the topmost buckle. I can't look up from them, I really can't. But I can picture his face. He's got these dark gypsy eyes that try to draw you into his world, and thick sultry lips. He's small and intense, looks a little sad at times but you can tell underneath he's crazy. Too much shit in his head. It's written all over him. He's very fuckable, and he knows it, but that's never been a problem for me.

However, he isn't wearing British Army assault boots, Soldier 95, and Lee is.

"Sir," I repeat in a strong voice. "I want to polish these boots till I can see my reflection."

They've heard me loud and clear. No one speaks. We all stay in silence, my voice echoing in our seven baffled brains. All of them are looking at me and I'm looking at them; or more specifically, at their feet. I don't know what to do. I don't know if I'm supposed to, you know, expand on my desire. Maybe some bull about how ashamed I am? Condi's always doing this, saying nothing till it gets so awkward someone cracks and breaks the silence.

But I don't say anything, nor does anyone else, and I wait and wait until eventually Condi says, very kindly, "Spitshine, you don't need my permission to do that."

This isn't very professional of him. He shouldn't be the first to speak but I figure he's bored or hard, and he wants some action. But it was the wrong thing to say and now I'm totally paralyzed. Permission? He thinks I lack the ability to act without permission? Jeez, I don't think he even *read* my essay, did he? I've been taking permission since I was fourteen years old, grabbing it by the neck and just damn well taking it. Hell, it's that kind of behavior that gets you locked up in the first place.

I'd heard rumors about what goes on in here. On the outside they call it the Pervs' Penitentiary though officially it's the Correctional Rehabilitation Academy for Venereal Extremists (CRAVE). They believe in aversion therapy, just like my dad did when he caught me stealing one of his cigarettes. He took me out into the yard and made me smoke till I was sick.

I will never get sick of army boots. I will never tire of polishing them. But now I can't act because Condi, with his dumb-ass reverse psychology, has effectively given me his permission, and it's making me feel nauseous.

So once again we're steeped in the silence I'm getting used to: the troubled silence of a bunch of alienated, incarcerated deviants, freaks and paraphiliacs, all of us with hope in our hearts. It's powerful stuff.

We're only in here because we ran into a little bad luck. Me?
They caught me heisting boots from a military surplus store. I
ought to have stayed home, working on my smile, but I got the
urge for more. I was careless, and got busted. And they thought
that gave them the right to shine a torch into my soul. I
remember a time when people used to have civil liberties.
Not that long ago, either. Lee? Jeez, I dread to think what
they caught him doing.

After a while, I glance up and catch his eye. I see his Adam's
apple bob in his throat and I have to look away. Lee is so
beautiful. His hair is velvet-short and though he's big and
strong, there's a kind of fraught melancholy to him. His brow
has a permanent low-grade pucker, and he wears an expression
of someone forever on the verge of getting hurt.

It's because he's always thinking about pussy.

I look at his boots, wanting to slide my tongue into creases
he's created with years of walking, marching, running, living. A
bee buzzes nearby, growing loud and soft before fading to
nothing. The sun beats down and I can smell baked earth
and grass. It's lucky my wrists are strong because this position
could take its toll. Beneath my dress, my back is slicked with
sweat. I see a twitch in the material of Lee's camouflage pants.
His hands have been resting obediently on his thighs, and I
guess he felt the need for a readjustment. Wow. Just . . . wow.

In the silence, I hear him swallow. My groin is thickening and
every breath I draw seems to last forever.

Then Lee says, "Polish my boots, Spitshine." His voice is
cool and steady, though a little uncertain. "Crawl at my feet and
polish my boots." It's growing in confidence now and making
me hot, all the hairs standing up on the back of my neck. "Polish
my boots, Spitshine, until you can see your reflection. Until . . .
until they're shining like black mirrors. Until the toes are like
glass, so bright, so . . . so fucking bright that I could see your
pussy in 'em." There is a silence. "Shit. I'm sorry, Kel. I'm real
sorry."

There's no need for him to be sorry because I'm right there at
his feet, trying not to overbreathe. I unlace his boots. This guy's
going nowhere. I've got my kit with me and from it I unfold my

crumpled, polish-smeared sheet of instructions and lay it on the grass, held down with a couple of brushes. I know these instructions off by heart but that's not the point. I still need to read them, still need to have those sentences telling me what to do. Like right now, I'm buffing with my horsehair brush and those instructions are whispering to me: *Abuse it. Work it hard.*

It's like a voice inside my head. Oh, and I abuse it and I work it till the boots are shining nicely. But it's not the shine I want. The shine I want is a spitshine, and a spitshine takes time.

My hands are trembling as I pour water into a little bowl. The sound is so refreshing. I'm in the kind of mood where I could dip my head to it and lap like a pretty kitty but I don't want to risk confusing the guys with cross-kinks.

And the instructions say to me: *Wet a section of the cloth and wring it out. You want it damp but not dripping wet.*

I twist the cloth and droplets tinkle into the bowl. Lee's legs are solid, and his camouflage-clad shins don't move an inch. His boots gleam, and the leather ripples around his ankles like fabric petrified mid-fall. I glance up. In his BDU pants and tight white vest, he's a statue of flesh, bronzed shoulders practically rigid as he breathes long and low, gazing down as I kneel at his feet. He doesn't look at me. He looks past me, staring at a patch of grass. But I know what he's thinking about. We *all* know what he's thinking about, day and night, night and day.

I edge into a good position and flip the lid on the tin of polish, inhaling that dirty chemical smell. I wrap the damp cloth around my first two fingers, gripping it to make a nice taut surface, and I read my instructions. *Dab a SMALL amount of polish on the cloth.*

Done. Sir.

Begin lightly stroking the surface of the leather in small circles, working a section at a time. Small circles, over and over. Small little circles.

This is the part that makes me spin, and all my spitshine dreams are being realized. I cup Lee's heel and start rubbing at the back, small little circles, just like the voice tells me. The polish streaks at first then it starts to smooth out, the shine rising. I do those circles over and over, more and more lightly, and the gloss starts to come. I dip my finger in the water, pinch the cloth, take a dab of polish and on and on I go, making my beautiful little circles.

It takes a long old time. Leather is skin. The polish layers have to be molecular, next to nothing, and you have to work and work, keeping it so gentle. There are no shortcuts here, no quick routes to brilliance.

When I spitshine, I swear it's like I'm becoming the boots. It's calming and sexy, and I slip into a kind of trance. I'd like to describe it as "spiritual" but I'm turned on and that seems awfully blasphemous. It's tough to explain. Okay, let me try. It's sort of a hot, horny, meditative vibe where I'm zoned out and tuned in simultaneously; and all the arousal I ever knew is resting in my groin and a river's running through me, so slow and so warm, and my clit is beating like a little heart, like new life, and my lust is spread across the starry starry night, thin as my layers of Parade Gloss; and no one can reach me and I'm ravenous, and that little beating heart is right at the center of the entire fucking universe.

Yeah, that's about how it feels.

By the time I'm working on the toes, I am God. And God has a very swollen clitoris.

Finally, my face appears, distorted and shrunk in the toes of Lee's boots. It stares back at me twice, like this is some tiny hall of mirrors, and I know I'm nearly done here. It's taken over an hour and that high polish is so sharp I could come.

Tomorrow, I'll work on Steve's combats. The day after, Louis's jungle boots, then José's jumps and Bobby's tankers.

If you ask me, I'd say aversion therapy is no way to cure a fetishist, especially when the counselors don't bother dishing up the bad shit with the good. You know, like electrodes to go with your psychic over-investment in panties? I swear, this institution would've been closed down years ago if it weren't sanctioned by a bunch of deviants who get off on administering phony treatments.

But I warm to the whole deal later that evening when I'm queuing in the mess hall for dinner. The place is a freak show of people in rubber, latex, fur and feathers, diapers, body harnesses and white surgical coats. Some folk have a hunted look. They haven't realized what a blast it is in here. Others who know better carry a certain glow, like cats that got the cream.

I notice his boots first, the brightest blackest things in the hall. They look liquid, as if they're made of ink. I can't look him in the eye. He sidles in behind me with his tray, an irregular GI Joe. He doesn't say a word and I don't turn around. I can sense him. I can feel the presence of his big solid body. Then he bends close, his breath tickling my ear, and in a voice full of shyness and secrets, he says, "Kelly, I want to spitshine your pussy."

And I melt. I just melt.

And I gaze at his boots, figuring I ought to offer him a little therapy because Lee and I, we understand each other, and together we're gonna let it shine.

Narcissi

N. J. Streitberger

He couldn't remember the exact moment he had fallen in love with his sister. And while "fallen in love" may have been an elaborate phrase, it was, he believed, an appropriate description of his feelings. Passion was involved. Yes, passion it was and it had crept up on him from behind like a mugger.

Josephine didn't know, of course. It was a love undeclared and consequently unrequited. But it was becoming harder and harder to keep secret.

Aside from a tendency to stare at her for longer than was usual and the erection he got whenever she approached him, Joseph had come close to blurting out his love for her on an increasing number of occasions. So much so, that he had taken to avoiding her as much as possible when at home with their parents. He couldn't begin to imagine the consequences of suddenly declaring his love within earshot of his mother.

Father was a heavy hitter in the City and his income provided plenty of money to support a large house, two fine cars in a garage and plenty of great holidays, some of which he even managed to attend himself.

But it was their mother who really brought them up. She was the parent he knew best. He knew her neuroses, witnessing her anxieties and addictions to prescription drugs and cosmetic surgery. Which is why he had to keep his infatuation a closely guarded secret.

Still, something had to be done.

He took to watching his sister in secret. He began sneaking into her bedroom at night, when he was sure she was asleep, to stand staring at her. It was he thought, as he watched her face, relaxed in repose, like looking into a mirror.

Josephine was older than him by three minutes. Apart from the fact that they were different sexes, they were absolutely identical. They shared the same dark, lustrous hair, arching eyebrows and smooth white flawless skin. Then there was the strong jaw, the aquiline nose, with an almost imperceptible kink, and the generous lips. They were exactly the same height and, aside from the obvious, the same build.

As children, so Joe recalled, they loved the fact that people could never tell one from the other and delighted in playing the game called "Guess the Twin".

The game came rapidly to a close when Josephine developed breasts and, although they continued to share the same general presentation, they gave up on the attempts to fool visitors as to their individual identity.

Maybe it was then that Joseph's desire for his sister began to germinate. He wasn't entirely sure. One day it wasn't there – the next day it was. Desire.

Joseph sought out books and literature and any material that might shed light on his condition. He underlined a passage in a biography of the actor Montgomery Clift, whom he was amazed to discover had a twin sister. The troubled Clift had revealed to a friend that he often woke up in the morning not knowing which twin he was. It echoed Joseph's feelings with extraordinary accuracy.

One day Joseph locked his door, stripped off all his clothes and stood in front of the mirror. He cupped his hands over where his breasts would have been, tucked his cock between his legs and admired himself as a man on the verge of womanhood. It was the most exquisite sensation, seeing himself as his sister. It took very little imaginative effort. There she was in front of him. All he had to do now was to step through the mirror.

He had to devise a strategy to discover whether Josephine had any similar feelings towards him. He couldn't just keep staring at her in the hope that she would say something that might encourage progress towards the consummation of his desire.

Among the books he had squirrelled away on his bookshelf was *The Taxi* by Violette Leduc, a tantalizing novella about a tragic sexual liaison between a brother and sister conducted in a closed carriage as it took them through the streets of Paris. It was the easiest way to send a veiled message to Josephine.

One night, he crept into his sister's room like a ghost, breathing in the atmosphere of her fragrance, so different from his own. He stood by her bed, as usual, and held the book in his hands. He looked down at her and once more thought he might have been looking in a mirror, or a pool of water.

Josephine opened her eyes and stared up at him.

– What are you doing?—

"I, I . . . er . . ." he stammered, "I just wanted to leave you this. I've just read it and I, uh . . ."

– It's late.—

"Yes, I know. I couldn't sleep and I've just finished it and I wanted to . . . you to have it straight away."

– Oh, thanks. Just leave it on my bedside table. There.—

"Well, goodnight, then, Jo. Sleep well."

– Mmm. Night.—

He returned to his room and crawled into bed where he lay shivering and sweating over his folly. Eventually he fell asleep and dreamed of her grey eyes.

His birthday was one day away. He would have to think of what to get her. Depending on her response to the book, he would find something personal and coded or something sisterly and simple.

That evening, Joseph was in his room when Josephine walked in without knocking. She held the slim volume in her hand and shook it at him gently.

– Why did you give me this?—

"Didn't you like it?" he asked.

She looked at him curiously and placed the book carefully on his table.

– No.—

"Oh," he couldn't hide the disappointment in his voice, "why not?"

– They died. It was unnecessary.—

She looked at him but her expression was unknowable. She turned and walked out, soft as a cat.

For a long time that night he lay in bed, hot beneath the sheets in spite of his nakedness. She had read the book. She hadn't liked it. But what hadn't she liked? The idea or the execution? The concept or the denouement?

– They died. It was unnecessary.—

He tried to sleep.

Three hours later, in the early hours of the morning, he was still awake. He was staring at the ceiling when the door opened softly and she walked in. She closed the door carefully and walked over to the bed. He could hardly breathe. He swivelled his eyes sideways like a man paralysed.

She stood over him, staring into his grey eyes with her identical ones.

– I want to see you.—

She took the sheet and pulled it from him, uncovering him entirely. On a reflex, he tried to cover himself but something made him stop and he let his arms drop to his sides. He watched her as she gazed upon him, taking everything in from his feet to his strong legs and his upright, hovering cock, up to his smooth chest with a light sheen of sweat. Until, finally she reached his face.

– Now it's your turn.—

She unbuttoned her silk pyjama top and slid it from her shoulders. She pulled down her bottoms and stepped out of them, revealing herself.

He looked at her with his mouth open. It was like looking at himself transgendered. She was utterly beautiful.

She bent over, pushed him slightly and climbed onto the bed beside him.

– I just have one question.—

"What?" he breathed, barely audible even to himself.

– Why did you wait so long?—

She leant in close to him and kissed him lightly on the lips. He felt her body against his and they trembled together. She kissed him again, longer this time and slid beneath him, staring up into his eyes.

He raised himself above her and marvelled again at what it was like to look at her. He stroked her dark hair and she sighed with pleasure, closing her eyes. He explored her body, savouring every taste, every smell. Each part of her delivered something different.

Her mouth was sweet like Parma violets, her neck and ears exuded coconut, her armpits smelt of talcum and musk, her breasts – pale as porcelain with nipples like dolls' thimbles – were scented with vanilla and milk. The tiny secret of her navel, in which he dipped the tip of his tongue, tasted of candle wax. And finally, her cunt, her beautiful cunt, tasted of so many things, salty, sweet and sour all at the same time – the sea, lassi, ginger.

He used his tongue gently, opening her up, allowing her time to relax. She moved her hips upwards, offering herself to him. She moaned and stroked his hair until she tugged him gently upwards bringing him face to face with her.

– Kiss me. I want to taste myself.—

They kissed and she reached down and held his cock gently in her hand, guiding him between her thighs.

– Now, Joe. Now.—

He pushed inside her gently until he met the expected obstruction. She looked at him with her eyes shining with confidence.

– Yes, Joe. It's all right. Please.—

He pushed harder and he broke through, sliding deep inside her. She squeezed her eyes shut and gave a little shudder, clutching him tight against her, and he lay down upon her and stayed still, stroking her hair and her sides until the pain subsided.

When he felt her shift against him, hungrily pushing her hips upwards to drive his cock deeper into her, he began to move. He raised himself onto his elbows to see her face and she looked up at him as they gave each other equal pleasure. He put his lips on her nipples, tugging lightly with his teeth, he licked her ears, she stroked his back, running her fingers down between his buttocks, pushing a fingertip lightly inside. And all the time they moved together, as one.

– Joe, Joe, Joe, oh Joe, it's the best Joe, oh wonderful.—

"Jo, Jo my darling, Jo you are so beautiful, look at us, my cock is inside you and it's . . . Oh Jo!"

Their ecstasy rose in tandem and they came together, holding one another, jolting and shuddering as they emptied themselves into each other and each filled to the brim by the other.

They lay fused together, quiet, for a long time. When light started coming through the window, Joseph reluctantly unpeeled himself from his sister's skin and turned to get out of bed. She leant over and whispered in his ear.

– I knew. I knew. I knew it would be like that.—

"Darling," he said and kissed her tenderly.

– I am so lucky. It was the best thing. It was like making love to myself.—

She had plucked the words right out of Joseph's head.

His mother was waiting for him in the kitchen. She smiled brightly at him but there was a sadness barely concealed behind her eyes. Joseph sat down at the kitchen table. His father had left early, as usual. He was more absence than presence in their house.

His mother brought a tray over to the table that flickered with lights. She placed a large cake with sixteen candles in front of him and a tiny fairy cake, with just one candle to his left.

"Happy Birthday, darling," said his mother. She kissed him on top of his head and wiped away a tear.

Joseph was puzzled. He looked up at her and then at the cake with one candle.

"What's that? Who's that for?" he asked. "Where's Jose . . ."

"Oh, darling," interrupted his mother, eager to get her annual ceremony of remembrance over with. It was a difficult time for all of them. "It's for Josephine. You know."

"Yes, but . . ." he glanced at the ceiling, expecting her to come running down the stairs at any moment.

"Sixteen candles for the years you have spent on this earth," said his mother, lowering her eyes. "And one candle for the precious hour that Josephine had," she choked on her own sentiment and ran out of the kitchen.

Joseph heard her weeping. He looked at the cake again. Ice water trickled down his spine.

Josephine, his twin sister, older than him by three minutes. His identical twin sister who didn't live longer than an hour after her birth? How could that be?

It couldn't be. It was a mistake. Mother had always struck him as a bit disturbed, a woman whose medication kept her just the right side of hysteria.

He blew out his candles and went back upstairs to his room. He stood outside the door. Maybe it was he who was mad? Maybe . . .

All doubts evaporated when he opened his door.

Josephine was lying on his bed, totally naked. She looked at him with a desire that bordered on the infernal. She opened her thighs in surrender, ran her fingertips over the tender cleft between her legs and blew him a kiss.

– Happy Birthday, Joe. Happy Birthday to both of us.—

Supercollider

Chad Taylor

Carrie Factor waitressed nights. She worked late shifts and spent the early hours of the morning alone in the restaurant, cashing up. Once the phone rang and she answered and it was some old guy asking what she was wearing. She nestled the receiver in the crook of her shoulder and continued pressing bank notes flat as she told him: I'm wearing my black Mary Janes and black pantyhose and a black skirt and a black bra and a white shirt and a green-and-blue striped tie. The old guy sounded especially excited when she mentioned the tie. Why are you wearing those clothes, he wanted to know. Because this is a restaurant, she said, and I'm a waitress. He thanked her very much and apologised, because really he was after a domestic number.

After closing the till Carrie would lock up the restaurant and catch a taxi eight blocks to the premises of one Louis Cloud, whom she called Lou and fucked on a regular basis. Carrie and Louis first met at the restaurant: he booked a table for one and dined slowly and alone. When they were the only people left he paid with cash and offered to escort her to the taxi stand.

They were walking a polite distance apart when, approaching the TV rentals store, he reached out and clasped her arm. My favourite window, he said, directing her to the stack of display monitors flickering behind the glass. Then he snapped his fingers and the television screens began to flash off and on. They switched channels and jumped to full volume, screamed alternate sound bites and hissed and glared. Carrie giggled. Louis grinned and showed her his palm. Learning remote, he explained, returning the device to his pocket. And they carried on walking, their stride leisurely, his apartment nearby.

On the way upstairs she put her arm through his, the old giggly schoolgirl trick. He opened the door to rooms without the usual things. No photographs of family or girlfriends, no hallway mountain bike. There was a large European brand television. And some Scotch, to which she said yes.

Carrie sat slightly forward on the red leather sofa, rolling the glass in her palms, and looked impressed by practically everything he told her. He'd become slightly nervous, flashing around paraphilia and anhedonicism and prototypical kleptomania like a Dunhill lighter. Gradually, buoyed by her expressions and gentle silences as elegant as any jargonese, he settled on discussing the more basic parts of his study: new drugs, hopeless cases, non-scientific techniques. When she unbuckled her shoes and raised her stockinged knees beneath her chin, he stopped talking for a minute and stared over her shoulder. What's wrong, she said. Your drink, he said, taking her glass. And also your shoes, he added in a quiet voice: I'd like you to put them back on. If you don't mind.

She said she didn't mind that at all.

Now after the restaurant she returned to his place more often than she went to hers, a three-bedroom flat that had yellowed with boredom and disuse until it consisted only of a bad couch and a forgotten pot of vanilla yoghurt at the back of the refrigerator. Whereas Louis' apartment was clean and permanently new in her mind. He owned a bed the size of a large dining table and when she walked in at one in the morning he was always in it.

It was part of the deal that she never, ever took a shower. She clambered onto his body wearing her work clothes, her shoes catching the sheets, and licked his nipples until his cock turned hard, and after or during that he would wake up and turn her over and press her on her stomach. Louis liked tearing the crotch of her hose and taking her through the rent. He liked leaving marks on her skirt, and especially her white shirt. He liked to pull out of her just in time to make them.

It was petty to inflict it on someone who wanted nothing more than to be filled with something better than frayed thoughts, but he did it to be petty and she withstood it out of respect for pettiness in general.

Their heads were full of questions. They'd met making commonplace declarations in an uncertain tone: I don't know if this will work; This is the first time in ages for me; I'm not looking for commitments; I'm this, I'm that, I'm feeling really really something – the usual culprits. In the beginning conversation was something that kept your brain from admitting that your body was doing all the work. He loved to watch her mouth, and her eyes. Some people undressed you with their eyes and others just stood there naked. She was the standing there type.

Afterwards she took off her clothes and had a shower. When she came back to the bed he was deeply asleep wearing her torn and sodden pantyhose. He liked pulling them up around his legs as he listened to her in the shower, the water drumming against the basin, the metal popping as she shifted her weight between her feet.

In Louis' mind Carrie stood as tall as him, sometimes taller. As well as her underwear he could fit into her jeans and most of her dresses. There wasn't any ceremony attached to the wearing of them: he simply picked them up off the floor, put them on, checked in the mirror, and then took them off again. She tested his cock as he did so: nothing happened. She liked shaving his face baby-smooth with a razor and applying new brands of foundation to compare them. She painted lipstick on him and licked it off. He rouged her nipples and her pubis while her hands were tied, painted her toenails as she was pinned unmoving to the bed. She confessed to a failed adolescent dance career. He bought her pointe shoes.

Ticking off on his fingers the clichés that inspired him to erection, pointe shoes were the middle finger. Adjacent digits stood for gags blackened with saliva; shaving her cunt; white ankle socks; and her hair, freshly cut.

The haircutting thing began in the first month of winter. She'd spent months growing it long: he gagged her with a handkerchief and shortened the right side by an inch. The crisp sound of the blades was loud in her ears. That night few male diners at the restaurant noticed her shortened bob. Every woman did. She felt herself turning hot with embarrassment. She dropped a plate. She stood before the mirror in the staff washroom and worked herself furiously with her fingers, biting her lower lip until it bled.

The thing about cutting hair was that it couldn't be done gradually. If it wasn't a shock, then nothing had been imposed. A week later she turned up for work looking like nothing on earth. A bad punk, a crazy girl, a villager convicted of wartime collaboration.

He'd cut it by first tying her to the bed and securing her neck in a prone position using a curtain cord. Then he knelt with his legs on either side of her chest and took a handful of her deep black fringe and felt beneath the mattress for the scissors, producing them with a flourish. It didn't seem real to her until he made a chop, taking her bangs back to the roots. Quickly, the numbness in her stomach took over. When he was finished he licked away the tears from her face and released her. She lay back and felt the sheets with her outstretched arms and stared at the ceiling in silence, unable to move.

She liked that. She liked having the words removed from her mouth and the obvious wiped from her brain. He counted a good two or three minutes after fucking before she could string an original sentence together. When she did manage to say something it rarely concerned the events of the previous hour – the sweating or the obscenities or the clothes she was left wearing. Changing the subject was an indirect eulogy. It proved there was nothing left to say on the matter of making love.

The remnants of her $90 coiffure lay scattered on the floor. Standing up he found her locks and off-cuts sticking to his bare feet like straw. He scuffed his way to the kitchen and edged a frozen block of vodka bottle out of the freezer. Back on the bed, he poured her a shot. She needed it.

He smiled as she rubbed the tearstains with the back of her hand and ran the other through her crooked shock, and wondered what it would be like to live in the courts of the Russian czars. They swapped childhood memories of millefiori paperweights, coral frozen in a bubble of glass, and failed interrogations thereof using a hammer and a cement garage floor. She twisted her head towards the dresser, her buckled school shoes leaving black marks on the sheets, and pressed him for details about lighter-than-air transport and *Star Trek* movies. He balanced his shot glass against his lips as he put his thumb inside her cunt. She closed her eyes.

He wouldn't release her until she was late for work.

She stood up slowly, rubbing the circulation back into her limbs, and checked herself in the mirror. Bored with her reflection as it stood he rolled onto his back and watched her upside down, his wet cock fat against the gully of his groin and the warm artery she had licked, pressed against with her ear. He counted down the bumps in her spine from her arse to her head, mentally levelling her clean and beautiful shoulders and the ragged crop of her hair. She wasn't taken aback as much as she'd expected. She was a worse sight than she'd made in the staff washroom a few nights before, but then again a lot better.

She walked around the bed collecting the pieces of her uniform. The shirt was crumpled: she spread the creases flat, pressing down her breasts. She straightened her tie and asked to borrow a pair of jeans. He said they were too big and she said that didn't matter. She unhooked the fly buttons and shook them out by the belt straps. Then she stepped into them and tugged them on. She cinched them with his belt, notching it at the last hole, and walked over to the mirror and turned around and around, watching her arse and her crotch, her flat ashen stomach, her small breasts. He watched her from the bed, monitoring her reflection and her face which wondered: do you think this is a good thing?

Finally she rolled up the cuffs and put on her make-up. Thickly. She bent over and bussed him goodbye. The shape of her lips stayed behind on his throat.

He listened to her footsteps down the hall and going out the door.

Her shoes were the first and last things about her: first thing he noticed, last thing he heard. Once he unbuckled the left Mary Jane and rested it against her cunt. She probed it with her fingers for a while, then invited him to fuck her with it, the kid-lined heel cupping his balls, his cock bowed inside the toe pressed flat against her pubis. She spent weekday afternoons in factory shops purchasing her favourite styles in a larger size. Salesgirls invariably asked who for. My boyfriend, Carrie would say. He wears them when we fuck. Meanwhile Louis waited outside in the car, counting the seconds until she appeared with a shoe box and a hungry look.

He wondered initially if this was therapy: if, after completing a special number of perverse scenarios, their true selves would surface. Months later, he realized their true selves were in fact awake and hard at work. They had arrived at the same point too easily for it to be a secret or obsession. They weren't titillated by it. There was no giggling or trembling lower lip. Louis and Carrie shared a language, and they had a lot to talk about.

Louis got up and started cleaning the apartment.

When the head waiter saw Carrie's hair he sent her home for the rest of the week. She disobeyed, and went back to Louis' house. She passed the TV Rentals shop without pause, although the memory of it still danced in her brain, and entered the hall she'd stepped out of thirty minutes before. He was naked and vacuuming the floor, using the long narrow nozzle to get right into the corners. He gave her a puzzled look. She pointed to her hair. He nodded. She said she'd do the dishes.

He was cleaning the bathroom when she entered still wearing the washing-up gloves and took his cock in her hands. She began to squeeze and pump it, marking its progress. Hot water from the wet yellow rubber was turning the dry flakes around his groin back into mucus.

He unbuckled her belt and undid her – his – jeans and tugged them down. She let go of his cock and rolled around and pushed her arse out towards him and he took her on the side of the bath, his teeth clenched, her rubber gloves squeaking as her outstretched fingers slid on the enamelled steel. The only time they'd made love in her house it had also been in the bathroom on a floor the colour of a sidewalk. He remembered pressing her face forward and making her lick the tiles.

As soon as her hair had grown enough for her to slick it down she returned to work and spending the last hour of each evening cashing up alone while at home he dozed in her pantyhose and the shoes she'd bought, sleeping on his stomach if his back was too badly marked. Around one, she stepped into his bed complaining she was bored – not with you, darling – and he put his mind to it. They decided to get out of town for a while. They decided to leave their clothes behind, pretty much. He cocked the hammer on his credit card. They could have driven down but they booked a plane, and they could have dropped in to see several groups of mutual friends, but they kept their arrival quiet. They weren't going away to see people or new places. They were going away to see each other.

But after stepping on to the aircraft and stowing hand luggage in the marked compartments and following the safety procedure and ordering a couple of stiff gins they gradually realized they weren't feeling themselves at all. Louis wondered who they'd be facing by the time they arrived at the hotel. Carrie spread the in-flight magazine flat across her stomach and stared out the window, waiting for his fingers to slide beneath the pages. It didn't take long. A little girl sitting across the aisle watched the whole thing, slurping on chocolate milk.

The city seemed bigger than they'd expected and the hotel room smaller. Carrie threw her bag on the bed without much effect. I haven't got any clothes, she said, you haven't got any clothes. He fucked her in the clothes she did have. She slept wearing his Y-fronts. He thought she looked better in them than he did. He sat up watching giant ants consume Los Angeles, the television's flickering light picking out the shape of her body beneath the sheet. He ran his finger along the elastic band of her underwear. She didn't stir. He began stroking between her buttocks and she sniffed and bit her lip, waiting.

The morning was cold. He stepped out wearing her torn pantyhose underneath his jeans. She was bare-legged in her skirt.

They started in the men's wear stores, buying her a pair of jeans in his style. They bought three pairs of boxer shorts in her size, with extra stitching around the crotch and a pronounced arse. She bought a narrow business shirt that spared no room for her bust and a pair of sideburn clippers with extra blades.

She picked out lipsticks and foundation, perfume and T-shirts. She had her face done in two different department stores. She listened attentively to sales pitches for depilatories and face cream. On the spur of the moment she had her earlobes pierced a second time, wincing at the counter of the corner chemist.

He didn't enjoy buying things directly. The necessary conversation slowed things down. Instead he discussed options in detail with her as they travelled the sidewalks and, once inside, indicated with a nod or a shrug before slipping away to another part of the store. She bought him calf-length lace-up mules and T-bar dance shoes. She chose white ankle socks and bicycle shorts, dog collars and elbow-length gloves. They bought matching oilskin hoods without the accompanying raincoats. She picked out the longest pantyhose and swimsuits, and upholstery ribbon by the metre. He sat in a dance store reading a magazine while she tried on black ballet slippers, her stare fastened on the saleswoman's hands tightening the laces. Louis watched a little girl go up *en pointe* for her mother. He could have sworn it was the child from the plane. Carrie came up to him clutching her new shoes wrapped in tissue paper and looking as if she was going to cry.

In the hotel room they ordered room service – steak sandwiches and salad and two bottles of good red wine – and settled down to tearing open the packages. Each item in turn was laid out and inspected. Naked and warm from the shower, they tested lacings and each fit, tried walking and breathing, compared the sheen of leather and cords and the smell of shoes unworn. He put her in the boxers, testing the crotch with his hand, and demanded that she piss in them so he could watch the dark shape spread and chug yellow down her legs. She tasted her ballet shoes and then the inside of the mules before cinching him into them, running her finger up the back of his calves. A lizard stomped across the television and splintered Tokyo. Her fingernails tested the Lycra around his legs, rasping. She cut the upholstery tape into two-metre strips and tied him to the bed. And later released him so he could bind her. She wore the ballet shoes, newly anointed, and the business shirt. He found a belt in his luggage and tested it against the air, the hide whistling. She bit into the pillow.

They ate and drank. The late night transmission died. Deprived of quality viewing they turned off the lights and opened the curtains. They counted the stars between the hotel awning and the apartment block next door, a black ribbon speckled with white pepper and the blue warmth of the street lights. She lay in her wet boxer shorts, feeling the damp creep into the mattress. He cradled his chin in the evening gloves, the fingers spotted with mucus and semen, his groin raw. Her nipples ached.

"I love the stars." She arched her head forward to sip her wine. "Looking at them makes me feel small."

"I started off doing physics at university," he said. "I wanted to do that instead of medicine."

"Why didn't you?"

"The inhumanity of it." He shook his head, his voice thick. "You have to do something practical."

"You don't believe that."

"It's true."

"That's your mother talking, I bet. Your parents."

"Pssshhhh." He let his breath out slowly. "Pssssssssshhhhh-hhhhh."

She strained to form another sentence. "Why did you like physics?"

"The drama." Balancing his wine glass on his chest, he held his hands wide apart, opposing forces. "Great things happen in moments of collision. One force meets the other, atoms collide. Bang!" He clapped his hands. The wine spilled. She laughed. In a cracked voice he told her the story of the Hindenburg at Lakehurst airfield in 1937, how the big airship had circled to land when static electricity ran up the mooring lines and burned it to the earth in thirty seconds flat. Static, he explained, or the spark from a flashbulb. He snapped his fingers. "The hydrogen. Just went up."

She rubbed the crotch of her underpants back and forth, up and down. "I don't know what I would have done if I hadn't met you."

He turned his head to face her. The moonlight held the silhouette of her face like curled white paper. She had never introduced the subject directly before. Given the circumstances he didn't think she would raise it again, and he found himself trying to think of what to say, how to cup it in his hands without having it burst.

"You would have met someone."

She raised her feet until the slippered toes touched the window ledge. "I love these shoes."

He felt his cock harden. "I know."

"I want to sleep in these shoes." She reached across for his groin. "These tights feel good. Is it nice wearing them?"

"Extremely."

Her finger searched the broken fabric. "Do you have to make the hole with your hands?"

He smiled. "I could use scissors."

"I'd like it if you used scissors."

He ran his fingers through her hair. "I could use the clippers."

"Yes."

He counted her eyebrows. "Do you think it's important for girls to have hair?"

"For good girls, yes."

"What about the others?"

She was finding it hard to breathe.

"Carrie?"

"I don't think they should have any." She touched the rim of the wine glass to her lower lip. "I don't think anyone bad should."

He waited for her to ask.

"Could you please get the clippers?" she said, finally.

He smiled and kissed her and sat up. His cock was fully hard, now, and she rolled over and kissed it and buried her face in him. The glasses tumbled to the floor. She was still buckling on his dance shoes when he came. The semen hit the right side of her face. She caught it with her hand and tasted it and then he lifted her up to kiss her and slid into her again and held on for just long enough.

A breeze washed through the window, gently curling the curtains. She arched back on his cock, testing its firmness every few seconds. He kissed her nipples. And then they fell apart, spread on their backs. He thought about getting up to find the clippers. He was thirsty.

"Is there any wine left?" Carrie wanted to know.

"We finished the bottle," Louis said. "We can order more." He wondered where they'd put the phone. "Red or white?"

"I can't decide."

"I'll get both."

"Not just yet." She found his hand. "Stay with me. And then order the wine."

"In a minute, then."

"I love the stars," she said again. "It all looks such a long way away."

Silently they compiled the things they desired. Each dot of light a possibility, the only respite the blackness in between.

"Is your cock hard?"

"It's sore."

"What would it take to make it hard again?"

Together they lay there, watching the sky.

I am Jo's Vibrator

M. Christian

I am a Rabbit Pearl vibrator: five inches long, one and a half inches wide, used for the enhancement of sexual pleasure. Manufactured in Japan, I was purchased for approximately $90 from Good Vibrations while the couple vacationed in San Francisco. I was selected from among other similar devices for my "playful" (according to Jo) and non-threatening (unspoken but clear from Patrick) appearance.

I resemble less a realistic depiction of a phallus than I do a child's toy. Halfway down my main shaft, for example, is a ring of several dozen plastic pearls, which energetically vibrate when I am activated. Below this band is what appears to be a comic representation of a rabbit, with fluttering ears to stimulate the clitoris – thus the English interpretation of my Japanese name.

In addition to the rabbit component's buzzing ears, I vibrate and oscillate, thanks to a special mechanical arrangement in my shaft that gently corkscrews. All of this is controlled by a simple mechanism at the end of a thin power cord.

For a few days after my sale to Jo and Patrick, I felt that my purpose was going to be unappreciated. But later, when they got home, I was pleasantly surprised when my darkness was pulled away revealing sparkling green eyes. "Come on, let's try it," Jo said.

Batteries were inserted into my control box and, with a slide of one of my switches, she giggled, nearly hysterically. Patrick, though, grinned but was obviously less enamored of me than his girlfriend. It was at that moment, she laughing, he smiling but tense, that I decided I would be Jo's vibrator.

"Here," she said, joy never leaving her lips as she slipped off her T-shirt. "Touch me with it." Reaching down, she cupped a small but beautifully perky breast, pointing a dark, rosy nipple out at him.

Cautiously, he reached out with me, grazing the hardened knot with my gently buzzing head. At the contact, she squealed delightfully. "Oh – I'm sorry," he said, turning me off.

"No, no – just a bit of a shock, that's all. Try it again." Her voice was rich and throaty, a warming purr. Hand away, she pulled her shoulders back, enthusiastically offering both her breasts.

Biting his tongue in concentration, he slid my switch, taking a long moment to adjust my vibration. Then, stroking my humming tip along the underside of each breast, he glanced back and forth from the sight of me sending undulations through her silken skin to her face for the tiniest flick of discomfort.

But she was certainly not uncomfortable. Arms flexing as I was touched to more or less sensitive areas, her breath quickened and her eyelids fluttered with quivers of pleasure.

"Okay," Jo said, fanning her fingers in front of her nipples in mock surrender. "Whew," then they were fluttered before her face, a pretend swoon.

"You like it?" Patrick said.

"It's weird – but nice," Jo said. Thumbs into sides of panties, she slid them down. Sitting on the side of their bed she gently spread her legs. "Try it here."

"Just a minute," he said, coughing between words. Putting me on the bed next to her, shoes were kicked aside, pants dropped, shirt pulled off and tossed into a corner, shorts following suit. Aroused, he leaned forward, kissed her as only new lovers can, grazing a hand across her breast and hardening nipple.

Breaking the kiss, she said, "Come on, try it on me." Leaning back, she displayed herself. "Right here." A finger at the top of her mons, pulling gently back, showing her deep purple hood and the red bead of her clitoris.

Prudently he brought me down until my vibrating head was just above her and then down. Contact made.

Puckering up her mouth, she sang a long, simple melody of "oooohs" and slowly bucked the muscles of her ass in

accompaniment. In response, her other lips puffed, moistened, spread. After a moment her eyes opened, after being
shut in concentration, and she uttered a few real words:
"Wow, that's nice. Try it all the way."

"Okay, if that's what you want." Down from her clit, gliding
between those slippery lips, and there hovering at the entrance.
"Ready?"

"Uh huh," she said, fully reclined, legs up and apart, excitement prominent.

In then – head first. Guided in with care, just enough force to
part the inner ring muscles and, with a warm wet slide, within.
Virgin no more, my own pleasure was as unmistakable as Jo's: a
change in mechanical tempo mirroring her own escalating rate
and shallowness of her breaths, flexing of her muscles. Mine in
purpose fulfilled, hers in being filled by my Japanese-designed
purpose.

Out then, and back in, and back out, a steady humming rhythm.
Discovery, then Patrick mischievously slid one of my controls,
and activated my band of pearls. Discovery, for her as well, as they
acted against that sensitive area just an inch or so within her
vagina, and Jo reacted with a deep, powerful moan of delight.

Her orgasm was as delightful as it was loud and strong: legs
stretched out and stiff, hands clutching clumps of bedspread, at
first she hissed between tightly locked teeth but then amplified
to a soulful, bass bellow of ecstatic release. Coming, having
come and fading to gone, she fell back, body glowing with
sweat, her panting easing in volume and duration.

"Oh, wow," she said, giggles spilling out after the words.
"That was intense."

"I'm glad," he said, turning me off and putting me aside. "I
was kind of nervous at first, that you'd like it too much, you
know? But seeing you like that . . . it was such a turn on. I liked
it, too. A lot."

Arms wrapped around him, she planted a flurry of kisses on
him. "That's wonderful – I hoped you would be. It was lots of
fun, but only because you were on the other end of it." Sly grin
on her glistening face, Jo added: "You know, there's a lot of
other places we can try it – on you, as well as me."

"I'm game," Patrick said, sweet smile on his face. "Let's play."

I am a Rabbit Pearl vibrator, who resides when not in use in a bedside table. I am certainly a tubular pink plastic device five inches long, one and a half inches wide, and was manufactured in Japan.

But I am not just Jo's vibrator. Instead I am a device used for the enhancement of sexual pleasure by both Jo and her boyfriend, Patrick – and they, and I, couldn't be happier.

Amour Noir

Landon Dixon

I stood in the rain, looking at the sign in the window, "Man Wanted".

Then I shoved the door of the diner open, was blown inside by a wet gust of wind. The door sucked closed behind me, and I gave the joint a once-over: red vinyl-cracked stools fronting a white counter, red vinyl booths with white Formica tables along the wall, black and white tile on the floor. The place was lit too bright and reeked of grease and urinal pucks, completely deserted except for a small, oily character dressed in white perched on a stool next to the cash register, reading a paperback.

A real Sioux City hot spot.

But it was way past midnight, and I was way past hungry. With still eighty-five miles to go before I reached Sioux Falls and the Tri-State County Managers convention.

"Sure coming down out there," I said amiably, slipping off my raincoat and tossing it over the back of a booth bench, sliding in opposite.

The little guy squatting by the register lifted a pair of liquid brown eyes and looked at me. His dark, shiny hair was parted down the middle, a brown, unlit cigarette dangling from the corner of his mouth. The nametag on his chest read: "Sinjin". He blinked his long lashes a couple of times and then bowed his head back down to his book, *You Play the Black and the Red Comes Up*.

I plucked a stained menu out of the rack on the table and opened it up, hoping the food was better than the service. Then the service got better, way better.

A red, plastic catsup container rolled across the floor, bumped against my foot. I looked up, and there she stood, in the swinging door to the kitchen – a cool, tanned blonde in a blazing white skirt and blouse, slender arms and legs gleaming bare, honey-blonde hair cut shoulder-length, wavy and glossy. Her eyes were blue, and they sparkled, her high breasts bobbing as she walked my way. The whole package dazzled these sore eyes.

"See anything you like?" she double-entendred, bumping up against my table. The nametag on her chest read: "Chrissie".

"Weeell," I said, getting in on the game. "Matter of fact, my appetite's really picked up."

Her moist lips curved into a smile. "A hungry man's good to find," she cooed, tossing a disdainful look over her shoulder at Sinjin. The guy had his foreign-made coffin nail lit now, was puffing up a storm.

"Food's pretty cheap here, too, eh?" I said, glancing down at the menu. "I hope it tastes—"

"You won't find anything *cheap* around here!" Chrissie retorted, eyes flashing.

I couldn't come up with any other pithy come-ons, so I ordered the hamburger steak platter and a cherry Coke. It came and went, lying heavy in the pit of my stomach as the blonde dish pushed out her chest and asked, "Dessert?"

"Something sweet and sticky?" I suggested.

"Pie?" she responded, wagging a smooth, brown leg back and forth, toeing the tile.

"Sure, what kind of *pie* do you have, Chrissie?"

"Cora."

I looked up her leg, to her chest. "Cora?"

"That's the ticket, Frank," she giggled, all sweet and sticky.

I didn't know what kind of a game we were playing now. My name isn't Frank, and hers wasn't Cora. But I let it ride. "Uh, the kinds of pie?" I reminded her.

She hooked a red-tipped finger into her crimson lower lip, blue eyes twinkling. "Hmmm, I can't quite seem to remember. They're all in the kitchen – come and see for yourself."

The place was empty now. Sinjin had skulked off five minutes earlier, the joint going up a full star with his exit. The only sounds were the night rain washing against the steamed-up windows, the wind rushing down the empty ribbon of wet asphalt outside. And the thumping in my chest.

I climbed to my feet.

"Cora" led the way, round hips swishing, mounded buttocks sluicing, lithe legs whispering. Through the swinging door and into a cramped, confused kitchen. She halted the parade in front of a flour-strewn counter and turned to face me. Slender fingers brushed across her soft throat, toyed with the top button on her blouse.

"Where's the pie?" I asked, looking around. I do like my pie.

"You're a drifter, aren't you?" Cora breathed. She fluttered her eyelashes, unbuttoned her buttons. "A stranger in town."

"Uh, actually, I'm heading for—"

"Don't talk, Frank," she cut in, pressing a finger to my lips. "You rang twice, and I'm here. That's all that's important."

The woman's eyes were elsewhere. And so were mine, because she had her blouse open now, revealing a white, satiny bra that packaged her pair of cupcakes beautifully – up and out. I licked my lips, the babe's sweet perfume flooding my good senses. I didn't understand any of her role-playing rigmarole, and I didn't care.

She ensnared me in her arms, kissing me, her breasts pushing warm and insistent into my chest, soft, wet lips sucking the breath out of me. I grabbed her and hungrily kissed back, grinding my swelling cock into her warm belly. She moaned, running her fingers through my black locks, then clutching at my hair, really digging her hooks into me.

"I wanted you from the moment I saw you, Frank," she murmured.

She was off in a world of her own, but the reality of her heaving chest was very near and dear to me. I grasped her breasts, squeezing the pert nubbins, forcing groans of pleasure from her lips. Then she popped her bra open at the back and I went skin-on-skin with her bikini-pale tits, kneading the smooth, heated flesh, pinching her pink nipples.

"Suck my breasts, Frank!" she implored.

I bent my head down and flicked a nipple with my tongue, watching in amazement as it instantly grew in size and rigidity. Cora's body quivered in my hands. I lapped at the undersides of her rubbery nipples, swirled my tongue around and around their pebbly aureoles.

Cora squirmed in my arms, then dropped right out of them, down to her knees on the floor. She quickly unbuckled and unzipped me, dragged my swollen cock out of the tangle of my underwear and out into the steamy open. We both watched it grow rock-hard in front of her, her hand pulsing its heartbeat.

I flooded with heat, trembling. She smiled up at me, then sent her silky hand sailing up and down the throbbing length of my prick, sending shivers of delight radiating all through me. She stroked and stroked my cock, raw and hot and honest. Before finally squeezing the pulsating shaft and sticking out her pink tongue and swabbing the tip of my straining dick with the tip of her tongue. I flat-out vibrated with the wet, erotic impact.

Then I smelled smoke. I twisted my head around – there were puffs of white, acrid smoke billowing through the crack in a black curtain that marked off the entrance to some sort of storage room. I'd smelt that smoke before, scared now there was going to be fire. "What the—"

"That's just my husband," Cora stated, winding her tongue around the bulbous hood of my cock. "Sinjin likes to watch."

I started to say something, started to tuck my hard-on back in and beat a hasty retreat from that greasy loony bin. But before I could finish anything I'd started, Cora inhaled me almost right down to the roots. And all bets were off.

"Jeez!" I groaned, ablaze in the wet-hot cauldron of the woman's mouth. I weaved my fingers into her yellow hair and hung on for the ride.

She eagerly bobbed her pretty head back and forth, velvet lips sliding along my gleaming, vein-popped pole. She sucked and sucked on my cock, pulling hard and long, fingering my tightened ball sack, building and building the pressure, setting me to shaking with sensation.

Until just as I was about to blow sky-high, she suddenly pulled back, dropping me dripping out of her glorious mouth.

She jumped to her feet, up onto the counter. And I shoved her back, unthinking, just doing, yanking off her skirt and panties and exposing her dewy blonde need.

"Fuck me, Frank!" she exhorted, crushing her bare breasts in her hands.

I shouldered her legs and recklessly steered my cockhead into her bush, through slick petals and deep into hot, wet, tight pussy. She rolled around in the flour, moaning, as I churned my hips, fucking her.

The counter creaked and the flour flew, as I pumped the writhing woman, the smoke from our puffing voyeur hazing the kitchen but not quite muffling the tangy, desperate smell of sweat and sex. I gritted my teeth and flung my hips at Cora, pistoning granite dong into gripping cunt. I was on fire, out of control, body and balls tingling way past the point of no return.

"Yeah, Cora, yeah!" I hollered, fucking the blonde in a frenzy.

Then I was jolted by orgasm, my thrusting pipe exploding inside her sucking pussy, filling her with white-hot ecstasy. She screamed her own joy, legs shaking against my chest and body shuddering, fiery orgasm engulfing the both of us.

I stayed longer than my budgeted one hour for dinner in Sioux City.

I soon came to realize why I'd never met anyone like Cora before: most people who thought and acted like she did were locked up somewhere, safely away from square johns like myself. The woman had some serious delusions – about movies. Not girlish crushes on matinee idols like Brad Pitt or Tom Cruise, or displaced dreams of being the next Scarlett Johansson or Catherine Zeta-Jones. No, this offbeat babe had a living, breathing, all-encompassing Film Noir fetish.

She told me all about it, gushing it out with the same intensity she'd gushed earlier. All about the black and white shadowy lighting, the furtive characters and seedy locations, the sexy, sinister themes, the motion pictures and movie actors and studios; an alternative rain and tear-streaked chiaroscuro world of brooding heavies and smoldering femme fatales, doomed lovers and desperate loners. A strange, exciting, flickering world that was her escape from a shabby Sioux City existence, I supposed.

Sinjin indulged her fantasy role-playing, as she indulged his fisted voyeurism. And now I'd become the third pointy-head in the whole crazy lust triangle. I'd been caught between the nutty dame's legs and she wasn't about to let go.

We hooked up again the following evening, the setting: an abandoned warehouse overlooking the misty banks of the Missouri River. I was costumed in a flimsy trenchcoat and a wrinkled fedora, playing the rogue cop, "Bannion". While Chrissie/Cora was now the bad-girl gangster's moll desperate to redeem herself, "Debby". Sinjin held down his usual supporting role as the peeping, puffing Tom in the shadows.

Pipes dripped unknown liquids and tiny feet scurried about, towers of crates creaking ominous warnings, as Debby set the scene of dangerous love by scrambling out of her little, black moll gown and up onto a pile of coiled ropes. She wagged her bare, tan and white bottom at me. I moved in behind, gripping the glowing orbs of her bum and sinking my shaft into her pussy. Her desperate cries and my urgent grunts echoed in the gloomy, cavernous confines, Sinjin's cigarettes burning bright orange behind a rusted metal pillar.

The next night, the scene shifted to a dank alley that ran into oblivion alongside a sleazy bar. I was the hardboiled private dick, "Sam", who plastered soft, willing, manipulating "Brigid" up against a grimy brick wall and tried to hose some truth out of her. Sinjin was third garbage can on the right, watching and puffing and pulling in the dark.

Night after rainy night it went on and on, through the dog-eared celluloid catalogue of con-men and suckers, vulnerable good girls and brassy broads. It all became way too much for me. I'm a Kung Fu genre fan, myself, and not much of a ham. Not to mention the fact that my boss back home was really wondering why it was taking so long to "get my car fixed" in Sioux City.

"It's been a lot of, um, fun . . ."

"Phyllis."

"Phyllis," I broke it to the blonde hottie, as she drove us to a seedy downtown hotel through another liquid night. "But I've got to get back to work. I can't afford to lose my—"

"No one's pulling out!" she sneered, strangling the steering wheel. "We went into this together, and we're coming out at the end together. It's straight down the line for both of us."

We skidded to a stop in front of the glowering hotel and rented Room 1313 from a nebbish desk clerk wearing a leer the size of all Iowa. Phyllis unlocked the door to the ratty room, unloaded a bottle of rye from a paper sack. She filled a pair of dirty water glasses, and drank from both.

"I'm crazy about you, Walter," she breathed, standing on tiptoes and smothering my mouth, drawing blood with her teeth.

I was the hapless stooge trapped in the erotic clutches of the calculating femme fatale, hopelessly playing a game I didn't even know the rules to, or the players. Phyllis shoved me down to my knees on the threadbare carpet, ordered me to polish the four-inch black stiletto she had strapped to her feet – with my tongue.

I looked up the smirking woman's slim, stockinged legs, up and under the knee-high, black skirt she was wearing without the benefit of panties. She gestured impatiently, and I hung my head, licked the rounded tip of her shoe.

A gold anklet encircled her left ankle, glittering in the light. I coiled my trembling fingers around it and lifted her foot, ran my tongue all along the high-polish leather of her shoe, tasting the rich, smooth texture. Then I lapped at her other high heel, licking the shimmering bridge of her foot where it humped out of her shoe.

Phyllis stripped off her pink sweater, baring her breasts. She cupped and fondled her handful tits, rolling engorged nipples between her fingers. She stuck a spike heel in my face and I dutifully snaked my tongue around it, then sucked on it, desperate to please.

When I'd worshipped at her feet long enough, she unhooked her skirt and slid onto the bed. She spread her legs and beckoned, and I crawled across the floor, in between her silken stems. I stuck my tongue into the damp, blonde fur of her pussy without hesitation.

"Yes!" she moaned, clawing at my hair. "Eat me, Walter!"

I gripped her taut thighs and lapped at her slit, anxiously tonguing her from bumhole to mound-top, over and over. She was wetter than night. Her spicy juices and musky scent made my addled brain spin even faster.

"Enough!" she commanded at last. She gestured at me to stand up, strip off my clothes.

I wiped off my mouth and stood, stripped, shooting a quick glance around the dingy room for that telltale smoke. Phyllis pointed at the cracked mirror on the wall, which I took to be of the two-way variety. Then she grabbed me and spread me out on the bed, herself on top.

She grasped my cock and speared it between her slickened lips, sitting down on it. "Mmmm, that feels good, Walter," she exhaled, digging her scarlet fingertips into the hair on my chest and moving her bum.

I gripped her hanging tits, tried to meet her urgent bouncing with my own upward thrusting. But I didn't have the strength, or the stamina. Phyllis vigorously shifted her ass up and down, riding my achingly hard cock, fucking me with her pussy.

The sagging bed squealed in agony, the blonde picking the tempo up to frenzy mode. The headboard cracked against the ragged wallpaper until the whole room shook with the ferocity of her passion. I lay there in a pool of our sweat, body limp, cock surging with sexual electricity.

"Yes, Walter, yes!" Phyllis screamed.

She tore at my chest, bouncing around like a madwoman. Until her dewy body spasmed with the wicked orgasm she pulled from my cock. Her joyous shrieking overpowered my breathless whimpering, as I spurted semen inside her in an orgasm long and loose and full of juice, but utterly lacking in feeling.

Then the door burst open. A man stood there, a huge, angry bear of a man. "I knew you was cheatin' on me!" he roared at Phyllis. "You're gonna die, asshole!" he roared at me.

Phyllis sunk her fingernails into my flesh, pinning me down.
She slow-rode my cock, eyeing the brute crowding the doorway
with total contempt. "So, you finally caught on, huh, Nick?"

The big man gaped at her, big, hairy hands clenching into
big, hard fists.

"Walter, meet my husband, Nick," Phyllis/Brigid/Debby/
Cora/Chrissie said to me.

Then kissed me deadly.

I woke up screaming, pushing the black angel away with a
superhuman effort. I jumped to my feet, cock and balls flapping
on empty. I didn't know for sure what the hell was going on, but
I knew one thing: I was being cast for the real-life part of patsy,
pushover, and fall guy all rolled into one, the clay pigeon. The
big knife was out and the big heat was on; this was the breaking
point, the set-up. I was going to be the accused, abandoned,
beyond a reasonable doubt.

The man filling the doorframe suddenly started shaking,
spluttering, body and soul, his beefy face burning purple.

"Remember your heart condition, dear," his wife jeered,
with more than a touch of evil. "Keel over from a coronary,
or tear my lover limb from limb and go to jail – either way,
Sinjin and I get the diner, and each other."

I shot a look of despair at the born-to-be-bad piece of blonde
ice. But it was too late for tears. I barrelled straight into the
third man, sending him slamming backwards into the hall
clutching his chest.

I raced down the stairs and out into the dark city, the asphalt
jungle, between midnight and dawn; the night-runner shooting
through a nightmare alley and across a street with no name. I
scrambled up a grading and by a narrow margin hooked onto
the side of a thundering boxcar, swinging inside, railroaded out
of town.

A poor sap on the run now, on dangerous ground, in a lonely
place. A guy who'd taken a detour into a roadhouse, a dark
passage, and was DOA as soon as he'd stepped through the
door. Was there ever a shadow of a doubt?

Hair Trigger

Nikki Magennis

Frankie came out of the blue.

In the bar where they met for the first time, he beckoned Sal over to where he sat – a booth in the quiet section. He had a lavish smile, and blew smoke around them as he talked, so that the dark corner of the pub filled with a blue haze.

"You're beautiful, did you know that?"

Sal smiled, and sat down. She took a sip of her gin-and-soda, held the ice cube in her mouth until there was nothing left but a cold, sharp sliver.

"But I'd be more beautiful naked, right?"

"Perhaps. Actually, I was thinking I wanted to see you with your hair down."

Automatically, Sal's hand flew to her hair. That night she'd straightened it, rubbed wax into the tips, and swept it up into a chignon. A few loose strands swam around her face.

"Why don't you take it down, sugar?"

Sal crunched the ice sliver in her mouth. Locking her eyes on his, she reached up and pulled out the clip. Her hair tumbled loose, a long black curtain falling to the small of her back.

"Much better." He nodded. "Now, let's talk about the naked part."

He leaned forward, hands nearly touching Sal's on the table-top.

When he reached out finally to touch her, to pull one lock of hair between his fingers, she knew what would happen next. Still, she loved the anticipation, how the atmosphere grew heavy and shimmered with wanting.

"What are you doing Friday night?" he asked. On Friday Sal
waited for him. Her door buzzer went off at precisely eight-
thirty, and she jumped like she'd had an electric shock. She
forced herself not to run to answer it, tried to keep the shake out
of her voice as she spoke.

"Hello?"

"Rapunzel, Rapunzel, let down your hair," he said.

Within an hour they were in bed.

It became their Friday game. As he asked, every week Sal wore
her hair up, perfumed and shined with serum, artfully tangled.
She dressed in elaborate outfits: stockings, basques, lace-
trimmed slips. High heels and immaculate make-up, ribbons
and hooks and small pearl buttons. Frankie liked her prepared
like this, so carefully primped. Ready for him to unravel.

He'd arrive at eight-thirty precisely. Never early, never late.

Sometimes Sal would suggest they go out for dinner, catch a
movie, but Frankie brushed her ideas aside.

"Let's just stay in," he said. "I prefer you naked."

After a few weeks, she stopped suggesting they do anything
else. After all, she was as hooked on their Friday night game as
he was. She burned with the tension of waiting. Each time the
week swung round to Friday, she felt the dark, strange magic of
their ritual take hold. It was like a drumbeat that echoed faintly
in the background all the time, even when she couldn't hear it,
until the end of the week, when the rhythm would start to
pound. By eight-thirty, she was deafened by the noise.

She'd fixed her hair with pins, and a couple of black enamel
combs. When he said the word she turned to the gilt-framed
mirror over the table. She knew he liked to watch her, pins in
her mouth, arms raised, undoing her hair so it fell around her
shoulders. And she'd watch him in the mirror, his eyes following the long trail of her hair, reaching halfway down her back.
She shook it free. The smell of coconut filled the room.

Still standing in front of the mirror, she waited.

"Strip."

Her hands shook as she fumbled over her buttons and wriggled out of her clothes. She let them fall at her feet – kicked aside the puddles of cloth to stand naked before him. He didn't allow her to cover herself.

"Keep your hands at your sides."

She knew he liked the contrast – dark hair, pale skin. The parts of her that never saw daylight, they were the parts he liked the best. That's where he'd linger, with his hands and his tongue and his teeth. He'd stroke her long neck and the delicate skin on the underside of her arm. The crease of her breasts. Her sex.

She shaved herself so smooth and hairless her pubis was as soft as soap to the touch. A small tuft covered her clit, just enough for him to tug at with his long piano-players fingers. After a few days, she'd get a rash and the small hairs would grow back red and angry, but oh God it was worth it for Friday nights. To see how his eyes would darken. To feel those soft lips press against her bare pussy.

When they fucked he held her down, slid into her like a knife, moved so slowly she felt herself falling into a deep and endless space. It was sex like the night sky, silent and expansive. And his skin – his honey-coloured skin – was taut and perfect. He pressed himself against her and they were two leaves of damp paper, stuck fast together. Cleaving.

When it came, the orgasm broke them apart, a supernova rending the universe: white-hot; cold and dazzling. Sal spun out into the void, alone in her private blissworld. As though she ceased to exist for a few moments, she was elsewhere. Blank, yet ecstatic.

Afterwards, they lay in a ruck of damp sheets with his hands tangled in her hair, his mouth against her ear whispering words she couldn't hear.

She should have picked up on the warnings, of course, but who can really tell danger from exhilaration? She had nightmares: grotesque animals spilling out of closets; electric cables wrapping round her ankles; phone calls with nobody on the other end of the line. She'd wake up gasping.

Two, three months passed. Without her noticing, the landscape of Sal's life changed. It was as though a curtain were pulled over her weekends. Fridays were inviolate, a sacred ritual. Her weekly dose of Frankie's adoration doled out in one sweet, concentrated night.

Afterwards, when they slept, he'd wrap himself in her hair, as though they were bound together, as though they were weaving a subtle net around the hours of sleep. Sal felt him bury himself in the crook of her neck and wondered if he was as trapped as she was.

The rest of the week grew colorless compared to Fridays. Sal went out less, telling herself she needed rest to recover from the intensity of the weekend games. She wouldn't admit the real reason – she was waiting for his out-of-the-blue phone call. She should have known. He called on Thursdays, at seven sharp. Never early, never late. Week after week, his ritual never varied. Yet she waited, hovered, hoped.

The night she turned up at his flat unannounced, overnight bag trailing behind her like a cumbersome pet, she wore her sheerest black top, a tight pair of culottes, and silk underwear. She'd chosen the ferociously high heels, the ones that made her walk with tiny little steps, ass thrust out, hips swaying.

His eyes narrowed when he opened the door. It was a Wednesday. They weren't scheduled.

He was in a suit – shirt open at the neck, phone in his hand.

"What's wrong?" he asked, eyes flicking to the stairwell behind her.

"Nothing," she said, smiling. "Just wanted to see you."

Inside, her heart was shrinking and leaping at the same time. The smile was plastered to her face. She stood there holding the strap of her bag and felt like a door-to-door salesman, begging for a little time. Behind him, the light in his hall was yellow and warm, spilling out the door.

"Didn't you think of phoning?" he asked, holding the door half-open.

She shook her head, and then in a moment of inspiration, reached up to pull the clip out of her hair. She sighed, like she'd had a hard day. Shook her hair out.

"I've had a hard day," she said. "Gonna let me in?"

A split second too long passed. The smell of coconut hung in the air between them.

"Sure," he said, stepping back.

Frankie's flat was unknown territory. Her heels clattered on the polished floor as she followed him, padding barefoot in front of her. He showed her into the kitchen, poured a glass of tap water, and left her.

"I have to take a shower," he said.

Sal sat and stared at the pistachio-green walls. She heard the lock on the bathroom door slide shut, and then the faint hiss of the shower. The kitchen was sparse. There was chequered linoleum on the floor and strip lighting overhead. A jar on the counter that held whisks, cooking spoons and scissors. Pinned to the wall, an art calendar showed Venus coming out of the sea, her face sweet and perfect. Underneath dates were marked in different-colored pen; red crosses and black crosses. Sal stared at his coded dates and shifted in her seat. The shoes were pinching her feet.

Hit by a flash of queasy inspiration, she slipped out of her high heels. In stockinged feet, she crept into the hall and checked the closed doors. Like a cat burglar, she considered her options, and finally pushed open the door at the end of the hall.

His bed was large, and sat in the middle of the room. The covers were messed up. She always thought of Frankie as obsessively neat, and the sight of his unmade bed gave her a pang of tender feelings, as though she'd caught a glimpse of some secret folded in among the creases of white linen.

Moving fast, she stripped off her top and culottes, and placed them in a pile on a chair. In her whore's underwear, she climbed into Frankie's bed, and lay on top of the rumpled covers. Her daring excited her, and she felt the welcome rush and tingle between her thighs as she grew wet.

Sal took a deep breath – and noticed a scent clinging to the sheets. A sweet, bitter and musky smell, something both familiar and strange. When she pulled back the covers, it rose up into her nostrils, and she breathed in the scent of another woman:

her perfume, her sex. Curled across the pillow was a long, fine red hair. Sal picked it up and held it between her fingers, mesmerized. Frankie opened the door, skin still damp from the shower, a towel wrapped loosely round his hips.

"Fuck," he said under his breath. "You're beautiful."

He walked to her, and pushed his fingers into her hair, pulled her to him to kiss her long and deep. Sal felt the wonderful softness of his lips, his warm, wet mouth, the heat of his skin.

She pulled away. Stood up.

"Lie down, Frankie," she said.

"You're giving orders now, sugar?"

Sal smiled lavishly.

As Frankie lay down across the unmade bed, she slunk into a stripper pose – hips tilted, head cocked provocatively. Bending down, keeping her movements slow, Sal unclipped her stocking fasteners. With swift movements, she pulled her stockings off, and held them in front of Frankie like she was dangling a gift.

"A striptease, huh? I'm liking this surprise," he said, coal-black eyes fixed on Sal's every move.

When she came around the bed he lifted his arms to reach her, and she caught them swiftly. As he strained to kiss her, she danced away from him, pulling his wrists together and pinning them to the wooden rail of the bedstead. Only then did she lean down to press her mouth against his, distracting him as she slipped a stocking through the bars, wrapped it around his wrists, once—

"Sal, babe, I didn't know you were into this."

– twice, and tied it firmly.

Next she moved to the end of the bed. Frankie laughed and she smiled sweetly back at him as she bound his ankles. There was an edge to his laughter, half-expectant, half-uneasy.

He was pulled taut across the bed.

"I can't move," he said.

"I know."

Sal undid the clasp of her bra and dropped it on the floor. When she started undoing the silk ribbons of her knickers, Frankie licked his lips.

She approached, carrying the fabric scrap of her knickers.

"Now what are you doing?" Frankie asked as she trailed them up from his ankle, over his thigh, brushed over his stiffening cock and lifted them to his face. She let him inhale her scent, and then she tied them over his eyes, using the ribbon to fasten his blindfold tight. She leaned in close.

"Now you can hear me, and feel me, but you can't see me," she whispered.

This time, Frankie didn't laugh. He swallowed.

Over his prone body she draped her hair, pulling it across his skin till it trailed behind her like water. She wrapped his cock in it, brushed it over his balls. He moaned. With slow, hypnotic movements, she swayed back and forth, letting the tips of her long hair drag over him. His cock lay across his belly, long and swollen. A bead of moisture leaked from the head of his glans and wetted the tips of her hair, so that she painted his skin with clear, shining strokes of pre-come.

Frankie rolled from side to side, lifting his hips up as he begged for more. But Sal kept up her gentle torment, the feather-light stroking of his torso and the wave of her hair over his cock. When his cock started leaping and twitching, she stopped.

Walking silently, barefoot, she slipped away.

In the empty room, Frankie tugged at his bonds, straining to feel the heat of her body against his, murmuring her name.

Moments later, Sal reappeared, and leaned in again to Frankie's ear. She held the kitchen scissors close to his face. *Snip, snip*, she rasped the metal blades against each other. Frankie's body went suddenly rigid, and his mouth fell open.

"Sal?" he asked, turning his head towards the sound and then involuntarily pulling away when he heard her make the cold *snip, snip* noise again. "What's going on—

"Shhhh . . ."

She laid her finger on his soft lips and silenced him.

Sal swung herself over his body, straddling him with the scissors still in her hand. She positioned her cunt over his thigh, where she could rub her clit against the fine hairs on his leg. Then she started moving, grinding against his skin, so that he could feel the hot wet fire of her cunt inches from his cock.

As she rocked back and forth, Sal lifted the scissors.

"Sal, what are you doing?" Frankie asked, but she didn't answer.

Her breathing grew faster as she started to cut, lifting handfuls of her hair and shearing them, an inch from her scalp. The cuttings fell over Frankie like a tree shedding its leaves in winter. She knew he could feel the slight weight of her hair piling over his body, tickling and caressing, but not giving any release. She knew he could also feel the kiss of her cunt on his thigh. Her clit was swollen, and chafed against his skin like an axe against flint, showering sparks.

Her orgasm was coming, and this time she wasn't spinning out into the cold blank blissworld. She was somewhere much closer, coming home to herself, her orgasm multiplying, amplifying her body. Frankie's belly and the messed-up sheets of the bed were covered in the ragged clippings of her hair, and she dropped the scissors as she rode his thigh hard towards an orgasm that he wouldn't share, wouldn't even be able to watch, only hear and feel her as she came down to earth hard, was buried in the sweat and flesh of her body, alive now, lighter, naked and shorn.

When Sal climbed off Frankie, he begged. As she dressed he started to plead, yanking at the twists of nylon that held him fast, raging at the scrap of dirty knickers covering his eyes. Sal's hair covered him like a dry black tide, itching and tormenting him, bringing no relief to his untouched, desperately shining hard-on. Sal rubbed her hand over her head absentmindedly as she looked around for her clothes.

She left him there in his bed strewn with hair, a headful of her black tresses and one single long, curling and treacherous red hair.

He could have it all, she thought, walking to the station with her head held high, the spring breeze fresh on the back of her neck. Bare legs, no underwear, cropped hair. He could keep it. For the first time in months, she felt free.

Spin Dry

Sam Jayne

"Pile of fucking crap!" Kay hopped off the top of the washing machine to boot the failing contraption. It was more or less dead, held together only by industrial tape. There was no argument, a new one was needed, but continuously it packed up at the most crucial moments and Kay thought sometimes it was simply taking advantage of its power over her. She growled in frustration, her groin burning, and kicked the washer with as much force as she could muster. Almost instantly it span back into action, vibrating manically, louder than an aeroplane taking to the skies. Kay bared her teeth and vaulted back to her seated position on top of the machine. Ten seconds later she orgasmed fiercely, moaning in pleasure as the appliance worked its magic. Such great effort must have drained the last dregs of energy out of the device because, concurrently with Kay's climax, the washing machine exploded.

"Shit."

Kay, who had been thrown to the kitchen floor, stared at the mess as she sat in a puddle of soapy water littered with burnt-out wires and foul-smelling clothes. She sighed angrily at the thought of the expense which loomed ahead of her. How much did washing machines cost nowadays anyway? No doubt they came with all the frills – an inbuilt fax machine, telephone and internet connection. Perhaps she should just buy a high-powered vibrator instead. Clothes could always be washed in the sink. But no, the washing machine was important. She had never even come close to rising to such heights of pleasure without it. It would need to be replaced.

"Fuck it," she muttered and, peeling a sodden pair of pants off her head, she hauled herself upright and staggered out of the kitchen to contemplate her washing machine crisis.

Kay lived a simple life. Her flat was plain and almost devastatingly minimalistic. There were three rooms; a kitchen, a lounge-cum-bedroom and a bathroom. The lounge, her current location, was made up only of a ragged mattress and blankets – to serve as a bed – laid out on the rough wooden floor, and a small television set in the corner of the room. Kay didn't care for art or ornaments. Pointless frivolities, she thought. She enjoyed her own company, though she did admit her washing machine had become something of an unlikely friend. This realization provoked a short bout of grief over its unpleasant demise, but her mourning period was over as quickly as it had begun. It was time to move on. But how? She needed to find – what? – a couple of hundred pounds for a half-decent model with sufficient spin-dry speed. Kay didn't have that kind of money. In fact, she didn't have any kind of money at all.

Depressed, she grabbed her shoulder bag from the floor and trudged out of the flat to partake unenthusiastically in a spot of window shopping. The mess in the kitchen remained. She would clean it later. The prospect of viewing expensive washing machines through prisons of glass was all she could take right now. Mopping the floor beforehand was asking far too much.

Old Edward's Square was a dismal place to be. Crowds swarmed in every direction and, more so, it stank of meat and fish which was being sold on the open market. As a vegetarian Kay found it difficult to refrain from gagging at these odours. It wasn't a love of animals that prevented her from eating meat, but the thought of such putrid fatty steaks and fillets entering her body. And even without the butcher stalls and the hundreds of people, the square was still horrendous. Kay preferred to avoid shopping like the plague whenever possible. There were few occasions in her life when she had ever been gripped by an overwhelming urge to shop. Mostly she stayed close to her own flat and bought food from the corner

Co-op. The corner co-op didn't sell washing machines. This was a shame. Kay was sure they would be dirt cheap if they did.

"My girl!" A bulk of a man slapped the unprepared Kay across the back of her head.

"What the fuck do you want?" she snarled, clenching her fists as if to prepare for battle.

"Eh, I dunno. Blow job would be nice. I'd pay extra for full sex."

Kay scowled. Jed was the epiphany of sleaze. He was obsessed with sex and, unfortunately, equally obsessed with her. She had never understood this. While she was slim and reasonably attractive – with dark cropped her and almost deathly pale skin – she also exuded hatred and anger. She didn't consider herself to be a pleasant person or a good friend to anyone and she had never wanted to achieve this status. Why Jed – a burly fool at best – was so transfixed on fucking her was a mystery. She could only guess some men must enjoy the risk of being castrated at any moment.

"You could never afford me," Kay spat.

Jed grinned toothily. "Wanna bet? Just won two hundred and fifty on a scratch card! Think you're worth more than that?"

Kay was about to walk away. She didn't need this today. However, as she turned her eye caught a gleam in the display window of an upmarket homeware store. It was the kind of gleam you see in films – an unearthly glow focused around something so appealing the onlooker is momentarily dazed. She knew in that instant she had found her replacement – a high-speed washing machine so alluring to her it should really have been hidden away in a sex shop. The price tag was a hefty two-four-nine.

Tearing her eyes away from the vision of loveliness, she glanced back at Jed.

"What would you expect for two-fifty?" she asked him.

Jed had never believed he would enter the home of Kay. The beautiful Kay who he had been certain he would never fuck. Most girls he knew were easy and he'd taken them countless times. Not Kay. She had resisted him without relent and Jed had almost accepted this. He was glad he'd pushed it today. His scratch card winnings were a small price to pay for some time with this striking enigma.

"My washing machine exploded," Kay muttered as a half-hearted explanation for the mess in the kitchen. "I like to sit on it until I climax. It's the only thing that interests me sexually, so don't think I'll enjoy my time with you. I will be detached and unexcited. I'm reserving my passion for my new washing machine."

Jed thought this was fair enough and seemed unperturbed by the flooded kitchen. He followed Kay into the lounge and obediently sat down on her mattress while she disappeared into the bathroom. When she re-entered the makeshift bedroom his heart was thumping. She stood in her underwear – a black lace thong and bra – and brandished a cat o'nine tails which Jed had purchased from an adult shop on one of the backstreets leading from the square.

There was no hesitation as Kay pushed Jed's head forward roughly so that he lay on his stomach on the mattress. She stripped him down to his boxer shorts then, with little regard for any pain he might feel, she tied his wrists and ankles tightly with detached bra straps to nail heads which stuck out of the crude flooring. His legs were forced wide apart, exposing the bulge in his boxers. Kay almost smiled. Initially she had hoped this encounter would be over quickly so she could be paid and buy a new washing machine before the shops closed. She had no inhibitions about sleeping with this man for money – she was not a regular prostitute but the offer had been too tempting to decline. Anyway, now that she stood in this position – with the fate of Jed in her hands – she felt a sadistic thrill running through her veins. She had never liked Jed's attention much but had also never imagined he would enjoy being dominated. This opportunity to cause pain and torture to someone who had consistently irritated her for the last few years should surely be savoured.

"Worthless scum," Kay hissed as she drew back the flogger and lashed Jed for the first time. He grunted as the whip struck his body, his buttocks clenching in the confines of his shorts. "Useless dog! Here's another . . ."

This time Jed couldn't contain a more audible yelp as the whips stung into his flesh. Again and again Kay brought the nine tails of the flogger down onto his back, reddening the skin until it was visibly sore. Then she stopped the lashing, leaving Jed to grit his teeth in anticipation for a few seconds before she slithered on top of him and softly pulled down his boxers so they hung rather pathetically round his bound ankles.

His bottom was tense as he awaited his next round of punishment and his swollen testicles rested, uncovered, between his legs. His hard cock had found its way between his stomach and the threadbare mattress. Kay was sure this was uncomfortable for him, but not as uncomfortable as she would make it.

Gently she squeezed Jed's balls and he moaned in pleasure. But this delicate approach was shortlived as Kay drew back the flogger again and thrashed her captive's buttocks, making doubly sure the ends of the whips kissed icily at those bloated testicles. He screamed out in pain, desperate to clutch his throbbing groin but unable to do so with his hands tied as they were. His body spasmed as Kay whipped him again, refusing him the chance to recover from the previous beating. He was groaning continuously now, but the agony aroused him beyond anything he had experienced before. His crotch felt as if it were on fire as a result of both the thrashing and his excitement. His balls were bursting for release.

"I detest you," Kay growled, only half role-playing. She lashed Jed one more time before crawling onto his back, her weight only adding to the pressure he felt. With her fingernails – regrettably not as long or sharp as they could have been, but effective enough – she clawed at the welts she had created with the flogger. Jed groaned, not wanting to show too much weakness. Then, in one swift movement, Kay slid to the side of Jed, tugged away the straps that bound his wrists and forced him to roll over onto his back. Kay smiled cruelly as she eyed up his manhood. Average size. Nothing extraordinary, but she could tell he was painfully aroused.

"I don't usually eat meat but I'm going to eat you," she declared quite seriously, then bent her head down to take in the length of Jed's cock. She sucked him tenderly to start with, her head bobbing as she increased the speed. Jed whimpered in ecstasy, his climax ever more imminent by the second. Kay realized this as pre-come seeped out onto her tongue. She lapped up the salty fluid, paused, and then bit into Jed's rock-hard member. He screamed out, unable to control his agony any longer, and also unable to control his excitement as hot ejaculate flooded into Kay's mouth. She forced herself to down the thick liquid in one gulp. This wasn't something she liked to do, but as the man was paying good money spitting was out of the question. In any case, the teethmarks indented into Jed's penis more than made up for her dislike of swallowing. She was, however, fairly surprised – and in a way impressed – that Jed had once again become hard so soon after his eruption.

"So you want more?" she grinned, and pulled off her own underwear before directing Jed's hands forcibly to her waist and allowing him to massage her body. Kay was damp with moisture between her legs and, for a moment, she felt slightly embarrassed that this session was turning her on. She had never before expressed any interest in domination or, indeed, in men at all. But now, as Jed rubbed eagerly at her clit, she could feel the excitement welling up inside her.

Kay's nipples were erect and Jed took one between his teeth now, kissing and sucking it softly, for he dare not treat her with the same disrespect she had shown him. She was his mistress and he was simply a slave. Being permitted to pleasure her was a privilege he had desired for so long.

"Enough!" Kay roared, swatting Jed's face away from her breasts. She would have liked him to continue for a while longer but she had been forced to suppress a groan of enjoyment out of stubbornness and didn't think she could continue doing this for much longer. Instead she held Jed's throbbing cock upright and mounted him, thrusting her body back and forth, pleasuring herself in the process.

Jed fought hard to prolong his peak as they fucked, determined to bring Kay to orgasm first. And it happened. Despite her best attempts at remaining calm her breathing was becoming fast and frenzied and her desire was escalating to unbearable levels. For the second time in a day she threw back her head and climaxed in a powerful spasm. A few seconds later Jed followed suit, his come spilling out into her body.

"Shit," Kay snarled, still breathing heavily. She was not entirely sure why this word escaped her lips. Déjà-vu, perhaps.

"That was . . ." Jed began.

"Yeah, yeah," Kay panted, regaining her composure and pulling on her clothes. "Got my money?"

Jed's face dropped slightly. He felt hurt by this instant dismissal, but a deal was a deal. He had promised to pay up. "In my trouser pockets," he muttered.

Kay hunted through Jed's clothes for a second, before pulling out a wad of notes and dashing out of the house, leaving Jed where he was, still tied to the floor by his ankles. There was only half an hour until the shops closed. She needed to buy the washing machine so the store could deliver it that evening.

As darkness fell Kay stared happily at her new washing machine. It fit perfectly in her kitchen, which was now mopped and cleaned. No taped-up parts. No impending breakdown. She couldn't wait to try it out.

Turning the controls to the fastest spin-dry speed, she grinned as the machine buzzed into life. On top of the washer Jed sat helplessly awaiting his torture. Kay could not pretend she hadn't enjoyed the afternoon and was damned if she was going to let this man get away so easily. With a smirk that promised pain she produced the cat o'nine tails from behind her back and prepared to catch Jed's cock with each vibration.

Jed shook his head, not quite believing his luck. Who'd have guessed the mysterious Kay was a closet dominatrix? Certainly not him, but there was little time to ponder this now. Duty called. Tensing his buttocks, he held his breath and braced himself as best he could for his very first washing machine thrashing.

An Early Winter Train

C. Sanchez-Garcia

"Where is your wife?"

She was lying on top of the blue comforter next to the window, in her cotton pajamas. Her beautiful thick hair, black and streaked with gray, was spread out over the pillow. She reached up with her hands, searching.

I wonder if it's the jasmine that brings this out in her, he asked himself. He sat down on the edge of the bed next to where she lay, and looked at her despondently. A small electric fan was set in the window and drew in the cool night air, filled with the scent of the jasmine vines they'd planted together years ago, when the kids were still teenagers. It filled the room with a sweet erotic scent, combined with the fresh earth smell of the rain that had just stopped falling. Far away in the kitchen, the radio was playing a Frank Sinatra song.

"Where is your wife?" She would keep asking this until he answered her.

"She's right here, Aimee." He reached over and caressed her hand. "Don't worry so much."

"It's terrible." she said.

"I know."

She tried to sit up, with a trace of fear building in her eyes. He took her hand and gave it a little squeeze. "Everything's fine. Don't worry so much."

She looked at him with a hint of panic now. "Where is your wife?"

"She's right here, Aimee. You're my wife. You know that." He said it evenly and confidently, choosing the tone of his voice with great care. He was pleased to see the fear leave her eyes and she settled back down. "Hey – how you doing, honey? You doing okay tonight?"

"It's terrible."

"What's so terrible?"

"Everything." she murmured.

He took her hand firmly and squeezed it to remind her he was there, that she wasn't alone. "Don't worry so much. I'm here. You worry about everything too much."

She looked at him, holding her hand, as if she had just discovered he was there. "Oh." He felt her squeeze his hand and hold on it, like a baby holding onto a finger. "I'm sorry." she said.

"It's all right."

"I'm sorry."

"It's all right." He held her hand and waited for her to calm down. When he felt her hand relax, he let go of it and stood up. The weariness of the day sank against him and he felt tired and lonely. The jasmine was certainly getting to him too.

He stretched and took a quick glance over at Aimee. She seemed all right for the moment. She rolled over to her side and the plastic adult diaper crackled inside her pajama bottoms. "Now you stay there," he said. "Okay? You stay there, okay?"

Obediently, she rolled over onto her back and folded her hands on her bosom. "Now that's my girl, you stay that way. I'll be right back. Okay?"

"Are we in Mobile yet?"

That question stopped him a moment. Mobile? What, Alabama? This was a new tangent, one he'd never heard before. He wasn't sure what she needed to hear from him. "Soon."

She smiled and closed her eyes. Evidently it was the right answer. He turned away, feeling too painful to look at her.

"The way you wear your hat . . . the way you sip your tea . . . The memory of all that . . . no, they can't take that away from me . . ."

Yes they can, he thought. Boy, they sure as hell can.

He yawned and for a moment thought of turning off the radio, but at least it was company and he headed for the bathroom instead. He opened the medicine cabinet and took down his toothbrush and the toothpaste. The bottom shelf was lined with amber bottles, mostly Aimee's medicines. They cost a goddamn fortune, and as near as he could tell they weren't doing shit for her, not any of them. Next to his own was her pink toothbrush, and he couldn't remember – damn, if he couldn't remember one way or the other – had he brushed her teeth for her tonight? This kind of thing always scared him. Soon it'll be me in diapers, he thought. Silently he recited his social security number, and then his cell phone number. A few years ago, when all this was new to him, the doctor had said that usually with Alzheimer's you forget the numbers first. Remembering strings of meaningful numbers was his frightened little talisman against Aimee's fate.

He closed the cabinet and squeezed a line of toothpaste on the brush. He checked his teeth in the mirror. They were fairly yellow from the coffee and tea, which he had no intention of giving up. But those were his teeth, by God. Every one of them nailed firmly in place until his dying day. No dentures, no bridges. He began to clean his teeth.

"Are we in Atlanta yet?"

His mouth was full of foam and he ignored her. They'd be hauling her off to the nursing home soon, and then what? Start over? Were there Internet dating sites for guys his age? The thought chilled him with guilt, and he threw cold water on his face. He stared into the sink, listening to the radio. Sonovabitch. That's your woman in there. It's not like she's dead, you horny old bastard, can't you even wait?

He thought of her in there, lost in her train ride. It's not my fault. I have needs too; I'm still a healthy man. Not too bad a looking man. And maybe in her own way she is dead really. She died when no one was looking, and it's just her body hasn't gotten the news. It's not her anymore. The woman I loved, she's gone. Not this big baby she left me with. It's not my fault.

He took some mouthwash and poured it into the cap and tossed it into his mouth. Bad breath had always been a problem for him, because his mouth was so dry, but there was no one to care about it any more.

How could he have fixed it? It was mostly genetic, the doctor had said so. Genetics. Nobody's fault, not when it's genetics. Your daddy loses his marbles, you do too. Can't fix genetics. Genetics are just the cards they deal you. Bad blood is what it is. Genetics are this little time bomb that goes off in your head and there's nothing you can do but watch all the fucking genetics turn to shit. Shit for brains. A big whoop-de-damn-doo doctor in *Time* magazine had suggested it was related to stress. It made him want to yell at this guy who knew so damn much.

Okay Dr Asshole, what stress had been my fault? Hadn't I made enough money? Maybe I hadn't spent enough time with her or maybe the kids? No? Maybe I'd been too stressful for her with my little demands and discontents. Maybe if I'd gotten her a goddamn dog with lots of fur to pet. Maybe if the kids hadn't driven us crazy from time to time, dumping the grandkids on us when things got rough, moving in when they couldn't find a job and then moving out and then in again. Maybe I'd secretly wished it on her without knowing, like a silent voodoo curse. Or maybe, just maybe what's really the scariest fucking possibility of all, Dr Asshole, maybe this universe is a big runaway train with winter ice on the tracks and with no God or Jesus or anybody else at the fucking wheel, and no justice or mercy or even kindness – goddamn kindness! – and the most awful shit happens to the very nicest people out there, and maybe . . . and maybe who knows what I could have done differently. I didn't want this. Hell, that could be me in there.

That could still be you in there, big buddy, said a voice in his thoughts. Would you like that? Some nice little lady in a nurse uniform to take your dick out for you, because you – a man – can't remember where to look for your dick any more, and maybe hold it in her nice warm little hand and aim it for you so you can pee? How about them apples, big buddy? Change your diapers for you when you're all full of shit and stink like hell? Want to see that look on her face? Maybe all that's waiting down the road for you too.

He spit out the blue foam and wanted to hammer his head into the mirror glass. Who knows how any of this shit really works? he thought.

"Are we in Mobile yet?"

What was it about Mobile tonight?

"No, Aimee, not yet." he called back to her.

In the kitchen Buddy Holly was on the box, rocking out about Peggy Sue and singing with that weird hiccup thing he did. They had seen Holly play at their high school auditorium in Duluth, way back in the day. Aimee had been in the drama club and played in "The Glass Menagerie" on the same stage where Holly had played later. After that show, Holly and his bunch had moved west working their way towards Moorhead and a couple days later they were mostly dead. He and Aimee hadn't been going together then, that came much later after they met at a class reunion, by which time they'd both scored a divorce each.

He put away the toothbrush and the toothpaste and tried to remember again if he'd brushed her damn teeth or not.

She was better off now, he knew, because they were long past the terror. It was worse in the beginning stages, when the episodes of forgetfulness and fugue began, when the long-faced doctors would come around with their goddamn grim-looking X-rays pronouncing the sentence of death, death in slow motion. Her terror of knowing she would helplessly lose herself. Her wordless rage at God in a restaurant, at seeing an old woman being fed by a health care worker and knowing it would soon be her. The anticipation of having all her life erased out from under her. "Just shoot me, Ron," she whispered to him that night in the dark. "If I get like that, promise me you'll just fucking shoot me." He hadn't said anything.

"Is your wife at home?"

"No!" he shouted at her. "Just shut up!" His throat tightened at the sound of his own voice and the tears began to burn his eyes.

We don't shoot people here, Aimee.

He turned off the bathroom light, but still couldn't bring himself to turn off the radio. He let it babble on, talking and singing to itself, as he went back into the bedroom. The air still smelled heavily of jasmine and she was standing up beside the bed with her hand up against the wall. "You all right, honey-bunch?" At the sound of his voice she turned to look at him, with that fearful trapped look in her eyes again.

"Where is your wife?"

"She's right here, Aimee." He reached over and took her hand from the wall and held it. "Don't worry so much." She smiled for him and for a moment seemed to know him again. He gently wrapped his arms around her and hugged her close, feeling the swell of her breasts as she moved against him. She was still a damn fine-looking woman. He should give her diaper a little check before lights out.

It bothered him that she was standing up already. That was a sign this might be one of her wandering nights, and blundering in the dark was how she always hurt herself. There was the little drama of waking up in the night to find her gone from the bed, and then to have to search the house for her, to see where she'd landed, what she'd broken, or what nasty business she'd deposited on the carpet. Releasing her, he took the edge of her pajama bottom and pulled it out to take a peek inside. There was a strong whiff of urine. Too bad if he was a little tired, but it would be mean-spirited to leave it for the home health aide in the morning to change, and the piss would aggravate her rash again, just when it was starting to clear up.

"It's terrible," she said.

"What's terrible?"

"Everything." She waved her hands.

"It's okay," he said. "I won't leave you alone. It's all right." She nodded. "Okay. That's good."

"Listen, we need to get you changed, and then we'll go to bed. Okay?"

"Okay. I'm sorry. It's terrible."

"It's okay, Aimee. We just got to do it, is all. Let's go." He put his arm around her waist, gently rotated her around and began leading her docilely, a woman with a master's degree in Italian classical literature, toward the bathroom. As they passed the towel closet, he paused and snatched out a fresh diaper from the box.

When the cold floor tiles touched her feet, she hesitated and stumbled a little. He held her firmly by the waist and steered her toward the toilet with the hamper next to it. She allowed herself to be lead, and her passive dependence on him he found strangely arousing. She would easily do anything he asked of her, on this night with the air full of jasmine.

It had been hardest for both of them in the beginning, as she felt things fading on her, constantly discovering herself in strange surroundings. Then she rebelled against everything he did for her. A few times she became violent, hitting him and collapsing in wild crying fits, in this very room. The kids had been pushing her out the door to the nursing home, because they said all this was too hard for him. In a way it was, but they didn't know shit about hard. Once he had come home and discovered her in the shower stall there, trying to cut off her hair with these big office scissors and muttering something about Dante and the "Inferno". She'd taken a vicious swing at him with the scissors when he'd tried to help her. That was what hard really looked like. Now she was – what? Submissive? Was that what all that weird shit that some people did with the handcuffs and the black leather was about? Just to have a fellow human being go where you lead them, do what you tell them? I can sort of see it, he thought. On nights like this, I can sort of see it. There was definitely something in her gratitude and her perfect trust of him, this kind and familiar stranger who guided her through her fog, that did inexplicable things to him.

He positioned her next to the toilet and the hamper. "I'm sorry," she said.

"You're fine, honeybunch. Everything's fine. Just got to get you changed. Get it done and get to bed.

"Thank you."

He looked up at her in surprise. She had never said that before. For a moment there was something of his woman back in her eyes, and then it faded. "You're welcome," he said, hoping she could still hear him before she went away again. He took the diaper, unfastened the tape, and put it by the sink. "Here we go. Ups a daisy." He lifted her arms away from her waist so he could reach her pajama bottoms. Then he remembered that the visiting nurse had said she should try to do these things herself, to keep the motor wiring going as long as possible. She was standing beside the sink, holding her arms out like an obedient child, her good breasts tenting the front of her pajamas.

He spread out the fresh diaper and turned to her, but the words that came out of his mouth were "We need you to take off your top, honey." She looked at him blankly, and for a moment he felt ashamed. But she was looking at him, and he was waiting for her. She lowered her arms, and tugged at the hem of her pajama top. As she was lifting it she became confused and stopped. "Please, honey," he said. "It needs to come off. Pop it off for me, please."

"Are we in Mobile yet?"

"Mobile? No, not yet, soon. We'll be in Mobile soon."

She took the hem of her top and lifted it over her breasts, catching it for a moment on the tips of her large nipples, and then tugging it over her head and off. Her body was still slender and strong. Her large matronly breasts rested on her chest, pointing slightly down, but heavy and glowingly pink. Even in her misery, her fog and her confusion, she was still the most desirable woman in all the world to him. All the more beautiful, because they were at peace with each other and she needed him and trusted him completely. She had lifted it off for him, just because he had asked her to. She held the top in her hand and waited for him to give her directions. He took it from her gently and stuffed it in the towel rack next to the sink and looked at her for a long time while she waited for him to tell her what to do. He ran his hand gently over her bare belly and savored the soft warmth of it, touched the faint scar where she had had a Caesarean for their daughter's birth. Amazingly, he saw her nipples swell and respond to him. He let out his breath, which he discovered he had been holding and his hands were trembling as he caressed her.

"Doctor?"

"No, Aimee, it's just me."

"Where is your wife?"

"You're my wife, Aimee. You're my wife and I still love you fine."

"Is everything all right?"

"It's all right." She was standing like one of those topless marble statues she had doted on when they went to Italy on vacation. Those are the good nipples that nursed our babies, he thought. She let me taste her milk when they became too full. Those were good times when she was nursing. We could fuck bareback without the condoms, which neither of us liked. Her breasts were so big and full, and she was so all heated up on her hormones that she came real easy, and came good and hard too. She came like a woman. When she came strong like that, all scratching at me and shouting and begging and crying against my chest those nipples would squirt milk everywhere and we'd laugh like hell. That was my Aimee. She came a lot in those days and there were nights in Italy she could just about wear me out.

He stood in front of her and admired her semi-nudity. "You remember that island, what was it, Bisentina something. They had that little hotel we were at. Back then the power blacked out and we went into the garden in the middle of the night and the sky was full of stars." His hands reached out to her breasts and caressed them, but she seemed not to notice and looked away from him while he lovingly ran his hands over her. "The garden had those very same jasmine vines climbing the walls. You smelled that jasmine and pulled me down onto the grass. You did all the work that time. You pulled down my pants, and took off your panties and slipped me in good and solid with people eating in the café just on the other side of the wall. And when you came you were so loud those Italian men heard you over there and they stopped eating and really applauded for you. That's when you got interested in the jasmine vines, I'll bet.

"You were always a great fuck, Aimee. Did you know that, honey? You were the most fabulous piece of ass any man ever had and you were all mine. Do you understand what I'm saying to you?"

"I know. I worked there."

"Well, anyway, you were pretty hot stuff in your day."

She smiled. "Okay."

Her skin seemed to heat at his touch, to flush pink, and glow in the fluorescent light of the medicine cabinet. He teased her nipples and they began to stiffen and rise under his fingertips, blossoming out amidst the goose bumps of her swelling aureole. She seemed to notice for the first time what he was doing to her. She lifted her breasts and held them out to him like a gift in both hands. He took one in his hand and hefted the warm bulky feel of it and placed his lips softly over her nipple.

"Bobby?"

Bobby was their son, whom she had breast-fed over thirty years ago. He had no idea what she was thinking, this woman who had once wanted to try out as a porno star, but his thoughts were consumed with the tension of her nipples which were standing out fully now. Taking the weight of her other breast in his other hand, he buried his face in her generous bosom.

Then there was the rising whiff of urine again and he felt like cursing God.

He released her breasts and turned his attention back to the job at hand. The bottoms would have to come off, and the diaper would have to be changed. He picked up the new diaper and held it up for her to see. At the sight of it, the bright glow that had been rising in her eyes also seemed to vanish. "Got to do this thing, Aimee. Okay? Got to get it done and go to bed. Get you cleaned up and ready for bed."

"What about Mobile?"

"I don't know anything about Mobile or Atlanta or any of that business . . ." he felt himself choking up again. Goddamnit, he didn't want to cry in front of her. It would upset her terribly. "I just . . . I can't . . . just fuck it. Just fuck it, okay? We need to get you changed."

He took the top of her pajama bottoms and lifted them up and out. She stood straight as if trying to be helpful, and he walked them down first one leg and then the other, lifting them past the crinkly edge of the diaper, and down and down, past her mighty thighs, and her knees to her strong honest calves. He patted her calves firmly. "Lift up." She became confused and tried to sit and he grabbed her and lifted her up. "Lift your leg." She tried to sit again and he grabbed her and pulled her up. "You got to lift your fucking leg, dummy." She just stood and suddenly he just wanted to haul off and smack her a good one. He wanted to slap her hard for doing this to him and discovered his hand raised against her to do just that when he caught himself. He turned away and felt the hot tears begin, while behind him she stood, baffled, nude, with her pajama top in the towel rack and her bottoms bunched around her knees looking like some lost and molested child.

He put his hand to his eyes and hid his face against the shower curtain, trying to keep the sobs of his weeping quiet and buried away from her. His shoulders shook and he pressed his face against the sour-smelling plastic, waiting to calm down. Behind, he heard sounds of Aimee moving, and the sticky snaps of tape. He took a deep breath and wiped his face on his sleeve. When he turned and looked, she had the wet diaper off and was holding it out to him. She was looking at him with great concern. "Thanks," he said, and took it from her and dropped it in the hamper.

She held out her arms to him. "I'm sorry." she whispered. "It's all so shitty." He put his arms around her and they held each other. She was warm, and big and sumptuous, and he loved her all over again and grieved for her. She relaxed against him and after a moment he felt able to return to the business at hand. She was still wearing her pajama bottoms around her ankles. Gently he patted the back of her thigh and she looked down. He put his hand behind her knee and pulled up and she understood at last and lifted her leg. He pulled her pajama off, and she lifted the other leg and stepped out of them. He stuffed them with the top on the towel rack.

Just a quick wipe off and a change would be enough. He folded the diaper into a bundle and taped it tight and dropped it back in.

He reached into the shower and took the soft thick washcloth he bathed her with and ran warm water and a dab of soap over it. "Step your legs open, honey." He held up the washcloth and patted the insides of her thighs. She understood what he wanted, spread her feet apart into a heroic stance and put her hands on her hips. The sight of her made him laugh. She was magnificent, an ageing Wonder Woman in the nude. For a moment he imagined her with a golden lariat and a tiara.

He kneeled down in front of her, as though he might pray to her, or beg her forgiveness. With the washcloth he washed the smooth skin of her inner thighs, rubbing his hand indulgently against the nest of her damp hair. He washed the hair, as attentively as a hairdresser, stealing touches against the skin of her labia, caressing them with the cloth, a necessary thing, and rinsing the hair, then the muscular cleft between her thighs and her pussy, making sure everything was clean and perfect. He washed her butt cheeks gently and soothingly, lingering there to run his hands over them, that ass, that big gorgeous ass, heavy and resilient, cuter to him than most girl's faces. He ran the cloth down the outside of her strong thighs, grooming the ruddy pink skin, and marveling at the strength left in them. Returning at last to her bush, he pressed his face, his nose, deep into the springy jungle depths of it. The feeling was electric, and instead of resisting, she moved into him, and he breathed the clean animal aroma of her, adoring her as she had once been. Her hands were on his head, and her fingers were in his hair and he felt very confused. Everything about this felt wrong to him, perverted somehow. But she was his woman. Who would know how beautiful she was, if not for him?

The baby powder was on the toilet tank. He picked it up and squeezed a small snowdrift in his hands. Spreading it on her ass, her inner thighs, he explored her all over again, making her dry and perfect. As his hand passed over her labia, he wondered. Running an experienced finger over the lips he explored them to see. Yes. A little bit. Not completely dry, some slickness there, something going on there. She was in there somewhere, standing stiffly in her Wonder Woman posture, while he kneeled to her as though worshipping her. She was a lush Hindu goddess, a primitive fertility goddess who had forgotten herself and wandered the earth believing herself to be a mortal.

"Are we in Mobile now?"

"Do you remember," he whispered to her pussy, "when we lived in Barton Street, that walkup near the little store? I lost my job. No money, no rent. No food. We had this fight. You don't remember, but you were going to drop out of school. I wanted you to stay, and we had that fight. You said you were sick of housework. You hated ironing, you hated cleaning my stupid shit everywhere. You were tired of everything and all that, you know the way you get sometimes. You don't remember, no, but I took the ironing board and told you I was going to do all the ironing from now. And you did this thing, this amazing thing you did. You had curlers in your hair, like a damn space satellite. You went behind the ironing board, and got on your knees, and I couldn't believe it, and then you just took my dick out and I still couldn't believe it and you just started sucking me off right there under the ironing board.

"Did I ever tell you? Did I ever tell you, you were the sexiest woman I ever knew? I think of you like that every day now, you there working away on me under the ironing board, curlers dropping out of your hair, bobbing up and down getting me off, because you were sorry. I came in your mouth for the first time then and burned a hole in the shirt cause I just forgot everything I was supposed to be doing. That's what you could do to me in your day, Aimee. Make me forget everything that was bothering me. I kept that shirt for a long time till you threw it out, because looking at the hole in the sleeve always got me hot for you. It's not fair, you don't know now. That makes me want to die, cause you can't remember what a great woman you were. That was such an animal kind of painful thing for you to do and I sure wish you weren't all so crazy now. Aw hell, I can't stand you this way."

He squeezed an extra puff of powder and worked it into her hair, dusting the skin around her sex lips and pausing to kiss the inside of her tensed Wonder Woman thighs. "Maybe that's why you get married to someone anyway. You just want a witness to tell the rest of the world you were there. You were here with me, Aimee. I knew you."

Tentatively, he caressed her pussy lips and felt them lifting open for him. His fingers were wet.

"This is Mobile, isn't it?"

He raised his head and looked up at her. What the hell was this Mobile all about? She was smiling down at him and her eyes were full and fiery.

And then he knew what he was seeing there in her eyes. The revelation of it struck him so fiercely he had to get up and sit on the edge of the bathtub to take it in.

Fog or not, she had remembered clearly something he had forgotten until now. Mobile, Alabama, on the train to Savannah. Savannah was where they would have their honeymoon, and the train was where they were on their wedding night. Although he was eager for her, she wouldn't let him fuck her until they reached Mobile. It was what she wanted. It wasn't the first time they'd had sex. That had been on their second date, sloppily and impetuously on the sofa in her sister's apartment, trying not to wake the family. That was when he knew this was the woman he would marry, this virtuous, intelligent, sturdy Republican with her ravenous appetites. On their wedding night, they'd rattled through the dark countryside in their sleeping car, groping and driving each other wild, but there was something about Mobile she really didn't like, and she was forcing him to wait. And then the tobacco barns changed into buildings and he wouldn't wait any longer. She peeled off the rest of his clothes and then her own. She turned on all the bright room lights, and threw the curtains open wide. He'd taken her as she directed him to, hard up against the brightly lit window glass for all the world to see, his stiff cock all up in her tight, naked and urgent and insane, and the train vibrated and rattled their bodies as they moved against each other. Outside rail lights flashed red and bells clanged as they whizzed through the barred crossings, packed with lines of cars, cars with white folks and black folks, good God-fearing families and children and grandmothers and babies and dogs watching her brazen female Whore of Babylon ass as he pounded it good and hard up against the glass, putting on a big show for the good folks of Mobile, courtesy of the rolling iron of the Southern Pacific. He came in her as they leisurely clanked through a crossing in the downtown, and she had the presence of mind to take out his wet cock and press it against the glass, waving hello with it to the people standing on the sidewalk gaping.

Now that was goddamn Mobile for you.

"Is this Mobile?"

"Yes, baby," he croaked. "You know, I think it is."

She smiled wickedly. "Good."

"Are you ready for Mobile?"

"I'm ready!"

"Let's go then. Let's stand by the window. That's what you want, isn't it? That's what Mobile is, right?"

"Mobile!"

"Anything you want, Aimee. Let's go to Mobile together."
He herded her into the bedroom with his arm around her waist.
He marveled at how she seemed filled with purpose such as he
hadn't seen in her in a long time. When he released her, it was
Aimee who threw the curtains open. She frowned. "Where're
we going?"

"Wait," he said, searching quickly for the answer, desperate
not to lose this moment without a fight. Then he realized, the
back yard was dark.

He stood her against the wall. "Wait. I'll be back."

Faster than Clark Kent, he unbuttoned the first two buttons
of his shirt and had it off in one pull. One more pull and he'd
jumped out of his pants and underwear together in one motion
and he was naked, his eager cock hard and ready. She was
staring at his erection with interest.

He ran around the room turning on every light and lamp he
could find. "Just stay there!" he called, holding up his hands.
He ran to the kitchen, his penis waving in the air, harder than he
had felt it in years.

He turned on the kitchen lights and turned up the radio.
Little Richard was screaming "God Golly Miss Molly! Sure
like to ball! When you're rockin and you're rollin can't hear
your mama call!"

The back yard lights? The switch was outside.

Oh hell, he thought. That's the whole idea isn't it? Let the
neighbors yell, let them call the cops, that's all. Or let them tell
Bobby and Frannie to haul me off to the nursing home too.
Tonight is the night I get to fuck my woman. By God, I'm going
to fuck her.

He threw open the back door and ran out into the night, his
boner waving in front of him like a herald. He threw on the back
porch lights and then the yard lights, reveling in the chill night air.

Mobile, by God. Ladies and gentlemen, present your tickets
to the conductor, we are in goddamn Mobile and the entertainment is about to begin.

He went back inside and passed through the kitchen. There
was an insidious moment of doubt. What would he find in the

bedroom? That she had forgotten the glory of Mobile and wandered off? Gone to sleep in the closet, or fallen down and hurt herself? Or maybe just didn't know who this old fart was and why he was trying so hard to stick his dick in her.

But she was there and waiting for him near the window, in her wide-legged Wonder Woman pose. His wonderful Aimee, with her secret porno star soul all aglow like a child on Christmas morning, the back yard lights lighting up the contours of her wonderful naked body, all lights and camera and waiting for the big money shot.

"Mobile, Aimee! It's Mobile!"

She opened her arms wide for him.

He threw himself against her, and her arms captured him, and her tongue was in his mouth. She squatted and wiggled her hips under him and like magic his cock had slipped into her slick and easeful depths and she held him tightly and without awkwardness. She threw her arms up over her head, her old signal for him to kiss her breasts. He mauled her big motherly breasts in his hands and took hold of both of her nipples and placed them in his lips together and sucked hard on them.

For the first time in ages, she was there for him, completely present for him; her legs were wide and she was there for him; and she was working her hips in rhythm with his and she was there for him as he struggled to keep sucking her nipples, and together their breathing soared and became ragged and filled with animal sounds and she was there for him, and the gasping turned to cries and she continued to be there for him, even as he felt her legs go rigid, and her pussy pressing down and she shivered in bliss and she was there for him, falling against him as her knees went weak and she was there and she was still there for him as he surrendered to the raw carnal energy of her lost amnesiac pagan Hindu fertility goddess power and let it wash over him. He felt his seed exploding in her, driving him hard into Wonder Woman Aimee, and she was there for him, and this was her lover's gift to him alone for his loyalty, for his nights of faithful celibacy, and the nights cleaning up after her little accidents, and to thank him for being there with her through her terror and hallucination, and occasional deadly violence, when he had to hold her down hard and whisper to her, and weep with her, and console her, and lie to her and tell her everything was going to be just fine – sure it would – when they knew he was all bullshit lies and God had abandoned them on this fucking runaway train of humiliation and fucking oblivion and the world was cruel and all they had was each other and everybody could go to hell including him, he could go fuck himself too goddamn you phony smiling sonovabitch bastard I'll kill your ass, but no, Aimee, I won't leave you, not never no, sir, no. For all of that and more, she held him tight to her, hugging her powerful thighs around him so that he would never ever leave her even when she had finally left herself.

They relaxed against each other and he slipped out of her and he felt her arms fall away. He looked into her face and it broke his heart all over again. She was neither offended nor frightened. Only lost again. He hugged her and rubbed against her but she was the lost docile love doll again. He stepped away from her and she had that worried look, discovering herself excited, nude and wet, while he drew the curtains closed.

Were the neighbors watching? Would this come up in the next homeowner's association meeting? What can they do to us anyway? At our age, lust is more of an achievement than a vice.

"There," he said to her, gesturing toward the bed. "Why don't you just sit a second and I'll fix all this up. I'll get . . . aw shit, Aimee. Aw shit. I'll get your diaper, hon." She stood where she was, uncomprehending and he kissed her on the cheek. He led her over to the bed and pressed on her shoulders until she sat. There was a small trail of his spunk coming from her pussy and he took some Kleenex from the bed stand and offered it to her. She looked at it. He tugged a few more tissues from the box and pulled at her hips to bring her back closer to the edge of the bed. She looked down and watched as he wiped away his sauce from her pussy.

After a moment it was clean. He couldn't resist and kissed her belly, and then got down on his knees and softly pressed his face against her damp delta of wiry hair.

"Where is your wife?"

"Right here, Aimee," he murmured into her cleft. "She's right here and I love her fine. That's you, Aimee."

"Oh," she said, with what sounded like surprise. "Whoo hoo!"

He looked up at her with tears in his eyes. "Sure. Whoo hoo."

"Yes." She smiled and for a moment her eyes were bright with recognition.

"Think of it as a prayer," he whispered. Slowly he rose to his feet again, and his knees hurt, but he felt happy and relaxed and infinitely lonely. "Diaper time, Aimee," he said, more to himself. "Lay down. Please. Lay down on our fine big bed, Aimee. Wait. Let me look at you laying down for a minute. I just want to see how you look that way."

Aimee laid across the bed luxuriously, lifting a knee, letting her legs fall open for him to see, her fine and generous breasts spread out over her chest and he stood over her, enjoying the view, loving her. She saw his eyes on her and raised her arms over her head and smiled to him, seductive, obscenely pliant and open to him.

In the kitchen on the idiot radio, sang Bob Dylan. ". . . with her fog, her amphetamine and her pearls . . . She takes just like a woman. Yes she does, and she makes love, just like a woman . . . Yes she does . . ."

"Time to rest, Aimee," he said. "Maybe we'll pass through Mobile again in the morning."

"Sure." She smiled slyly and raised her arms higher, half-closing her eyes for him.

He went into the kitchen to turn off all the lights and the radio, and to bring her a fresh diaper.

Smears

Robert Buckley

He was at the edge of slumber, his mind reeling off a loop of jumbled images too inchoate yet to qualify as a dream. Her voice – her cry – echoed through the white noise in his brain once, and then again. He broke the surface of wakefulness doubting he had actually heard her. Then it came to him clearly, a sob dissolving into a despairing whimper.

"Linda!" He sat up. Silence.

"Oh – noooo!"

"Linda!"

He flung his legs off the bed and stumbled barefoot to the stairs. He bounded down, missing a step and nearly sliding onto his ass. He recovered and careened around the landing to the bottom.

She was in front of the desktop computer. She seemed unaware of his presence, frozen, her hands covering her face, shoulders hunched – everything about her body language communicated – what? Guilt? Shame? Fear? Certainly surprise.

"Linda, what is it? What's . . .?"

She turned, startled. Then, with fumbling desperation, she repeatedly clicked the mouse.

He started toward her, but she turned, pleading, "No!"

The Web page dissolved into the desktop.

He was behind her now. His hand rested on her shoulder. "What the hell is wrong?"

She looked up at him, her eyes filling. "Oh, God, Tim. Oh, my God."

"Linda – Jesus, honey. What . . .?" He looked at the screen. "What did you see?"

"I–I was just . . ."

"Yeah, just what?"

"I Googled Rossin College."

"Yeah . . . and so?" His wife's alma mater, a small school in Virginia, had sent her a homecoming notice. He'd seen it atop a pile of mail. She was not one for attending reunions, and he had never seen the place himself. He met her about two years after each had graduated from colleges at opposite ends of the country.

She shivered, and her chin trembled.

"Jesus, what's going on?"

He slipped the mouse from her hand and opened up the browser. Then he clicked on "history" and scrolled to "in order visited today." He moved the mouse to the last entry.

"No, Tim. Please."

"Shhh." He clicked and the page opened up. His eyes widened at the sight of his wife. A much younger Linda.

Her dark hair draped over her shoulder in a thick, lustrous pony tail that continued down and out of the frame. She was grinning – a dazzling smile, and her dark brown eyes, the ones he fell in love with the day he met her, caught the light.

A girl, a blonde about a head shorter than Linda – she had come to their wedding – stood beside her, and seemed to be straining to . . . lick her cheek.

Linda's face and the other girl's – he'd forgotten her name – were streaked with some sort of white translucent gel.

There were other pictures – it was a gallery. Above the pictures a red banner screamed: FACIALIZED COEDS.

"It – it's a porn site." His last words came out in a raspy whisper.

"Oh, Tim, it's not – I mean, I'm not . . ."

The subtext below the banner read: Horny lesbo Rossin College comesluts lick jizz off their freshly drizzled faces.

Tim stepped back. Linda? Come slut? Lesbo? Was he dreaming?

"Tim – you don't – you can't believe . . ."

It took him a moment to gather himself. "Linda, how in hell . . . what is this? Where'd these pictures come from? How did they . . .?"

"Oh, God, I don't know, Tim. I remember when they were taken, but it isn't what they say it is. Oh, my God. What if people see these?"

"Okay, just try to calm down, and tell me what you can. You say you remember these pictures?"

"We were – I don't know, I can't even remember if we were seniors or juniors then."

"That's okay; just tell me how these pictures came to be."

"We were just, you know, a bunch of girls living in a dorm. It was a dull night. We used to do silly stuff like, you know, like everyone in the dorms did, all the time."

"What were you doing?"

"One of the girls used to like the frosting that comes with those cinnamon rolls, you know, that come in a little paper cylinder – you get them at the supermarket. You smack the side and the dough pops out and you put them in the oven and . . ."

"Yeah, yeah, I know the kind you mean."

"Well, she used to steal the cup of frosting that came with them, you know, that you're supposed to spread on after you take them out of the oven."

"Uh-huh."

"Well, it drove everyone crazy, so one night, just to teach her a lesson, we went into town and bought a whole case of cinnamon roll dough. Then when we got back to the dorm we held her down in bed and smeared a ton of frosting on her face and hair. It was just a joke – I mean, we weren't being cruel, she was laughing and going along with it."

"Okay, but what about the pictures?"

"Brenda – you remember Brenda? – she had a Polaroid, and she took a picture of Ali – that's the girl we frosted. But then we all got silly and started smearing the frosting on each other. Brenda kept taking pictures."

Tim began to scroll down the rest of the page as a despairing whimper rose in Linda's throat. Another picture, a pretty ass bent over a chair, smeared in frosting, and two girls licking it off each cheek.

"Jesus!" Tim said in a long exhale.

"Oh, God, Tim. Please believe me . . . we were just being silly girls."

Tim's eyes narrowed as he focused on an array of moles and freckles. "Jesus Christ, Linda . . . that's you – that's your ass!"

Her eyes overflowed and her sob emerged unfettered and doleful.

He held his head in his hands a moment, then he hugged her. "Okay – okay. Honey, shhh, I know you were just being silly. It doesn't mean anything. God, it was twenty years ago."

"But – but – but . . ." She could barely speak through her sobs as her throat spasmed. "Someone will see, they'll think – think – think . . ."

He hugged her tighter. "Okay, let's not worry about that. The chances of anyone we know seeing them are pretty remote."

"But, I Googled Rossin. Anyone doing the same thing will see them."

"Yeah . . . well . . ."

She began to sob again.

"Well – then – if anyone asks, we'll just tell them the truth. Our friends will understand."

"But, what if someone at work . . . my boss, if he were . . ."

"You didn't put them on the site, so what could he do? It's *your* privacy that's being violated."

"Can't we do something? Can't we make them take them down?"

He thought about it. That would be the ideal solution.

"I don't think so, honey. These sites – well, there are so many layers, you could take forever finding out who really owns them, and you might draw more attention to them."

"But, Tim, we have to do something."

"Look, Linda, these sites change content all the time. A week or a few from now they'll have some other photos up. I think – well, I think we should just go on as if we don't know a thing about them. If someone should bring them up . . . well, we just act like we don't know what they're talking about."

"Oh, God, Tim . . . look, there are comments."

"What – where?"

Linda pointed a trembling finger at a thread beneath the gallery.

Tim read the comments silently. He knew Linda was reading them too as her breathing got louder, and she trembled in his embrace.

– Fine fucking blow-job lips on Ponytail . . .

– Looks like she can suck cream out of a baseball bat.

– Love to put my ten-inch dick up her ass while she ate her girlfriends pussy.

"They're writing those things about me. Tim, God, look what those filthy men are saying about me."

Tim didn't answer. He was mesmerized. A sense of unreality took hold of him – those filthy comments from men – who knows who they were or where? – saying they wanted to fuck, gag, come all over Linda. His wife, the mother of his children?

"Oh, Tim, we can't just do nothing."

He had to force his eyes away from the comments. "Honey, I don't think we can. Look, I'll check around, maybe call our lawyer, but I think he's just going to tell us to ignore it and let it blow over."

"Blow over?"

"What if we took them to court? We'd just draw everyone's attention to them. Okay, so they put them on their site without your permission, but the fact of the matter is, Linda, you allowed a picture to be taken of your dorm mates licking your ass. And, it ain't gonna make a bit of difference that you were just a bunch of girls acting silly, that it was all – innocent."

Her shoulders slumped. "Oh, Tim, I feel so dirty . . . so violated."

"I know, honey, I know."

"Who would do such a thing? How'd they get hold of those photos?"

"Linda," he shook his head. "No one had any inkling what the Internet would become. You couldn't have imagined them showing up where a whole world could see them."

"Oh, Tim . . . the whole world."

"You said Brenda took the pictures. Would she do it? Was she mad at you about something?"

"No. God I haven't even heard from her in five years."

"Well, then, who the hell knows. Maybe an ex-boyfriend

stole them off Brenda. Or she tossed them in the trash and the garbage man scooped them. Fact is, anyone could have gotten hold of them and posted them to this site, or any site. They keep stealing content off each other."

"Tim! You mean my pictures could be on other sites?"

"I'm sorry, honey. There's no way of telling. Once they're out there . . ."

"God." She ran her hand through her hair. "From now on, if I get passed over for a promotion or a raise, I'll always wonder if it's because someone saw that picture – lesbo-comeslut Linda."

Her shoulders heaved with fresh sobs, and then she wailed, "What if the girls see them?"

He tried to console her. "They won't . . . c'mon; our kids don't look at that kind of stuff."

"But how do we know, Tim?"

He held her in silence until her sobbing subsided. Thank God the girls were off on a school trip. He'd erase any trace of the site from the computer before they came home.

"C'mon, Linda, let's go to bed. We'll work it out after a good night's sleep."

"How am I gonna sleep?"

He helped her upstairs.

Tim lay still with his eyes closed as Linda tossed beside him. She couldn't fall asleep, and who could blame her? The pictures of Linda reeled behind his eyelids like a slideshow, along with the lurid captions. What a mess, he thought.

At least she wasn't naked in them, except, of course, for the shot of her ass, but no one who wasn't intimately acquainted with her moles and freckles would recognize it. But, then it struck him like a rifle shot. Linda had dropped her pants and let a pair of girls lick her ass – lick her ass, for crissakes!

Okay, kids in dorms did screwy things. He did. He had a roommate who used to drink himself into a stupor and piss out the fourth floor window. He participated in a dick-measuring contest himself – thank God they were all too blitzed for anyone to think of taking pictures.

It wasn't like Linda had been a wanton slut, not the woman he married. Not buttoned-down Linda who was too modest to wear a two-piece bathing suit, never mind a bikini. But the photos, and their context – the context created by the people who put together that Web page – somehow it was as if they had created an alter ego of his wife. An odd notion began to gnaw at his brain that the porn-site Linda existed, perhaps lurking in the shadows, eager to emerge.

The thought made his cock twitch.

Linda tossed again. He reached over and laid his hand on her hip, then leaned closer and kissed her shoulder. Her body was tight, rigid. He slid his hand beneath the waist of her pajama bottoms and over her ass. The picture of her ass on the Web site loomed large in his mind.

She turned onto her back and his hand slid over her belly, fingertips fluttering the edge of her patch of dark hairs leading to her pussy.

"No, Tim. Please, I'm too upset."

She abruptly turned onto her stomach. "Just rub my back for a while, please."

His cock had poked its way out of the fly of his pajamas, but he sighed and said, "Okay, honey, sure."

He slid his hand over her back slowly, lovingly, taking an occasional detour over the rounds of her ass. After a while her breathing became relaxed and regular; she fell asleep. But he had a raging hard-on. He considered jerking off, but eventually fatigue overtook him and his cock and he fell asleep.

Linda was already up and gone when his alarm sounded. He had wanted to take her to breakfast, but once sleep took hold it did not yield its coddling grip easily.

He showered and dressed and was about to head out the door when he stopped. Like a guilty schoolboy he tiptoed to the computer and fired it up. Again he opened the browser and then clicked on History. Another click and the notorious Web page was again displayed on the screen. The thought again occurred to him that none of the pictures showed Linda naked, or flashing her breasts.

But this was just a preview page. He had to pay to get inside. Damn if he was going to give out his credit card number to these sleazeballs just to satisfy his curiosity. He gripped the mouse to click the browser closed, but his eye caught the thread of comments. There were new ones. Christ, the page was getting some heavy traffic.

He read the latest entry:

> She needs a big-cocked cowboy to grab that ponytail and ride her ass hard.

"Fucking bastard," he muttered. But, an image of Linda on all fours being taken from behind by some anonymous man flashed in his head. He shook himself, more determined to turn the damned computer off, when something else nagged him.

He clicked the History button again. He counted how many times the page had been opened and when.

"Linda!" She must have viewed the page before she went to work.

That evening he found her curled up in her robe and slippers on their bed. He decided to let her nap and went to work to fix dinner for them. Later, he gently shook her shoulder.

"Hi, hungry?"

She stirred. "Yeah, okay." She sat up and stretched, and he caught a glimpse of nipple as her robe separated. Instantly the thought intruded that the pay site harbored photos of her in more explicit states of undress. He forced it from his mind and followed her downstairs.

She sat at the table as he filled her plate with roasted chicken and vegetables. She was silent, a faraway look in her eyes as she ate.

"I talked to a couple of people today – just hypothetically," he said. "They pretty much told me what I already suspected: we'd be creating more trouble trying to get those pictures taken down, than just letting it go."

She nodded. "It's just so surreal, seeing myself. Those awful comments."

"Hey, honey, those guys have no idea who you are. You're just a fantasy woman. They wouldn't know you if they passed you on the street."

She looked at him, an eyebrow cocked. "Do I look that different now?"

If sounded like an accusation, and it took him a moment to respond.

"No – of course not, Linda. It's just, well, you were twenty then; you're forty now. Yeah, you've changed, but you're still the beautiful girl I married. You turn guys' heads, I've seen them."

She shrugged, then forked a piece of chicken, raised it to her mouth and began to chew with an absent expression.

"Your hair," Tim said. "I had no idea you wore it so long, it must have reached your waist."

She nodded, but her eyes were still unfocused, her thoughts far away.

"You wore it shoulder-length when we met," he persisted. "I liked your hair long."

He gazed at her as she chewed and nodded silently. Her boy-cut hair was attractive, but he began to imagine it long and draped like a shawl over her shoulders.

She swallowed and said, "I talked to Jeannie about it."

His back stiffened at the mention of Linda's best friend – divorced and gratefully childless Jeannie.

"Do you think that was a good idea? The fewer people who actually know about the existence of this site, the better."

"Jeannie's not going to tell anyone. Anyway, she thought it was funny."

"Funny?"

"Uh-huh. I gave her a lift home and she asked me to come in for a while. We looked at it on her computer."

"And she thought it was funny?"

Linda shrugged. "She lived in a dorm – she said she did a lot crazier things. She didn't believe me, though, when I told her there were no pictures of me – you know – naked. So she used her credit card to get past the first page."

"I wouldn't have taken that chance. Who knows who these people are?"

"Yeah, well, if you did you would have gotten a good look at Brenda's boobs."

"Brenda?"

"I'd forgotten. Someone grabbed her camera from her, and we got her top off and smeared frosting all over her chest."

She said it off-handedly, but then she froze. "Oh, God, I can't believe I told you that."

"Honey, can you be recognized, you know, touching her tits?"

"Huh? Oh, no, just our hands. Brenda had huge breasts; they filled the frame."

"Linda, is there anything else about these pictures I should know?"

She looked at him as if the question was entirely ridiculous. He shrugged and let it go.

"Jeannie laughed out loud at the comments," she said.

"Yeah, well, she has a weird sense of humor."

"She had me laughing at them too after a while, but something she said . . ."

"Huh? What did she say?"

"Something about how there might be guys all over the world . . ."

"Yeah . . . what?"

Linda's face flushed. "Jerking off to my pictures."

Tim at once was aware of a cool wet spot where his cock nestled in his shorts.

"Well . . ." He cleared his throat. "I wouldn't think about that."

"I can't help but think about it. Tim, it's like there's another me that exists somewhere, some filthy little sluttish . . ."

She didn't finish her thought. Instead, the faraway expression came over her face again.

She was quiet the rest of the evening. She got up while they watched television and, without as much as a good-night, went to bed. Later he slid in beside her and let his hands roam over her hip and thigh. She turned onto her back and his hand slid down her belly to her pussy where his fingers dabbled with her clit.

Her hand covered his. "Stop it, Tim." But, her fingers manipulated his as they stroked her folds.

She abruptly turned on her side and clenched her thighs together. "Not now – I'm really tired."

He was left again with a painful hard-on. And perplexed, the tips of his fingers were moist.

As her breaths became soft and regular, the slideshow of images reeled behind his eyelids, this time including an imagined shot of Brenda. He remembered her, and her bosom, straining against the dress she wore to their wedding. Her breasts were so large, he thought a chest cold could prove fatal.

Linda had touched those tits. Spread frosting over them. Had she told him everything? The other girls licked frosting off Linda's ass cheeks. Had she licked frosting off Brenda's gargantuan tits?

His cock tented the bedclothes. He got up and went downstairs.

He opened the browser and immediately clicked to the Web page. There were more comments from anonymous visitors. They echoed each other, they wanted to gag Linda with their cocks, fuck her up the ass, make her eat pussy while they fucked hers. After a while Tim's eyes glazed over.

"There isn't an original idea in the bunch," he mumbled to himself, then chuckled mirthlessly. "Morons."

He gazed at Linda's picture, the one with the blonde girl licking her cheek. Then the thought formed in his brain: what would you like to do to her?

His hand slipped beneath his pajama waistband, over his nest of hair and closed around his cock. He pulled it through his fly and leaned back in the chair. He imagined Linda naked, held down by her dorm mates, straining against their restraint. Her pussy was pink and glistening as he laid the knob of his cock against its slick folds.

She pleaded, "Please don't fuck me." But he knew she really wanted him too. So did the girls, as they broke into giggles.

He was stroking furiously now, ravishing slut-Linda in his mind.

"Tim!"

He hadn't heard her come down the stairs. He wasn't even sure he'd heard her voice. He sat up and tried to put his cock back in his drawers, but it might as well have been spring-loaded. He turned; his face felt like it was on fire.

"Linda – Jesus – I'm sorry, I was just . . ." He stopped, knowing any attempt at explanation would be lame.

Linda's expression was fierce. "Is that how you think of me now?"

"Linda, no, please . . ."

"Maybe you want to believe it – well, do you? That I let men come on my face."

"Christ, no! Of course not . . ." But he was talking to her back. She had turned and was running up the stairs.

"You can stay down there!" she shouted from the landing. "You'd better."

"Oh, for crissakes!" But there was no appeal. He heard the bedroom door slam.

He was ashamed, but then his shame turned to self-pity, and then to anger. Didn't she and her girlfriend have a good laugh over the site? Yeah, a good laugh thinking of maybe hundreds, thousands of anonymous guys whacking their dicks looking at her pictures. So, he was horny – she'd turned him down twice two nights in a row. And hadn't he jerked off to *her* picture, for crissakes, and not some anonymous, whale-titted Internet bimbo?

In the morning, she got dressed, came downstairs and walked past him on the couch without a word.

He sat up at the sound of the front door closing and tried to stretch the stiffness from his back. "Aw, fuck her."

From the moment he arrived at work people gave him a wide berth. He wanted an excuse to vent on someone. Hell, he'd have knocked the boss on his ass if he'd said the wrong thing. He was glad to be out of there at the end of the day, but he couldn't make up his mind about going home. He spotted a bar. But to hell with that. His anger rose again. He headed home.

He walked through the front door. Her purse lay on top of the kitchen table. He pulled off his overcoat and suit jacket and draped them carelessly over a chair.

The computer was running.

He clicked history, then counted the number of times the Web page had been accessed. Damn . . . she was looking at it too. Was she getting off on the comments thread? Or maybe reliving some fond memory of licking and getting licked by another girl?

He ascended the stairs bounding two steps at a time. The bedroom door was open. She appeared to be just shedding her work clothes. She stood staring at him a moment, then she rushed to shut the door in his face. He pushed it and her back.

"Leave me alone," she demanded.

"We have to talk."

"I don't want to talk."

"No?"

"No!"

Her blouse was unbuttoned almost to her waist. The bra she wore pushed her breasts up and apart affording him a view of shadowed cleavage.

Her eyes followed his. "I mean it, Tim."

He responded by pushing her back on the bed.

"Get out!"

He grabbed the lapels of her blouse and pulled them apart sending buttons flying.

"Tim, stop!"

He lifted her onto the bed and fumbled with her skirt trying to locate a zipper.

"Stop, c'mon, you'll rip it."

He might have if he hadn't found the zipper. He tugged it roughly until the fabric lost its tautness. He yanked skirt and panties down her legs and off. She began to flail her legs – but she didn't kick at him. He tugged at the bra until the clasp failed and it catapulted onto the floor.

"You want to know what I think of you, Linda? Huh? This is what I think of you."

He unbuckled his belt, and tugged his zipper down. His trousers fell away and he kicked his boxers off and climbed between her thighs.

"No! Don't, I don't want you to. Noooo!"

He fell onto her, pressing his lips to her neck, then turning to her breasts, sucking roughly at her nipples.

"Don't – don't . . ." But she clenched handfuls of his hair and pulled him against her.

Her pussy was sopping. "You don't want it?"

She whimpered at his mocking remark.

Hips swiveling, he drilled his cock under her belly. She cried, her protests weakened, and her legs closed behind his knees.

"Bastard, bastard . . ." her voice trailed off. But it released his trigger. Spasm after spasm, he strained to empty himself into her. Her body trembled beneath him, then trembled again; her cunt clenched, relaxed, clenched again, as if she were squeezing the last remnant of fluid from him.

They were both breathless, spent. But he managed to push himself off her and onto his feet. He stood for a moment looking down at her. Her hips at the edge of the bed, her legs dangling over; his come drooled out of her cunt.

He wiped his brow with the back of his hand. "I'm not sleeping on any fucking couch tonight," he declared, then walked to the bathroom and shut the door.

He stepped into the shower and let the heat pour down his back. He let his mind go blank – no more thinking.

When he finished he wrapped a bath towel around himself and stepped into the hallway – just in time to hear the front door slam.

"Aw, shit! Now what?"

He hurried downstairs with just the towel tied around his waist, then stalked from den, to kitchen, to living room, where he stood alone, seething. The towel slipped off his hips.

"Stupid," he muttered, but remained in one spot, shivering, naked, and feeling foolish.

Where had she gone? Maybe to Jeannie's to commiserate, have a good cry – or maybe a good laugh. At him.

Maybe he should call – no, fuck that.

He lifted his hand to his forehead and rubbed a thumb against his temple.

"Asshole! You don't rape your wife. What a shithead," he admonished himself.

But a voice asserted itself, in counterpoint to his shame and remorse.

Rape – bullshit! She was hot for it too. She had fucked him back – fucked him hard – and then she came so powerfully he thought her bones would shatter. He also knew she was continuing to access the site, knew that something had overtaken her, as it had overtaken him.

"But . . ." he whispered at the empty room, "you don't treat your wife that way . . . not your wife . . . do you?"

He thought again to call Jeannie, just to make sure Linda was there, that she was all right, but decided against it. Better to let her yak it out with her friend; don't interrupt; don't interfere. But the hours passed and a weight settled in the pit of his stomach.

He pulled a robe around himself, but nothing else, and paced. It was 10 p.m. Where the hell was she?

As it closed in on 11 p.m. he was entirely frantic. He'd call Jeannie.

But there was no answer. It was Friday night – single girls went out on Friday nights. Was Linda with her – had she been there at all? He thought about calling the police, imagining the conversation with a jaded cop: "So, you say you had a fight with your wife? Give her time to cool off, pal."

At least, he thought, he could ask them if there had been any accidents reported; ease his mind on that score.

It was 11:20 when he picked up the phone. He had punched in one number when he heard her car in the driveway. Thank God. He was relieved, but now he was angry.

He heard her keys rattle in the lock, then her steps as she turned to close the door behind her. Her heels clicked on the tiles in a pattern that indicated a casual, unhurried gait. When she stepped into view his chin dropped.

She wore a leather jacket he hadn't seen her wear in years, and a black miniskirt she once said she'd never fit into again. But she had, just barely; high on her thighs, it possessively hugged her hips. A pair of high-heeled, over-the-knee-high boots completed her look.

But her face – she appraised him with a smirk, amplified by a garish shade of red lipstick. It was smudged at one corner of her mouth.

Her eyes traced their way from his chin to his hips. He shook himself out of his spell and realized his robe had fallen open.

"Been entertaining yourself again, Tim?" Her sneer curved into a mocking grin; she tilted her hip like a pro advertising herself on a street corner.

"Where the hell have you been?"

She shrugged and stepped toward him. What was that on her face? – Something sticky, white-translucent. There was a dribble over her left eyebrow, and another, reflecting the light, on her right cheek. She unzipped her jacket – she wasn't wearing a thing under it. There were more slimy streaks, over her collarbone, and between her breasts. Another over the curve of one breast looked like it had dried and become tacky.

He struggled to find his voice. "Linda – what . . . what the hell?"

"You wanna know where I've been, Tim? Well, I just thought I should be the girl you want me to be."

"Huh? What are you talking about?"

"What they said I was: a come-drizzled slut. Wasn't it?"

"Linda, for crissakes . . ."

"I found a bar, Tim. And I didn't go in there to drink, but I found what I was looking for. The biggest one – well, he was leaning against the bar. God, looked like he hadn't taken a bath in a week, but I could tell he had what I needed."

"Linda! Jesus, what are you saying?"

She let her jacket slip off her shoulders, revealing more streaks and smears over her belly, her ribs.

"I just tapped him on the shoulder and said, 'I want to suck your cock – okay?'"

Tim's heart skipped a beat, then it began racing. Blood simmered in his ears.

"I like it when a guy doesn't waste time thinking – doesn't look a gift slut in the mouth – sort of speak. Before I knew it he had me down on my knees – God, I almost choked on it. And when he came – well, I had to gargle."

Tim felt his brain cooking, synapses firing off, circuits shorting out, and electricity arcing behind his eyes.

"They had a crappy pool table there, husband. See, he wasn't finished with me. Not he, not his friends. Must have been at least a half-dozen of them that tossed me up on that table like a piece of meat, spread my legs and fucked me – Christ, they fucked me. And all the time they called me slut, whore, cocksucker. It just got me wild – I begged them not to stop."

Tim's ability to think, process what she was saying, was reduced to a level of passivity that follows shock. He heard every word, every nuance, but oddly it left him unable to move or speak – paralyzed – a prisoner of the lurid tale she was telling.

"They flipped me over when they were done with my cunt. Being fucked in the ass was something I'd never imagined before – I was afraid it would hurt. But the bartender greased me up with some margarine – well, they said it was margarine."

She unzipped her skirt, and with some pushing and hip maneuvers, it reluctantly let go of her body and pooled on the floor. Now she was naked except for the boots. She took a step back. "They kept my panties for a souvenir – my T-shirt too. They're hanging over the bar if you want to drop in sometime and see them."

Her grin widened and she licked her lips wickedly. "God, I thought my eyes would pop out when that first cock went up my ass. But then he started to really fuck me, then another took his place, and another, I lost count how many times I came."

She crossed her arms over her breasts and dabbled a finger in a streak of goo on her shoulder.

"They were just going to leave me there, but I asked them for one more favor. I said, 'Guys, my husband is going to be awfully disappointed if you don't come all over me.' Well, as you can see – they were happy to oblige."

He assessed her, still standing with her hips tilted at a saucy angle. There were streaks on her thighs, in her pubic hairs; slime clung to the rim of her belly button.

"Well, husband? Isn't this what turns you on, your wife – what do they call it – a jizz-drizzled slut?"

His rage asserted itself now, growing, pulsing hot in his chest, but controlled.

"What are you trying to prove, Linda?"

Her expression changed a moment. He tried to read it; perhaps a momentary twinge of regret, fear, remorse?

He stepped back, but she stepped toward him, closing the distance until they were nearly nose to nose. Now she resumed her tart, taunting demeanor.

"Well, Tim, I might have room for one more. You up for – what do they say – sloppy seconds?"

He grabbed her elbows and pushed her onto the couch. Before he could take a step toward her she drew her legs beneath her, kneeling; she flung her arms over the back pushing her breasts out. Tim bent and slid his hands beneath her folded knees, lifting her as he knelt, hefting her into his lap.

"Go ahead," she sneered.

His cock was rigid, maybe it had been since she began her tale. But right then it ached to penetrate her. He drove himself into her cunt without preliminaries. Her channel was hot and slick. Had she really fucked them – was he plowing through their slime? He pummeled her like a piston, harder, faster, rage and lust fueling his assault on her womb, but she met every thrust. She straightened her legs, and pressed her thighs around his waist. He could hear the squeak of her boots rubbing together.

Their eyes locked, each glaring, furious, burning into the others. Then Tim's glance shifted to the gooey streak over her cheek bone. Linda's sneer reappeared.

"Go ahead – you want to. Lick my lover's come off my face. Do it!"

He snarled, and hesitated. Just a taste, to prove one way or another – what? – that his wife was still his? Could he stand the answer? Could he pay the price to find out?

He pressed his lips to the spot and swirled his tongue.

It was sweet, it was sugary – it was frosting.

"Bitch!" he cried. She'd played him, but what did it matter? She had goaded him into tasting it, and he had done it. He fucked her furiously – he wanted to explode inside her.

Her shriek about shattered his eardrum, then he launched his fluids. Tremors seized him and his arms tightened around her.

Somehow – neither would ever be able to recall – they made their way upstairs, fell into bed, and fucked . . . and fucked . . . and fucked, until exhaustion overtook them and they surrendered to dreamless oblivion.

In the morning he reached for her, but felt only the still-warm depression where she had lain. He roused himself, wincing in pain. He must have pulled a muscle – maybe a couple of muscles.

He stepped into a pair of jeans, pulled on a T-shirt and gingerly made his way downstairs.

He found her in the kitchen, wrapped in her quilted robe, sitting at the table, absently stirring a cup of coffee.

He approached her until he stood right behind her, his hand hovering over her shoulder. She had not acknowledged his presence. Tentatively he rested his hand on her, closed his eyes, and said a prayer. It was answered an instant later when she laid her hand on his.

He walked around her and turned her to face him, then he knelt on one knee.

"Linda – I . . ."

A vigorous shake of her head told him there was no need to talk, no need to analyse, and certainly no need to apologise – for anything.

He laid his head against her bosom and closed his arms around her back. She reciprocated.

Something had changed, something that frightened, but excited them. They had walked through a door, and there was no going back. They would have to adapt to and embrace whatever lay ahead.

He whispered, "I love you, baby."

And though he couldn't have imagined her being able to hug him any tighter, she still managed to fortify her embrace. And that told him, wherever this new journey led, they would make it together.

The Threshold

Polly Frost

"Cameron, what's wrong with you today?" Janine asked me.

We were walking down our high school corridor towards class.

"Yeah," Tia said, narrowing her gorgeous black eyes at me. "You're so pissy today. What gives?"

"It's just this G-string I'm wearing," I said. "I hate the thing."

A group of senior guys strode toward us. Janine swirled her head around to see if there were any of St Theresa's teachers or nuns around. The coast was clear. She pulled her skirt down so her bright pink G-string showed above the gray flannel.

I kept my own skirt where it was, but Tia wiggled hers down until it was lower than Janine's.

"Kill me with a G-string!" one of the boys said, as they passed by.

"I love you, Janine!" said another.

"I want you, Tia," the cutest one said.

Janine gave them one of her come-on smiles accompanied by a "fuck you" sign. She saw one of St Theresa's teachers ahead and hiked her skirt back up.

"Good morning, Ms Sobowski," Janine sweetly cooed.

We rounded a corner and marched down the main hallway among the hordes of other uniformed students.

"I don't know why I have to wear this thing up my butt crack," I said.

"Resign yourself to it, Cameron. It's your fate as a woman," Tia said, adding with a laugh, "or at least it's your fate as a friend of Janine's."

"Besides, how many times do I have to explain that you're never going to get laid if you go around in baggy old undies?" Janine demanded.

"They were perfectly decent bikinis of mine that you threw out!" I said.

At Janine's insistence, halfway through sophomore year we three friends had sworn to always wear G-strings under our Catholic high school uniforms. When the moment was right – when no teachers or parents were around – Janine would signal for us to hike the straps up so they showed over the tops of our strict little uniform skirts.

"And lucky you are that we rescued you," Janine said. "You were headed toward the sad, dull sexual life of everyone else in this town."

Tia took over. "They don't know what a good fuck is. They marry practically the first person they sleep with and start having babies. And then it's all over. They sit around in front of their TVs and get disgustingly obese and never have any sex again."

"I know, I know," I said.

And boy, did I ever know! My own parents probably hadn't done it since they'd conceived my younger brother, Tim. My mother was still pretty but she wore shapeless beige pants and overblouses, or mid-calf skirts made of fabric that was wrinkly on purpose. As for my dad, he was always talking about trying to lose his belly, but he never did.

How yucky it was to think of my parents even kissing each other, let alone fucking! It seemed as though their lives were already over and they were dead but no one had thought to bury them. I would never be like them, I told myself. I would stay alive for a lot longer.

And maybe Janine was right. Maybe I did need to get on with my sex life if I didn't want to end up like my folks.

Still, even though Janine had been so persuasive, I wasn't sure she was right.

"Speaking of sex, as we always are," Tia said. "How's 'Project-Lose-It' going?"

"Well, Mike wants to do it with me," I said. "So I guess Saturday night will be it."

I flipped back my hair and tried to sound nonchalant. The truth is, I was anything but calm. I was feverish in the inexplicable way I always was when the subject of losing my virginity arose.

Janine turned and pushed up her white shirt sleeves. She did this when she was about to give me her standard pop-the-cherry lecture. "You're the only virgin left at this high school, you know," she said, her voice dripping with disdain.

Tia nodded in energetic agreement. "Yeah. We've been so patient with you."

"But I'm not sure Mike is the right guy to do it with the first time," I said.

I'd gotten used to talking frankly with my friends about intimate body matters. How could I not? It was all that seemed to be on anyone's mind: it was on TV, in the magazines we bought, all over the internet. I had certainly seen a lot of porn. Tia's father and her step-mom kept an ample stash in their bedroom drawer. I knew how people fucked from blow jobs to ass rimming. Yet when it came to thinking about my first time I couldn't keep my skin from flushing red.

I heard a click of fingers.

"Cammie!" Janine snapped. "Where are you?"

I brushed a strand of hair off my face and hoped the sweat I could feel wasn't visible to my friends.

"Sometimes I think you don't care about our friendship," Tia said. "Because if you did, you wouldn't embarrass us by refusing to get laid."

What would it take to get them to leave me alone?

"I'll do it with Mike. This weekend! Are you satisfied?"

My two friends raised their eyebrows at each other.

"We would be if your attitude was a little better," Tia said.

"Cammie's trying, Tia," Janine said. She turned to me.

"Do us a favor," she went on. "When he fucks you the first time, just do it in some boring position like on your back. Don't get fancy. Because you don't want to embarrass us by bleeding all over everything. We don't want to hear about that throughout these school halls."

"Oh, God, yes. That's really excellent advice," Tia nodded.

"I'd almost forgotten what it was like. And you have to make sure you don't become the stuff of locker room jokes."

Tia had lost her virginity over a year ago, and to us three teens it was as if the event had occurred in prehistoric time. "You don't want your blood everywhere. And, you know, there is likely to be blood."

Great, I thought, staring at the ground, hoping that my emotions on the subject weren't too apparent, though by now I was pretty well resigned to being made fun of for my virginity.

"Anyway," Janine went on, "it'll be over before you know it. A little pop, a little pain, a little mess."

"Ouch," Tia chimed in. "Then: ooooh."

I shuddered while my friends burst into giggles. Why did the whole thing seem like such a cosmic hurdle to me and to no one else?

"I just hope you're right that it's best to sleep with a guy you don't care about first time around. Like Mike."

"Well, of course we're right!" Janine's brown eyes were wide with indignation. "Haven't you listened to anything I've said?"

I swung my blue backpack around and clutched it to my chest as though for protection.

"Sure," I said, still keeping my eyes on the ground. "It's just that sometimes I wonder if it isn't more special than that."

I tried to sound confident, but I felt humiliated by my emotions. Why was I so damn vulnerable on this subject? Why did talking this way – even thinking about this subject – make me feel as though I was on the threshold of something extraordinary?

"No, girl, you don't want it to be special," Tia said. "Special is bad. Special is demeaning. That's like something our grand-parents would think."

The three of us turned the corner and headed down the long corridor to history class.

The truth is, I did worry about whether or not I was emotionally disturbed about the subject. It shouldn't be a big deal, going to bed with a guy for the first time. But talking – or even thinking – about the moment when I would lose my virginity made me start to tremble with an avalanche of emotions.

A familiar male voice startled me out of my thoughts. "Hey, Cammie," Mike said, catching up with me. "So we're on for Saturday?"

"Sure," I replied. Tia and Janine stood back respectfully, exchanging little significant glances. Mike didn't seem to notice.

"Awesome," he said.

He looked pretty awesome himself in his loose jeans and T-shirt, leaning a muscled arm against the wall. Nothing like playing three sports to keep a guy in shape. Even in the boring school uniform Mike's looks made my body stir. He was really an okay guy, too.

But I couldn't help feeling there was nothing special between us as people. He ran his eyes up and down my body, licked his lips and lowered his eyebrows at me.

"You know you're looking good, baby."

I glared at him indignantly.

"Hold that expression – I like it when you get riled. Well, gotta get to math," he said.

"What a hottie," Tia said, looking after him as he ran down the hall.

"The way he moves," said Janine.

The two girls exploded in laughter as I once again blushed furiously.

History class turned out to be a video about the Christian conversion of pagan cultures.

As I sat in the dark and watched the images of chalices and robes, I thought about my upcoming date with Mike. He had a driver's license and would pick me up at my place. Then a restaurant. Maybe a movie.

Then afterwards . . . that was the big question. I was secretly hoping his parents would be out for the night, so we'd have his house to ourselves. Otherwise we'd be stuck in the car, and that seemed a little tacky. At his place, there were beds, sofas – towels, too, for easy clean-up.

But my mind was operating on two levels, and as I methodically and practically tried to anticipate what was to come on my date, another feeling entirely was moving through me, its origins not in my head but my body.

And then it took over my brain.

Everyday images of school books and desks and students were flushed out, and different images took their place. I was floating above myself, watching.

I saw myself in a lovely white gown, lying on my back. The sleeves were trimmed with antique lace. As I looked down at myself I saw that I was beautiful, with my hair flowing around my face and onto the black and gold marble slab on which I lay.

My eyes were open, stunned and terrified. For a moment I stared at this image of myself. Was it a dream me? A future apparition? But now I was inside whatever it was, looking out. The fear I thought I saw was, in fact, a feeling of awe. I was in the presence of a power greater than any I had ever known.

What was that around my ankles? My arms and legs were manacled. And even as I struggled to get free, I worshipped the strength of the steel and chains that bound me.

I could not escape whatever was in store for me. I heard the heavy steps of boots, followed by the staccato sound of high heels. I fought against my chains now, my body writhing in my elegant prison as much from excitement as from fear.

Then I felt the soft, sweet touch of a woman's hands on my head. She put a blindfold around my eyes, and kissed me on the lips. I greeted her tongue with my own. I could not see who she was, but I gave myself to her completely. Now where was she? Ah, I felt her hands running over my breasts. My dress must be made of a deliciously sheer material. I arched my body up to meet her touch.

But she pulled away from me. I wondered where she could be. Then I felt my blindfold being removed and I saw a man in a hood suddenly before me!

He loomed like a giant – naked, muscular. And the size of that thing! His dick was enormous. The woman was now pulling my legs apart, roughly, no longer soothing. The man was stroking his cock as he moved between my knees. And it seemed to grow even more.

A leather strap appeared in his hands, and he wrapped it around his balls and cock. I glanced at the man. And once again his member grew. It would hurt like a knife slicing through me and yet this was how it was supposed to happen . . .

I felt a thwack! on my arms and popped out of my fantasy. Janine was leaning towards me, rolling her eyes.

"Jesus, what's with you today?" she whispered. "You've been off in Cammie-land for the last fifteen minutes!"

The video was still running on the screen in front of the class, showing images of native children taking their first Communion.

I straightened myself, then saw Sarah Walker, the new girl at St Theresa with the strange, English-sounding accent. She flashed me a knowing, private smile.

While my two friends peeled off toward geometry class, I hurried to the bathroom.

Thank God no one was in there. I picked a stall, went in and closed the door. I was still hot and flushed from the images that had possessed me.

There was no way I could get through another class while in this state. I hiked up my skirt, sat on the toilet, slid my hand into my crotch, and gasped at how wet I was.

My breathing grew shorter. I entered into the sensation, trying to stifle my moans. I moved my fingers in the wet tangle. I was growing sweaty, tense, excited and confused.

In my mind, I struggled with the image of the large naked man and his leather strap and my legs forcibly parted. I needed the images to feed my excitement, yet they caused me such shame that I fought them back at the same time. As I remembered the thrusts he gave me in my vision, I slid my fingers into me. They couldn't begin to give me the rich and brutal pleasure the man had. I quickly searched through my purse and got out an elastic hair band and wrapped it around two of my fingers. I looked at it, imagining it to be the ring on the man's cock. Now I poised it at my needy hole.

I heard the bathroom door open. I stopped and peered through the crack in the stall.

Great, Sarah Walker. She had begun attending St Theresa's only two weeks ago. There was an air of mystery about her. First, there was the accent. It was British, but as though she was born in some far more exotic country.

Then there was the fact that nobody could figure her out. Was she rich? Was she poor? No one seemed to know. I knew exactly where the rest of my classmates stood. Who was spoiled, who had two after-school jobs, and who was somewhere in-between. Janine claimed to know for sure that Sarah's family were actually trailer trash and doing their best to disguise it with their fancy way of speaking.

Janine might put her down, but I thought Sarah was amazingly sophisticated with her short, chic cropped hair. I suspected the blackness of it was a dye, because Sarah's skin was so fair. And her posture! It made the standard Catholic-school uniform look like a fashion statement. She didn't sex up the look the way Janine and Tia did. Yet, Sarah was hotter, like someone who'd just dropped in from the best party in a big city. Nobody this rad could be trailer trash.

The bell for the next class gave its shrill ring.

I hated being late. I jumped up and wiped my crotch as dry as I could. I gave my G-string a fast spray of perfume and pulled it on.

"Hello, who's in there?" Sarah asked in her crisp yet seductive accent.

I emerged from the stall, doing my best not to look red-faced. Fortunately Sarah seemed pleased to see me.

"Oh, it's you, Cammie dearest. I'm so glad," she said, giving me an inquiring look. "My goodness. You look as though you're running a fever. Are you all right?" Her voice was a crystalline purr.

"Yeah," I said. "Though I don't know. Maybe I'm coming down with something."

Sarah marched over and put her hand on my forehead. I flinched, then let Sarah feel my temperature. Her hand was pleasantly cool.

"You are a bit warm, and even sweaty," said Sarah.

"Oh, gosh, I'm so sorry," I said, covering my mouth. "I don't mean to –?"

"I'm hardly concerned about a few worldly germs," Sarah said.

She clicked open the plush scarlet purse that she always had with her. It was a red velvet clutch – the kind of un-hip thing no one else would have dared carry in high school.

"I have just the thing for you," Sarah said, removing an old-fashioned jar. I gasped at its beauty. "Isn't it lovely?" she said. "It's cloisonné."

As Sarah daintily unscrewed the gilded top, I stared entranced at the exquisite, bejeweled little jar, with its latticework and tiny symbol-like curlicues.

"It's so amazingly beautiful," I said.

"I know," said Sarah. "Now hold out your left hand."

I did as I was told, and Sarah gave the jar a gentle shake. Tiny glistening lavender-colored flower petals – or were they butterfly wings? – fell into my palm. They seemed weightless. "If we put this on your eyelids, it will make you feel much better."

With her index finger, Sarah touched the dainty heap of glistening things in the palm of my hand. The petals – or whatever they were – turned into an iridescent powder.

"Let me help you," Sarah said.

I obediently lowered my lids, and felt the slight pressure, as the English girl applied the strange powder.

"There," Sarah said. "Now take three deep breaths, and you will start to feel better."

And did I ever! My feelings of franticness and vulnerability flew out of me. My breathing got deeper and calmer with each inhale and exhale.

"Wow, that's amazing," I said. "What is that stuff?"

I opened my eyes and glanced at myself in the dingy bathroom mirror. I even looked better. The thick pale purple color Sarah had put on my eyelids wasn't something I would ever have thought to wear. Yet it brought out the blue in my eyes, and it did something else too. What was it? In any case, I adored how I now looked.

"It works for you," said Sarah. "Isn't that enough to know?"

I nodded happily. I was no longer the embarrassed virgin who felt she had to apologize to Janine and Tia. Here was an image of myself I could really go for: womanly, a little mysterious, triumphantly beautiful.

I looked over at Sarah, who jokingly batted her eyes. She was wearing the same shade of purple shadow. She entwined her arm in mine. We coolly walked out of the bathroom, down the hall and into art class.

When we entered the room late, I expected to be reprimanded. Instead everyone looked up at us. With awe.

"I like this eye shadow," I whispered to Sarah, as we sat down next to each other.

She touched her hand to her eyes and mouthed back the words, "Looks pretty on you."

During the class, I noticed that Sarah was making the strange little shapes she always did. It didn't matter if she was molding clay, or painting, or doing water colors. It was always the same – they looked human, but with three eyes and long extended limbs.

Sarah worked on her little creations very hard, and her work on them was extremely detailed. They looked like their limbs had been twisted so hard that the veins were popping through the skin. She modeled the flesh so it had scales and hideous knobs.

I myself loved being creative, and today amused myself by painting large, swirly, swoopy abstract images. As I moved with my brush, my imagination drifted off.

In my mind, I was in an English garden. I saw myself in one of those large, flower-strewn hats and a long white dress. There were flowers bordering an expanse of grass. It must be spring, I thought, because the air had a newborn quality to it, not plumped up the way that summer air can be, but like a first, pure breath.

And all of the blooms were shades of purple: rows of deep blue-red roses, lines of lavender tulips, beds of white and purple striped petunias. I walked among the abundance of flowers, strolling, finding a Victorian parasol in my right hand.

I caught a glimpse of my skirt and saw that it was transparent and realized I wasn't wearing anything underneath. I could see my pubic hair. I gathered my voluminous sheer skirt around me, bunching it up to cover myself as best I could.

And yet when I glanced around the garden, I saw dozens of aristocratic women, all adorned in the same sheer way. You could see their pubic hair, and their breasts. They wore their revealing skirts proudly. They strolled elegantly, carrying parasols. They wore enormous hats that had long feathers and ribbons.

They held their heads high, so why shouldn't I?

And there was Sarah, laughing and chatting with them. What a glorious day! I was so happy to be there. Sarah waved at me, her own dress not white, but a stunning shade of lavender and I could glimpse her body through it. She raised a parasol and flirtingly twirled it, while smiling enigmatically. Then she walked on, winding her way around the lawn. There was a mansion behind her – one of those many turreted and chimneyed things.

I suddenly realized that it was Sarah's family estate.

How nice of her to have invited me over! I was having the loveliest afternoon.

I waved at Sarah, let my skirts waft in the gentle breezes and leaned down to take in a rose. I startled at its perfume. It was exactly the way my pussy smelled when I had touched it in the bathroom, but instead of wanting to disguise the odor, I breathed it in.

I saw in the distance that Sarah's funny little humanoids were in the garden too, serving tea, playing croquet – but they didn't seem odd. They seemed as elegant as everything else.

I felt something nipping lightly at my ankles. Could it be an insect? It was a far more pleasant bite than a bug or fly. When I looked down, I saw that some of Sarah's humanoids were running in and out of my skirts.

At first they sent delicate itchy shivers through me.

Suddenly, my imagination broke free. It, rather than me, now ran the show.

I tried to regain control. But all went dark around me. I blinked my eyes, trying to reconnect with the reality of my art class. I couldn't.

I was in a pitch-black place where I could see nothing.

The little humanoid things now swarmed over me. A couple of them scrambled up my thighs and humped me the way our family's dachshund often did. They were making their way to my crotch and I swatted at them, but the feeling was strangely good, like being tickled, or loved. It made me giggle and swoon. As I did, my pussy relaxed, and I could feel several of the creatures scurry into my cunt.

"You can't go in there!" I cried.

Yet my pussy had a mind of its own and welcomed them in. It was so pleasurable, not at all like anything I'd ever felt before.

At that time, I was ashamed to admit it, even to myself, but the truth was I was a very bad masturbator. When I tried to make myself come, I strained and agonized, and got tense.

Now, I could feel the little beasties in me. The muscles of my cunt were relaxing. I felt like I was melting. Feelings were sweeping me off, effortlessly.

Still lost in my fantasy, amazed at the reality of it, I watched the scene shift. The writhing in my cunt subsided, and my fantasy now extended before me.

I was in a long narrow corridor swathed in red velvet. It was the red velvet of Sarah's purse! The lush material billowed like slept-in sheets. I walked among the flowing red waves, my white dress a sharp contrast.

"Come with me," a voice whispered into my ear, a woman's voice, self-possessed and seductive, with an English accent.

It was Sarah, of course. Her arm circled me.

"We're so delighted to have you here today," she said. "Have you been enjoying yourself?"

I didn't have to say "yes." She knew I had loved the afternoon. She led me down the plush scarlet tunnel, moving me toward a candle-lit opening I could barely see.

As we drew closer I gasped at the beauty of it: the walls were covered in black satin. In the center of the room stood a shiny marble slab.

"Come here," Sarah said.

She settled me slowly, slowly onto the marble. It was so cool to the touch. When I was on my back, Sarah smiled, then she pinned my arms down. She ran her red fingernails between my legs, parting them. I felt the cold metal of chains and manacles. I knew where I was now. The man with the cock ring would soon appear.

I struggled against the chains. I could feel myself sweating. I'd put on my usual heavy dose of anti-perspirant that morning, but it was no use. It was no match for my body's desire. The smell grossed me out at first, then it filled me with a wicked pride. I struggled against Sarah's bindings no more.

The chamber was suddenly filled with a blinding light. I heard familiar voices murmuring concern. I blinked, and when I reopened my eyes, I saw that my classmates, art teacher and a priest were peering down at me.

I was lying on the floor of my art class.

"She must have fainted," I heard my art teacher say.

I felt my head, yet it didn't hurt from the fall. My body still tingled with evil bliss. Were my hard nipples showing through my white uniform shirt? I raised my head and saw my legs were still parted the way they were on that marble slab. I quickly closed them. I stammered as I tried to explain myself.

"I have no idea what happened," I said.

Sarah winked at me. Then she took control of the situation.

"Right before class Cammie told me she thought she might be coming down with the flu," Sarah announced.

My teacher insisted that I see the school nurse, but instead I hung out in the courtyard. I felt okay, I really did – I actually felt amazingly good.

At lunch hour, I dodged Janine and Tia. I didn't need to have them pestering me with questions about the incident. It wasn't difficult to avoid them. They didn't want to catch whatever I might have. My best friends swerved around me, keeping a good distance away.

I wandered back into the girls' bathroom. Two classmates stood applying mascara. They looked at me as I entered, then abruptly packed up their makeup and hurried out, whispering and giggling as they did.

I stood at the sink and splashed water on my face. Would I never stop being tormented by my fantasy life? And then I glanced at my eyes. That purple eye shadow really was lovely but I had to wipe it off. I wet a paper towel and rubbed my lids. It stubbornly remained, not even smearing.

The door opened. I knew who it was even before I heard the deep clear tones.

"You didn't have a good time in art class?" Sarah asked, walking toward me.

Something in me snapped. "It was that fucking eye shadow you gave me! What's in this stuff? It's evil! I want it gone!"

"All right," Sarah said.

She made a curious motion with her index and little finger. And I saw that the eye shadow disappeared from my lids. I reeled around.

"Stay away! You're too weird!" I stammered, trying to get past her and out the door. "Janine's probably right about you!"

"That what – that I'm trash?" Sarah said. "From the back-woods? That's what everyone says about me, isn't it?"

She was standing right next to me. Our hips touched slightly. Sarah raised a hand and ran a gentle finger down my face.

"The truth is we sort of do live in a trailer park," Sarah said. "We are only here for a while and then we will have to move on. But you know why we're here, don't you?"

I shook my head, but I felt a strange rush. I gasped for breath.

"We want you. We want you because you have sacred blood," she said. "Do you understand the word 'sacred'? It's something that you shouldn't be wasting on Mike."

I backed away from her. But I was now far away from the exit.

"What are you talking about?" I asked.

"Why do you think I transferred to this school?" Sarah murmured. "We smelled your virginal essence a continent and a century away. We came to help you through this passage so that you can realize your eternal female power."

Sarah urged me into one of the stalls as we talked. I tried to get past her, but found myself swept along. I heard the click of the little lever as she flipped it over. We were locked together inside the stall.

"Here," Sarah said, taking her hand and moving it down to the top of my skirt. "Let me show you what I mean."

"But people are going to come in here," I protested.

Sarah shook her head. "I don't think so," she replied.

"Don't you hear that?" I said. "Someone's in here."

I whipped my head around at the noise, but Sarah drew my face back to hers.

She pushed me against the wall until our lips were only an inch apart. Was Sarah going to kiss me? Janine had often extolled the virtues of messing around with other girls – had hinted, in fact, that she'd had one or two lesbian sessions herself. Tia claimed to have made out with another girl at camp when she was only fourteen. She bragged about it, and made sure all the boys in school knew about it. But the most I had ever done was dance with other girls and try to masturbate to a few girl-girl fantasies. But now I was growing hotter and more confused by the second.

Sarah merely talked and whispered into my mouth from a half an inch away, her breath warm, sweet and dizzying.

"You can have some guy from this school break your lovely hymen – and face the most ordinary of lives ahead of you. Look at your parents. Because that's what you'll become. Or," she said, her voice growling seductively, "you can pass over a different threshold. If you come to my house you will spend the day in the greatest luxury you'll ever experience. You and I will go to the mall together and shop. You'll dine at our table on a feast you've never imagined. I will prepare you myself for the moment. I'll bathe you in the milkiest waters and slip a white silk dress on your oiled and perfumed body."

The words were like little bites and licks. I involuntarily opened my mouth, desperately wanting Sarah to kiss me.

But again, she only spoke. "And then you will be taken to the most special chamber in all the universe –"

"It's black and candlelit, isn't it? And it's down at the end of that corridor," I whispered.

"Yes, I took you there in art class so you'd have a little taste. And you liked it, didn't you?"

I swallowed hard and helplessly nodded yes. I could hear the voices of other students outside the door. I hoped they'd come inside and rescue me and yet at the same time I longed for them to go away and leave me with Sarah forever.

"It's locked!" one of them cried.

"Locked? But it's never locked," another voice shouted. "And I really gotta go. Oh, let's go get the super to open it."

I heard them march off. And that was it. Sarah and I were truly alone.

I now felt the length of her body press against me more closely. Something was forcing its hot way into my mouth.

Oh, God, I thought, I'm being kissed by a woman.

And in my mind, I was propelled back into the black chamber. The man with the leather cock ring was fucking me, and I could feel the soft caress of the woman holding my head. The combination of the gentleness of the woman's touch combined with the sharp pain of the man's thrusts . . . I writhed. Was this what it was to get close to orgasm?

In my fantasy, I opened my eyes in rapture, only to see the woman above me. Or was it Sarah's face? Yes, it was Sarah. And in her hands was an enormous knife . . .

I struggled my way back to reality.

"You're planning to sacrifice me, aren't you?" I cried. Despite my fear, my voice still groaned with excitement, an excitement I hadn't known I was capable of.

"Kill you?" Sarah said, her voice dropping into a dark rich purr. "Why would we do that? What do you take me and my family for – backwoods serial killers?"

She laughed, relaxed her physical tension, and opened her velvet purse. She took out a long slender knife.

"How'd you get that past the school security?"

"I never went through it," Sarah said. She held the weapon to my throat.

"Don't kill me," I pleaded. But I was moaning, too.

Sarah ran her other hand up my thigh, and under my school-girl skirt. Her fingers lingered over the G-string straps.

"Mmmm, very sexy," Sarah murmured. "Straps become you."

She moved the cloth aside, and a finger slipped between my vaginal lips and found my hot little button. Sarah massaged it expertly, until I thought I would faint or die. Then she stopped and withdrew her hand. She raised it between us so I could see: there was menstrual blood on it.

"Oh no!" I said, "I'm so embarrassed. I'm not supposed to have my period now. Not for another three weeks!"

Sarah laughed and made a gesture. The blood crystallized into a crimson gem that sparkled and cast a red glow around us.

"Now do you realize what kind of precious blood your hymen stores?" Sarah asked. She took the knife away from my throat and replaced it in her purse. "Give me a call when you're ready," she said, sticking out her tongue and placing my blood stone on it. Her eyes gleamed with rapture.

"You're crazy!" I said. "I wouldn't go near your house. How do I know next time you won't use that knife on me?"

"You don't," Sarah laughed. "And that's exactly why you want to come to the black chamber and find out if I will."

The door swung shut as she left.

I went to the sink and tried to steady myself. One of the stall doors opened. It was Janine.

"Were you there that whole time?"

"I sure was." Janine's brown eyes were wide like flying saucers. "And, whoa, did I just hear what I thought I heard?"

"I don't know," I said.

"Divine blood? Essence? I mean, that's crazy stuff! It's also kinda hot. But talk about kinky! Wow!"

The two of us paused. I leaned against the wall to catch my breath. As I calmed down, the path before me suddenly became clear.

"So, what are you going to do?" Janine asked.

"I need to get laid by Mike on Saturday. And then this whole thing will be over."

"Do you really think that'll get rid of her?" As usual, I couldn't tell if Janine was upset for my safety or thrilled at what she'd overheard.

"Don't worry," I said. "It's just the blood from losing my virginity she's interested in. It's a weird fixation, but she doesn't care about anything else. I wouldn't go near her place. As soon as I get laid, the spell will be broken and she'll lose interest. But you can't tell anyone. Promise? Really. It would be dangerous if Sarah found out my plan."

"Of course, of course. We're friends for life, remember?" Janine drilled. She was getting more agitated. It reminded me of how she got when she'd had too many Diet Cokes. She jumped around, gesturing with her hands, blabbing at warp speed. "I always said she was trash. I was so right. Ooh, but shouldn't we check it out? Notify the police or the school paper or the local TV news?"

I put my hands on Janine's shoulders to steady her.

"No," I said. "This must be done in complete secrecy."

On Saturday night as I prepared for my date with Mike, I wondered what to wear. Jeans, or the miniskirt? Oh, the skirt, of course. At the key moment, it would be much easier to manipulate. I put it on and checked myself out in the mirror. Good!

The fantasies that had possessed me receded, and were now safely held in a locked cage at the back of my mind. Where they would stay forever, I thought resolutely.

Soon it would be over. My virginity would finally be a thing of the past. And, I thought, I would be safe from Sarah. What a weirdo! "Precious hymen blood" my ass.

Thirty minutes later, when I hopped into Mike's SUV, he seemed impressed.

"Hey," he said. "You look awesome!"

"Thanks," I said. "You look pretty good yourself."

He didn't start the car.

Why wait, I thought. "Look, we both know what we've got in mind. Let's go somewhere and do it right now."

Mike looked startled. Had I been too blunt? Boys' egos were tricky things.

"I want you really badly," I said in a hurry, to make him feel better.

"I don't know," he said. "I was kinda planning on a movie and dinner first."

So he was going to drag his feet? I couldn't believe it. Weren't boys supposed to be horny all the time?

"You do want me, don't you?" I asked.

I licked my lips in what I hoped was a seductive way.

"Yeah!" he said. "But what about the date part?"

"I can't wait that long!"

Mike turned the key in the ignition, then put his right hand on my thigh. "That's so cool you're horny. I like that. But let's take it one step at a time, okay?"

I took his hand and moved it under my skirt and up to my crotch.

He pulled his hand away. "I really do want you," he said. "I just need to have something to drink first." He pulled a can of beer out from under the seat, took a big slug and handed it to me.

"Take me somewhere to make out," I insisted. "Don't be such a wimp."

"Sure, sure," Mike said. "My parents will be out of the house after eight o'clock. Maybe we could go there."

"I don't have the time. There's got to be some place to park in this town."

"What's the rush, baby?" asked Mike.

But he drove off. A few minutes later, we turned right onto the road that led towards the farms on the outskirts of town.

Despite the urgency, I backed off for a few minutes to let Mike get his pride back. He seemed to need to talk on about things that had nothing to do with sex. Where was the cocky stud he always seemed to be at school?

We passed the last of the suburban enclaves. Beyond were fields and thick woods. We drove on.

Feeling impatient with his blab about teammates and hockey, I sneaked a look at my cell phone. I had a message from Janine. I pressed the retrieval key. Mike just kept talking.

"Cammie," Janine was saying with unusual emotion in her voice. "I don't know if you've lost it yet, but there's something you should know. Call me ASAP."

I turned my phone off and stuffed it back in my purse. Janine probably wanted to lecture me about putting a towel down for the blood. Forget her.

"Why don't we stop here?" I said, pointing to a clear area on the side of the road.

"The cops roam this road, you know," Mike said.

"Yeah, but I'll make sure we're through before they get here," I said.

I glanced out the window at the thicket of tall pines beyond. In the moonlight I could make out branches moving in the wind.

Mike seemed reluctant, but he parked the car and turned off the headlights. I helped him put down the back seat so there was a long flat area for us to make out on. Mike had brought no pillows or towels, so I pushed him down on the carpeted surface, and climbed on top of him. I took off my skirt and top. Mike licked his lips at the sight of me in a thong and bra.

"I was going to do this strip that Janine taught me, but there isn't time," I apologized.

"It's fine, really," he said. "That was wild enough."

He sounded as nervous as he did excited. I gave him one big kiss, and started to unzip his pants.

"Hey, hey, hey!" he said, pulling my hand off.

"What's going on?" I cried. "Don't you want to fuck me?"

He looked up at me. He seemed incredibly shy. Was that shame I saw? Or pride? "I've never done this before," he admitted.

"What?" I almost screamed. "You haven't? You're supposed to be the school stud!"

"It's all rumors," he said sheepishly.

"Great! Another virgin!"

"I'm sorry," he said. "But can't we start over? I like you. I really do and I would like for us to make it, but not like this. It sounds weird, but I think that having sex for the first time is special, not something just to be gotten out of the way."

I was stunned. It had all come screeching to a halt. At the same time, a deep thrill was passing through me. He'd spoken a secret password and had opened up my soul. I climbed off him and lay next to him.

"I agree totally," I said. "It's like everybody wants to make you feel weird about it if you think the way we do."

"So if we both feel special about losing it," he said, "maybe that means we're perfect for each other."

I was silent for a moment. My insides were becoming silky and calm. I felt like I could tell Mike anything. "Do you know Sarah Walker at school?"

"Sure," he said. "The strange chick with the even stranger accent. Everybody knows her."

"Well, don't laugh at me but she's some kind of demon, definitely. And this may some completely insane, but she wants to have her people – or family, or whatever, I don't really know – do it to me for the first time."

"Wow," Mike said. So what if he wasn't very articulate, there was real sympathy in his voice.

"Yeah," I said. "She says I'll be totally pampered and treated well beforehand. And then I'll be dressed up and led to this amazing black chamber where I'll be tied down. Only – and here's the bizarre part – I think they might kill me."

"Fuckin' freaky shit," said Mike.

I nodded. My nipples were hardening – was it because of the intimacy of the moment with Mike? Or the memory of Sarah's knife at my throat and the feeling of Sarah's fingers in my cunt?

"This is so sick but I can't get it out of my mind," I said. "The thought that I might die while fucking for the first time just turns me on like nothing ever before in my life."

Mike seemed to be brooding.

"What?" I said. "Tell me what you're thinking!"

"You're not the only one," he said.

"What?"

"Everybody at school knows her. And everybody who's still a virgin has been asked by her to do it that way. She's got designs on a lot of us. And let me tell you – there are more virgins at school than you'd think."

I suddenly felt totally let down! What was wrong with me? Why was I feeling disappointed when I should have felt relieved? Did I really want what had happened in the bathroom stall to have been special? I pulled myself together and said, "That's amazing. What should we do about it?"

"I don't know," Mike said. "I've been thinking about that myself, and thinking about what she told me she'd do to me as well. God, can that bitch brain-fuck or what?"

I saw the front of Mike's jeans bulging. I couldn't help my reaction. I reached over and squeezed his hard-on. Mike groaned, so I squeezed some more. I was getting wet as I felt my power. We leaned our heads together and indulged in a long soul kiss.

My heart was thumping when I raised my head. Outside the moon was still glowing, the countryside was still dark, the branches were still moving . . . only something was different. I looked around again, my head clear. Definitely some moving shapes. Only now I knew they weren't branches or trees or bushes.

"Lock the doors!" I said.

"What?" Mike asked. "But there's no one around – oh my God."

Now he saw them, too. Shadowy, tall figures in long, flowing black coats, walking purposefully down the road toward us.

Mike burst into action, scrambling around, hitting buttons.

At the head of the clan was Sarah, wearing a long black coat. Her milky skin was translucent in the moonlight, her cropped haircut proud and sinister.

"Did you really think you could do this without us?" Sarah screamed. She was still in the distance, yet her voice reverberated within the SUV.

"Shit, it's the bitch, and she's got her family with her!" said Mike. "We've got no chance. They're going to take us off. We'll be human sacrifice."

"I should have figured Janine would blab! But we can get through this," I said. "I know what we have to do."

"You have a gun? Or what?" said Mike.

"We've got to fuck, and pronto."

"Just like that?"

"It's the only way," I said, looking deep into his eyes. "Once we've lost our virginity, they'll have no interest in us. Now get to work."

"Easy for you to say," said Mike. "How am I supposed to perform in these circumstances?"

In a flash, I unzipped and yanked down Mike's pants. I set to sucking his cock and sexily squeezing his balls. It was as though I'd always known how to do this.

"Oh, Christ, Cammie, that feels so good," gasped Mike. "Oh, Jesus, I'm getting really hard. Oh, that's the best sensation ever. Shit!" he said suddenly. "They're getting closer."

"There. You're good and hard. Now get to work. We've got to do it as fast as possible," I said. "Otherwise we'll be theirs."

I looked out the car window. I figured Sarah and her family would be running toward us. Yet they were slowing approaching, still a good twenty yards away. Sarah smiled, strolling the way she had in that English garden I'd seen in art class. And now she was wearing that same flowing lavender dress, and the men were all in old-fashioned suits.

Mike saw it, too. "They're playing us," he said. "I don't know what to do."

I sighed impatiently. "Lie down," I commanded.

He did as ordered. I checked outside. Sarah and the men had disappeared.

"Where are they?" Mike asked.

There was pounding on the SUV glass. They were pressed up against the window leering at us. I saw the man from the black chamber.

I shuddered, but I knew I had to remove my thong. The man ran his enormous, bright red tongue along the glass as I did. I kept on my bra.

"Better for you to close your eyes," I instructed Mike.

"What about a condom?" Mike said. "Fuck, I didn't bring one. I thought we'd be going to my house where I can raid my older brother's stash."

"This is no time to worry about unsafe sex," I said.

I got on my knees and straddled Mike's hips. Sarah's family leered at us.

"Damn you," Sarah screamed. Her face was a shrieking mask from some horrifying biblical painting.

"This will never work," Mike said.

"I'll make it work," I told him.

I took his cock in my hand. I positioned my hips, then quickly tried to settle my weight onto him. Sarah and her family began to rock the SUV. Mike and I were separated as we rolled around the back of the car.

"You can't do this without me!" Sarah screamed.

Her flock of weirdos tilted the SUV until it was nearly on its side. She flashed her eyes and the moonlight vanished. It was completely black.

"Oh no," I said. "She's taken us to the chamber."

And we were there.

"Oh yeah," Mike said. "I can feel my ass on that cold marble slab."

"Hold on!" I said.

I could see Sarah with her knife, coming at us. I climbed on top of Mike. He was having trouble keeping an erection. I pumped him a couple of times until he was hard. I aimed his shaft at my virgin entrance.

The tingling nerves in my pussy could sense the plush head of Mike's circumcised cock as it pressed its way in. I gasped as my body welcomed his pulsing urgency. I felt like the most glorious angel floating on high, I felt like a devil burning in flames – and then something snapped.

"Oh, God," I gasped.

"I'm in," Mike said.

I could feel the heat of my blood as it began to run out of me. "Oh, it does hurt," I said, falling onto Mike's chest.

When I pulled my head up, I saw we were once again inside the SUV and it was no longer rocking.

Outside, Sarah stuck her tongue out. On it, pulsing red, was the blood jewel she had taken from me.

"Why aren't they going away?!" Mike cried. "I'm inside you, but they're still there."

Sarah let out a banshee shriek.

"It's you," I said. "They want your virgin soul."

Mike valiantly pumped his hips, thrusting his cock over and over again into me, deeper each time.

"I don't know if I can stay hard with them out there," he said. There was the noise of shattering glass as a fist punched through the driver's side window.

"Just imagine you're tying on a cock ring," I whispered. "Now tell me about it."

"Oh, God, Cammie, if the guys on my team ever heard me say that –"

"Come on, Mike!"

"Okay, okay," he whispered. "I'm tying on the . . ."

He couldn't say it. I heard something sharp against the driver's window.

"Mike, you've got to," I said.

He cleared his throat and rasped. "I'm tying on the cock ring!"

I heard glass shatter. The huge man put his hand through the broken window. He licked his bloody wrist, then unlocked the door.

"Oh no," Mike said, his confidence fading fast. I remembered some advice Tia had once given me. I reached around and squeezed Mike's balls.

"The cock ring is making your dick twice its normal size," I whispered.

And it was true. I could feel Mike growing inside me, stirring feelings I'd never had before. Was I about to have my first orgasm? Yes. My eyes were locked with Sarah's as I rode the wave of my sensations.

The man climbed into the car. He had Sarah's knife, the one she'd held against my throat in the bathroom. He aimed it at Mike's throat. I pumped as hard as I could. Mike groaned and gasped his way into his own orgasm. I felt him thrust one more time.

Then I heard him scream "Awesome!"

I watched an amazing transformation occur. The beautiful Sarah, deformed by her rage, started to give way. The man growled and shook as his knife froze in midair.

Enormous bumps were forming all over Sarah and her family. Limbs and sinews could be seen bulging under their flesh. A head with three eyes popped through Sarah's fine, white skin. She was weeping, and turning into one those humanoids she was forever making in art class.

"Baby, I love you," Mike groaned.

I could feel his sperm mingling with my blood and trickling down my thigh, and as it did I saw my blood jewel burst in Sarah's open mouth. Blood cascaded down her lips and neck. And then she and the men dissolved into the moon-filled night.

Mike and I were lying on the floor of his SUV, a wet, sticky tangle. The SUV looked untouched, except for the mess our sex had made.

We drove back into town. We'd talked about what to do next. We decided not to call the police. What would be the point? Who would believe us? Besides, now we were safely out of Sarah's reach.

When we entered the comforting lights of suburbia, we became silent. I shivered as I thought about how close we'd come to dying. Wasn't it wonderful to have survived? On top of that I was now a real woman. I could hold my head up at school. No more jokes about being a virgin from Janine and Tia.

I took out my compact, and adjusted my makeup. In the tiny mirror, I tried to find the sophisticated woman I should now be. I did look different. What was it? Yes, that was it. For the first time, I saw how much I resembled my mother.

I snapped my compact shut.

"Everything okay?" Mike asked.

"Sure, sure," I said.

"I bet you're happy to be alive," Mike said. "Like I am."

"Yeah," I said. I was happy to be alive. I just didn't feel happy the way Mike felt happy about it.

We drove past the giant mall. I'd always been so proud of it: the biggest in the tri-county area with the most up-to-date fashion stores. Couples milled about the movie multiplex. As a kid, I couldn't wait to be old enough to go on dates there.

"Hey," Mike said. "What do you say we take in a movie next Saturday night?"

"Sure," I said. "I'd like to see that new Spiderman sequel. Although, it'll seem tame after what we went through tonight."

"That'll be fine by me," Mike said.

I saw that he really did feel that way. As for me, I couldn't help wondering what Sarah and her crew would be doing next Saturday night. She'd probably leave this area. Maybe even this century. Sarah could go anywhere, forever.

I, on the other hand, would be going to the multiplex.

We turned the corner toward my house. "I'd like for us to be a steady thing."

"Why not?" I said, then realized I should be more enthusiastic. "That would be nice," I added.

"Don't worry about your blood in the back of the car. I'll take care of it."

"Thanks," I smiled.

He put his hand on mine. I glanced down at our fingers resting on each other and for a moment, I saw my parents' hands instead of ours. I shuddered harder than I had all evening.

"You okay?" Mike asked.

I remembered something.

"I should check my messages," I said, pulling out my cell phone.

"Sure," Mike said obediently, as though we were already an old married couple.

I pressed the message button and listened to my friend's voice.

"Hello, Cammie? I just wanted to tell you something," she was saying in a breathless voice. "I . . . I don't know how to say this . . . but . . . well, okay, here it is."

Janine's voice paused. I knew what my friend was about to say before I even heard the words. I felt my heart beat furiously with a mixture of fear and unwanted envy.

"I have something to confess. I told Sarah Walker about you and Mike. I didn't mean to, but she kissed me and the next thing I knew I was telling her everything!

"And there's something else I have to admit. I guess that makes two things I'm confessing, right?

"So here's the second one. I . . . well, I've never actually slept with anybody, Cammie. That's right, I'm a virgin. It's all been a big act, my stories about being so experienced.

"When Sarah was feeling my breasts, I couldn't help it. I just had to tell her that, too. I thought she'd laugh. But she was really, really nice and totally sympathetic!

"So here I am now at her house. It's extraordinary. I mean, outside it's just a trailer in a trailer park. But inside! There's velvet and candles and marble. And she has the most wonderful family. And I'm so bummed because they're going to be leaving town! I wish I'd gotten to know Sarah earlier.

"Anyway, they left for a while earlier this evening, but now they're back, lavishing me with attention I never thought possible and I'm so sorry I called her trash. Oh, I've only got a second more to talk. They're about to come get me.

"I'm all ready for them. I'm in this amazing white gown Sarah gave me. She's going to walk me down this red corridor to a black chamber. Cammie, this is the coolest moment of my life. I'm about to lose my virginity! I'm nervous, sure. But Sarah tells me I'll be over the threshold in no time. And I can't wait to find out what's on the other side."

A Night in Cameroon

Kelly Jameson

SIMPLE HARMONIC MOTION = Motion that repeats in a regular pattern over and over again.

I don't need to look far for a piece of physics. Or for a piece of ass, either.

I never finished high school, but I *know* about energy and momentum. Make more money stripping than the girls in my high school who went to college to study things like teaching nursing psychology and can definitely afford a flashy ride with all the bells and whistles, but I'm loyal to my dented midnight blue Ford Escort. Living among a drew of popcorn tenants in a jittery little place in the city: got my ass as far from the state of opaque suburbia as humanly possible.

At thirteen rebelled against authority when they called me bad. Bad for developing breasts, for sucking cigarettes and beers, bad for sitting half-naked with boys on the top of a hill, watching for shooting stars, trying to forget the Ds in geometry, not caring about *The Great Gatsby* and not understanding the adults surrounding me like bombs, the world fucking blowing up in my face orange red blinding white. How a wet beer bottle and my first pair of motorcycle boots and boys' eager hands taught me to forget about music, forget my dreams to be a pianist, the wet wind slog crunch of my parents sixty-hour weeks, our refrigerator covered in magnets photos art coupons prescriptions report cards shopping lists standing like a grotesque Christmas tree. Taught me finally they were afraid, their faces place holders where something might have been.

Never looked back. Danced and felt the cooling night air on my face, a beer in my hand; learned to look for shooting stars and wondered does anyone else? and I haven't seen one in a really long time, but I keep trying, and when I was nine and did see one, I made a wish. I wished I could fly away from this place where something used to be.

No surprise I'm practical as the everyday fog resting on the collarbone of this smudged city, no-nonsense as a bank teller cashing checks and taking deposits with transactions in the back room of the club. It's not really about transactions anyway. When it's right, like spontaneous perfectly choreographed dance, it's about connecting, about falling; up down sideways but shooting together, coming together, all the parts of your lives, grabbing every possible particle of time together. It's not about thighs asses breasts, cocks; it's about feeling alive, in the moment. In the thick throb and stream of my flesh.

Never personally felt that way for anybody but I keep looking to the sky. Want to swallow it all.

Tuesday night. A steady rain. It didn't let up, continued into early morning, tapping on the roof even after the last patrons departed for home and soggy, airless, tight-fisted dreams, hoping to snatch a few winks before heading to sterile offices for coffee and idiotic business banter playing earnestly at back-nine politics.

I play cog in the closing-time machine at the club, hanging in the sudden calm of the emptiness. Still in glitter top, G-string, white stilettos, I stop and stand beside the grand piano against the back wall, counting the waxy green bills pressed against my flesh by groping hands during the course of the night. I think, as I count them, that the grand piano may be the most complicated hand-made mechanism in the world. I once read that it has 12,000 parts, mostly wood and most fashioned by manual labor, and can take up to four years to go from tree to concert hall or living room or strip club. Stroking the silken wood, wondering what it'd be like to fuck one of the men who made the parts, suck the fingers of a man who forged a machine capable of producing the greatest sensitivity to the artist's touch, deft fingers that part, stretch, cram my aching cunt. Handled by a man whose world is the focused delicacy of hammers, strings, tuning pins, woodwork. Sounds.

Whoa, look what we got here . . . the mouth. Rumor is she and the boss used to run with the same bunch of bikers . . . seems she was the service cow . . . turned her out for a this and that . . . mostly mouth jobs . . . blowjobs to strangers to keep the gang in cigarettes . . . say she once blew twenty guys in a men's room in a bar for free brews for the boys . . . now the gang's dead or in prison . . . 'cept the boss who ended up with money to buy this club . . . and the mouth here . . . guess that makes her a handmedown fucktoy . . . still passin her round . . .

Lingering in the cigarette haze of the damp bar, I press a few keys. Sound gradually dissipates; weaves into the pedals and trap work of sex and lust and dancing vibrant in the club only an hour before. Fitted with a hydraulic lift operated from the stool by another sort of player, this particular piano rises slowly to the ceiling and lowers again in a kind of harmonic entrapment, a prancing young woman atop it shaking her breasts, baring everything to the men staring up. An expensive prop, popular with the dancers and men in business suits and ties and dark, sweaty work socks who fancy themselves strangled by clocks, mortgages, kids, and ever fatter wives.

old serviceable cunt but running that mouth all the fucking time . . . boss says it don't bother him . . . just keep it full he says . . . then can't say nothing but mumph . . .

I've danced on it. When I was ten years old I could play. *Fantaisie Impromptu, Liebestraum, Unfinished Symphony, Pathetique, Minuet in G.* I've forgotten most of what I learned as a kid.

thinks she's smart . . . bit long in the tooth for this business . . . least here in the City . . . the only one puts out for the boss, boss's friends, high rollers . . . spends a lot of her life on her knees in the backroom . . . men's room . . . boss's office . . . seems to like it . . .

Thinking about lying across the piano, fucking above the guts and strings of the great symbol of civility, legs spread, flesh tuned to sound and movement, moisture and maleness, hammer-rush of wetness between my legs. Why I haven't done it atop this modern incarnation of the invention of a harpsichord maker for a

Florentine duke, a man of the early eighteenth century who knew, though he couldn't yet hear it, that there existed more to the world of sound than strings plucked to coerce vibration—

She could always work in Dubuque or some such shithole in the hinterlands but I don't think she'd be up to it . . . can't see her blowin in the men's room in Dubuque . . . then again easy to see her doing truckers at those all night stops just the thing for the old bitch's retirement.

"You thinking what I'm thinking?"

I lift my fingers from the keys (generally made of spruce or basswood and not ivory. Ivory-yielding species endangered, protected by treaty) and look up to find Jones, the muscular, tattooed bouncer standing beside me, six-foot-two, two-hundred thirty-five pounds. Jones and I, we compared scars and tats one night after closing. He wears a lot more than I. Jones began piercing parts of his own body when he was fourteen. I asked him what it felt like to get his penis tattooed. He said explosion of pain, like time and his dick stretched out infinitely.

well, she puts out . . . just about the only one here who does . . . everyfuckingbody been in that nasty cumbucket . . .

We talked, drank vodka, decided everyone loves to be used. If I stretch my imagination – a lot – Jones reminds me of a Florentine duke. He's a man who failed to win riches and fame from the world and doesn't care; plays life with carelessness not beyond his charm. I tried explaining to him how electrons pair up in copper-oxide materials that superconduct at temperatures above 100K; he tried to explain to me the NHL 1992–93 longest losing streak of the San Jose Sharks. I told him about breast ironing, body modification practised in Cameroon. Pubescent girls' breasts flattened by their mothers to make them less attractive to men, believing it'll prevent rape and early marriage. Apply grinding stones, belts, pestles, breast bands, heated objects and press or beat down the forming breasts. Local organizations try to stop it. I told him four million girls probably experienced it, cried from the pain, developed blisters and abscesses or worse, cancer even. End up pregnant and maybe married anyway.

man, she talks the dumbest shit . . . talk, talk, talk . . . ignore most everything comin outta her mouth . . . let'er ramble on . . . what gets shoved in that's interesting. Particularly my meat. She likes that fat tattooed dick . . . that stenciled thing gets me in a lot of cooze . . .

Jones didn't know what to say, so he didn't say anything. I didn't say anything. We drank more vodka. He asked, "Where's Cameroon?"

"It's a unitary republic of central and western Africa. People know it mostly for its national football team. They use a wooden pestle to flatten the breasts, the same thing they pound tubers with. Or they use heated bananas and coconut shells."

"Oh," he says. "God. God." never says no to me . . . she don't wanna fuck she sucks me off . . . sucks it all down . . . no hesitation . . . loves that shot in the mouth like any of the boys prowling the bathhouses.

Kind of ironic he's a bouncer whose job it is to keep me from being raped by horny drunks every night. I've fucked him before and it was nothing to complain about. Never on this piano, though.

"There's always time for a little physics," I say.

Physics. What the fuck's she jabbering about physics? . . . she don't know shit about physics . . . quantum this, relativity that . . . she so good at that shit why's she blowing high rollers in the boss' office and shaking that tired old ass and those beat floppers laying flat on her chest . . . workouts ain't cutting it for her like used to neither . . . that sagging ass. But she is one horny bitch . . . nasty . . .

I'm tired but fancying a cock perks me up, begging for it, groveling, having Jones, like Gottfried Silbermann – organ builder and clavichord maker from Dresden credited with constructing the first two pianofortes in Germany around 1730 – moving over me and inside me, looking for the music inside me, demanding, as Johann Sebastian Bach once did, better sound, searching, maybe, maybe, maybe this time we'll find it.

. . . dick's drooling just thinking of the men she's done today what's it been? five, six, fifty? good we're alone in the club cold wet spot sticking to my crotch hair . . .

Pull his pants to his knees, quadriceps darkly downed sprouting from his knees like twin tree trunks, menacing tree trunks in my face christ the slut's grabbing my dick before I say a fucking word what a pig for dick the first soft taste of him in my mouth as he swells, bristly hair rough on my face, musk man-smell . . . listen to that moan busts my nut like no other bitch already in her mouth Jesus licking strands of dick drool like glistening spaghetti hanging from her hole craving something hard to paint with my lips tat of black panther wrestling a cobra over part of his rippled abs down his penis cobra twisting around the erection fatter with the stiffening filling my mouth now pubic hair the snake's basket rising alive in the black jungle cat claws red eyes glowing back in the throat bitch shove it in there . . .

I'm in the rut needing the tattooed cock, all tongue and mouth and heat and square jaw twist my tits yank my hair tell me suck me off slut twist my nipples hard make me beg to swallow like a whore strong and hard too hard diamond fuck a venomous fuck against the neon-crusted world where everything's gamble and glittering freak show. This – it – it's what I want. Bitch in heat, sucking cock throbbing purple, angry, swollen. Lips ready to slip it in, rough and quick and hard. Quivering erection feel blood pulse. Ooze from the tip. I'm dripping wet. . . .

"You do plenty you oughtn't whore, how many'd you do today?" she moans again digging remembering on her knees sucking off the fat old shits "answer, slut."

His fat dick bobs beneath my lips. I drag my tongue up his belly, up his warm chest, his neck, kiss his Adam's apple, feel the blood beating, his pulse beating against my lips, taste the hardness of his firm jaw, finally move them over his ear and whisper and beg and lick, "I'm a bad, bad girl. My cunt wants to suck at you now." I don't look into his eyes when I beg. No faces.

. . . not into fucking this old thing yet . . . use that mouth . . . "not yet, cunt suck me off . . . earn it bitch . . . you deserve dick in that fuckhole? how many old dudes you suck up today already slut . . ."

I bend down, pull at his dick with my lips, suck hard so my mouth aches, gurgle and slobber long viscous strands, mewl like a baby. He yanks me up by my hair. His steel fingers spear my cunt, sharp pain parting and pulling my pubic hair. He jerks out his fingers and forces me to suck my own juice. I grin; the girl in me, the one who masturbates in the shower thinking of pot-bellied old men all gray chest hair and hard cocks watching me play with my pussy talking dirty stroking themselves dripping, and I'm dripping from the warm water of the shower, my legs spread apart, and they're spurting. I stand weak with lust, legs like water, and he squeezes my mound with his other mammoth mitt. I groan around the fingers in my mouth.

"I'm not messing around, bitch . . . you gotta get back to it . . . suck . . ."

"Fuck me now, Jones, now," I moan.

"shut up cunt. I'll fuck you when I'm good and ready . . . I ain't heard you beg yet. Bitch . . . you beggin bitch? . . ."

I kneel, lick inside his muscular thighs, nibble the soft layer of hair. He moans. I kiss his skin to ease the pain. "I can't hear you bitch . . . beg slut with that nasty mouth . . . show me louder . . ." I lick his cock and suck him, slurp, gurgle his juices and my saliva in tiny bubbles smack my lips polishing the knob spit on this dick catch his juice; he yanks me to my feet, strips off my glittery top and G-string. Impatient now, he kneels at my feet. All I'm wearing are my white stilettos. He spears my curls. "Christ, you're wet" sucking his own fingers this time.

"Please, please . . . fuck me." I beg. "Fuck me now before I come all over the floor."

He tosses his clothes, muscle shirt jeans briefs socks sneakers; carries me to the piano.

I imagine he's a man expelled after the sack of Rome in 1527 for lewd acts with all sorts of women. A distortion of the history in the texts, but I imagine he's a man from a long line of Italian music patrons who will restore the luster of his family name, a musical chapel of bone, muscle, sinew, and lust.

He pushes me down on the piano and climbs on top. I notice his beautiful feet. I wonder if they're pedicured.

I think how being on my back is my least favorite position; I prefer on my elbows, ass in the air. In position, no choice but to bare all, forced to give all my smells, the faint smell rising from just above my cunt – between shows I shit; used moist wipes after but didn't take time to shower between sets. I want to be dominated, fucked hard so I feel him burst from my throat, forget for a while I'm getting old for this, that the beer tastes stale, that I haven't seen a shooting star for years.

The cock of the man inside me? Genealogy complicated by innumerable illegitimate offspring and by the tendency of some of the members to dispose of each other by assassination. A dangerous man of experienced lips and hands, squeezing my breasts, painfully tweaking my hardened nipples; in haste to mount me his feet clumsily strike keys emitting crushed chords. He pushes inside me. Sonorous echo of discordant cacophony, jumble of randomness. Black and white inside my head, I am sharp, I am flat, I am the metal frame of the piano, the strings struck by hammers.

My Italian count is no patient man. Already he sucks air through his teeth. He repositions himself, somehow flays his legs outward and I think I hear the strings inside the big piano vibrate even though no keys have been struck. I think I hear moans of a thousand peasant women from the fourteenth century as the count rams inside me. If I had the dick, I'd wear him out. I'd wear him out.

"quiet . . . the bitch finally quiet . . . the place quiet . . . goddamn she's wet and sloppy . . ."

He thrusts harder.

"you're a dirty whore . . . beg me for it bitch . . ."

He strikes into my core and soon I actually feel as if I'm ascending. Strokes deliciously rough and panicked. His mouth over mine, jaw bunched and strained; veins in his neck bulging blood lust vitality.

"I wanna fuck you in the ass bitch . . ." breathing into my neck, he always wants to fuck my ass. "Forget my ass" clench tight around his erection until he moans "God," he holds there a sweet suspended instant "I'm going to come. . . . need . . . stop . . . a minute . . ." I realize we really *are* ascending. The ceiling looms closer. Jones must've knocked the switch with his foot. It's out of reach back at the stool. He doesn't realize what's happening fucking me hard, grunting with effort, lost.

Grand pianos have a special repetition lever in the playing action. This lever, as I understand it, a separate one for every key, catches the hammer close to the strings as long as the keys are played repeatedly and somewhat fleetly. In this position, with the hammer resting on the lever, a pianist can play repeated notes, staccato, trills with more speed and control than on a vertical piano.

I kick at him, bite him, harder than before, but this only drives him to frenzy. He pumps me like he will rip me in two. I scream and bite his ear enough to draw blood.

"What the fuck bitch? . . ."

He looks over the side of the piano. He looks up, realizes there's only a foot or two until the piano crushes both our bodies into the ceiling.

. . . holy shit this fucking thing's going up . . . goddamn the floor's down there a long fucking ways . . . the ceiling Jesus the goddamn ceiling's inches away . . . we'll be stuck but the goddamn thing can't push that hard . . . we'll be okay . . .

"Shit! . . ."

It's all he says.

He looks into my eyes, his pupils ironed dark marbles of shock.

"Shit! . . ."

He's still inside me when he runs out of room and becomes intimate with the ceiling. One of the heels of my stilettos snaps off. Sounds like bone breaking.

DOPPLER EFFECT = As an ambulance speeds toward you, sirens blazing, the sound you hear is high in pitch because the sound waves in front of the vehicle are being squashed together by the moving ambulance. This causes more vibrations to reach your ear per second, resulting in a higher pitched sound. When the ambulance passes you, the sound becomes lower in pitch. Behind the ambulance there are fewer vibrations per second, and a lower sound is heard. This change in pitch is known as the Doppler Effect.

Goddamn pressure . . . gonna push me through the goddamn
ceiling . . . can't breathe . . .

Two hundred thirty-five pounds of male flesh compressing
my chest as we crush against the ceiling; can't move anything,
not chest, hips, legs, arms. He's inside me; impaled and bound
and now something wet inside me running down my legs crack
of my ass, smell like shit sperm piss rot decay death blood, God
I see us as just two more damned in those paintings by that
crazed Dutch Flem Hieronymus Bosch. *Welcome to the religious
brotherhood of our lady.* . . . Oh God Jones tries to speak . . .
only grunts. And then spittle. He gasps, tries to speak; crushes
against the ceiling features twisted face distorted eyes bulging
mouth open only liquid no sound emitting vomit brown soup
atop a piano, run-of-the-mill strip club jazzed up with levitating
piano-and-girl act painted reality by Bosch.

Numb, octaves above the fundamental, heat wetness liquid
something, don't want to think how things compressed inside
Jones, fetid air liquid slop trickles from anus and mouth oozing
to drips God no gushing please God. Medieval torture devices,
people crushed by other people because of religion or views or
words, crushed to jelly, flesh lacerated to bone. Crushed for
fucking. Dog snarling at poverty-stricken old man. Something
gives, his bones piercing his flesh with excruciating slowness,
his marrow gushing out. I cry. Feel trapped in an Italian tourist
trap, hundreds of people pressing down on me, mouths with
black, rotted teeth, gaping open, heavy and hot and stinking,
laughing at an exhibit in a museum that houses ancient torture
devices operated by demons birds beak frog legs legless feet. I
think I hear something, some sound, far away. Wailing? Skates
scraping ice? Sails flapping ships of fools. Coconuts pounding
small breasts flat, coconut milk dripping flopping glopping onto
flesh? Shallower and shallower breaths; think about how Jones
was a star defensive tackle in high school and start to see
pinpricks of light behind my eyes, little shooting stars, and
high school and even this morning and even just five minutes
ago a long time ago now.

I had this science teacher in middle school, he told our class
about an experiment suffocating dogs by placing air-tight

rubber mask over their heads and it only took eight minutes for the dogs to cardiac arrest. It made me feel so sad. Jones the sound of mud sucking at the boots of a man. The dogs convulsed before death. Jones convulsing.

I want to pull him close – ha! – and cover his almost screams with a kiss, only I feel like a damper pedal under a giant foot, stationary, and I realize I am trying to scream but nothing comes out of my mouth. Fat ugly whore swallowing the sky . . . I've just had a man die inside me, his cock still inside me, at least I hope he's dead, and why am I still breathing, air escaping my lungs in little meteor streaks, small spirals of milkshake-through-straw-breaths? Shooting stars are a bonus of stargazing, if I watch the sky on a dark night for half an hour they say I should spot a few brief streaks of light – meteors mined, dog barking in the distance, all I need is a blanket, a clear view of the sky on a dark moonless night, a cool beer, but if I watch too hard I'll never see them. I'm not sure how long we've been up here. It's been more than eight minutes for sure. It feels like eight hours. I see shooting stars now . . .

Someone hits the switch and the piano lowers to the floor. (Shooting stars are grit from space colliding at high speed with air molecules. That's all. What are these?)

"Don't get up." A paramedic peers down at me. They start to carefully pull Jones' body from me. One of them says, "Wait," realizes Jones' penis has been crammed inside me for hours, or however long it's been, and they talk quietly together.

"You'll experience a sudden change of blood pressure when we move him," the paramedic says. They talk again in low voices and I feel another little death as they disconnect Jones from me.

"We have to determine what kind of injuries you have. We'll be flying you to the trauma unit."

"I'm alive?" I feel an irresistible and illogical urge to scream, "Sex is good for you!" That would've made Jones laugh.

"Just relax and trust us, okay?"

"Okay."

"Is he . . .?"

"I'm afraid so. You were damned lucky. He was crushed against the ceiling but his body cushioned yours."

I am riches come through combat. I wonder if Jones kept his football trophies from high school, if they are in a box in a basement somewhere, collecting dust. Grit. The shooting stars are gone.

I'm lucky? My breasts are flattened like pancakes. I think of the girls in Cameroon and I know them now. I know them now. There are tiny indentations from Jones' body and bones and chest hairs on my skin, like a bed of nails has been *lying on me*. I amaze everyone when I sit up and try to walk away. Except I forget about my broken stiletto, and naked, stumble into the arms of a waiting paramedic. "Easy," he says. "Easy." Still, I let them take me to the trauma unit and put me through their tests. Nothing is broken. No other injuries. They prescribe horse pills to ward off any infection that might be caused, say, by having a dead man's penis inside me for eight hours or so. I will try not to think about this later as I sit at my tiny kitchen table in my tiny apartment, eat my Fruity Pebbles with skim milk, drink my tiny darts of black coffee.

A few weeks later and I've finally mustered courage to dance at the club. The night is over and I'm getting ready to leave. I know I'll never dance on top of the piano again. I see the owner of the club talking to a rough-looking man.

"So, this is the infamous piano," he says. With his rough hands, he plays something beautiful on the keys, then shakes his head. "It's out of tune. What a shame."

The piano tuner is like I imagined he would be. Not handsome. Not careful in his appearance. Past his prime. A bit of a belly on him. We lock eyes. And though I'm wearing tight jeans and a tiny white T-shirt that leaves nothing to the imagination, he doesn't spare me or my tits a second glance after he's introduced to the piano. After she spreads her lips for him like a dime whore, he can't look away from her strings, her guts. His jeans are worn, his hands calloused, his knuckles uneven and gnarled. I know I will fuck him until I am pushed so far out of consciousness that I almost won't exist, and the sleepiness afterward, staring at the sky, watching, breathing gulping looking swallowing shooting stars, waiting for something to connect, something that makes sense of accidents. I imagine my buttocks in the air, legs spread wide as he pumps me with his fat cock, those rough fingers spreading me apart so he can examine me as he examines the grand dame piano. I can't explain it. So I won't try. What's there to fix? What is there to be punished for? I am who I am intended to be.

Cristoforo? The Italian count who invented the first piano three hundred years ago? He died in obscurity. Jones will be remembered for some small time to come.

I look at the piano tuner. The piano and the man are the perfect blend of art and physics. In his startling imperfection, he is the most beautiful thing I've seen. He looks like he could take the devil – or a grand piano – in a fistfight. I can't explain it. So I won't.

I stay up. Watch the Weather Channel. Sleep late. The next night, I drive into the canyon, park my dented midnight blue Ford in a patch of grass and sand; the tires settle, send up little puffs of grit. I grab the blanket and beer I've brought and, on foot, climb a little higher.

I spread the blanket under a cavern of domed sky, sit down where the wind drags itself roughly across my face. I open a beer and take the first long, cold sip.

When I was a young girl, my father, before he and my mom split, brought me here. We sat on a blanket like this one and looked up at the sky. "People see stars differently," he said, ruffling my hair with his big hand. "So until you learn the sky, you aren't going to know what you're seeing."

He told me stories about clusters of stars, myths and legends, about groups of young women, sisters, wandering the sky. The sky. A late Gothic painting. In some of the stories, the sisters were lost. Like the Pleiades. Seven sisters. With the naked eye, you can only see six. The seventh, the story goes, the youngest and missing sister, sheds tears that dim the light from her eyes. Or, she cries because all of the sisters except her have married gods.

My father, a man who worked a pharmacy, who scraped slid counted medicines into plastic pill bottles all day, his fingers and the dark hairs on his wrists covered with the fine white powder of pills, taught me about goddess lore and when I was a junior in high school left my mother for a man. The Pleiades are a cluster of stars in the constellation Taurus. Electra is the youngest sister, the one nobody can see. "Maybe once she shone more brightly," my father said. "Maybe once there were seven sisters in the sky."

The seven sisters:

Alcyone – seduced by Poseidon, the god of the sea.

Asterope – raped by the god of war.

Celaeno, seduced.

Electra, seduced.

Maia, seduced.

Merope, married a mortal man.

Taygete, seduced.

I take my clothes off and lie naked on the blanket, absorb the earth's heat. It's like being on the ocean. I listen to the wind's hot breath through ledges of stone, feel it rock and lick my body. Orion is near. My sisters before me knew this. But they ran away from him. I wouldn't have run from a man like Orion.

The earth groans beneath me as if it can sense my thoughts.

Naked, I am time and space and accident, the youngest sister, a cellular memory, a star seduced by a sea god. I imagine Cronus throwing the severed genitals of his father into the ocean, the salt water churning and foaming about them, Aphrodite rising up from the sea foam.

I lift my fingers from between my legs to the sky and trace their forms. The sisters. I listen for their croaky whispers.

Astrologists say the constellation of Taurus rules the throat. I can still taste Jones. See him in the liquid pool of time that is the club. Bosch is pronounced Boss in Dutch. I've never minded being drenched in black light, moving center stage, silvery and animalistic, men's chairs in a circle pointed like stars toward my center. Bouncers like Jones circumnavigating the space. I sit up, sit for a long time until the sky bears the faintest trace of lighter blue, like the veins under a pink tongue, drink beer, get dressed, take a last look at the sky without feeling anything, anything anything, walk back to my car. I grab Jones' shirt off the passenger seat and press it to my nose. He left it at the club and I took it, well, *after*. I wanted something of his. How long before his big, ungainly, male smell fades from the world? I drive down, out of the canyon, with elastic slowness.

I haven't seen a shooting star in years. I wonder, has anyone else?

Shooting stars are grit from space colliding at high speed with air molecules. That's all. And you're a shit if you believe anything else.

Over the next few weeks, I get a tattoo that covers both breasts and meanders down my torso and inner thighs. When I'm naked, it looks like I'm wearing a kimono. I fall in love with pain. And veils. The back seats of taxis. Hypocrisy. People magazine. And Jones all over again.

When I dance, I imagine I'm the corpse of a young African girl; I'm starting to burn. I fly around the village market, frightening the vendors into upsetting their displays of produce as they flee in fear. I am drums, song, food, palm wine. People bring offerings of pineapple, bananas, sugar cane, a live chicken. We all bring what we have.

At the club, a Pygmalion thing standing in the street between an old church and a crack house like a giant erection, men watch me dance, their eyes eager for a flash of wet pussy, their hands eager to squeeze a mound of tit, their dicks straining at their zippers and eager to be sucked. I am, with my hot red dragons burned into my soft flesh, a church of sorts but only in a mathematical sense. Norwegian stave churches have dragons at the tops of their multiple roofs just in case the spirits of Viking ancestors aren't happy with the Christian activities inside. The music changes, the light changes, and now I'm a white heap of cotton waiting to be harvested by long tan fingers of a peasant thinking only of the coolness of a mosque that awaits. A colorful fiber prayer mat with oil spots ground into it. I wash myself in a river of light. God's done waiting for me to fuck up. And if you believe anything different, you're a shit.

I like the taste of men. I like the clumsy, twisted mess of my underwear drawer. The rooms are big here, the ashtrays dirty. Pubic hair clipped down to stubble with a Mohawk along the mons. Nails of electric blue polish part and spread pussy lips. Light harsh and artificial, and I love it. My breasts are burning.

Am I scary? I'm not always pretty. Most of the time I'm not pretty at all. You know, I could be you . . . could be. Here, in this light, where the whole world strains against me.

The Inner Vixen

Saskia Walker

Daniel is kneeling before me. I walk around him, my paces measured, my long leather boots making a quiet but insistent sound as they brush together. They're all I'm wearing. Daniel is stripped to the waist, his arms cuffed behind him. I'm admiring his body, so leanly muscular as he kneels on the floor before me, resting on his haunches, his torso upright and proud. As I consider the fact that he is mine, my willing pet, power plumes through me. As if it were a heady sexual elixir, I thrive on it. My core tightens and my sex grows damper with each passing moment.

His head moves imperceptibly as he watches me, and I revel in his adoring gaze. His cock is hard inside his faded black jeans, but I know he likes that confinement, just as he likes his wrists bound behind his back while I survey him. He's so alert, so taut with restrained desire. I feel it pouring out of him and it empowers me more.

As I walk on, circling him, I reach over, pull a chair close behind him, and sit. Over his shoulder, I see our reflection in the mirror. He's looking too, and it's the perfect image of woman and lover.

I trace one hand down his back. His muscles ripple and I know he's longing for more, for a more vivid assault on his senses: the whip. Making him wait, I sit back in the chair, lift my foot, and rest one stiletto heel between his shoulder blades, edging him forward. He pivots against it and groans aloud, his body arched. I know just how much pain he wants, how much he needs. My body responds to his reaction, heat rising to the surface of my skin. My inner vixen is revving up to full throttle, the essential me – the inner woman that Daniel recognized and introduced me to.

"How did you know that I would respond?" I asked him the night we met.

"I saw her, your inner vixen. I wanted to know her. I wanted to experience her."

So did I.

That's how it began.

We met at an alternative music event. I was there to photograph it for a guide promoting local gigs. I went alone, which I usually did when I was working. I dressed strong, which meant people wouldn't bother me – Doc Martens, black combat pants with a studded belt, cropped sports bra, bare midriff, my tribal tattoos on display.

It was a hot night and heat was rising from the pavement. Inside the pub venue I found the performance room was a large space upstairs, filling fast with the alternative crowd, black-wearing fetishists and goths. I stationed myself by a pillar near the front, where I had a good view of both stage and audience. The atmosphere was already humming with energy when the music kicked off.

I was busy photographing the first band when I became aware of someone watching me. I scanned the crowd. The man caught my eye and, as he did, he acknowledged me, quickly smiling and walking over. All in black, he was a studious type with shaggy hair and a lean, whip-strong countenance.

He ducked in against my head to speak over the music, introducing himself, commenting on what I was up to. "Nice camera, is this a hobby?"

"Started that way. It's work, this time around. I'm photographing the gig for a new music magazine."

He nodded. "I haven't seen you in the scene before."

"I just moved from the other side of London." I nodded my head to the people behind him. "Looks like a fun crowd."

"You better believe it." His smile held so much mischief that I was immediately affected by it.

Looking back at how events unfolded that night, I often contemplate how surprised I would have been if I had known where it was going. I tried not to get too distracted from the job as I answered his questions. There was something compelling about him but I couldn't put my finger on it. Was it because he was looking so attentively at me?

During the gap between the bands I took a break to chat properly. He started to talk about astronomy, of all things. He was intelligent and amusing, and I was quickly laughing, unable to stop enjoying the rapid-fire conversation he initiated. The crowd moved around us, a parade of peacocks, a blur of black, velvet, shiny, metal-studded – a visual feast for the senses. The DJ music between the bands had my pulse racing, or was it because of Daniel's attention and the fact it was all mine? All mine. Like a devotee. Oh, yes, I was hooked, even though I didn't yet know why.

When he made the move, he did it subtly, never breaking his conversation. He reached inside his biker jacket and pulled out a small, soft leather object. He turned it in his hands, attracting my attention to it. I saw that it was a leather head mask. He looked up suddenly, and stopped talking.

He was measuring my reaction to the object he held.

My pulse tripped and then raced on, fascination flickering inside me.

His eyes narrowed, glinting, his smile wickedly mischievous and attractive. I couldn't stop myself from returning it. Behind him I saw that people were looking our way. Part of me wanted to walk away. Whatever game he was playing with me right there at the front of the venue was going to attract attention. But he triggered something inside me, and it was because of his demeanor, somehow respectful, and intrinsically sexy. It tugged at my curiosity, and aroused me.

"Will you lace me in?" He paused, his eyes scrutinizing me as I considered the remark.

Something was unfolding inside me, and it was something big, overwhelming.

I nodded, still smiling. I'd never done anything like this before, but the adventure had me firmly in its grasp. He pulled the mask over his head. It moved easily into place, pushing his hair down and outlining his head starkly. The leather was polished black, reflecting the stage lights as he turned and dipped down to let me tie the laces that ran down the back of his skull to the nape of the neck.

Oh, how that simple act affected me, fuelling me for what was to come.

My camera dangled from my neck as I moved into place. The laces felt good in my hands, and I enjoyed the feeling of control I got when I pulled the soft leather into place. It hugged tightly to his skull, enclosing him. Even though I tried to concentrate on the task, I was acutely aware of my own reaction to it, as well as the attention we were generating from the crowd beyond. People were watching, and somehow that made it all the more arousing.

When I was done, he turned back to me, his eyes twinkling through the peepholes. Incredibly, he unzipped the mouth and continued his conversation as before. The second band came onstage. The singer, a striking punk in leather jeans and a studded corset, strutted the stage as she sang, twin keyboard players behind her moving to the drum and bass sound. Daniel and I shifted to the music at first and then, without warning, he dropped to his knees before me. Resting back on his haunches, he looked up at me adoringly. Laughter escaped me and his eyes twinkled as I reached out and instinctively put my hand on his head. I could almost feel him urging me on. Something certainly was, and I was getting high on the rush it delivered. After I stroked his head, he rubbed it against my thighs in an affectionate, catlike way, first one side, than the other. It was an incredibly sensual thing to do and my pussy was getting hotter and damper all the time. Arousal and self-awareness of the observers affected me strangely. I couldn't quite believe it, and for some reason I couldn't stop smiling. It was different from what I had thought it would be, though, because it felt so . . . right. Something inside of me was responding to him, and it felt good.

"You're diverting attention from the band," I teased, when he stood up, speaking close against his head so he could hear me.

"Ah, but they don't mind, they're friends." He looked toward the stage and as he did I realized the singer had been watching him and she was beaming. She winked at me. I felt welcomed, part of it, and oddly at home.

Daniel reached inside his leather jacket again, his hand resting there. *What would it be this time?* I wondered with anticipation. From the pocket, he pulled out a whip, a cat-o'-nine-tails with its leather strands wound tight around the handle. *A whip.* I watched as he ran the strands through his fingers, untangling them. My heart was pounding. I couldn't imagine where the situation was going next. Just thinking about it set me on a roller coaster of emotions. Over his shoulder, I saw that several members of the audience were completely riveted. Men. Hungry men, with envy in their eyes. Did they think we were together? That we were part of the show?

Before I had time to wonder any more, the singer jumped from the stage and strode toward us as she belted out the lyrics of her song. She took the whip from Daniel and pointed it at the ground. I watched, riveted, as he knelt and curled over. Moving to the music, she thrashed his upper body through his leather jacket. As he pulled the jacket tight I became aware that there was something under it. Daniel was wearing a bondage harness under his clothes. My pussy clenched.

The singer handed me the whip and smiled, before leaping back onto the stage. She hovered at our side of the stage, where the light poured down onto us. There was a moment of fear, a moment of confusion, and then it happened: a rampant urge to do it, to take control, rose up inside me, as if a switch had been tripped. I knew what to do, and why. I stepped over to where he was crouching, looking up at me with expectation. I clenched the handle of the whip, running the strands of leather across my other hand. What would it feel like, whipping a man? My body told me how it would feel: good. Any doubt I had was pushed aside as I reminded myself that he wanted it, and he enjoyed this. So would I.

The audience had created a semicircle around him, and I stepped in front of them, facing the stage. Music pounded in my ears, powering me up even more. My senses were being over-loaded, and yet I was strangely honed and clear-headed. I was in this scene. More than that, I was in control of it now.

Oh God, how good it felt. I was wet, my sex clenching.

I ran the strands of leather across his back, testing it out. The line of his bondage harness was obvious now. As I considered how it might feel for him, and for me, something flared inside me: need, and desire. I thrashed him across the back of one shoulder, then the other, moving in rhythmic patterns. He flinched at each thrash and my pussy gushed. The rush of power I got, heady and deviant, startled me with its intensity. Pleasure ripped through me. I bent down and put my hand under his jacket and T-shirt, grasping for the harness. Pushing my fingers under it, I gripped, applying enough tension so that he would feel it all over his body.

His hands went to the floor, bracing himself, and I knew I had tuned in to something. "You naughty boy," I said with delight against his head.

Shame poured out of him.

I lifted and stepped away from him, returning to my pillar at the stage, the whip dangling from my hand. My heart was pounding. I couldn't believe what I'd just done and, most of all, I couldn't believe the way it made me feel. Daniel rose to his hands and knees and padded over to me, like a pet panther. He stayed by my feet for the rest of the gig, his head rubbing against me affectionately. As I stroked his head in between taking photographs of the band onstage, a feeling of inner calm washed over me. Even though I was still aroused, startled, and confused by my reaction, it was like a feeling of honesty and true realization.

This has empowered me.

The whole experience had been like sex itself, with its arousal, its peak, its transcendence. I'd had no clue I would enjoy dominating a man, whipping him publicly, but I had. And, judging from the adoration at my feet, it was a two-way street.

As the gig ended, the lights went up and everyone was suddenly far too real for me. I didn't want the staring eyes anymore. I needed a drink. I needed space to think through what had happened to me. The band members were with Daniel; he was on his feet, chatting. Maybe if he hadn't been with me, he would have gone to someone else. Whatever his reason for choosing me to approach, it had altered my life. Grabbing my stuff, I headed to the bar downstairs, where I ordered a double shot and downed it quickly. My legs were like jelly as I put down the glass and made ready to leave. Daniel was on his way down the stairs, and the mask was gone.

I wanted to go home and think about it, savor the strange sense of euphoria that had overcome me back there. But if I left now, would I ever see him again? Unsure how far I wanted to go along this path, I headed for the door and out into the street. It had rained and the street was different from when I had gone inside. So was I. I ran up the hill, passing underneath the railway arches toward the station. When I heard his footsteps echoing under the arches behind me, I knew it was him. I stopped and turned back to look at him.

He held up his hands in a sign of peace. "I wasn't going to come after you, but something made me."

I nodded. I wasn't afraid of him; I realized it was me that I was afraid of. The unknown me who had risen up so quickly, so unexpectedly. My inner vixen, as I would later identify her.

"You were so good," he whispered and reached to stroke my arm affectionately.

"Why did you come over to me?"

"I could tell you wanted to play. You did, didn't you?"

He was right, but he had known and I hadn't. That was unnerving. He was still stroking my arms. I noticed that we felt like equals now. In fact, his seductive movement against my skin felt as if he was taking charge of me. Uncertainty reigned. "I have to go."

"Don't go. Don't deny it." He smiled hopefully, but I saw a flicker of regret in his eyes. He thought I was leaving.

"I've never done this before," I confessed, needing him to know that.

He stared at me, and then after a moment he stepped closer, that mischievous smile of his surfacing. With his hands around my upper arms I felt strangely secure, and yet curious and aching for more. A complete stranger had this effect on me? It was because he recognized his opposite in me. The thought crossed my mind, and I didn't reject it.

"Did you want to do it again? Did you want to do more? Somewhere private, perhaps?"

Images flashed through my mind; images brought on by that suggestion, images of fantasies I hadn't ever recognized that I had, but were suddenly growing fast and multiplying in my mind, assailing me with their erotic potential, their absolute promise of pleasure.

"Maybe," I murmured.

We stood there in the gloom of the damp tunnel, with the sound of cars driving down the rainy streets surrounding us. There was no need to say more. When his head dipped and his lips brushed over mine, my inner vixen whispered to me: *Don't turn away.*

I didn't.

I couldn't.

And so here we are, months later, and I am so glad I didn't turn away that night. Reaching down, I unbind him before I grab the whip. The mark of my heel on his back is like the center of a bull's-eye. I use it to focus me, because whipping him gives me such a rush that I need that anchor. When I'm done and he's shuddering with need, I step in front of him.

His forehead rests against my pussy. "Thank you, Mistress."

I feel his breath on my skin, the brush of his forehead across my naked mons. I want him to fill me, physically, as he has filled me emotionally and spiritually. "Lie down," I instruct.

He rolls onto his back, opening his fly, knowing what I want, never once breaking eye contact with me. His cock bounces free, long and hard, oozing. Climbing over him, I lift and lower, taking him inside, my sex hungrily eating him up while my boots bite into his flanks. Looking down at him, I know that what Daniel saw in me may never have been revealed by anyone else, and that makes me snatch at him, my nails driving into his shoulders as I grind down onto his cock. He recognized her in me before I did. He told me he could see her, showing me the real me.

I make love to him fast and hard. Taking him, using him, devouring everything he gives, until his body bucks up under me. He spurts inside me and then I come, with loud and determined force, reveling in the sense of power and release. The inner vixen, risen and reigning supreme.

Matthew, Mark, Luke & John

Alison Tyler

I didn't mean to fuck all of them.

Matthew, Mark, Luke, and John
Guard the bed that I lie on,

I'm generally not that kind of a girl.

Four corners to my bed
Four angels round my head,

If anything, I'm fiercely monogamous . . . or always have
been in the past.

One to watch and one to pray
And two to bear my soul away.

But I'd never tutored four guys before. Never found myself
attracted to four different men at the same time. In my defense,
it simply couldn't be helped. They were each so unique, and so
willing. And once I'd taken one into my bed, I found turning
the next one down too difficult to fathom.

Of course, other people saw the whole situation in a different
light:

"Why in the hell are you taking *that* class?" my mother had
asked sternly, when I'd read off my schedule.

"French? I've always wanted to learn French."

"Not French," she huffed. "The other one."

"Ancient Greek Art?" I tried next, grimacing at the audible sound of her anger steaming through the phone receiver. "You know I was hoping to go to Athens next summer . . ."

"The religious one," she interrupted. "The *Jesus* one."

I'd signed up for the 8 a.m. Christian Iconography class because it suited my schedule, not my spirituality. I was done by 9:30, able to make 10 a.m. French three days a week, and then finished until my late afternoon Art History lecture, which gave me time for my job at a weekly newspaper.

"It's indecent," my mother insisted. "A nice Jewish girl like you, taking a class like that . . ." FIX THIS . . . She wanted indecent? Indecent had nothing to do with the class, and everything to do with my fantasies.

The iconography class was my last choice, but the only one still open by the time my lottery number for class sign-ups was called. I kept reminding myself that it was important to take the appropriate amount of credits each semester. I even pretended that Christian Iconography was bound to be useful in my future life. Although how useful in my future *love* life, I couldn't really appreciate.

Three days a week, I found myself walking down the steep hill from dorm to quad, trying desperately to memorize the various icons we'd been discussing. For a non-practicing Jewish girl, the subject might as well have been in Greek. (Except I was doing fine in Ancient Greek Artifacts.)

"Do you like it?" my mom asked after the first week.

"Sure," I told her. "What's not to like?"

Matthew, Mark, Luke, and John
Guard the bed that I lie on.

I sing-songed the nursery rhyme as I headed into class.

Four corners to my bed
Four angels round my head,

And I took my standard spot at the back of the lecture hall, to-go coffee cup in hand, ready to learn more about art with a Christian perspective.

One to watch and one to pray
And two to bear my soul away.

The truth was, I couldn't focus fully on the slides, or the droning words of the professor. Couldn't focus properly because of my fellow classmates. Well, four to be precise. The handsome jocks in the row in front of me, who always showed up late, and who seemed to have found themselves in this lecture for the same reasons I did – nothing else was available.

I listened to them joking with each other, never saw them open a notebook, never even saw them glance up at the slideshow. And I nicknamed them: *Matthew, Mark, Luke, and John*. The dark-haired "Matthew" was the man. Redheaded "Mark" was the lion. "Luke" had shaved his head, punk-rock style, and sported more than his fair share of tattoos. He was definitely the ox. And "John," the quietest, most delicately drawn, the eagle.

Matthew, Mark, Luke, and John
Guard the bed that I lie on.

In spite of their intrusion into my fantasies, I tried my best. I took copious notes. Created flashcards. Posted assorted images on my bulletin board and over my bed. I was determined to show my disbelieving family that I could ace a class I had no interest in. Although my interest grew the week before mid-terms, when the foursome sent over "John" to ask me a question.

"Study with us?"

"Excuse me?"

"We're rancid at this. Seriously. We lost a bet and had to take the class. I have no desire to take it over again, and even less of a desire to fail without trying. You look like you know what you're doing. Will you study with us tomorrow night? Cram with us. Help us out."

"Group studying has never worked for me," I told him honestly.

"You'd rather do us one on one?"

The way he asked the question made me wonder if he might actually be suggesting something else entirely. But I pretended not to hear the innuendo, and I nodded. "Sure, that would be better." And I watched as he made out a little study schedule for the week we had left. Matthew on Monday and Thursday. Mark on Tuesday and Friday. Luke on Wednesday and Saturday.

"That only leaves Sunday for you," I said.

"I'm the smartest of the four of us," he grinned.

When the first one showed up – twenty minutes late, with a brown paper bag in hand and no backpack in sight – I started to get the feeling that maybe betting on classes wasn't the only gamble this little group took.

"I've got flashcards," I told him, ushering him into my dorm room.

"I've got vodka."

"I don't think that's going to help you pass," I smiled, trying not to sound too condescending.

"But it might help me get *there* – " he nodded toward my bed.

"I heard you lost a bet. That's why you're taking the class."

He nodded. He didn't look the least bit sheepish about this information.

"So you're a gambler?"

Another nod as he opened the vodka.

"Then let's place a bet of our own. You name the items on the flashcards – get at least ten correct – and I'll have a glass of that."

"I didn't bring glasses."

"A swig then," I said brightly. But "Matthew" had other plans. "Let's try this," he countered. "You take off your clothes and lie down on the bed. I'll cover you all over with the flashcards. If I get one correct, I'll take the card away. Until you're totally naked."

"How's that going to help you ace the exam?"

"I'm doomed," he said. "I just want to have a little fun."

Against my better judgment, I stripped down and placed the cards strategically over my body. Matthew turned away, gentlemanly, while I got comfortable. When I was ready, he came up on the bed at my side, gazing at the images on the cards, doing his best to try to remember what each icon represented. He failed miserably, but was such a good sport, that I wound up laughing, giggling, as the cards fell away, and then stopping when I saw him staring at my naked body.

> *Matthew, Mark, Luke, and John*
> *Guard the bed that I lie on.*

The words spiraled in my head as he slid off his own clothes and met me on the mattress.

"Who would have thought Christian Iconography would be such a fucking turn-on?" he growled right before he came.

On Tuesday, I vowed to be better prepared. I had books spread out on the bed, so that there was no chance for foul play, or *fore*play. And I dressed myself in a type of no-nonsense costume – clad in my oldest gray sweats, my dark hair scraped back in a pony tail, my glasses in place. "Mark" didn't seem to notice. He showed up with his backpack, unlike Matthew. But it didn't hold books, a binder, notebook, or even a pencil. Instead, as I watched, in awe, he drew out the sexiest little lingerie set, tags showing that he'd correctly guessed my size.

"I've got this thing for brunettes in black," he said, handing over the lacy outfit. "Especially ones who wear those cute little intellectual glasses like yours."

"Why would I put that on?" I asked him. "We're supposed to be studying."

He gave me an evil smile. "Yeah? Just like you did last night?" And embarrassment flooded through me. "Mark" was handsome, with his long gingery hair and easygoing smile. He located my CD player while I snipped the tags and put on the outfit, and in moments, Pink Floyd came rumbling out of the speakers.

"Don't you want to *try* and study?" I asked.

"You can't teach me half a semester in a night," he said softly.

"We've got two sessions," I tried valiantly. "We could get you a decent score."

He shook his head. "I've got no head for those slides," he said. "And you look good enough to eat in that thing."

Who was I to argue with a lion? He had me up on my desk in a flash, my slim legs spread as he lapped and licked me along the seam of the black satin panties.

Four corners to my bed
Four angels round my head

I saw stars when he made me come, and then he lifted me off the desk, spun me around, and pulled down my sopping panties. He fucked me hard as I stared at the bulletin board over my desk, at the images of angels with their luminous halos, then at the study schedule John had carefully laid out for us. It would definitely take a miracle for these four boys to pass.

But it took much less than a miracle for him to make me come.

Wednesday brought Luke.

And Luke brought pot.

"I thought the pictures would look prettier if we were blasted," he said.

"Prettier, maybe," I agreed, "but I don't think you're going to learn anything."

"Oh?" he asked. "I don't think that's true at all. From what I've heard, you're an excellent tutor."

Once more, I felt myself flush, and that made Luke smile, as if he'd just won an A in a difficult class. I watched as he expertly rolled a joint and lit the tip, inhaling once before handing it over to me. When I shook my head, he gripped the nape of my neck and pulled me close, kissing me and exhaling at the same time, so that my lungs filled with the fragrant smoke.

He was right. The pictures in the books *were* prettier when we were stoned. We looked at all of the lambs. We looked at the ancient frescoes, the colors faded but beautiful all the same. And then we looked at each other and started to laugh.

"I'm usually high in class," he said, "that's why I never take notes."

"You don't take notes because you don't care about anything but punk rock and football."

He studied me for a moment, then grinned. "Sounds like the title to one of our songs," he said, "you're very observant."

I shrugged.

"But have you noticed me watching you?"

"Yes . . ."

"And wondering what you look like under your clothes."

My heart started to race. I'd promised myself that two was my limit. *Matthew* and *Mark*. That I had no room in my bed for three. But I'd lied. "Luke" was persistent. Sweetly stroking me through my jeans before slowly undoing the button fly. The scent of pot surrounded us. And that led quickly to the scent of sex.

Who did I think I was, forgoing studying in place of pleasure? Did I think I could keep up a schedule like this? Truthfully, I didn't think. I tried to plan educational lessons, but for six days, I wound up in bed with my pupils. One after another. I knew I'd feel responsible if these four boys failed the class. But as soon as one had left, I found myself daydreaming about the next.

Sunday should have been a day of rest. Instead, I prepared for John. I found myself wishing that he had been first. Because there was no way I was going to sleep with him. I'd worked my way through the other boys – twice each. They had to have told John what we were up to. And he had the brains of the bunch. He wouldn't give me a second glance now that he knew I'd been with his frat brothers.

Would he?

John seemed prepared to study. He liked my flashcards. He liked my color-coded notes. And he liked the way I kept glancing over the top of my glasses at him. At least, that's what he said.

"And who are these four?" he asked finally.

I must have turned the non-erotic hue of a beet. "Matthew, Mark, Luke, and John," I told him, wondering if he could possibly guess that those were the names I'd given him and his buddies. Monikers I couldn't shake, even when we were fucking.

"And what are these notes about?"

"Each one is represented in a different way," I explained, trying to keep my voice steady. "The man, the lion, the ox, and the eagle."

"Which one am I?" he persisted, and I realized that yes, he was the smartest of the bunch. He'd found me out.

"You can guess, can't you?"

His blue eyes lit up.

"I could guess, but I'd rather have you tell me."

"No," I shook my head. "Match them up. *Matthew. Mark. Luke and John. Guard the bed that I lie on. Four corners to my bed. Four angels round my head . . .*"

There was a knock on the door then, and I felt a change take place in the boy at my side. He slid the notes away. He slowly turned off the desk light. And then he went to the door and opened it, letting in the trio, waiting there for me.

I sucked in my breath. There was no way.

No way . . .

But, of course, there was. The angels, coming in, lifting me up. Setting me down on the floor instead of the tiny twin bed. Taking off my clothes. Wrapping me up in their bodies and their warmth. The man. The lion. The ox. The eagle.

John, taking his time, letting the others prep me before positioning himself on top. Arms tight, pumping hard.

One to watch and one to pray
And two to bear my soul away.

Had I taught them anything?

No. They were the ones who taught me. Giving me the most extreme pleasure in that single evening. Drawing out our actions. Painting pictures with their lips on mine, their fingertips on my skin.

We didn't study at all, but we stayed up all night. Stumbling into class with bleary eyes. Laughing as the exams were passed out. Feeling as faded as one of those old frescoes, but as beautiful.

John laughed when the slides of the four apostles came up.

And I knew he'd get at least one question right. One out of many.

But you want to know all of the test results, don't you?

Well, I won't lie. They failed. One more dismally than the next. With their study habits, they couldn't possibly pass. But that was okay.

You see, it was only a mid-term.

We had plenty of time to cram before finals.

The Unattainable

Livia Llewellyn

. . . one thousand one . . .

There's a dream I once had long ago, a girlish fantasy I'd almost forgotten – and now I'm remembering it again, today of all the lonely days I've lived. I stand alone on the flat dirt of an arena. The flame-eyed stallion stares me down, foam-flecked lips curled back. He rears, slams his weight into the earth: I don't move. I know that by seeming not to see or care, I make myself the unattainable, the thing he longs for most in all the world.

And after time passes, the wild thing approaches, fear subsumed by curiosity. We dance in the empty center, limbs weaving rhythms hesitant, intricate, until I've mounted him. Now I'm astride his wide torso, hot muscles shuddering between my legs. He bucks beneath me, fights my weight against his heart. Yet I hold on, I will his fear to pass.

And it does, because he wants to be under my command, he wants to be broken. But it's only when I've ridden him pain-wracked to the ground, and still he pleads for my touch, do I know I've won. In the calm center of submission, when all that binds him to me are the reins of trust and love, I press against his steaming neck, and whisper in his ear:

"Now you're mine."

Of course, there are no feral things in this world. There are no flame-eyed stallions, no dragons to bestride. Nothing wild exists; and I'm old. Twenty years of bad jobs and nothing to show for it, except to turn tail and run across America, back to my old hometown. I'll fall into the void of my twilight years, and no one will remember me. At least, that's what I'm thinking as I drive the long curve of 97 into I-90. The hills part, and Ellensburg appears in the valley, backlit by the gold of the setting sun.

Twenty years haven't made a difference. College buildings still rise like neo-Gothic queens from the flat expanse, challenged only by the subtle mound of Craig's Hill and the white alien spine of the stadium. Cars stream ahead of me, ruby lights flowing into the town's throat. I roll down the window: hot air rushes over my face in dusty sheets. It's a wide and clean smell, like the scent of my first lover's skin, the night I lost my virginity on a sagging dorm room bed. He was a cornfed stud, thick-limbed and heavy-cocked. I forgot how much I loved that smell, the taste of it in my mouth and lungs. I've forgotten so much, I realize.

Bright hoops of lights shine at the town's darkening edge, candy-colored tops gyrating above houses and trees. They disappear as I drop further into the valley, but now that I've seen them, I know what to listen for. Calliope music, high above the hum of traffic and wind, laced with the roar of a grandstand crowd. The sounds and lights mean the fair is in town, and with the fair comes the rodeo: horses and horn-crowned bulls, and all their men.

Tomorrow I'll cross the Cascades, drive to the house I was born in, slink inside. I'll sit by the window, remember all the things I lost in life because I was always dreaming of something else. This little town below me is the last bead on a necklace that's been falling apart for years – soon it'll slip off with the rest. All I'll have left is the wire that binds me to nothing, except useless childhood dreams.

That's when the old fantasy floods my mind, pushing reality aside. I shift in my seat, trying to shake off the weight of the late-August heat. Sweat trickles under my clothes, pools between my legs. I need a shower. Something wild, that's what I need. A pleasurable ache blossoms inside as I think of cool water, the rough hands of a stone-faced stranger running soapy hands over my breasts, while I lift one leg, guide the red tip of his flesh into—

A burst of horn snaps me out of the daydream. Wincing, I fall back, letting the car I almost back-ended disappear in the traffic ahead. I rub my hands on my dress, clench the wheel and concentrate. And yet, my mind drifts. One thing I never did in Ellensburg, all those years ago. One last bead, one last sparkling jewel. One last chance to catch it before it falls.

Hotel names float through my mind, but they'll probably all be full. It doesn't matter. I already know, wherever I end up, I'm going to stay the night.

. . . one thousand two . . .

Parking on the north campus lot takes half an hour, and the ride to the fairgrounds just as long. By the time I stumble down the shuttle steps, it's that odd hour before twilight, when a thin veneer of silver coats the shadows, sharpening the edges of everything. I pay the price and walk through the gate, stopping to look at the brick-red back of the grandstand. Crowds surge and disappear inside. The bulls will be in the arena tonight, the rankest beasts in the nation. Only eight seconds for each rider to hold on in order to place – but I know too well how eight short seconds can turn into a lifetime.

To my left, Memorial Park has been transformed into the midway, with Tilt-A-Whirls whipping screaming kids through the air. The stately O of the Ferris wheel hovers like a portal to another world. Odors of popcorn and sawdust, barbeque and leather saturate the air. It's like a big family picnic. I feel out of my element, clumsy – a middle-aged woman in a limp cotton dress, trying to get out of everyone's way. Wandering through the stalls, my eyes fix on men young and old. Men with children, men with wives and girlfriends, men with their buddies and friends. Stetsons and Levis, clean-shaven faces and light-colored button-down shirts. All of them, with some-one. A couple walks past, high school kids. The boy's hand is hooked into the girl's jeans, revealing smooth, tanned skin. Her hand rests on the back of his neck, playing with strands of hair. They're in love.

In a panic, I slip to the side of a cotton candy stand, away from everyone. What was I thinking? I don't belong here. This little fair isn't the Puyallup, where the midway blots out half the sky, where crowds of ten thousand clog the grounds. I could get lost there, unseen in the crush. But here, I stand out for what I am. A big-boned woman on the make. Floozy. Whore. Inside my dress pocket, the grandstand ticket crumples into a tight ball. Somehow it slips to the ground as I walk away.

A volunteer tells me where the exhibits are. She also points me to the beer garden – the look in her eyes tells me this is a woman who knows about the booze, because she'll be hitting it after the midway shuts down. I thank her and move on, determined to reach the stock barns before they close. Maybe I'll find someone there, some dirty stable hand who won't mind five minutes of humping in a cobwebbed corner with a desperate woman on the run from herself. It's a depressing thought, but it keeps me going.

I pause at the race track surrounding the stands. Behind the high chain-link fence, a horse approaches at bridle pace, the rider steering her down the dirt. A rush of noise from the grandstands, drowning out the announcer's metallic voice. Did someone get thrown, or did they win? I turn away, just as the cowboy catches my eye. Not that I wasn't looking. But it's the horse that makes me pause – a roan, glossy and tall, perfect form. She's a wonder, and when the boy hears my gasp of pleasure, he smiles.

Yeah, a boy. Barely out of his teens, so bright and flush with youth that it hurts to stare at his face. Yet when he winks, I blush and grin like a little girl. He's not my type, he's far too pretty and young, but I'll take what I can get, nowadays.

"She's beautiful," I say. The horse tosses her head, dark eyes looking me over from under a fringe of hair. *I don't submit*, her mouth implies, firm against the bit.

"Don't let her know that," the boy replies, as he steers her over to the fence. "She thinks too much of herself."

"May I?"

"Sure. She's gentle." The boy watches as I stroke the long muzzle, his eyes never leaving me.

"You do know you're headed in the wrong direction," he finally says. "Rodeo entrance is that way."

I point in the opposite direction. "Yes, well, the beer garden's that way." The boy laughs, and touches his hat.

"Well, ma'am, maybe I'll see you there later."

"I highly doubt it. You don't look old enough to drive."

"I'm driving her, aren't I?"

Now I laugh. "Oh, I think you have it backwards."

The boy winks. "Believe me, I'm old enough to do a number of things. I just might prove that to you later on." He guides the roan away, leaving me rolling my eyes even as I revel in the flattery. Turning away, flustered and unseeing by my small victory, I run smack into—

The words freeze on my tongue. The man standing before me stares me down with a face so sharp and cold, it's like being punched with black ice. By the time I've caught my breath, he's slipped into the crowd. People push past as I stand transfixed, shivering in the heat. All I remember of the face under the dark Stetson reminds me of Mount Everest, in the black slits of his eyes, the weathered angles and peaks of his profile – a face I could kill myself on. And why I should care to remember what he looks like, I don't want to think about. Yet, I can't stop.

At some point I'm moving again, although I don't know what my destination is, or what will happen when I arrive.

. . . one thousand three . . .

I can't see the land around us, when his truck finally stops. But I know I'm near Kittitas, the small town just east of Ellensburg. I found him in the barn with the Black Angus bulls, and it took longer than eight seconds to get his attention. Yet somehow I convinced him, made him take pity on a woman with no home, no place to stay the night. So when the floodlights dimmed and the gate closed, he let me follow him out of Ellensburg and down quiet roads to his home – a small white bungalow surrounded by large trees and endless clear sky.

I cut the engine. As it ticks the heat away, silence blankets me, the kind found only between mountains, in the sleeping valleys and plains. It's like someone just took the pillow off my face, and let me breathe again.

He's already out of the truck, a large sheepdog groveling at his feet. A peaceful pleasure radiates from his face, erasing the sharpness of years. I watch him caress the dog's soft ears. Goosebumps and prickling nerves, like my skin is on fire, like my first date in high school – I never thought I'd feel that way again. I grab my bag and get out of the car. I'll make him forget about that dog, if only for this night.

Following him across the dirt drive, I walk up several steps to a sleeping porch. Face hard again, he opens the door, motions me inside. I slip past, feeling a bit like I'm trespassing. Honestly, I didn't think I'd get this far. He drove to his house so fast, I was chasing him most of the way.

"Have a seat." As I perch on a worn brown couch, he hangs his hat up, runs his hands through his hair. Without the wide felt curve framing his eyes, he loses a bit of the severity. He wipes his palms on his jeans, stares at the floor. One boot rubs at something invisible. Is he nervous?

"Beer?"

I nod, and he disappears into the kitchen. I sit for a minute, all polite and mannered, then decide he's giving me a chance to snoop. So I circle the room, gleaning for clues. What kind of man is he? Well, he's not stupid. The bookcase next to the TV set is full. I run my fingers along the spines: Pynchon and Kerouac sit next to McCarthy. Below them sits a shelf of thick technical manuals on agriculture. Several posters hang on faded cream walls – country landscapes, an Ansel Adams photo of the Rockies. No photos of him, though – nothing personal at all. I still know nothing about him, other than that he wants me here. I think, that is. If he wants to fuck, he hasn't shown much interest.

"You a reader?"

He stands in the doorway, beers in hand. There's a look on his face – amusement? Well, I can't pretend I wasn't snooping.

"Not much anymore. I got rid of most of my stuff when I had to move. The books were the first things to go."

He doesn't reply. Anxious to keep the conversation going, I slide one of the manuals out from the shelf.

"*Guidelines for World Crop and Livestock Production.* Light reading?"

"I'm not a light reader." He sets a beer onto the coffee table with a thump. The conversation on books is over, it seems. Frustrated, I sit back down on the couch. He returns to the edge of the door and takes a long pull from the bottle, his eyes never leaving me. I drink my beer, feeling self-conscious. It's like he's sizing me up, the way he'd size up a horse before deciding if it was worth the ride. It's a territorial stare.

Gathering up my courage, I stare back. His hair is longer than I thought, but there's also more grey in it than I noticed before. Dark brown eyes, and fine lines running from nose to mouth. My age, maybe older. Not beautiful, but compelling. His mouth *is* beautiful, I decide. Not the plump wet lips of a boy, but hard and dry, experienced – the mouth of a man. A sudden urge to feel that mouth moving over my breasts, between my legs, sends a violent shudder through me.

"Cold?"

"No," I mumble, playing with the label on the bottle as a blush warms up my cheeks. He saw me stare, knows why I shivered. Time to act coy. "I'll need sheets for the couch, though."

He shoots me The Look. I know that look. It's a sardonic half-smile, accompanied by raised eyebrows and the slightest of eye-rolls. It's the look my mother used to give me when I lied about not touching myself. I knew he wasn't going to make up the couch, that I wouldn't be spending the night there. We both knew it. And so he gives me The Look. It's like waving a red cape before a bull. I sit up, back stiff, face tense.

"What." It's not a question. It's a challenge.

He says nothing. Now it's a contest. But my impatience makes me crack. I keep my voice light, but I can't disguise the anger.

"What? What did I say that's so amusing?"

He shakes his head. "Please. You didn't follow me all the way out here just for my couch."

"Well, I didn't follow you out here because I'm a slut, if that's what you mean." I spit the words out like bullets. My mistake. His whole body shifts, like a snake's casual recoil before striking.

"Don't pull that shit on me." His low voice oozes polite menace. I ignore it.

"What shit is that? Enlighten me, please."

"Acting like you don't know why you came here. You're far too old to pretend you don't know what's going on." A slight twang has entered his tone, a bit of the country. I'd laugh if I wasn't so unnerved by him – yet I can't stop goading him. Fucking up my life overcomes my fear, every single time.

"Well. If I'm too old to understand you, then I guess I'm too old to fuck. Problem solved." I sit back and pound the rest of the beer.

"Put that down, bitch, and get over here. I don't have all night." He eyes his watch. "Some of us actually work, you know."

That's it.

"Fuck you!" I slam the bottle down and grab my bag. It's only five steps to the door, but I don't make it. All of a sudden he's just *there*, arms around me, same way he's probably done it a thousand times with animals wilder and stronger than me. As he spins me around, covers my face in hard kisses, I'm surprised by how good it feels to be grabbed, to be handled. There's no poetry in it, it's all need. I still want to hit him, but I was oh so right about those lips of his, and my whole body rocks with the desire to fuck him. He slams me against the door – I match the grind of his hips, panting as I spread my legs, rub my crotch against the hard bulge in his jeans. But when I reach for his zipper, he breaks away and drags me across the room, hand clamped firm on my arm. I stumble behind, lips and cheeks burning from his rough stubble, as if a ghost of him remains locked against my face.

The bedroom is dark, and he keeps it that way. The moon is bright, though, and I see everything: hard muscles, beads of sweat, the flame-red spark of his eyes . . .

. . . one thousand four . . .

There's no foreplay. He takes off his clothes with absolute economy of movement, while I let my dress fall to the floor, pushing it aside in a flowered crumple. I fall back on the bed, but I'm barely off my feet before he's crouched over me. Two thumbs hook into my panties, and they're ripped apart, gone. He's not looking at me, not touching me, not caressing me. I'm not here.

In the dim light, I see the ragged line of a scar across his lean stomach, glowing white against tan. It reminds me of that last sliver of light above the mountains, before the sun disappears. He spreads my legs wide, then places a hand against my shoulder, as if he thinks I'll bolt. He's not wrong. This isn't what I wanted, though – he's in complete control, there's no taming of anything happening here. Straining my neck, I catch a quick glimpse of his cock, long and hard as he strokes it, before he lowers and blocks my view. I close my eyes, grimace as he enters me. One expert stab, and I'm pinned to the sheets like a butterfly on wood. A gasp of pain escapes my mouth, but the hint doesn't take. He's fucking the hell out of me, and he won't slow down. But he doesn't make a sound – no grunts or groans, nothing to indicate pleasure.

The speckled ceiling overhead catches moonlight from the open window. I watch shadows dance in tiny patterns but they can't distract from the pain. I raise my arms, thinking if I put my hands against his chest, he'll slow. The movement triggers a violent reaction: he grabs my wrists and holds them against the mattress. I kick out, but he ignores me, probably doesn't even feel the blows. His cock pumps in and out, methodical and sure. Instinctive, against my will, my hips arc up in slight thrusts. My traitorous cunt contracts, grows slick. The pain doesn't lessen, but it doesn't grow worse. I'm not thinking of the ceiling anymore.

He presses down harder, crushing my breasts. Sweat trickles from his hot skin to mine, and I smell him, sharp and musky. A foreign scent, not unpleasant. He buries his head into my neck and hair. Hot breath floods over my skin as his mouth moves against me, murmuring some strange language I can't hear. Fear and anger dissipate, replaced with slow wonder. He's gone, somewhere so far away that I can't follow. Does he see me there? Am I in that dreamscape of his? He chose me. Even with that face, those dagger eyes, he could have had anyone. He wanted me. But, he's not with me.

"Stop," I say. He doesn't, and I try again. "Just stop for a second. Where are you?"

His sudden grab at my face is the last thing I expected. Two large hands hold my head tight. His lips brush mine as he speaks.

"What are you talking about?"

"Wherever you are, I'm not there. I'm right here."

He doesn't answer, only sighs before thrusting in again, like an engine that can't stop. I struggle against him, trying to keep him still, but he's too strong. He pushes down, pinning my arms between the both of us.

"You're hurting me," I say.

"Then make me stop. What are you afraid of? I can take it." The intensity of his words, the clotted growl of need and desire confuses me. Now I'm the one with no answer. Does he want me to punch his face, twist his balls until he does what I say? That's not my fantasy.

"Please, just slow down a little."

"Make me."

"What?"

"*Make me.*" Pleading.

This is unsettling. "I can't *make* you. You're twice as strong as me."

"Goddamn, you're stubborn." Is he laughing at me now, or is it from despair?

"Fuck you. I'm not livestock. You can't break me."

"I've broken everything." Desolation and sorrow in his voice, so deep I don't think he even knows they're there.

"You can't break me," I repeat, voice cracking. Tears well in my eyes, but I refuse to cry. "You won't win."

A moment of silence. Then, out of the dark:

"I always win."

His mouth covers mine, tongue sliding inside. Protestation forms in my throat, but it dissolves. His cock demands my full attention, hammering away as if it had never been interrupted. God, it's so painful, and it feels so good. I can't help it – it's the way he moves his hips, the way the base of his cock and coarse hair rubs up against my clit, the slick pole of flesh filling me up.

A perfect fit, like he was born for me. My nails dig into his back, barely able to keep a grip, mouth biting his shoulder as I come, thunderstruck into stiff spasms. A few more thrusts, and he stops – abrupt and matter-of-fact, like he lost interest. He rests on me, our hearts pounding in time together, with my muscles wrapped so tight around his cock, he couldn't leave me if he tried. All that, and he never uttered a single moan. He never came.

His head lies against my shoulder, breath light and untroubled. Do I dare? With the lightest touch, I caress his damp hair – a cautious attempt to show warmth. But the moment he feels it, he lifts up and pulls out of me, then rolls over, curling against the side of my body like a child.

He's asleep.

. . . one thousand five . . .

I stare at the ceiling. Beyond the roof of the house, stars run across the cloudless valley sky in silent flight. Everything sleeps below, dreamless and deep – horses and horn-crowned bulls, and all their men. Everyone safe at home, except for me. My hand creeps down to the matted hair, the throbbing folds of flesh. No one's ever fucked me as hard as he did, but I've never come like that before. I think of waking him, hoping he'll slide his arms around me, hold me tight – but the thought of his impersonal brutality keeps me still. And why didn't he come? Why did he fuck me with such violence, and for no apparent pleasure of his own, save that he could?

Well, that must have been the point: the bastard could. Leave it alone, I think. Let him sleep, before he wakes up and beats me to pulp. I was lucky he didn't – I haven't been so lucky in the past. Rolling away from him, I slide the edges of the sheet over my worn flesh. I shut my eyes, concentrate on the wind in the trees, the passing of the stars.

But the hours drag, marked by electronic ticks of a digital clock on the bedstand beside me. I can't sleep, and now I have to pee. He hasn't moved, except to slip one foot over mine as he sinks further into dreams. If I get up, I'll wake him. But I really have to go, so I move, trying not to rock the bed as I pull my hair from under his head. He shifts, says nothing. I don't look back to see if he's awake, as I creep into the pitch-black bathroom. Only when the door's shut do I fumble for the light switch, and let out a sigh of relief.

The bathroom is sparsely decorated, much like the rest of the house. Under the glare of the light, I sit on the toilet and stare at the plain shower curtain, the half-curled tube of toothpaste on the counter, a chipped glass holding a single splayed-bristle toothbrush. Nothing on the walls except a mirror over the sink, and a small wreath of dried roses and crumbling greens. Not something a man like him would have bought in a million years. There was a woman here, once.

Flushing, I hobble to the sink and run the water till it's lukewarm. Wetting the corner of a bath towel, I pass it between my legs, ignoring the pain. It'll pass. In less than a day, I'll be home, and this will all be a distant memory, just another foolish, fucked-up dream –

I pull the towel away. The dull ache pulses like a second heartbeat. It's blood, rushing through all the secret places he once was. It's all I have of him, the pain of where he filled me up, where he left me. Do I want to erase it so quickly?

I empty the chipped glass and fill it with water. As I drink, my reflection catches my eye. The woman staring back is a strange but familiar one – the young girl of my past. A quick-silver ghost, fine-lined around the eyes and mouth, but all the more beautiful for ageing. A pale face, surrounded by messy brown hair, red-tinged cheeks where his stubble burned the skin off, and a bright sheen drifting across dilated pupils. A drop of water hangs from my swollen lower lip. Is this what he sees? I imagine him standing behind me, hands cupping my breasts, mouth pressed against one shoulder in soft worship – an image so strong, I glance to my side to see if he's really there. I look back at the mirror.

What I could be, with him. If I want it to be.

"Stop it, Katherine," I whisper. "It's just another dream."

But the image, the feeling, remains.

. . . one thousand six . . .

A knock at the door – the image dissolves. "I'll be just a minute," I start to say, but he's already opening the door.

"You alright?" He looks up and down my body, his face neutral.

"I'm fine. I was thirsty."

"Took long enough." He gestures, indicating that he wants in. I let him take the glass as I sidle past him, careful not to indicate my impulse to run.

"Don't fall asleep," he says before closing the door. I notice he keeps it open a crack. The thin line of light guides me across the mattress to the headboard, where I curl up and listen to the sounds of running water. Night pours in through the window like a river, in the rustling of leaves, the distant howl of a dog. The light flicks out, and I sigh. I don't want this again, all this rough handling, the impersonal stabbing of flesh. My heart pounds, unmoored and drifting – I curl up tighter, afraid it'll break through my ribs and float away.

He moves across the room, graceful and invisible. My body senses him standing over me, staring. I'm clutching myself like a child hiding in the closet from the monster outside. I want to shout *no*, my muscles ache, I'm battered and bruised. I want to cry, having him kiss the tears away. But he won't. He lowers.

The second time is like nothing I expected.

My hair slides back from my face – he's caressing it in careful strokes as he tucks it behind my ears. My eyes have adjusted, and I see all the sharp angles of his face softening. One finger traces my jaw line, moves up to my lips. His other hand rises – I brace myself, but don't turn away. His fingers suss out a length of hair, separating and smoothing it into three pieces. Something catches in my throat as I recognize what he's doing. He's braiding my hair, gently working the pieces into a single plait. His touch is comforting – inch by inch my legs unclasp, fall against his. Together we sit, heads bowed. Static crackles, and he licks his fingers before slicking the unruly strands down. My mother used to do that.

When he gets to the end, he ties it off – a hard and neat knot my fingers wonder at, while he turns my head and starts another braid. I shift closer, draping one leg over his. His knee rests against my cunt, soothing to the sore flesh. My left hand lowers onto his thigh, casual. He doesn't push me away. Inch by inch he works the plait, and I glide my palm up to the dark center, where he's all silky curves and tight curls. My fingertips find a home in the tangle of hair right at the base of his cock.

He ties the knot, then runs his hands over my face. Heat flares inside my cunt. His knee shifts, and I press against it, leaving his skin wet. He thrusts his hands into my hair, grabbing the braids, drawing me in. I don't have to see to know where his lips are – I draw his hot breath in on a sigh, let it seep back from my mouth to his.

"Don't go," he whispers. "Don't go." Each word is a kiss, a sigh, a plea.

"I'm not going anywhere." Inside, my heart sinks. Is he going to start this all up again? But his response surprises me.

"Don't go home." More kisses, and his hands drop to my waist, running over the wide curves. "Stay here."

"I can't stay, I have to get home –" The sentence trails off, disappearing in the other conversation between our lips.

"Your home's not there." His words are cruel, and true. Firm palms slide up to my breasts, where his fingers and thumbs begin rolling my nipples into stiff points. "You're running to nothing."

I have no answer, for him or myself. Just let him have his say. It's worth it. My hand travels up his hardening cock, to the plump tip. I rub at the small hole, working silky liquid out over the soft skin. He gasps, but shifts away, his cock sliding out of reach. Lips move to my nipples, then lower. As I fall back onto the pillows, his wet mouth courting my cunt into delicious submission, it finally sinks in: this is a competition. An event. He's going to make me come like the animal I am, then walk away before I can give him one second of pleasure: because he's the one in control. And I'll be left naked in the dust, pleasure and pain ringing my bones like bells.

I've broken everything. I always win. Isn't that what he said?

He wraps himself around me, sinks into me, and once again I drown. He doesn't come, and he won't tell me why. Hot tears and pain follow the orgasm; but this time he holds me, rocking me like a child as the night bleeds into pink dawn. Exhausted, liquid-limbed, I sink into delicious half-sleep, floating through fragments of dreams. The land lies all around me: I am the Cascades, ice-capped peaks covered by his star-shot skies. And somewhere in between, three words thread their way through us, a radio whisper of the heart drifting from one slumbering body to the other. *Let me submit.* I reach the black lands of sleep, a frisson of fear pushing its way in with me, as I realize I don't know where the words came from – from me or him, from the mountains or the sky.

. . . one thousand seven . . .

Sunlight and birdsong. Before I stretch out, open my eyes, I can tell he's already gone. The wake of his leaving fills the whole house with bittersweet calm.

A thin plaid robe lays on the edge of the bed. It wasn't there last night. Folds pressed into the fabric tell me it hasn't been worn in years. I slip it on, and raise a sleeve to my nose. His faint scent clings to the fabric. I smell him on my skin as well, and in my hair. My tongue glides over my lips. He's there, too.

I pad through the living room, reverent this time, as if I'm in church. The windows are shut, and dust motes hang in the air like dead stars. From the kitchen, a clock ticks out the seconds. I follow the sound. Midday sun drenches the room, bleaching the curtains white. I smell coffee and the sulphur whiff of eggs. A mug sits next to the pot – I pour a cup and lower myself into a chair, still a bit stiff from last night. I don't feel bad, though. I haven't felt this calm, this balanced, in years.

He left a note and a map on the table, under a candy-red apple. I slide the note toward me, and read. Neat cursive letters in blue pen rest on the lines:

Working the fair today. There's a plate for you in the oven.
Take what you need from the fridge.
I'll be home around eight.

A plate in the oven – I swing around, catch the handle and open the oven door. Warm air hits my face. A plate covered in aluminum foil sits on the rack. I grab a dish towel and pull it out, peel the foil away. Bacon, eggs and toast. He made me breakfast.

I pour another cup of coffee, and start to eat, staring at the note all the while. No "thanks for everything", no "it was great". Well, it's not his way. I unfold the map. He's drawn a dotted red line from the middle of nowhere, through Kittitas up to I–90. A note, an apple, and the way out. After all his protestations, he wants me gone. He wants me –

"Home," I say to the ticking clock. But the word doesn't sound right anymore. Maybe because, when I think of home, I don't know what it is I'm supposed to see.

My dad once told me that no man could live in an oasis. He could stop and drink, rest a bit, but then he had to move on, find his way home. This is only an oasis, I say as I wash the dishes and place them in the plastic rack. It was a place to lay in the shade, away from the burning sun. I stand in the shower, curtain open, staring at the wreath on the wall. It was only a place to get a little rest, before pushing on. The braids grow fat with water, and I don't undo them. My eyes blur – from the soap. I smooth down the sheets and plump the pillows, pressing each soft feather mound to my face before laying it on the bed. He'll sleep on them tonight.

I have to go.

I could have snooped through all his things, but I don't. He deserves better from me. But on the way out, I peek into the second bedroom, unable to resist. A flick of the light switch reveals boxes and cartons, an old steamer trunk, musty sheets covering tables and chairs. I lift a sheet, revealing a short bookcase. Trophies, plaques and ribbons, all proclaiming the same thing for the same event. *FIRST PLACE. FIRST PLACE. FIRST PLACE.* The dates – he won some of these in Ellensburg, the same years I lived here. We fought and bled and slept in the same little town, under the same starry skies. I let the sheet drop.

An open box sits high in a pile – I pull it down, and flip through a series of photos in cheap frames. A young man, jet-black hair framing a stern and determined face, riding bull after massive bull. Behind him sits a sea of faces: judges and grandstand crowds, with floodlights shining down on man and beast. Odd to see so much power and rage, muted behind framed glass. In one photo, the bull's kicked back so high, his hind legs are higher than the rider's head. But none of the photos show the rider falling. He's marking out his eight seconds, every goddamn time. The rage in the photos is the rider's, not the bull's. This is a man who always wins, who never lets go of the reins.

And yet he let go of me.

I pack the photos into the box, and balance it back on the pile. I'm careful to close the door behind me, just like it was before. My watch says two o'clock, I have to be on the road. A good six hours of driving are ahead of me, and I want to cross the pass before dark. The lights are off, the windows shut, and everything's tidy in the kitchen. I take the note and the map, leave the apple behind. I struggle to lock the front door, then realize it doesn't, and probably never did. There's no need for it out here. Amazing.

Throw the bag on the seat, rev the engine, and don't look back. It feels good to be on the road again, to be free. So it didn't turn out quite like I planned – when did anything? Buildings whoosh past in a blur as I speed through Kittitas, up to I–90. It was an adventure, something I'll remember when I'm old, when there's nothing else left to remember. One last bead from the string, flame-bright like the eyes of some rough stranger, caught in the palm of my . . .

. . . I stand by my car. It's parked on the lookout, a half-oval of dirt next to the highway, high above the valley. From here I see Ellensburg, see the glimmer of the Ferris wheel, the sparkle of windows and headlights caught in a late afternoon sun. Kittitas lies to the east, green jewel in a strand of ancient land left scrubbed by the Cordilleran floods. To the left sits Cle Elum, another small tree-dappled town. And in between, rivers of roads, a patchwork of farms and ranches. The land teems with life from the horizon's edge up to the snowy Cascades. This is no oasis. It's an empire.

I'll be home around eight, the note in my hand says. I've been staring at it for three hours now, almost four. My skin burns from the sun. *I'll be home*. He's a careful man, economical with words. That much I know to be true. Three things he wrote that I needed to know, and left the map for leaving. What purpose, then, in telling me when he'll be home? Why should I care if he's home around eight? That's when I'm supposed to be back. I won't make it now. He's won again. Has he ever lost?

Night's closing in. The sun's still high, but the light's changed. I look beyond the mountains and see nothing, feel nothing. The only thing I feel is in my hands – on a slip of paper, in a single cryptic sentence. Turning around, I reach through the open window and pick up the map. A dotted red line with two round ends. The circles look like the eyes of a bull, burning through paper streets. An animal who's always won, who's never been allowed to surrender. What would his fantasy of love be, then? What would be the unattainable for him?

Let me submit.

Traffic's a bitch. The fair's closing, and horse trailers and RVs clog the streets. I inch my way through Ellensburg to Kittitas Highway, then gun the motor till I'm back at the house, tires spraying gravel across the scraggly lawn. The windows glow pumpkin orange from the setting sun. Early evening winds whip the braids across my face as I unlock the trunk, root through boxes. At the bottom: thin leather straps and bronze workings, attached to six erect inches of polished wood. I could be wrong. What if he hits me – or worse? The note is damp with sweat. I clutch it, pray I'm right as I stumble up the steps into the house.

Everything's as I left it. I open the windows, turn on a light. He'll see my car, I can't hide. I don't want to. Let him know the rider is ready, the event's already begun. I leave the bedroom dark. By the light of the setting sun, I slip off my clothes, strap the harness around my hips, and climb onto the middle of the bed.

The clock ticks, the wind sighs. Shadows stretch across the room. I wait, patient – the apple my feet. The clock hands near eight. An engine, faint in the distance, growing nearer, until it throbs through the open window, then cuts. I don't breathe.

Footfalls against the earth, running. The slam of the door, the pound of boots against wood. He's rushing down the hallway, down the chute –

. . . one thousand eight . . .

There's a dream I had long ago, a girlish fantasy I'd almost forgotten – and now I'm remember it again, tonight of all the lonely nights I've lived. I wait alone on the flat white plain of the arena. My flame-eyed stallion stares me down, lips curled back in rage or shock: I am unmoved. Arms outstretched, erect, I look away. I know that by seeming not to see or care, I make myself the unattainable, the thing he longs for most in all the world.

And after time passes, the wild thing approaches, shy fear subsumed by curiosity, kissing my hands, my feet. I wipe the sweat from his skin, run my fingers over his body, passion flowing where once only loneliness lived. We dance in the empty center, bodies weaving rhythms hesitant, intricate – until, slowly, gently, I've mounted him. Now I'm astride the lean torso, hot muscles shuddering under my legs. He bucks beneath me, fights the pain, fights my weight against his heart. Yet I hold on, I will his fear to pass.

And pass it does, in the shower of pearl-studded pain: because he wants to be under my command, he wants to be broken. But it's only when I've ridden him pain-wracked to the ground, and still he pleads for the pleasure of my touch, do I know I've won. In the calm center of submission, when all that binds him to me are the reins of trust and love, I press against his tear-streaked neck, and whisper in his ear:

"*Now you're mine.*"

Late for a Spanking

Rachel Kramer Bussel

Laura is late. There's no escaping the fact that the clock tower outside my apartment has just loudly chimed six and my spankee has yet to show. I walk around my bedroom, running my fingers over the implements I've set out in preparation. There's a tiny slapper, a small, patent-leather nothing of a toy, one whose bark will always be worse than its bite. There's a ruler, an extra-long, coated one, for maximum impact. There's a shiny black paddle, stern and strong, like me. There's one with fur on one side, for when I want to soothe her, or just lull her into a false sense of security. There's a strap, my belt, a wooden paddle. I probably won't use them all on her, but I like to have them ready, just in case.

I pace around, trying not to get too angry. Our spanking dates are about fun, about mutual enjoyment as she bends herself over my knee or splays herself across my lap. Sometimes I sit in a chair, completely clothed, while she strips before me and then lies down, her long, black hair brushing the floor. I have to wait for her to become totally still; she's that perfect blend of nervous and excited that makes her body gently hum and quiver.

I pick up the strap and slap it against my hand. The noise and sting bring me back to earth. I look at the clock and see another ten minutes have passed. We've talked about this countless times; I've tried to instill in her the importance of punctuality, not just when she's meeting me, but generally. It's rude to be late, it insults the person you're meeting by prioritizing your schedule over theirs. She always nods contritely, and I give in to her, even though once I almost sent her home without her dear spanking. My cock was pleading with me to go through with it, though, and I did, though the lesson might've sunk in more had I been a stronger man.

My dates with Laura are about spanking and spanking only. You see, even though I'm dominant to the core, I'm in love with a sassy, whipsmart submissive named Evangeline. She knows she's got me wrapped around one of her tiny, delicate little fingers, and I actually like it that way. On the surface, I call all the shots, telling her when she can and can't wear panties, supervising her nipple piercings, exerting control whenever and wherever I can. I know it makes her wet when I give even the slightest command. "Spread your legs farther apart," I'll whisper in her ear on a crowded subway train. She'll turn and give me an infuriated, but utterly aroused, grin, as she does it. She's only playing at being mad because now her panties will be wet, her pussy seething, her mind racing for the rest of the day as she wonders what else I'll tell her to do later that night.

We have an open relationship, but the door isn't flung all the way wide. We keep it partly cracked, just ajar enough so other women, like Laura, can get in and get the spankings and punishments they, and I, crave. But, horny as they make me, Evangeline has forbidden me from fucking them. I've managed to work that energy and want into my scenes, even though it's sometimes very hard to resist those wet pussy lips I'm allowed to stroke but not enter. Laura's the worst of all, the biggest temptation, and sometimes she gets spanked extra hard because otherwise I just don't know what to do with all the pent-up arousal. Evangeline wins too because when she comes over after I've played with Laura, I fuck her so hard she can feel it for days afterward.

I finally sit down on the bed, my hand lightly resting on my crotch. There's no real way to simulate spanking a pretty, willing, needy girl's ass when you're by yourself. Watching videos just doesn't quite do it for me; I need flesh and blood, I need to hear her beg, I need to look down at her face and see the answers written across her features. At six forty-five, my doorbell finally rings. I have to admit, I've pretty much given up on her ever showing up. Maybe we'll never see each other again, and while

I'll be disappointed, what can I do? So I'm partly surprised, partly aroused, and partly annoyed when I open the door to see her standing there blowing her sweaty bangs up off her face, looking contrite and bedraggled but still goddamn sexy. She's pushing thirty but dresses like a schoolgirl – literally. She has on a pleated plaid skirt, strategically ripped fishnets, big black platform shoes, and a skimpy little white tank top and no bra, letting anyone who cares to look see the twin barbell piercings adorning her nipples. Her hair is in two braids, black eye makeup smeared around her eyes, red lipstick emblazoned across her mouth. Those lips are so tempting, even more than her ass; I've had many a fantasy about sinking my cock between them, letting her do what I'm sure she's brilliant at.

Just the way she makes her sorry face, her mouth open, eyebrows up, hip cocked, makes me want to fuck her. Since I can't do that, I let my annoyance show. "What took you so long?" I snap, blocking her entrance with my body, even though part of me longs to grab her and give her a hard, solid kiss.

"The train was delayed, and I forgot something in the house . . ." she seems to be making excuses, her voice getting whiny. When she looks up at me, her eyes blaze both apology and defiance. I know she hadn't been deliberately late so that I'd spank her harder; we don't need to play those kinds of reverse psychology mind games. She's genuinely tardy, as Laura often is; she just assumes whoever's waiting will be patient and forgive her. All her friends have gotten used to it, considering themselves on "Laura time" when they're meeting her. Even I, for the most part, have adapted, but our spanking dates are special. I've made it clear that she's to treat them with the utmost importance and care, if she's truly dedicated to our play.

Just because she wasn't late on purpose, though, doesn't mean she's above trying to tease me into going easy on her. She steps forward, pushing me until I relent and let her inside. Then her hand goes automatically to my cock. "Miss me?" she asks with a smirk as she massages my dick. The rules of our relationship are clear; I can spank her, and we can be naked together, but Evangeline doesn't want me touching her private parts or her mine. We've found ways to push the limits of those restrictions, but I take care to abide by them, even though it's maddening sometimes to watch her pussy get wetter and wetter as I smack her ass and not be able to feel just what I'm doing to her.

· I grab her hand and shove it behind her back. She's a feisty girl, and immediately tries to fight me, plunging us into a mock wrestling match I'm destined to win. "Aren't you even going to say you're sorry?" I ask, pinning her down so her hands are raised above her head, her cheeks flushed, her breathing heavy as she surrenders to my superior strength. I know that even that little bit of immobilization has her aching to be spanked – and fucked.

"Maybe," she says, her voice rising in the sexiest lilt I've ever heard. Even if she didn't have the slamming body and completely masochistic nature she does, her voice could do me in every time.

"Maybe? Oh, I think more like definitely. I'm going to make you say you're sorry, girl. You were forty-five minutes late! I really should've just left, and your punishment would've been to go home with your bottom just as pale and bare as it is right now. But I'm going to make you pay, don't you worry," I say, my cock stiffening as I speak the stern words. She sticks her tongue out at me, but rolls over quite willingly when I let up on her arms and nudge her over. I decide to start off right there on the floor, pulling off her shoes and tossing them into a far corner, where they land with a thud.

"You're going to get forty-five whacks – one for every minute you were late. I know, you think that's nothing, but those won't all be with my hand, I'm not that dumb," I say as I push her skirt up. I yank off her fishnets, the tearing sound ringing pleasingly in my ears. Usually she gets totally naked, but her skirt is so short I can practically see her ass, and the image of the tiny garment shoved up above her lower curves, with her white cotton panties around her knees, is too hot to resist.

My dick is pressing upward against her stomach as she does her best to make me come in my pants, wiggling and squirming. I shove my fingers through her mass of sleek black hair and tug, watching her neck bend backward just so. I tug harder, just enough to make her body ripple in pleasure. "Stay still, Laura; you'll like this better. You're going to count for me, and if you mess up, we'll have to start over, but I know you won't mess up," I say somberly. She gazes back at me with a look that would wreck a lesser man, her moist lips slightly open, her eyes wide and luminous, her nostrils flaring, her need to be spanked, by me, etched as strongly into her skin as a tattoo. Over the course of our relationship, I've figured out just what sets her off, and I know how to take her into that magical sub space with just the sound of my voice and a simple tug on her hair or snap of my fingers.

I let go of her hair, catching the gentlest of sighs passing from her lips. Her ass is right there, all mine for the taking, wide and round and pale and perfect. She's got just enough meat on her bones to make her rump perfect for spanking; girls who are too thin make me worry I might truly be hurting them, and I like asses that are wide enough to cover a range of smacks, ones where I need to hit them a few times to cover the entire cheek. I place my left hand on her lower back, letting my thumb just graze the upper edge of her asshole. I'd love to press it against her sweet puckered hole, but I save that for Evangeline. With Laura, it's all about hinting, dancing just around the edge of our desire, getting the most bang for our buck, if you will.

I press down against her body, ensuring that she won't jerk when the first blow lands. Then I raise my hand and bring it crashing down against her right cheek, hearing the boom, seeing her skin go from pale to pink in moments. "One, sir," she says, her voice loud and direct. It always starts off strong, like she's trying to show me just how powerful she can be even spread across my lap. By the end, I'll have her whimpering out her numbers – if I'm doing my job right.

I roll her slightly forward to get the best angle, then do the same to her left cheek. "Two, sir," she responds dutifully. I keep going until ten, my palm stinging as the heat roars through our flesh. I pause there, rubbing my palm against her curves, ready to take things to the next level.

"Get up," I tell her, unceremoniously shoving her off of me. My cock is pressing hard against my jeans, and I'm dying to whip it out and touch myself, even for a minute, but I know that could lead to dangerous territory. If her mouth goes anyway near my dick, as besotted as I am with Evangeline, I might not be able to resist, so I keep it in my pants, literally, and work out my arousal another way. She gives me that look again, the one that silently begs for more, the one that tells me, without even looking, how turned on she is. "Bend over the bed," I tell her, and she hobbles up, knowing I don't mean for her to change any part of her attire.

Not only do I like to see her bent over, but I also know this means her piercings press against her sensitive nipples, arousing her further. Her skirt has flipped back down to caress the curves of her ass, so I push it back up, noting how already in a few minutes the redness in her cheeks has faded slightly. I pick up the belt, wrapping its sturdy leather around my hand, then running it across her cheeks, tapping lightly. "Hmmm," she moans, her head turned to the side, her eyes closed, as if lost in her own personal reverie. I need to snap her out of wherever she is right now and bring her back to me.

I push the belt to her lips, startling her eyes open. "Kiss it, then tell me what number's next," I demand.

Something breaks open inside me, swelling not just my cock but my insides, puffing me up, when her lips purse immediately. She gave the belt a solid smacker, then says in her most matter-of-fact tone, "Eleven, sir," as if telling me what she's made for dinner. Her eyes watch me, this time not so much begging as seeking, staring back at me an equal partner in our game. She knows just how much I like to spank her, and I know how badly she needs it, but both of us go along with this game anyway, adding to the thrill. Actually, making the thrill happen; without me on top and her below, spanking her would be no fun at all, something a machine could do just as well.

"Get ready," is all I say as I move to the side so I can hover directly over her ass. Something about a woman's bottom makes it look even hotter when raised the way she has it, so round and firm and tempting, like it was made with just such a kinky purpose, and no other, in mind. I let the belt whiz through the air once, its snap, crackle and pop music to my ears. I strike the air again, right next to her ass, and she squeaks, a high-pitched noise that sounds as beautiful as any melody. Then I strike her for real, slashing the stripe of leather against her flesh, searing her skin in a way my hand simply cannot do. "Eleven," she chokes out in a robotic voice, as if it were not a number but the normal response when one has been struck dumb, literally. The pain blooms instantly on her skin, a pretty line that makes me want to lean down and kiss it. Taking away her pain is almost as enticing as causing it, but we have thirty-four more whacks to go.

I let the belt lash against the area where her ass cheeks meet her upper thighs, that never-never land of sensual flesh that is disproportionately tender. Like when I'm fucking and trying to hold off from coming, I have to think about something else for a moment besides the beauty of her welting curves, her do-me posture, her have-me stance, her I'm-yours body language. Sometimes I wonder if the constraints on our spanking dates aren't too much for either of us to bear. Evangeline has my heart, plain and simple, but my cock, my hands, my mouth, my power, those I would share with Laura, if I could. Instead, I must convey all that I want to do to her in these strokes, these beatings that take on so much more than their share of emotional energy.

She calls out the numbers as the belt slams against her ass, spreading her legs just enough to give me a glimpse at what's between them. I haven't told her to, but I haven't told her not to, and for the moment, I let it go, too pleased with the slick pink shine I see there to argue. I drop the belt at twenty-five, picking up the wooden paddle instead. I could insist on the blindfold, but I like the look on her face when she sees what I'm holding – half-horror, half-need. It's like the look Evangeline gets right before she comes, like she's tempted to push me away, to stay teetering on the precipice instead of dropping over the waterfall's edge. I know my job is to urge her on, for the reward is always so much greater than the risk.

The pain only lasts for a few moments, her ass smarting, but the pleasure will keep Laura going for days. I hold the toy that resembles a ping-pong paddle, only thicker, with holes to let air through, then tilt my wrist and let it fly against her reddened cheek. "Twenty-six," comes out muffled as she absorbs the blow. I pause, trailing the backs of my fingers along her skin, then pinching a bit between my thumb and forefinger. I kneel down behind her and pull her cheeks apart, staring at the forbidden fruit of her pussy.

I need her to come, but I can't interrupt the flow of our play. I deliver the final blows with the black leather paddle, the simple yet stern one, its shiny surface too cheerful for the kind of sting it delivers. Her voice rises and falls as my arm does the same, until her ass rivals her lips in terms of redness, even after she's gnawed on her lower lip while taking her punishment.

If she were Evangeline, I'd simply pull down my zipper, get behind her, and shove my cock deep into her waiting hole. She'd convulse instantly around me, tears of joy filling her eyes but not tipping over, while I marveled at how her heat seemed to travel into my body. I'd try, but fail, to wait, and simply pump my hot lava into her tight tunnel, the explosion truly feeling volcanic. But she's Laura, my play partner, my standing spanking date, my toy, even though she means no less to me where it counts.

Because it's her and not my girlfriend, I will wait to jerk off until she leaves. But she can't wait, and we both know it. "Lie down on your back," I order. It takes her a few seconds through the haze of arousal to get into position, but I let her have them, knowing the crisp, clean sheets are rubbing against her sore ass. She goes to remove her panties, but I still her hand. "Keep them on," I say, sliding them down to her ankles and hearing the fabric strain and rip slightly. I don't care. I stand between her legs, holding her feet apart as she looks up at my towering presence, my erection practically undoing my zipper on its own. She used to be tentative, taking light swipes at her clit, only really indulging in her masturbation ritual when a good half hour had passed.

Now, she gets right into it, shoving three fingers deep inside while her other hand tweaks her nipples into tight, fierce points. "That's it, fuck yourself for me, Laura. That's your reward for taking your spanking like a good girl, even though you were late and had no excuse and are really a very bad girl to the core." I like to punish and reward her at the same time when I can, plant a seed of doubt so she'll give me some reason to keep on spanking her, besides the obvious. "Picture my cock sliding into your mouth, right now, me climbing on top of you, your wrists tied above your head, your lips open and ready. Your friend Kira is fucking your pussy with a dildo at the same time, and I'm pinning you down with my dick so you can't move except to enjoy being filled in two holes at once." I know my words are getting to her from the way she clenches her fingers, the way her face convulses, her eyes fluttering open to look at me, then shutting when the intensity gets to be too much. I wait, feeling triumphant when her climax seems to glide over her, making her curl up into herself. I let her go, let the panties slide off as she does what she needs to do. I'm absolutely turned on, but also wistful, wishing I could touch her and help take her to that higher place.

She gives me her panties as a present, a souvenir to sustain me until next time, a little secret for me to hide away, a compromise between my allegiance to Evangeline and my unquenchable need for Laura, and her sweet ass. "So I'll see you next week, at six, right?" I ask as she steps into her gargantuan shoes, the height making her look older, wiser, but still just as needy of a spanking. She nods, and I grab her chin, holding her face and gaze steady. "Don't be late, or you may really get what's coming to you," I warn, trying to summon the proper vengeful tone. I can't quite get there, though, because no matter how late she is, I'll still want, no, make that *need*, to spank her, still lust after her and dream about her ass even when I have my girl's firm curves right before me.

And no matter what I use on Laura when she's bent over, no matter how firmly I plant my hand upon her skin as she's asking for it harder and stronger, she knows who really holds the paddle in this relationship. She's got me exactly where she wants me – on top, looking down at her, my hand raised, my dick hard. And if you want to know the truth, there's nowhere else I'd rather be.

Child's Position

Dawn Ryan

I always thought she had the most beautiful name. Even before I fell in love with her, the name planted a seedling and I was done for. I still can't really say it without plummeting head first into a pit of nostalgia or hear it without going silent, getting embarrassed, self-conscious like a pubescent, terrified that the name-speaker can read my thoughts and know how much in love I am still, despite the years that have passed and the small corner of a life our romance inhabited. It was huge to me, still is, like a mythical kind of lovers' chase that never panned out but will somehow torment the heart forever, an Orpheus-turning-around kind of pain. The afternoon we said goodbye I walked away and superstitiously kept on looking forward. I wanted to turn around and see her crying, but I didn't want to risk having the earth swallow her up and take her from me forever. I could always return and maybe we could rendezvous again some day. Five long years passed and this pathetic little desire still ate at me. There've been other, longer, actual relationships, a host of career endeavors, over a dozen failed attempts at learning how to play the guitar, learning how to watercolor, learning how to build a musical synthesizer from scratch – a motherboard out of particle board – a whole montage of life experiences that seem all together exciting and when I fast forward in my mind I really do like what I see; they're really good prodigal scenes, nearly Kerouac-ian. I've lived since Lily . . . liiiily . . . lilllleeeee . . . not really.

Had someone told me beforehand that the next time I'd see Lily she'd be bent at the waist with palms on the floor, knees locked and ass in the air, performing what looked like slo-mo acrobatics, I'd have beamed with erotic anticipation. I'd have thought up clever and nasty witticisms and I probably would have kept myself in better physical shape, maybe would have laid off the pot, laid off the chimichangas; I'd still be the strapping young Adonis on the verge of greatness who she fell for, wept over. But no one told me, and though seeing Lily in downward dog was objectively sexy, the only real feeling I had was the urge to stab myself in the heart, fucking rip the thing out of my chest, grab my knotted trachea from my neck and rip that out too. The earth hadn't swallowed her up, at least I didn't think so, since she was right in front of me, a perfectly trim and limber form, iridescent, almost glittering with whiteness, blondness, zero-percent-body-fatness. She was the picture of what we picture when we imagine health and beauty. An honest-to-God yogurt commercial.

I ran into her at a yoga slash tai chi studio downtown. I'd come back to Boston for law school, a last-ditch effort to validate my existence, give myself direction. It was my first year and I was already thinking about dropping out and going back to the union. I'd been working for the Justice for Janitors campaign the year before, mostly silk screening T-shirts and smoking pot in the bathroom. Mostly pretending to care. At least in law school I actually did care. I cared about not being the dumbest, laziest, and ugliest person in the lecture hall. I was pretty certain I was failing. I cared about fucking. I'd kind of turned into a lech, not deliberately or maliciously, but I guess I was still chauvinistic, no matter how desperate and hollow. When it came to women I had tunnel vision. Maybe it was my age or my godlessness or whatever other cultural ailments a person might suffer from these days, but all I ever seemed to want to do was ram my head in between a set of legs, push my way through the tunnel, come out on the other end of time. Fuck. I guess you could say I was restless. Real love, whatever I think that is, began and ended with Lily. I'm not sure what all the other stuff was. I think something ended for her too, the day I left, because not long after she wandered into this yoga studio, looking to clear her mind, reset her heart, and she never left.

There was a side to her I hadn't really taken seriously. I remember her reading *The Celestine Prophecy* and accusing me of stage six-ing her, vampirizing her energy field, but I thought she was kidding. Turns out she was dead serious. My Lily was a new-age junky, or, as she put it, "a missionary, a nun, and a workaholic," working seventy hours a week at the studio, selling kitschy Buddhist knick-knacks and useless ointments, promoting holisticism, mysticism, eating only brown rice, starving herself sexless, sleeping five hours a night on a mat on a floor, depriving her mind of dreams and oxygen; and she was living, actually living at the center, the New Dawning Fitness Center, and had been living there for the past four years. She was in a cult.

New Dawning Fitness wasn't an obvious sort of cult. It didn't have the usual indicators. There wasn't any male leader with long hair and a sexual pull on his members. There wasn't any isolated compound or sinister sense of Armageddon, no self-published pamphlets filled with an end to the world manifesto. New Dawning had yoga studios everywhere, out in the open, and offered free classes and healing sessions to first-timers. It had a business model, and its legions, as steely-gazed and loyal as any other religious bag of nuts, were celibate salespeople dead set on turning a profit for their centers. They were smiling, friendly, attractive young people who seemed to welcome everyone with open arms.

I have to admit, I've never had any real interest in yoga, I only went to the class because it was free and because of the flyer I saw at Starbucks. There was a picture of a gorgeous brunette swathed in white linen, sitting lotus and grinning euphorically. It was a black and white and not well designed, but my third eye could distinctly make out the shadowing of a camel toe. I bought a pair of tai chi slippers and took the train to Copley.

New Dawning was nestled between a Burger King and a Barnes and Noble. It could just as easily have been a Curves or a Kinko's or a fall-out shelter or anything else. I was greeted by a gazelle-shaped, shaved-headed girl no older than twenty-five. Her name was Daisy. Daisy rubbed my shoulder, felt my top chakra, and led me to a back room for a consultation. She laid

me down on a blue foam mat that smelled like the body sweat of
a million vegetarians. She spread my limbs crucifixion style and
placed a kidney-shaped, battery-operated vibrating device
along my abdomen, then my pectorals, disappointingly avoiding the nipples, then passed the object along my inner thighs,
onto the calves and down to the vulnerable cup of my underfoot.

"You have so many blocked meridians," she told me.

"I do?"

Daisy turned off her device and placed both of her hands on
my stomach. She pushed on my muscleless abs, kneading the
flab covering the swollen glands coddled in my pelvic girdle.
Probably a UTI from too much beer and sex.

"I can feel them, clear as day," she said, pushing so hard I
nearly pissed myself. "We can fix these for you. You'd be
amazed what a difference just a few sessions can have on your
overall health and well-being. Some of our healers have worked
miracles."

"I think a little cranberry juice will do the trick," I joked, but
she didn't flinch.

"If you sign up now we can get you four half-hour sessions
for only five hundred. They usually go for a hundred and fifty a
piece, but I can tell you have an open heart."

"Well, I came here for the yoga, mostly, but thank you," I
said.

"You don't have to decide now, we'll talk after the class." She
placed her hand under my head, closed her eyes and guided my
body in a sitting position. Her movements seemed like mock
dance, not the sort of grace that comes with true study and
training. She sat across from me, folded her hands and stared
into my eyes with what I took to be a deep and sexual intent. A
sales pitch? She took a deep breath.

"Have you ever wondered about your own power, I mean
really wondered about it," she asked. "Have you ever felt like
you had this personal wellspring of energy, deeply feel it pass
through you and out into the rest of the world, a sort of force
that you can't quite name, but you're just as certain of its
existence as you are of anything else?"

"You mean like a sex drive," I asked, flirting.

"Sort of," she said, maintaining her earnest, cocked-head, folded-hand cult-gaze, "but more of a love drive, or an energy thread, like a phone line, connecting us and allowing us to share information and wisdom."

"Oh."

"Have you ever heard that story about the monkeys," she asked.

"The bonobos?"

"I don't know if they were bonobos," she continued, "but there was a study published about these two islands with these two separate societies of monkeys, and one day, on one of the islands, a female monkey is eating this particular kind of fruit that grows on both of the islands, and she decides that instead of just eating the fruit straight from the tree she's going to wash the fruit in a stream first. So she starts washing her fruit before she eats it and teaches all the other monkeys on her island to wash their fruit too. After a while every monkey on the island is washing their fruit before they eat it, which is pretty amazing in and of itself. But the coolest thing is that soon after, without any sort of outside influence or direction, the monkeys on the other island start washing their fruit too!"

"Incredible!"

"Isn't it," she said. "It's irrefutable proof; it's undeniable – the existence of these shared transient energies that pass between us, unseen, guiding and influencing us, for better or for worse. Here at New Dawning we want to teach people how to harness these energies and use them for the better and learn how to reject the worst."

The monkey story sounded awfully compelling at first blush, but irrefutable proof of magical information waves? Telepathy? The flunky law student in me needed more precedent.

"But how do you know?" I asked.

"What do you mean?"

"How do you know it was this energy and not just that the fruit tasted better washed? Why does it have to be telepathy? Why not just a practical application by two separate ingénue bonobos?" I asked.

"I don't think they were bonobos," she corrected, "I think they were probably chimps."

"Bonobos are chimps," I informed her. "And chimps aren't monkeys."

"Well, either way, it was a published study in a scientific journal. It's agreed upon."

"What journal?"

"I'm not sure, but I can find out," she offered. "Let me bring you to the studio now." She stood herself up, hands-free, putting a halt to my questions and flaunting her tight and capable ass-muscles, "Today's complimentary class is being taught by this center's new management and one of our brightest masters. It's an introductory class to breathing and laughing."

It had never occurred to me that I had my breathing and laughing all wrong, that one day I might take a class to learn proper technique. It had never occurred to me that such basic functions of life would demand mastery, but I was open-minded enough to question my own Western paradigms of inhale-exhale and guffaw. I had no reason to be cynical yet and every reason in the world to press on. I was under the very false impression that my bald, pelvic examiner wanted me to fuck her. One way or another, I was going to dedicate the afternoon to our potential cosmic DSL connection. Also, Daisy had told me I had an open heart, which made the sad ape in me feel warm and understood. She'd reiki-stroked my ego, which, I've come to learn about myself, is all it ever really takes for me to sign up. The smallest hint of a compliment sends my heart aflutter, destroys all reason, and urges me toward a quest for vaginal subterranean ego eradication, anti-birth, clam diving. All she had to do was say I had pretty eyes and I'd have cut a check right then and there.

She guided me to the studio. There was calming music playing, and all the members hugged each other when they crossed paths. I felt idiotic, but lulled.

And there she was.

It's hard to say what it is that attracts us to certain people, what makes us think that one thing is love when another thing isn't. It could very well be something metaphysical. The only thing holy in my life had been this sense of other-worldly connection to Lily, this story I'd tell myself about my soul and her soul coming together once, meeting myself for the first time, and for the first and only time having the schism between myself and the rest of the world filled with the most thrilling peace. And I carelessly chucked it away for manifest destiny, I'd tell myself, but it was probably more out of fear that this fairytale wasn't real, that I was never bound to her, that my soul was still and forever homeless, and that there was no love at all and just the fear and the wanting of death, a quick and mindless coming. There was freedom and security in maintaining the myth and never pursuing the real thing. I imagine this is why seeing Lily the way I did, after so many years, caused the reaction it did. Downward dog, hair cropped, glossy-eyed, reciting some Sanskrit text (or was it Korean?) that was meant to influence the diaphragm. She was the master, dressed in linen, teaching. I couldn't learn how to breathe and laugh from Lily. We'd breathed and laughed together before, and though it was great, it wasn't skilled by any means. I took a spot in the back of the class and fought back some tears. The love of my life, the woman I'd hoped everyday to see again, hunched before me, and all I wanted to do was bash my head against a wall.

She was no Lama, I knew that. It wasn't possible that she could have reached enlightenment in such a short period of time, and how does one willfully go from finger-fucking in the bathroom stall of some dive to meditating under the bodh tree? And how does it become a for-profit enterprise? I hadn't even spoken to her and I was angry with her already. A master of what? A healer of what? The magic that had lived inside of me and kept me believing and hopeful, the image of Lily that had meant so much to me, The Virgin Mother herself, all her greatness and glory, was demolished the second I learned that she called herself a master, a healer, a missionary, a nun. My soul felt orphaned. She was selling it now, to anyone that could afford it, like some boogy love-hussy, just selling it to any man, woman and child off the street! Under the guise of yoga slash tai chi! I watched her hug complete strangers with the kind of prolonged urgency a person is supposed to save for foreplay. I watched her lay hands on pelvises during exercises, close her eyes and smile. I wanted the ceiling to fall on her, or me.

When I was younger I used to wake up early and walk along the river. There would be a group of Cambodians that met to walk together too, and I would follow close behind them, imitating their stride. They swung both their arms in the same direction and lifted them all the way to the height of their chin. I did this too, and thought for sure this must be the best way to walk, until I lost my balance and tripped over my own feet. I should have learned my lesson then, and maybe I did, because the class on breathing and laughing was a farce to the point where I feared for my physical safety. Lily instructed us to breathe fast and shallow while pounding on our kidneys with our fists and bouncing from the knees. I felt instantly light-headed, faint. She then had us laugh in a monotone, "huh, huh, huh." Next she had us chanting, "Funny kidneys, funny kidneys." We made our way to our liver and our heads and ended with our hands patting the insides of our armpits, shouting, "I love my armpits!"

I'd never done any yoga before, but I was certain this wasn't it. I was almost too dizzy to be freaked. There was a group of about twenty of us singing the praises of our armpits, without any irony.

I peeked around the room and spotted Daisy. She was bouncing with such vigor, and stroking her pits with such enthusiasm, nearly compelling me to believe I was accomplishing something. Tears were streaming down her face. An older Korean man stood by the entrance with his arms folded, nodding his head in Lily's direction in affirmation. His approval made her beam in such a way that made my comedic organs jeer. The Lily of my imagination didn't need the approval of anyone. She was an autonomous, brilliant professor of the arts, or maybe in medical school at Mount Sinai, working summers with Doctors Without Borders.

She ended the class with ten minutes of Child's Position, a yoga posture where we kneel and place our heads on the floor, during which time Daisy went from student to student, pressuring us to sign a three-month contract for their classes. I was shocked to see a number of people agreeing to pay the outlandish costs. Five hundred dollars for unlimited classes and a guaranteed personal relationship with your instructor. I was shocked when I saw my own hand sign the dotted line, but I couldn't help but believe the cosmos brought me here for a reason. I'd have done anything to be in Lily's company again.

Tea was served after we rose from position, and we began to mix. I took a deep breath and wandered over to Lily. She was giving hugs and praises to everyone who approached her. I stood in what felt like a line, waiting to get my touch. When we locked eyes she didn't recognize me right away.

"Lily, it's me," I declared. I opened for a hug; large dark circles of sweat revealed themselves from my underarms.

"Oh my God!" she shrieked, throwing her arms around my neck, vigorously kissing my face and head. "Oh my God! I can't believe it!" She placed her hand on my round stomach, gave it a pat. "It's been so long," she said. "Look at us. We've gotten old."

"Not you. You're fit as a fiddle."

"Well, it'd be bad marketing not to be fit in this place," she joked.

Despite my sweat, my nerves, and my revulsion with Lily's chosen profession, I couldn't keep myself from begging her to join me for dinner.

"I'd love to, but I need to run it by my mentor." She motioned toward the stone-faced Korean man in the doorway.

"You need permission?"

"No, I can do whatever I want. It's just a courtesy. We have meetings most nights, and we have classes most days, so I'm not left with much time for other things. But it's great!" She held my shoulders. "I want to tell you all, I want to hear all that's going on with you." She kissed me again and ambled over to her mentor.

Lily lowered her head when she addressed him and the conversation seemed to go on longer than necessary. I felt his eyes on me, summing me up, as if he were measuring my strength, what kind of threat I'd be. Apparently I wasn't any serious threat, because Lily returned with a smile.

"He says I can leave now as long as I'm back by eight o'clock. All the healers are learning a new form of fingertip therapy that's meant to alleviate symptoms of lupus, but that's another story. Oh, I can't wait to share!"

"Shouldn't you go to a doctor if you have symptoms of lupus?" I queried, but she didn't respond.

"So where are you taking me?" she asked. "Let's go to the sushi place we used to go to."

"I remember that place," I said. "I remember somebody drinking too much sake and getting frisky under the table."

"Now, sweetheart, don't get ahead of yourself."

"Do we have time to change?"

"Probably not," she said, throwing me a towel. "Just wipe your face and no one will be the wiser." She was still awfully cute.

Up to this moment I wanted to believe Lily hadn't changed much. I was also willing to believe there might be something to this new age hocus-pocus in which she was involved. More importantly, though, I needed to be alone with her. Now that I had her in my sights, I needed to hear from her what had been between us once, some kind of validation for all the longing I'd suffered and relished.

We walked to the sushi place and reminisced innocently. She even locked arms with me as if we'd time-warped to when we were in love. I was expecting greater boundaries, more nervousness on her part, but was quickly sucked into this rushed sense of trust and intimacy. After all, it was all I'd wanted for the past five years. It seemed too easy though, and after watching her embrace everyone at the center, willy-nilly, I was skeptical of the authenticity. How my heart hurt. And she was still so fucking sexy.

She told me about her new life. She told me that she was not just teaching yoga, but that she was part of a movement, a spiritual awakening. She spent two weeks in the red cliffs of Sedona sitting in an energy vortex and only moving to drink water. She didn't even move to pee. She told me about her mat on the floor where she slept, and how she shared a room with five other women. She said she hadn't had sex for at least two years, that it was sort of frowned upon, but everything was her choice because she'd never felt so happy in all her life. She told me about this pit in her core, how she'd had this empty, sad feeling at the core of her being, and when she started practicing New Dawning Fitness the pit was suddenly filled. I told her that I liked my pit; it keeps me in line with everyone else. She told me that just last week she'd spent eight hours doing a repetitive bow, from the ground on up, all the while chanting some text that's supposed to save the world. She'd done one thousand bows before, but four thousand bows really wiped her out. Lily also hinted that she'd given up all of her earthly possessions, hinted that she'd dropped out of grad school to pursue her messianic calling, hinted that she might like to have sex again some day. I hinted I might be the man for the job, and held the door for her as we entered the restaurant.

I ordered a bottle of sake and a giant boat of raw fish. She ordered a Perrier and a bowl of edamame.

"You can order whatever you want," I said. "It's my treat."

"This is exactly what I want," she told me.

She prayed over her bowl and then nibbled cautiously on her beans. I shoved whole colonies of salmon roe down my throat. I swigged a shot of sake, wiped my mouth and mustered the courage to speak.

"So let's hear it, Lily," I said. "What's this New Dawning Fitness really all about? It doesn't really seem like yoga at all. How'd you get involved?"

"Didn't I already tell you, about my emptiness and every-thing," she said, defensively.

"Yeah, but what are you after with this group," I asked. "What's the point of doing these exercises all day, every day?"

She wiped her mouth, cocked her head the way they all seem to, and pensively chose her words. "Can I tell you a story first?" she asked. "I want to tell you this story. Every time I tell it to myself I remember why it is I'm doing what I do, what I'm called to do."

"Of course you can tell me a story," I said.

"Well, did you know, as a child I never cried?"

"Never?"

"Never, until the age of nine. I remember clearly; I pressured my mother into a foot-race to the front door of my childhood home. Within just a few gallops I'd tripped, fell flat on my face and busted my chin."

"That seems like an appropriate moment to shed a tear."

"Yes! That was the exact thought I had, 'this is an appropriate moment to cry,' so I did, and I didn't just cry; I wept, I sobbed, I sang my woes in a shrill soprano, face to the heavens, sorrow aria. I couldn't stop. I didn't want to stop. When I felt like I was about to stop I shrieked some more. I screamed, rubbed the scrapes on my knee, stared at the small dots of blood on my fingertips. I was enveloped. I went nuts. I had what I now consider a religious experience."

"What did your mother do during all this?" I asked.

"She held my shoulders and consoled me, of course she did."

"But wasn't she shocked, I mean, she'd never seen you cry."

"She was alarmed, but it wasn't an isolated event. After that, I cried over everything. TV commercials, puppies, delicious foods, you name it. I only had one way of expressing myself. I turned into a cry-baby. I got teased at school. I could turn on the waterworks at any moment and everyone knew it. People became annoyed with me. I remember a tension in the room when anything profound or interesting was about to be shared, everyone was worried I'd start crying uncontrollably. The principal even scheduled a private meeting with me before my biology class was to watch *The Miracle of Life*, that documentary that shows live childbirth. She told me that I might be asked to leave the classroom if my emotions disturbed the other students."

"What did you say to that?"

"Nothing. I cried."

"Why are you telling me all this," I asked.

"I'm trying to shed some light on who I am. I don't think you really know. I don't think you ever knew. I'm a cry-baby, have been for years. Ever since that day I learned how to tap that energy, I've been feeling things on this deep, primeval, sub-cortex, cave-woman, Gaia sort of way. I'm different from you. I have this pain."

"I have pain," I told her.

"But you're not a cry-baby. You don't want to leap into it, really see how incredible this energy is, see that it's not pain at all, but a power millions of years old, located in our brains, giving us the ability to heal ourselves from within. New Dawning has taught me how to heal myself."

"So you don't cry anymore?" I asked.

"I cry all the time."

"I don't understand."

"You'd have to come to the mountains for the weekend to really get it. I could get you a partial scholarship. It would only run you a grand or two, but you'd learn so much about your self."

"Will you be there?"

"Sort of."

"I don't want to go if I can't be with you," I said, surprising myself with the youthfulness of my voice. It cracked a little. "I'll only go if you're there," I told her.

"Oh come on! None of us are really anywhere, and yet we're everywhere, all the time, and time isn't anything at all."

"Yeah, I'm not going." I shoved a yellow-tail into my mouth.

"Think about it," she said. She sucked the kosher salt off a bean pod ever so coyly, looked at her watch, and then she made a grimace that said "I really should be going."

"Wait, Lily," I said. "There's something I have to know. There's this question I've wanted to ask you, and I don't know even if I want to know the answer."

"You can ask."

"Well, I just need to know, because well, it's haunted me all this time not knowing. I need to know, were you, because I definitely was, I know I was, back then in love with you, and I just never got to know if you felt the same way."

Lily cocked her head at me, new-age, compassionate, therapist-like, and smiled. Her eyes were bluer than a robin's eggs, but her stare was like two swirling eddies vacuuming reality, spitting it back out rearranged.

"I thought I'd never stop crying," she said. "But that's just who I am." She stood, cupped my face with her hands, kissed me on the cheek, and in a Katherine Hepburn voice, she said, "Goodbye, lover."

I began to cry, not anything of any great sum, just a few tears and a sorry-sack expression on my face.

Lily laughed. "There ya go," she said, then turned to leave. I wiped my cheeks and thought about ordering dessert.

"Wait, Lily," I called out. "There's one more thing I need you to know."

"What's that?"

"I don't love my armpits," I shouted. "In fact I hate my armpits. I have fantasies of slicing them off of my body. I feel that way about all my parts actually. I don't think there's anything funny about my body. I have so much pain. I wake up in the morning hating myself. The second I wake I imagine a power drill coming through the wall and entering the top of my head and it's the only thought that brings me any relief. There's nothing funny about it."

Lily grinned, blew a kiss, and left.

I could hear the happy couple sitting next to me snickering at what I'd said. I muttered for them to fuck off under my breath. When the server came around I ordered some tempura fried bananas and green tea ice-cream. At the time I thought I was just being paranoid, but I was certain that one of the linen-clad Korean masters was pacing the sushi place, pretending not to be watching us, but when Lily left the man left with her, almost like an escort or chaperone. I soaked a banana in the melting ice-cream and thought about going to the restroom to masturbate. I was distraught, inconsolable. I was a flitting electron under the thumbnail of some horrible, moss-faced space alien; a sad little fish at the bottom of the ocean, blindly fertilizing the coral bed. What a terrible joke.

I had no intention of ever returning to New Dawning Fitness, but it occurred to me sometime the following week that I'd already paid five hundred dollars for three months. Maybe Daisy hadn't quite reached the celibate stage of cult-hood and I still had a chance. More importantly, though, I still felt this love drive, this telephone line connecting me to Lily. I didn't know what I wanted to say or do when I saw her; I just wanted to see her. All I've ever wanted for the past five years was to see her.

I brought my own yoga mat this time, and I wore a more breathable top. Daisy was standing at the front desk, appearing very business-like, filling out paperwork and organizing fliers. I walked up to the counter and greeted her.

"Remember me," I said.

Daisy cocked her head and revealed a subtle frown. "Yes, I think I do remember you," she said. "Would you mind waiting here for just one moment?"

She turned and entered a small door that read, "staff only." She returned with a very familiar-looking brunette. I recalled the flier at Starbucks, felt a rush of blood creep up my thighs. I was star-struck. Daisy had brought out the flier girl to address me personally.

I said hello, but the brunette did not welcome me back. She was clearly American, most likely of Irish decent, but she spoke in a choppy sort of way similar to the Korean masters she worked with. She cocked her head, sucked her lower lip and said, "We do not want you." I wasn't sure what she meant.

"New Dawning does not want your patronage," she clarified.

"But I paid," I told her. "I paid for three months.

"New Dawning will refund your money," she said. "We ask that you leave now."

"What the hell are you talking about," I shouted.

"Where's Lily, what happened to Lily?"

"She has been relocated. She does not want to be distracted from her journey. You make her cry and she doesn't stop. You take her chi. We worry you have bad chi. You are not ready for our methods."

"But I thought this was a yoga studio, I thought anyone could come here. What rules have I broken?" I was flustered and a little offended.

"You give us ten thousand dollars," she said, "you go to desert, you meditate with masters, then we reconsider." I told her she was out of her fucking mind and I left. I was infuriated. I wondered what legal action I could take against them. I ripped their fliers off of the telephone polls, decided to go back to Starbucks and get rid of those fliers too, but there was a new one posted when I got there, and when I saw it I began to sob just like an honest to God cry-baby. It was my Lily doing a bridge and hovering in outer space with Saturn and Jupiter. Underneath was the slogan, "Be the master of your own universe. Join New Dawning Fitness today."

I took the flier home with me. I tacked it to my wall. I begged and pleaded with whoever it is we beg and plead to. I went online and did research on New Dawning. It goes by many names to avoid exposure, but its business model is the same. It steals people, makes them think they're on the path toward enlightenment. There's a leader somewhere in Arizona who has his own golf course. He writes books that all the members must read. He likens himself to Jesus and Buddha, but those in the know refer to him as the new Revd Moonie. He has horse stables and his wife's neck is draped in gold chains. Supposedly he can train people to be telepathic, like the monkeys.

I couldn't read anymore. I went to my favorite porn site to clear my mind. It's called Horny Hot Female Doctors. I clicked on a video with two women and a male patient with an ace bandage around his knee. The busty and blonde female doctor and nurse seduce the male patient into a threesome. It's the same premise every time, just with different actors. I love it. I put the volume all the way up on my computer and listened to the young nurse moan while her patient did her from behind. The doctor, her mentor, sat spreadeagled on the hospital gurney and motioned for some girl-on-girl cunnilingus. Run-of-the-mill stuff, but something strange happened. Instead of going down, the young nurse went up. She and the doctor locked eyes; the doctor opened her breast to her and the nurse nestled her head in the cleavage. The nurse seemed to fall into a reverie. The doctor gently brushed the nurse's top chakra, kissed it, and held her tight, and then the nurse, perhaps in an attempt to be sexy, seemed to mutter something that sounded a lot like "mommy." Even the man with the sports injury, giving it to her from behind, was touched, and he began to fuck her more gently.

I would give anything to be part of that holy trinity.

Objects of Meaning

Savannah Lee

My face was so hot you could fry an egg on it. Despite that, I went ahead with my plan. I marched into Professor Gordon's office, threw my proposal down on his desk, and said, "My name is Julia Lowe and I want to suck your cock."

He went Cliffs-of-Dover white and dropped his pen.

Hand trembling, I tapped my proposal. "It's for my senior anthropology project. See? I'm supposed to bring participant-observer skills to bear on an aspect of community life, so . . . I picked the phenomenon of student-teacher affairs. Now, I don't mean we have to pretend to fall in love or anything," I reassured him. "This is going to be strictly a physical affair, and I'm going to observe the social adjustments we make to accommodate it. I plan to get started right away by crawling under your desk and fellating you."

Professor Gordon, now flushing almost as scarlet as me, picked my proposal up. He verified that this was in fact what it said – or maybe he was just trying to find something to do with his shock.

"I'm not wearing a bra," I added, to help him get in the mood.

He stammered something with the word "unethical" in it.

" 'Unethical' my white cotton panties! I'm not in any of your classes. I'm not even in your department. I speak absolutely no Russian and have no desire to. You will never be in a position to give me a grade or evaluate me in any way, nor will any of your close colleagues. That's why I picked you."

Actually that *wasn't* why. The reasons I'd listed were just blind luck. Truthfully, I picked him because he got the highest score on my Professorial Package Rating: a GHI (Gotta Have It) with Oak Leaf Cluster. For the past three weeks I'd conducted an exhaustive survey of professorial crotches, rating them from IBAA (Invalidated By Advancing Age) through EW (eeew!), EH (eh), NB (not bad), DT (definitely tasty), and the aforementioned GHI. Know that, in keeping with the practices of this institution and my own ideals, my survey was entirely equal-opportunity in regards to gender. The only difference was that, with female professors, I added the rating AWSD (Always Wears a Skirt, Dammit).

All right, can I make another confession? Gordon's rating came way before the project. Way before. I'd been wanting this bastard for a year now. And through my anthro seminar, I finally got the nerve to manufacture an excuse.

I'd been watching Gordon for *so* long. Or more precisely, I'd been watching that heavy, prominent bulge in his pants. We're talking *Mission Accomplished* prominent, despite lacking the crypto-bondage straps on either side to set it off – and, thank God, the right-wing delusions. It was almost too good to be true. I wanted him – but he was so aloof, so intellectual.

Then I'd had to come up with a project on social behavior, so I thought, well, intellect for the intellectual! It was worth my giving it a try. I could sell it as a lark. A joke, almost. If all else failed, I could say it was *Anthropology*.

The object of my simultaneous academic-erotic designs was now spluttering something about my age.

Well, I was prepared for that. I whipped out, you should pardon the expression, my driver's license; it demonstrated that I was twenty-two years old.

"No, I, I . . . I didn't mean to question your legality per se," he said. Oh, his confusion was so cute! "I just meant to say that, in relation to myself, you are . . ."

"Desirable and vital," I told him. "Don't lie." I came around and perched on his desk right near his chair. "How long?" I asked him. "How long since you've felt alive?"

He looked away. "That . . . that is irrelevant."

"Bullshit. It's everything." I moved in; I found his zipper. He tried to put me off. "Julia . . . you don't understand."

Taking a huge risk (this could be assault?), I put my hand in his shorts.

I stopped.

It was *cold*. Cold and inert, with a strange feel like rubber. It – it *was* rubber. It was fake!

I looked up in shock.

He wouldn't meet my eyes.

I stuttered, "P – professor – what –" Was he an FTM? Had he been born a bouncing baby girl with a bow in her hair? Were there shell-shocked parents somewhere, wondering where they "went wrong" with their little Georgina?

His voice came out crumbly and gray. "About ten years ago . . . I had . . . there was an incident."

I was too stunned to understand. "A what? What do you mean?"

"I mean an *incident*. You will forgive me if I don't go into details."

Scenes of horror – an attack by an unleashed dog, by a deranged human – burst into my brain like the ten o'clock news. "Oh my God," I whispered.

He took my hand and moved it up and to the side; I felt thick scar tissue. "It was a . . . prolonged event," he said, "and . . . very serious. My fiancée," he added, "rather disappointed me by not even making a pretense to remain loyal. Recently I've come to feel that she did us both a favor."

I was still flailing around mentally. "You . . . you mean you lost your . . ."

"Yes. 'I lost my.' I piss like a girl, though I don't feel like one. You probably think my little totem is pathetic. But it reminds me of . . . who I think I still am."

Well. I made the only reply that I could.

I tore his pants the rest of the way open, pulled down those tight briefs (now I understood why they were so), grabbed that thing for all it was worth, driving it halfway up his stomach in the bargain, and shoved it right in my mouth. Balls and all.

And I sucked.

I sucked to slap down my own shock and fear. I sucked to defy what had happened to him. I sucked to give the finger to that fiancée of his, who had *not* done them both a favor. I sucked for Jesus, because whereas Jesus might not have chosen this exact deed as the means, he in his loving kindness would have blasted – and possibly through me was blasting – mercy upon this man. I sucked for Jesus, then, and logos and cathedral and even old Sister Ancillita.

That's right, I sucked for church. I sucked for consecration. I sucked for ritual. I sucked for holiness. I sucked for profanity. I sucked to ignore how stupid I felt. I sucked for the thing itself!

I was, after all, an anthropologist, a student of artifacts and objects of meaning. Totems. Yes. I sucked for intellect: that dick which was not one. I sucked for Simone de Beauvoir. That not-one which was more dick than dick. I sucked for Robert Desnos. I sucked for my own mouth: inside it, the soft wet rubber was boundaries I didn't know I had, boundaries being shattered.

Amid the shards of them I began to suck because I was wet. Wet for *it*, God help me, for everything from its foul taste and its strange feel to its fakeness and its tragedy and its pride.

I was hot for Professor Gordon's rubber softie. I engulfed it, I gummed it like real balls, I licked and nipped and tongued it. For real.

"My God," he said in a strange new voice. "My God."

Something stirred against my chest. It was his remnant.

"Holy shit," I said. "What do I do, what do I do?"

"I don't know."

So I started licking across the jagged stumps and twisted scar tissue.

I remembered my first-year anthropology professor (Shepard, straight out of Ageing Hippie central casting, and I loved her). I remembered her saying *When I was with the Megono, I slept in the longhouse with the other women and the children. We were all on the floor together, and the children would pee in their sleep. I woke up soaked! And that was just how it was. Now here, of course, I would never tolerate that. But over there, the rules were different. It was another country.* And she stopped and really looked at us.

You always have to be ready to pack up and go don't you?

When he came, it was watery and diffuse and from the center of the wreckage. It didn't shoot out, like I was accustomed to, but gushed all over. I watched it spread with amazement and dismay.

"My pants!" he said.

We both started laughing. "Here," I said, and started licking it up. "Ack," I said. I wiped my mouth. "I'm sorry. I've never swallowed."

"Could have fooled me."

I stopped and looked up at him. One of the few times I'd really, truly looked into someone's eyes. They were bright, set in a fragile smile.

From this country there was no way home. No dirt road, no dusty airstrip could take me even halfway there.

"Oh . . ." I began to say, but, finding nothing where his name should have been, burst into half-tears. After this, how was I going to call him Professor? But I'd never called him anything else. (Never *spoken* to him before today. Strange to remember that; I'd watched him for so long.)

He made a laugh that sounded embarrassed, though his eyes were still candleflamed. Gently he said, "Call me by my name."

"George," I said. "George."

"Julia," he said, and took my hands.

He bent his head and kissed them. Somehow that was the most intimate thing. The feel of his lips on my knuckles and pads.

He was a strong kisser, exact and decisive, dry and warm. I thought, good God, what it must have been when he could lay you down and stick it in. When those driven lip-prints could tell you just what was coming. Was the devil jealous, George?

At last he buried his face in them, my hands, and held them to him. "Julia," he spoke into them. "Julia." No man had ever said my name like that. Like it was a vessel . . . into which he could put anything.

I knew that what he wanted to put in me right now was meaning. Hadn't I felt the same? There'd been so much I wanted to tell him when I first tried to say his name. I would have had to make up the words, because the words didn't exist, but right then I'd thought I could.

I knew better now. We were going to have to struggle, the two of us. But I think he'd learned a thing or two about that, living like he had. As for me, I'd trained for long journeys and learned stamina of mind by slogging through nights of prose that could only take me further and further away from what its writers tried to convey.

"Julia," he said again, thick-voiced with the fight.

"Shhh," I said, and freed a hand to stroke his hair. "Later. Later. Right now . . . let me see your eyes again." The only light in the room.

Funny. I didn't even know any longer where the object of meaning was that had started all this.

I don't know how long we stayed like that. But it is, dear Professor Maye, the reason why I haven't returned to class – any of them – and have in fact withdrawn from the college. I hope you'll understand. Please accept this, not so much as a paper, I suppose, but as a testament that what anthropology teaches goes beyond the relativism of external experience to the relativism of inner experience as well. What explorers like Maya Deren found in *The White Darkness* can be found right down the hall; I too was mounted by Erzulie in the end. I have gone inland to find what can no longer be contained in books, and only pretends to be found overseas.

P.S. In case you were wondering, Professor Shepard got an AWSD.

Skin Deep

Kristina Wright

It was the beginning of May and the beach was deserted. Michael preferred it that way. Sitting on the beach in Nags Head, North Carolina, reading the latest thriller, Michael looked like the contented bachelor he was supposed to be, except he kept rereading the same page because his mind kept straying to when he could go back to work, back to life.

Then he saw her.

She was pretty; dark hair brushed her shoulders and long, long legs that danced across the sand. It took him a minute to realize she was chasing after two little dark-haired children.

It had been so long since he'd had a date, he wouldn't have known how to approach her anyway. Rest and relaxation, that was what he needed. A solid month of nothing but his own company, doctor's orders. It should have been a dream vacation, but it felt like hell. Relaxation wasn't a part of his life, but life had a funny way of kicking him in the balls just when he thought he was on top of the world.

He hid behind his sunglasses as he watched the pretty girl on the beach. It didn't matter that she was probably half his age and was playing with two kids who were most likely her own and had a husband who was probably a big, dumb hulk. She was cute and sexy and his cock hardened as he watched her follow a red beach ball toward the surf. A little fuel for fantasy wouldn't hurt. If he couldn't get laid, he could at least daydream.

He saw her again the next day and this time the husband was there, too. He'd been right about him being a hulk – he was well muscled and as model perfect as his pretty wife. They seemed like the perfect little family, but the couple rarely looked at or spoke to each other. When they did, it seemed to be in reaction to something the children had done.

The kids and hubby wore swimsuits, the little girl in a bright purple suit, the boy and father in matching yellow trunks. The woman, though, wore shorts and a baggy pink T-shirt. The T-shirt hung low enough to nearly cover the shorts. She seemed to have a nice body, so he wondered what she was hiding. He looked down at his own white T-shirt and black trunks and shook his head. He needed to get back to work so he'd stop speculating about strangers' lives.

He spoke to her on the third day. The kids were nowhere to be seen and he'd come out earlier than usual because the afternoon promised rain. She was walking along the surf's edge, arms wrapped around her slender torso as if she were afraid the wind would snap her in half. It seemed as if it might. A gust caught the baseball cap she wore and tossed it across the sand in his direction. He ran half a dozen steps toward it before it was blown into the ocean.

She was breathless when she reached him, a healthy flush in her cheeks. "Thanks."

He gave her the hat and their fingertips brushed. "No problem. Kids inside today?"

She looked surprised for just a moment, wary the way women sometimes are when a strange man has taken a little too much notice of them. Then something in her face relaxed. Perhaps she remembered him from previous days.

"My husband took them to Kitty Hawk for the day. Some sort of kite competition, I think."

"Oh." He looked up at the sky, growing dark with thunderclouds. "Not a good day for kite flying."

"Probably not."

They stood there awkwardly. He wanted to say something witty, something charming, but he was about twenty years too old for witty and charming.

"I'm Michael Levine," he said, extending his hand, wanting to touch her once more.

She hesitated just a moment before extending her hand. It was cool and soft in his grasp. "Kate Gallagher."

"Is this your first time here?"

She shook her head, wind tossing the long strands of her sable brown hair in all different directions. "No. My in-laws own the house. We come down every year for a couple of weeks."

"Well then, we'll be seeing more of each other. I'm here for the month."

He couldn't read her expression. "How nice."

"If you ever need anything – I'm usually here, on the beach." He tried not to make it sound like a line, but he knew it did. He wanted her. It made no sense and wasn't based on anything of consequence, but after just a couple days of watching her, he knew how her body would feel beneath his, how her moans would fill his mouth when he fucked her.

"Well, I – um – thanks." She took a step back, smiling nervously. "I guess I'd better get back. My husband will be home soon."

He knew by the way she said "husband" that she was reminding him. He didn't need reminding.

Michael thought about her that night as he stroked himself to orgasm. Something about the way she kept herself covered, not showing much above the legs, made him want to strip her. Slowly. Teasing himself, teasing her.

When he came, he groaned her name.

He didn't see her for two days. It rained steadily, the ocean churning up in black, angry waves. He stood at the picture window sipping decaffeinated coffee and brooding. He wanted to see her again.

He pulled on his rain slicker and tugged the hood over his head. He had no destination in mind, he told himself, he just needed a distraction. Somehow he found himself walking down the beach in the direction of her beach house.

He knew he would make a fool out of himself, but he kept walking until he was climbing the rickety wooden stairs to her front door. There wasn't a car in the driveway and he felt a stab of disappointment when he realized she wasn't home. He started to turn away without bothering to knock when he saw her standing just inside the screen door.

"Hello," she said, as if she'd been waiting for him.

Today she wore a navy blue T-shirt that skimmed her thighs. He couldn't tell if she was wearing anything underneath it. She probably was, she didn't seem the type to be running around in just a T-shirt. There was something about her that was very proper. Ladylike. He thought it was sexy as hell.

"Hi," he said, jamming his hands in the pockets of the slicker. "I was just walking –"

"In the rain?" she interrupted.

"Yeah. Stupid, huh?"

A hint of a smile played at her full lips. "Actually, I think it's great. I used to love to walk in the rain."

He wanted to ask her why she didn't any longer, but he was afraid she would stop smiling, so he didn't ask.

"Well, anyway, I was walking by and thought I'd see if you and your family might like to come to dinner."

He didn't know where that had come from. He didn't want them over for dinner. Correction, he didn't want her husband and kids for dinner. He wanted her to himself, which was even more stupid than walking in the rain.

"Oh, well, I don't know."

"Right. Sorry, I didn't mean to bother you," he said, angry for being so foolish.

The screen door squeaked open. "Wait! I'm sorry, I didn't mean to be rude." Her voice was soft, warm. "Come inside. Have a cup of coffee with me."

He knew without asking that she was alone. "Thanks." He shrugged out of his slicker and hung it on a hook by the door.

He followed her into the beach house that was a mirror image of his own. The kitchen was to the left rather than the right, the living room faced the ocean just as his did, but the fireplace was on the opposite wall.

The house was dark and it made it seem more intimate to be there with her.

"Would you like some coffee? I just made it."

He didn't want coffee, he wanted to pull her close and learn the shape and feel of her body. He nodded. "Sure, sounds great."

She went into the kitchen and returned with two oversized pottery mugs. She sat in a chair by the window and he took the chair across from her. They drank their coffee in silence for several minutes, both of them staring out the window as the rain lashed the ocean.

"Where is —" He realized he didn't know her husband's name. "Where's everyone?"

"They drove up to Virginia Beach for the weekend. My in-laws live there."

"Why didn't you go?"

She didn't seem to mind his invasive question. "I wasn't feeling well. I thought a couple days' rest might help."

There was truth in what she said, but he could also sense the lie beneath it. "Well, I hope you won't be offended if I say I'm glad you weren't feeling well."

She didn't smile, but she didn't look angry, either. "Me, too."

Something shifted between them. The difference between strangers and friends was gone.

They continued to drink their coffee, but now they were watching each other. He saw the way her hand trembled slightly as she held her mug. Her gaze was steady though, watching him watch her.

"Are you married?" she asked finally, her soft voice cutting through the sound of the rain on the roof. "Kids?"

"Divorced. Five, no, six years." He shook his head. "Never had time for kids and too old now to think about it."

She sat her mug down and tucked her legs under her. "You're not too old. You could find some younger woman who would want to have children with you."

He tapped his chest. "Who'd want me? I'm fifty-six years old, I'm going bald, I've got bursitis in my shoulder and someone else's heart."

Surprise flitted across her face. "Really? Wow."

He hadn't meant to tell her, didn't know why he had. "Yeah.

I probably had a month to live, had gotten my life – and death – in order, when a heart came through."

"That's pretty amazing."

He sat his mug on the table beside him. "I guess. Sometimes I wonder what's the point? I'm alone, I can't do a lot of the things I used to do, and my best years are behind me. Maybe prolonging things wasn't a good idea."

She put her feet on the floor and leaned forward, staring at him intently. "But you're *alive*. That *means* something. That's everything. You're alive."

She said it so fiercely, with so much passion, he didn't dare argue with her. "Don't mind me. I'm grateful most of the time."

She sat back, as if content with his response. "I know. It's hard, isn't it?"

"What?"

"Carrying around the secret of your own mortality, knowing most people haven't got a clue."

He hadn't thought about it that way, but she was right. He would be out with friends and wonder if they had any idea what it felt like to know that today could be the last day. Or tomorrow. Or maybe a week from Tuesday, so there was no point in TiVoing *CSI: Miami*. He wondered if they even ever thought about dying. He hadn't, before. Then one day his heart started doing funny things and he'd given up all the foods he loved and quit playing golf and put on twenty pounds. He'd hated the thought of dying, then he'd accepted it and been ready to welcome it. Now he was back to hating it – and fearing it.

"How do you know that?"

She watched him, searching his face. Memorizing him, it felt like. "I've been there."

He was about to ask her what she meant, figuring they were already so deep in unknown territory that it wouldn't matter if he got just a bit more personal, when she stood up. He thought she was going to leave the room, or tell him to leave, but she didn't. Instead, she hooked her fingers in the hem of her T-shirt and pulled it up over her stomach.

She wore a pair of running shorts, just as he suspected. He

was startled by the paleness of her belly in comparison to her tan arms and legs, but his breath caught in his throat as she pulled the T-shirt higher, over her chest.

She didn't wear a bra. Her right breast was pretty and plump, the nipple a pale, creamy pink. Where her left breast should have been there was only an ugly, pink scar bisecting the left side of her chest.

The T-shirt hid her face as he stared. His eyes kept drifting from one side of her chest to the other, from perfection to deformity, from healthy to ill. Though he supposed she was as healthy as she could be, now that they'd removed the sick part of her.

After what seemed like minutes but couldn't have been more than thirty seconds, she tugged her shirt down. Her face was blank, expressionless, but he knew what it had taken for her to expose herself like that. Not just her flesh, and her scar, but the part of her no one else could see. The vulnerability.

She stood there, watching him. Waiting.

"Thank you."

She nodded sharply. "We're quite a pair, aren't we?"

"Yeah. We are."

"I don't know why I did that. I think I'm just to the point where I don't care anymore," she said softly. Her fingers played with the hem of her T-shirt. "Eric – my husband – he doesn't like to talk about it. He doesn't like to look at me."

"What do you want, Kate?" There was so much else he could have said, but that seemed to cut to the heart of things.

She didn't speak. She stood there with her baggy T-shirt hiding her pain and stared at him. Then she slowly reached out a hand to him. Her shell-pink nail polish was chipped at the edges, pretty but imperfect. Like her.

He leaned forward far enough to take her hand. A flash of something – surprise, maybe – flitted across her face before she let herself be pulled onto his lap. Once there, she nestled against him as if she'd needed that exact thing.

He enjoyed the weight of her, the way her bare legs rubbed against him and her arms slipped around his neck. The weight of her ass across his lap made him hard and he started to shift her so she wouldn't notice, but she clung to him, burying her face in his neck.

"Don't move," she breathed against his skin. "Let me feel you."

So he sat back and held her, his arms around her waist, his chin resting on top of her head. The scent of her – so warm and fresh – surrounded him. He was aroused, almost painfully so, but he wouldn't move. Not until she wanted him to.

She finally tilted her head up and looked at him. "Tell me if I'm making a horrible mistake."

He had no idea if she was making a mistake, but he had no intention of turning her away. "What do you need?"

"I need . . . I need . . ." Her voice trailed off. "I don't know. I just *need*."

Her voice broke, echoing the ache in his chest. He bent down and brushed his lips across hers, not waiting for permission. Soft at first, then harder. Hard enough to feel the press of her teeth behind her lips. He was torn between being gentle with her and being as rough as both of them could take, to erase everything they'd been through.

She didn't resist the kiss. If anything, she pulled him closer and kissed him harder. She shifted in his lap, straddling him, her thighs pinned between his legs and the arms of the chair. Her hands fisted in his hair, tugging, urgent. They kissed with a fierceness he'd never experienced, or at least didn't remember. His tongue invaded her mouth and his cock throbbed, aching to enter her body.

He slid his hands under her shirt, spanning her back, pulling her down on his crotch. She tensed for just a moment as his thumbs curled around her ribcage. One thumb grazed the velvet underside of her breast. The other thumb found only the ridge of scar tissue. It didn't startle him, he never broke the kiss. He knew what she was hiding and it didn't matter.

She broke away after a moment, both of them breathless. She stared at him. Her eyes were green with flecks of brown and gold, her pupils dilated.

"Is this – should we –"

He put his fingers against her lips, still moist from his mouth. "Don't ask that. Just don't."

She hesitated a moment, then nodded. She climbed from his lap and he bit back a groan as her knee grazed his erection. She extended a hand to him and it seemed a gesture of trust, of vulnerability. He stood and took her hand, letting her lead him down the hall.

He knew where they were going. His house was laid out just the same. The master bedroom was at the end of the hall, the door open. Before they got there, they passed the other two bedrooms, each strewn with toys and clothes. She looked straight ahead, as if afraid to acknowledge the other pieces of her life.

The bedroom was done in shades of blue and gray, much like the sky and ocean outside the large picture window.

"Just tonight." Her fingers skimmed down the front of his shirt as they stood in front of the bed. "This can't happen again."

He smiled, wanting to lighten her mood. "Just tonight? You have the weekend, don't you? Are you sure you want to give up *this* for the rest of the weekend?" he asked, thumping his chest.

She blinked at him, as if unsure how to take his words. Then a slow, easy smile touched her lips. "You're right. We'll see how tonight goes then, huh?

"Oh man, talk about pressure."

The rain pounded the roof, the deluge making the whole house vibrate. Kate climbed on the bed and knelt in front of him, her head level with his shoulders. She began to undress him, unbuttoning his shirt with slow, awkward movements.

He put his hand over hers, stilling her. "It isn't pretty," he warned. "I can leave my shirt on, if you want."

She looked up at him. "Do you want me to leave my shirt on?"

The vulnerability was there in her eyes. So powerful, he felt it in his bones. He shook his head. "No. I want you naked. I want to kiss every part of you."

She focused on his buttons, but there was a blush in her cheeks when she said, "Good."

Soon enough, his shirt was unbuttoned and she was spreading it open, much the way they'd spread his chest to give him a new heart. He waited for her to flinch. He hadn't been with a woman since the surgery, but he knew what it looked like.

She didn't flinch. She leaned forward and pressed a kiss over his heart. It was his undoing. He hauled her close, his hands under her shirt now, under the waistband of her shorts. She was naked under the shorts, no panties. That surprised him, excited him. He squeezed her bare ass under her shorts and kissed her until he thought his cock would burst through the front of his pants.

Once again, she pulled back. Her eyes were heavy-lidded, her breathing nearly as ragged as his. She reached for his waist and undid his jeans. The rasp of his zipper seemed louder than the driving rain. He was hard and heavy in her cool hand and he groaned when she squeezed the tip of his cock.

He watched her, a look of intense concentration mixed with lust on her face as she stroked him harder. It had been too long, way too long, for him to let her touch him that way, but he didn't have the heart to tell her to stop.

Somehow, she sensed his impending loss of control and slowed her motions. "I need you," she murmured, head bowed, and he wasn't sure if she was speaking to him or his cock.

He gently took himself from her grasp and pushed her back on the bed. Her shorts were already tugged down low on her hips and he quickly removed them. Her T-shirt still protected her modesty, but he didn't intend to let it remain that way for long. He stretched out beside her, his cock still poking out of his jeans. She threw a leg over his hip, his erection brushing against her thigh.

They both groaned. He tugged at his jeans and boxers, needing to get them off before the zipper bit his cock off. She watched him, amusement playing on her face as he eased himself free of the heavy cloth. She looked predatory, hungry, not at all the reserved woman she'd been in the living room. He wondered for a fleeting moment if he would be up for whatever they were about to do.

He reached for the hem of her T-shirt and she gently pushed his hands away and took it off herself. Then she lay back, her arms at her sides, and let him look his fill. It was a gift he didn't take lightly.

She truly was stunning. In the wan light of the thunderstorm, she seemed perfect, whole. Her healthy breast lay flat against her chest, the nipple hard and dark. Though he'd never seen her any other way, he mourned the loss of her other breast. It seemed a cruel thing to steal such beauty.

She lay there, her body tense, as if she feared his rejection. He smiled. "You're beautiful."

"I was."

"You are." He didn't give her a chance to argue. He covered her body with his own, pressing his scarred chest to hers. His cock nestled between her thighs, finding warmth and wetness. "I have to do this slowly," he said, almost apologetically. "I have to be careful of my heart rate, at least for a while."

"Can you do that?" she asked, her eyes wide and innocent.

"I can try."

She contemplated him for a moment. He could feel the tension slipping from her body as she eased her legs around him, opening herself.

He didn't push into her, he didn't need to. She was so wet and he was so hard, it was as if her body absorbed him.

She tangled her fingers in his hair and pulled his head down, taking his moan into her body the way she was taking his cock. With the barest tilt of her hips, he was buried inside her. Home.

He clung to her, arms wrapped around her body and tucked under her ass, as he drove his cock into her. When his thrusts became almost animalistic, he felt her fingertips soothe his shoulders.

"Easy," she whispered. "Slow, go slow."

He thought he was hurting her, then realized she was saying it for him. "Fuck it," he said through clenched teeth. "I need you."

She didn't argue as he plunged into her again, pushing her up higher on the bed. She wrapped her legs around him tighter, her nails digging into his shoulders. Her soft whimpers and moans drove him crazy; he wanted to fuck her until his body gave out.

Her body tensed under his and she angled her hips a certain

way. It limited his thrusting, but he knew she was doing it for her own pleasure and that pleased him. She slid her hands down to squeeze his ass and he let her control his hard, shallow thrusts.

"Yes," he panted against the delicate shell of her ear. "Come, Kate. Come."

She arched her back and cried out, his cock nearly slipping from her spasming cunt. His own orgasm hit him like a wave, dragging him under even before he could catch his breath. His heart jack-hammered in his chest, but he was beyond caring. All he knew was Kate's arms and legs around him, her warm body sucking him in, squeezing and milking his cock.

Finally, his breathing returned to normal and even his heart slowed to a rate that seemed safe. Kate trembled beneath him and he thought she was crying. He rolled off her and propped himself on one elbow. She was laughing.

"That's not exactly the response I was hoping for," he said, though her laughter was contagious and he found himself grinning like an idiot. "Hardly a vote of confidence for my abilities."

"I was just thinking, I'm glad your new heart is stronger than you led me to believe."

"Me, too."

They stared at each other, silence heavy as shadows took over the room. The rain had quieted, the sky growing dark as night came. Finally, she spoke.

"Thank you."

He laid his fingers across her lips and she kissed them. Then he gently trailed his hand across her cheek and down her neck. He felt her tense, but he soothed her fevered skin with a gentle touch, over her collarbone and down to the scar on her chest. It was smooth and cool to his touch, cooler than the surrounding skin. Older than his scar and not as raw-looking, but still a scar.

He watched her face, saw the tears come and didn't try to talk her out of them. He lay there, touching her ravaged skin and letting her cry.

She was right. They were both alive. That was all that mattered, really.

Slightly Ajar

Jeremy Edwards

First, she started to leave the door slightly ajar. More or less closed – but not, technically, shut. Open just enough so that the merry reverberations of her waterfall would squeeze through the crack, creating a subtle soundtrack to accompany the glowing sliver of bathroom fluorescence that I could see from across the dimly lit bedroom.

On the first couple of occasions, I attributed it to carelessness. I assumed that Bernadette had intended to shut the door but hadn't pushed hard enough. But soon a pattern emerged. The narrow stripe of light became a reliable indication that Bernadette was in there peeing. This was the only time the door was slightly ajar, neither really open nor really closed. It was what a statistician would call a one-to-one correlation, and a mathematician an "if and only if" statement. If Bernadette was in there peeing, the door was ajar; if the door was ajar, Bernadette was in there peeing. It was a logically airtight correspondence.

It excited me. I didn't know why it excited me to have two inches of bathroom light bring me closer to my own wife's tinkling, but it did. This was a woman I'd fucked almost every night for three years, whose most intimate areas I'd probed and explored and titillated and feasted upon till I knew every one of her erogenous hot spots better than I knew the back of my own cock. And yet it triggered a novel sort of arousal to hear her peeing with the door slightly ajar.

I became accustomed to this curious new habit of hers, and I waited to see what, if anything, would develop from it. Was something expected of me?

A few weeks after she had introduced the sliver of bathroom light into our relationship, she began talking to me through the crack. Now, we have a little rule between us that we try not to talk when we can't see each other's faces. We both grew up in homes where family members would shout to each other from the bottom of the stairs, from far corners of the house, or even from outdoors, through the screen windows . . . and we were determined to be more civilized than that. We'd learned early on how easy it was to mishear content or misconstrue tone in the absence of visual cues. So our rule is that if I have something to say and Bernadette is not in sight, then I will go find her, and vice versa.

Therefore, Bernadette had to know that if she spoke to me from her womanly perch on the toilet when the door was almost-but-not-quite shut, I would instinctively come through the door, so as to better facilitate effective communication. After all, *she* clearly wasn't going anywhere for the time being – so the burden would be on me to come to her.

The first time it happened, this instinct propelled me into the bathroom before I was fully conscious of the implications. But when I gazed on the sight of my wife, poised elegantly on the commode, her panties rolled slightly out of place – aptly analogous to the barely ajar door I'd opened – it hit me that I'd walked into a hitherto unknown space. I felt as if I'd entered a shrine. Though I was, of course, entirely familiar with our bathroom, it had become at this moment a sacred locus of feminine mystery: the place where a woman urinates.

She was asking if there were any mushrooms left. I'd made a stew the night before, and she wondered if I'd used them all up. It was a reasonable thing to ask at 6 p.m., with dinner on our minds. But did she really need to know the answer before returning from her brief visit to the bathroom?

As I stared at her bare thighs, which emerged with a jaunty raunchiness from her bunched-up skirt, I became conscious of my erection. And of the fact that I couldn't, for the life of me, recall the status of the mushrooms.

Though Bernadette had actually concluded her pissing be-fore I'd arrived, she didn't appear to be in a hurry to remove her bare ass from the seat. So we stayed where we were, while I muttered something about checking the refrigerator. I noticed that her smile seemed to have a special glow to it.

Finally, she reached behind and under herself to wipe her pussy dry, thus exposing me to a routine gesture of feminine maintenance – one that I naturally knew about, but had never before observed. She did it with such a graceful motion that it was anything but mundane. And it surprised me that she did it from behind, which somehow made it sexier. I felt a vibration in my groin that had an odd, sentimental quality to it. For some reason, this act of hygiene emphasized my wife's softness and put a tender finish on my libido. I reached for the vanity to steady myself.

When we made love later that night, I was thinking about what I'd seen before dinner.

Over time, the crack in the door began to widen. And the unnecessary conversations that Bernadette engineered became a frequent feature of her evening tinkles. These dialogues were always timed so that I'd enter her sanctuary shortly after her activity had trickled to a conclusion, but before she had wiped. I didn't fully understand her motivation, but I knew that the ritual was one that always left me tingling, and Bernadette glowing. And it gradually dawned on me that this, of course, *was* the motivation.

The timing of Bernadette's toilet-seat conversations changed momentously one evening. "Are you going to be able to drive me to work tomorrow?" she inquired. In this instance, she spoke just moments after she'd dashed out of sight. I had returned home only a few minutes earlier, and had found her waiting for me in the bedroom, but evidently ready to head into the bathroom without further ado. I'd noticed that she was already undoing the belt buckle at the waist of her denim skirt as she crossed the threshold.

Upon hearing her voice from beyond the unclosed door, I looked at the wide shaft of light as if it were a beacon of joy.

I entered.

She had not only dropped her denim skirt and powder-blue panties; she had allowed her feet to step out of them entirely.

Her legs were spread generously as she prepared to let go. From her navel on down, I could see everything.

She sat poised, exposed in naked glory. And here, as in the bedroom, she had waited for me. Not a drop had yet emerged to kiss her quivering pussy and journey down into the bowl.

I started to stammer something about tomorrow's carpool, when an impressive roar overtook me. How could I never have ventured in to watch before? How could I have missed such a wonderful, erotic phenomenon? Smooth thighs, sensuous bush, adorable nether lips . . . frame and backdrop for one of nature's most breathtaking miracles – a woman peeing. A woman spreading her legs and giving in to an insistent private fountain-head. Letting all her senses be overtaken by the aquatic bliss of the flow, and allowing – in effect requesting – that I watch every drop come out of her.

I was enchanted by the fact that it was difficult to see through the rapids to discern the actual source. I was fascinated by the illusion that the water was coming from everywhere at once. It was spectacular.

Bernadette, in her present guise as a urinating woman, seemed to exude a sexuality more potent than anything I'd previously seen her express. This simple biological process, in its feminine incarnation, threw her femaleness into such sharp relief, both anatomically and sensually, that I felt this might be the quintessential context in which to admire her. Bernadette, legs apart, immersed in this all-absorbing task, was perhaps the most beautiful Bernadette I'd ever seen.

Idiotically, I still felt obligated to address the question about who was driving whom to work the next day. I struggled to concentrate, despite the fact that I had my hand in my under-wear, stroking hard. "Uh . . . I have to be in the office a little early, so. . . ."

She interrupted at once. "Shh! Please, Derek. Shut up, honey. Shut up and watch me," she said rapidly. "Just watch me pee, for goodness sake." Her face was transfixed, watching me watch her. She attempted to spread her legs even further. It was physically impossible . . . but she tried, with a symbolic compulsiveness. Her cheeks were flushed and her eyes were

half-closed, though still focused on me. She was now squirming, clearly making the most of her intimate sensations. Then
she started to laugh – a strange mixture of delight and release.
"You're watching. Oh wow, you're watching." She was as
turned on as I'd ever seen her.

She grabbed herself. Her eyes closed as she cried my name.

She was still pissing forcefully across her fingers as the
orgasm cooked through her. I imagined how the warm waters
must feel against her hand. This was when I shot my seed all
over her thighs.

Testing the Waters

He didn't know it, but my obsession had begun the night our
friends Tammy and Craig came over to sample beers. It was
around midnight when they left, and – for the umpteenth time
on this lager-laden evening – I had to piss for all I was worth. I
ran upstairs, not even waiting till I was in the bathroom to start
sliding my panties down. Just as I closed the door behind me, I
heard Derek's footsteps on the stairs. By the time I'd settled
into place, I knew he was in the bedroom.

The water came out of me quickly at first, then slowly and
deliciously. And I realized, as all my muscles relaxed and my
nerves oohed and ahhed with the joy of peeing, that I was
seriously horny. After three years of marriage, it was suddenly
driving me wild to know that Derek was on the other side of the
bathroom door while I sat here, exposed and tingling.

I'd had quasi-orgasmic peeing sessions many times in the
past, but they'd always existed in isolation. It had never
occurred to me to relate them to my larger sexuality, or to link
them to my sex life with Derek. But now, as I pissed my pretty
ass off, I found myself craving something I'd never craved
before – that Derek could be in here watching me, sharing this
experience, seeing every pulse of pleasure travel from my crotch
to my face . . . dipping his hand into my water, touching my
nakedness and feeling my two wetnesses.

It struck me that with my legs spread immodestly and my pee
flowing freely, I was uninhibited, open, and sensually awake on

a level that rivalled or perhaps even surpassed the sharing of myself that occurred during sex. My entire body seemed united in the electric carnality of what was happening between my legs. I was peeing as only a woman could, feeling that special pleasure spread itself through places that only a woman has. I felt primally and holistically in touch with my own femininity. I felt like I wanted to piss forever. And I suddenly had a revelation that, as a sexual being, this was perhaps the ultimate, essential me – the horny, natural woman with water flowing out of her feminine juncture, whose intimate muscles and nerves were dancing euphorically around her stream. And it struck me that this was the woman I now desperately wanted Derek to meet.

I dragged it out as long as I could, until I simply couldn't pee anymore. While the warm, lingering drops still tickled my most sensuous zone, I brought myself off, trembling on the toilet seat with my panties at my ankles. I could hear Derek puttering around in the next room as I came. Afterwards, I tenderly licked my fingers dry.

That night in bed, I pounced on Derek even more enthusiastically than usual. As my cunt pulsated around him, I caught myself fantasizing that I was pissing in his presence.

I knew I had to test the waters. So I started "forgetting" to close the door all the way. I began chattering to him from the toilet, so he'd come into the bathroom just after I'd finished, when I was still cunt-naked on the seat. It made me slippery to play host to him while I sat there.

Then, it was time to take the next step.

I was wearing a short denim skirt that evening, I remember. I felt the slow, lazy beginnings of a need about thirty minutes before he was due to arrive home. Once I'd made the decision to wait for him, it became a pleasant challenge. I turned it into an autoerotic game, nurturing my kinky predilection for the thrill of "holding it" – something it was high time I told Derek about, I realized. (Would he get off on it?) I turned a reverent focus to the current dammed up inside me, and I paced myself through the passing minutes of anticipation and excitement. The need blossomed, and at moments I felt like I was about to lose it, to

wet myself wildly over the bedroom floor – and it further
aroused me to fantasize about Derek finding me in such a
situation. But then I'd re-cross my legs or wedge a hand into
my crotch . . . and immediately the impending flood would
become tame again, a force that I could control a while longer,
and whose pulsing tingle I could continue to revel in lewdly.
Like a skillful woman on the brink of an intense orgasm, who
prolongs that moment for as long as she can continue to milk her
pleasure from the tension, I was as reluctant to release as I was
certain that the release would rock me to the heels when I finally
permitted it. Every minute, half of me hoped that Derek was
about to pull up in the driveway and accompany me to the
commode for my cascade. But the other half hoped his arrival
would be delayed just a few minutes longer, so I could keep
squeezing my thighs and playing with that inner tickle.

He arrived at last, and I lured him into the bathroom by dint
of some inane conversation. I roared forth with a piss so
glorious that it made some of orgasm's greatest hits pale in
comparison. And Derek saw every fluid ounce of it. I was in
fucking paradise, sprawling there on the toilet for him. He was
very cute, trying to answer my irrelevant question about the car
while I showed him what it looks and feels like for a self-
actualized lady to piss herself giddy after deliberately playing
into thirty minutes of overtime.

It Never Rains But It Pours

After that night, my wife's routine need to urinate gained the
status of a featured attraction in our life. Our evenings now
often seemed to be structured around Bernadette pissing her
heart out while I watched, crouching on the tile floor. She
would finger herself, sometimes not even waiting till her stream
abated. I would jerk off, usually coming while she was still in
full flow. Sometimes it was my hand that caressed her wet
pussy, instead of her own. Whatever the details, the sense of
intimacy was indescribable.

It had always been common for me to look at Bernadette and
think, "She's so very beautiful." These days, this thought was

no less common; but it was often followed by the kinky corollary, "Will she have to pee soon?" I might have been troubled by this obsession, were it not for my confidence that Bernadette approved of it, and indeed had deliberately encouraged it. And I was not left alone to wonder when her panties would be coming down. For Bernadette had begun to keep me informed, with blushes and whispers, whenever she felt the liquid tickling up inside her.

When we had wine with dinner, I would watch her as she drank – study her face, her posture. "Is she starting to feel the need yet?" I would wonder. With every ambiguous shift in her position, with every swallow she took from her wine goblet or her water glass, I would anticipate the inevitable. And on the nights on which she opened a beer, I could barely contain myself as I envisioned the fluid consequences.

Imagine that you happened upon the banks of the Niagara River, and that the falls had been magically switched off. And imagine that you never knew that there were supposed to be falls there. You would, I believe, still find it gorgeous. But if you knew about the falls, you'd miss them. At times, now, this was how I felt about my wife's pussy. It was as lovely as it had ever been. But, at certain moments, what I craved most was to see it with her water pouring out of it.

It was when we were dining downtown with Tammy and Craig one Saturday that I realized how absolutely fixated I'd become on Bernadette's waterworks. We were indulging liberally in a selection of marvelous wines – with plenty of lemon-tinged water to accompany them – and I kept wondering when Bernadette would need to excuse herself. My attention wandered, again and again, to her body language – did I detect a pressure, a shifting of weight? I would be heading for the restroom myself before too long, and I was speculating that the rather pleasant sensations I was feeling behind my zipper were analogous to what she was feeling in her panties. As I communed with the familiar presence of my own beckoning reservoir – relishing that mixture of tension and titillation, that impetus to release which could, for a time, be cherished on a comfortable, gently swelling plateau

– I imagined her experiencing the same things, in the anatomically female variant.

I was irrationally resentful of the fact that I wouldn't be able to accompany her when she went. And it was a bit of a shock to note that I cared more about my visions of Bernadette piddling voluminously into the restaurant's sparkling toilet than I cared about the excellent wine, the five-star food, or the urbane conversation. What, I wondered, would our friends think if they knew that the better part of my consciousness was now turned toward meditations upon the joys my wife feels when she holds her pee, along with rich conjectures regarding what pleasures travel through her erogenous territories as she releases it? They might be less inclined to pick up the tab, I supposed.

Despite my social qualms, my mind was drifting farther and farther from the restaurant chitchat. I found myself entertaining the bizarre thought that it would be incredibly erotic for the two of us to eschew the restrooms entirely and simply wet our pants in unison – or, more accurately, in harmony, the alto and tenor ecstasies complementing each other. It had never before crossed my mind to seek sexual gratification through a fantasy of pissing in my clothes. But sitting there at the elegant restaurant table, I had a strong vision of how magical it could be to watch Bernadette quietly piss herself, while feeling a wet warmth in my own groin. I could vividly imagine how my own physical bliss would give dimension to the voyeuristic thrill of studying her face as she sensuously wet. Ah, to hold her hand across the table and watch her features relax as she gave in to her wetness. Ah, to look under the table and see her little knees twitch and her cute trousers darken at their feminine crotch, while I allowed a dedicated, complicit trickle of my own to approximate a shared experience.

Though this train of thought was making me hard, I was reasonable enough to see that this was a blueprint to file away for possible home use, and not one to bring to life in front of our friends in a restaurant. So I reluctantly set this fantasy aside before I came in my pants, peed in my pants, or both. It was then that my eyes met Bernadette's. She must have been observing my peculiarly preoccupied face, for her smile hinted at delight and curiosity.

She got up at last and headed in the appropriate direction for ladies who have been drinking much water and wine. I watched her handsomely trousered ass recede until she was out of sight. Then, while I feigned interest in a discussion of local jazz quartets, I wondered how thick and how forceful Bernadette's piss would be, how long it would continue, and how wide her smile would become as she enjoyed all the associated sensations. Would she touch herself, wishing I were with her? Would there be a woman in an adjoining stall who would hear a faint squeal of pleasure as Bernadette finished up? Would my wife's pelvis bounce as she made her last dribbles, or perhaps gyrate with tiny aftershocks?

My turn to leave the table came soon after Bernadette had reappeared, looking radiant. I had the men's room to myself. And, for the first time in my adult life, I elected to pee sitting down. In a convoluted twist on autoeroticism, I closed my eyes and pretended that I was Bernadette – pissing for me. It felt great; but I knew that we needed to go home and fuck before I drifted any further into an erotic haze.

By the time we arrived at the house, Bernadette was making it clear, with semi-masturbatory explicitness, that her bladder had long since forgotten the trip to the ladies' room. As had become typical, she made an uninhibited display of the enjoyable mixture of urgency and arousal that she experienced while holding on.

Hustling behind her jiggling ass as we traveled up the stairs, I felt that our splurgy evening out with our friends had been a mere prelude.

We entered the bedroom, and I turned on the light.

"Come on," she urged, pulling me forward toward the bathroom.

I stopped. It seemed so ridiculous, but I knew what I wanted. "Wait," I breathed. My heart raced to hear myself say it.

She giggled with a tipsy charm. "Derek, I'll wet my pants if I wait any longer."

"Yes," I said hopefully.

Her eyes widened.

"Unless you don't want to," I wavered.

I waited to see if she would rush for the toilet. But she froze in place. Her eyes lit up the room.

"Oh, Derek," was all she said when she dissolved into sensation. She shivered as she wholeheartedly relinquished control. An instant later, she was clutching frenetically at her pants, celebrating what was happening down there with bold, nurturing strokes.

Now it was my turn to freeze in place, as I watched her intimate waters seep through the crotch seam, rush down each leg, and puddle crazily onto the hardwood floor. It was, for the observer, a transcendent experience.

Bernadette was laughing, dancing, and chanting. She was totally enthralled by her own act of sensual abandon. She was wetting her fucking pants for me, and she was having the time of her life doing it.

Eventually, with the vigorous flow still continuing, she peeled the trousers and clinging panties down so that I could see the inside story. I marvelled at nature's sweet, gorgeous cascade. I admired it as it descended from the delirious pink pussy of a lady on the brink of knee-knocking orgasm, into the yearning geography of her woman-soaked clothing below.

It was Niagara Falls, with everything switched on.

Victoria's Hand

Lisette Ashton

London, England, 1890

The parlour was quiet enough so Victoria could hear the tick of the grandfather clock from the hall outside. Stark spring sunlight filtered through the net curtains to illuminate the elegant furnishings. The family's finest bone china was laid out on a lily-white tablecloth. The afternoon tea was completed with freshly baked French fancies. Sitting comfortably in one of the parlour's high-backed chairs, Victoria placed one lace-gloved hand over the other, adjusted her voluminous skirts, and stared down at Algernon as he knelt before her.

She knew what was coming.

She had anticipated this day for months.

Before he started to speak, she knew what he was going to say.

It was the first time they had ever been together without a chaperone. Unless he had come to the house with this specific purpose her parents would not have allowed her to spend any time alone with a suitor. The idea of her being alone with a man was simply too scandalous for civilized society to contemplate.

"Victoria, my dearest," he began.

There was a tremor of doubt in his voice. Victoria liked that. It suggested he wasn't entirely certain that she would say yes. His bushy moustache bristled with obvious apprehension. His Adam's apple quivered nervously above his small, tied cravat. His large dark eyes stared up at her with blatant admiration. He looked as though his entire future happiness rested on her response to this single question.

She was dizzied by the rush of rising power.

"I've spoken to your father," Algernon began. "I've discussed the matter with my own parents and employer. I've even gained tacit approval from the local bishop. But now comes the time for the most important response of all, my dearest. Victoria: I've come to ask for your hand."

She smiled smugly to herself.

Outwardly her face remained an impassive mask.

"Algernon," she murmured. "I don't know what to say."

"Say yes," he said quickly.

She allowed her lips to twist into a demure smile.

He fumbled in the pocket of his waistcoat and produced a small gilt-edged box. Almost dropping it in his haste he snapped the lid open and showed her a quaint ring that was encrusted with microscopically small semi-precious stones. She recognized it as one of the DEAREST rings that were currently enjoying popularity. The initial letter of each stone – a diamond, an emerald, an amethyst, a ruby, another emerald, a sapphire and a topaz – spelt out the word DEAREST. The eclectic collection of colours made Victoria think it looked more like a childish novelty than a genuine declaration of their betrothal.

"This is a mere token of our betrothal," he gasped.

"Yes," Victoria agreed. She made no attempt to take the offered jewellery. "It is a mere token. With the emphasis heavily on the word 'mere' I think."

He blinked with surprise.

She could see it was time to test his mettle. Straightening her back, quietly deciding she liked having Algernon on his knees before her, Victoria said, "Do you want me to consider you as a potential husband?"

"I'd be honoured."

"Then get your cock out. Let me see what I'd be getting."

The words hung between them like a thrown gauntlet. The grandfather clock in the hall outside continued to tick loudly. Algernon studied her face with an expression that was almost comical. "Victoria?" he whispered meekly. "I don't think I heard you correctly. Could you please forgive me and say that again?"

"Get your cock out," Victoria said flatly. "If I'm going to consider marrying you I want to make sure you're carrying something more impressive than that crappy little ring you just offered me."

His cheeks flushed bright pink.

She could feel the inner muscles of her sex clutching as she watched him squirm. His embarrassment and awkwardness were exhilarating to behold. Knowing she had inspired those responses made her moist along the line of her pussy lips. "If you want me as a wife I have every right to know what my husband will be bringing to the marital bedroom. Get your cock out and show me the goods, or I'll have one of the servants escort you out of here now."

Again he hesitated. It took all Victoria's restraint not to rub her thighs together and gleefully enjoy his dilemma. Inside the tightly laced bodice of her corset her nipples were hard and aching. A wave of light-headedness came close to making her swoon in the high-backed chair where she waited.

"Unbutton your pants. Show me your cock. Or go away and tell your parents, your employer and the bishop that I've rejected your offer. The choice is yours, Algernon. But make it quickly. The tea is cooling."

He began to fumble with the buttons at the front of his trousers.

The ring box fell to the floor and the gaudy jewellery dropped forgotten on the Oriental rug. Algernon's face was the shade of flustered crimson that Victoria had seen on the angered cheeks of drunks and brawlers. On his bookish face the colour was surprisingly fetching. She lowered her gaze as soon as he had exposed himself. The flaccid tube of his pink flesh hung innocuously from the front of his pants.

"It's not very big, is it?" she sneered.

"It gets bigger," he said defensively.

"Then make it bigger," she snapped. "Because at the moment that appalling little engagement ring looks slightly more attractive."

There was an instant where she thought he might refuse. If there was any point when he was likely to reject her authority, Victoria knew it would be this moment when she had insulted his gift and his manhood. To make sure he didn't take advantage of the opportunity and go scurrying back to the sanctuary of his friends and family, she tugged the frills of her skirt up and dared to reveal a stocking-clad ankle.

"Make it big enough," she coaxed, "and I might consider saying yes."

He began to pull on himself.

His gaze was fixed on her ankles and his concentration appeared hard enough to etch wrought-iron. His hand moved quickly up and down the limp length of his cock and she watched the meagre tube of flesh thicken and grow. His fist was tight around the shaft, trapping blood into the dark and bulbous dome. As his hand continued to work she saw that his fist had to travel further each time to go from the base to the end.

"Stop masturbating," she snapped.

He obeyed instantaneously.

She grinned at the eager way he had given himself to her control.

"It's an adequate length," she conceded. She hoped that her smile was not so wide that he realized she wanted him. If she was to accept his offer of marriage, this was a vital moment in their relationship. If she could make Algernon understand from this moment onward that she was the one in control he would be her malleable slave for the rest of their days together. "Do you know how to use that cock of yours?"

"I . . . I think I know wh . . . what to do with it," he stammered.

"You may carry on handling yourself while we discuss my terms to accepting your offer," she declared haughtily.

Automatically, Algernon's hand went back to his cock. He stroked himself slowly and eventually managed to tear his gaze from her ankles so he could study her face. Certain he would be more easily controlled if he wasn't studying her eyes, Victoria inched her skirts higher. She was showing off her shins, and silently proud that she had elected to wear her sheerest stockings today. As she pulled the skirts higher, Algernon stroked himself more swiftly.

"Are you attached to that moustache?"

He floundered. "It grows from my face," he said, sounding puzzled. "Is that what you meant?"

"No, Algernon." She recited his name with the impatience of a disappointed schoolmistress. "You know perfectly well that's not what I meant. I was asking if you would lose that moustache if it meant I would consent to being your wife." She hitched her skirts higher. It was a daring poise that revealed her knees. Another few inches and he would be able to see the tops of her stockings and the alabaster flesh of her thighs.

"Don't you like the look of my moustache?"

"It's not the look that worries me," Victoria purred. "I'm more concerned about the way it will feel when you lick my pussy."

He held himself rigid.

She understood he was on the verge of climaxing and admired the restraint he showed in holding off his potential orgasm. His eyes were momentarily glazed. His mouth hung open as though he had almost pulled too hard and pushed himself beyond the brink of reasonable self-control. Delighted by his torment, Victoria lifted her skirts higher.

Algernon's gaze fell to the tops of her stockings. She could see his eyes widen as he noted the pale flesh of her upper thighs. He licked his lips with appreciation when he saw the thatch of curls that covered her most intimate secrets.

Aside from selecting her finest hosiery for this appointment Victoria had elected to meet Algernon without donning any undergarments. It was a bold way for a young lady to deport herself but she understood her courage was reaping ample rewards. "Should we see how your moustache feels against me?" she suggested. "A young lady has a right to know about these things before making a commitment of this magnitude. Would you care to tongue my hole for a moment so I can decide whether or not you may keep your moustache?"

He nodded.

She sensed his excitement was so great he couldn't properly articulate his desire to do as she had asked. Still stroking his length, and shuffling awkwardly forward on his knees, he lowered his face towards her sex.

Victoria held her breath as his tongue squirmed closer. A part of her wanted to judiciously concentrate on the pleasure he was able to bestow. She wanted to fairly gauge the sensation of having his prickly moustache so close to the tender flesh of her sex. She was struggling hard to be the dominant member of their burgeoning relationship and wanted to behave in the manner she thought most befitting for an authoritative young lady.

But arousal constantly distracted her thoughts.

A soft tongue lapped at the outer lips of her sex.

She arched her back against the seat.

The warmth of Algernon's breath proved maddeningly exciting. He teased the dewy lips of her cleft until she was almost dizzy with the need for climax. She could tell he was positioning himself carefully, trying not to brush her most sensitive skin with the abrasive tickle of his bushy moustache. Occasionally an errant hair scoured her flesh but it was a small distraction compared to the bliss of his tongue travelling over her pussy. Nevertheless, she could see the facial hair might eventually present a problem.

"My clit," she insisted. "Tongue my clit."

It was a test. If he understood what she meant, and went on to find her clitoris, she would consider taking him as her husband. If he pulled back and looked puzzled she would push him away and tell him he was unworthy.

Algernon's tongue slipped to the top of her sex and stroked the pulsing bud of her arousal. The sensation was enough to make her groan. Victoria stuffed the back of her hand against her mouth to stifle a scream of delight. She pressed her shoulders back against the chair and thrust her pelvis sharply towards him. The urge for release had been strong before but now, as his tongue chased lazy circles against the throbbing bead of her clitoris, she realized she was only moments away from ecstasy. Knowing she had to show some restraint, determined that Algernon would not reduce her to a quivering wreck of satisfaction, Victoria steeled herself against the pleasure and said, "Now tongue inside my hole."

He was more obedient than she had dared to hope.

The tongue slid slowly from her clitoris and eased itself between her labia. The warmth was divine. The intimate penetration was so intense Victoria had to grip the arms of the chair to maintain her show of equanimity. His tongue slid deeper, transporting her to a plateau of unparalleled delight. And then she was cresting a cloud of satisfaction so strong that she couldn't hold herself back. Her inner muscles went into a joy-inspired convulsion. The fluid heat of her sex grew so hot she was momentarily seared by its brilliance. The shock of pleasure was so strong she wanted to scream with jubilation.

With a magnificent show of control, Victoria remained composed throughout the climax. Muted tremors shook her body but she wouldn't allow Algernon to see how strongly they affected her disposition. Pushing his face away she adjusted her skirts and easily regained her previous composure as she settled herself decorously in the parlour's high-backed chair.

"That was pleasantly done," she allowed. Glancing down at him, she saw his fist remained clutched around his thick length. The idea of having him thrust between her legs was suddenly so appealing it was almost overwhelming. He had teased her sex to a wet and wanton furnace and she could imagine him stoking those fires further as he rammed into her again and again. With an amazing show of self-discipline, Victoria pushed that thought from her mind and regarded him coolly. "Continue doing that while you admire me," she declared. "And I will set out the terms and conditions that you need to meet before I consent to be your wife."

He nodded eagerly. His hand slid slowly along his throbbing shaft.

"First," she said. "If you want me to be your wife, you'll provide me with a far better engagement ring than the piece of crap you offered before."

He nodded and apologised.

She spoke over him. "Diamonds," she explained. "Large ones are best. And I think they always sit more prettily in white gold. Second, and this is vital if you ever want to taste my pussy again: lose that bloody moustache."

"Of course." He started to tell her it would be shaved off before the end of the day but she was talking over him.

"Third, and this is most important of all, I want you to know that I'm in charge of our relationship. You may go to the races, and the gentlemen's clubs. You may pursue your career as best befits a gentleman of our times. But when you get home, you will get down on your knees when I tell you and you'll obey every instruction I give. Do you understand and accept that condition, Algernon?"

Victoria could see the hesitancy on his face. She watched his resistance flicker and die. She adjusted her voluminous skirts, giving him a brief flash of the sodden pussy lips he had just tasted, and knew he was won over by the sight.

"I understand and accept," he panted. "You shall be in control of our relationship."

Her smile was thin-lipped with satisfaction. She gestured for him to come closer and said, "Very well. You may leave shortly and go and tell your parents, your employer and the bishop that I have consented to be your wife." Her gaze sparkled with mischievous intent as she reached for his length. Encircling his shaft with lace-gloved fingers, she said, "But before you go and do any of those things, didn't you say you wanted my hand?"

Spider

Donna George Storey

Escape. That's why I left Tokyo, to get away from trouble – thrilling, addictive, going-nowhere sex with a married guy. I lined up a few English teaching jobs in Kyoto, rented a studio in a "mansion" apartment building in the western district, and planned to spend my free time contemplating life's transience at picturesque temples. No more desperate quickies in public restrooms, no more butt fucking in hot spring baths after midnight, no more blow jobs in a private compartment in the Shinkansen. Unfortunately, I forgot to add "no letting gorgeous neighbors tie me up and screw my brains out" to the list, but I didn't think of that until I was already in a bind again.

Oddly enough, my fall from virtue started when I went outside to do my laundry. The cold-water hookup for the washing machine was located next to my front door, and I always began by hosing off the week's accumulation of dust from the lid. That's what I was doing when I first met Ito.

Actually, what I was really doing when I met Ito was screaming my head off in terror. Because when I sprayed away some cottony cobwebs behind the washer, I suddenly made the acquaintance of a new neighbor I was none too happy to see – a very large spider. A fucking huge spider, as large as my outstretched hand, its hairy legs as fat as fingers.

I screamed and jumped about three feet in the air, screamed again and aimed the hose, my only weapon handy, directly at the spider's swollen brown body. This turned out to be a mistake, because the creature rocketed about six feet across the pathway and vanished in the weeds. No doubt it was already plotting a counterattack. And it knew just where to find me.

I was still whimpering when I heard a deep voice drifting down from the balcony above.

"*Dô shitan desu ka*?" What's the matter?

I looked up and saw a slim male figure leaning against the railing, cigarette in his hand. His name was Ito, although I wouldn't learn that for a few days, and I wouldn't call him by his first name, Toshima, until we'd already had several rounds of very hot sex. But at that moment, my heart pounding, my breath coming fast, I silently called him the most gorgeous hunk of eye candy I'd seen in some time.

"It was a spider," I replied in quivering Japanese. "Really big. This big." I held out my hand, the fingers clawed in a spidery pose.

Ito arched an eyebrow. "A spider?"

"A very scary spider." A *tarantula* was more like it, but I didn't have my dictionary handy to check for the Japanese word.

I admit part of me hoped he'd come down and help me out. It wouldn't have been the first time my beseeching blue eyes had lured an attractive Japanese man to my side. But Ito just gave me a cool smile. Far from offering to help a maiden in distress, he seemed to take genuine pleasure in watching me squirm.

For the next few days, I made a habit of peeking behind the washing machine before I went inside my apartment. I searched my room, too, my body tensed as I scanned every corner and crevice for a sign of that hideous, eight-legged monster. More than once I woke up to a tickling sensation moving over my chest, but since I never found any real spiders in my bed, I convinced myself that bit of trouble was gone for good.

I did see Ito again, though, by the mailboxes after my Wednesday night English class at Hitachi. I assumed from the salaryman's suit and tie that he was coming home from work. He looked tired and older than he had in his Sunday morning jeans – on our first meeting he'd struck me more like an insolent college student than an office worker drone – but when he saw me, a mischievous light switched on his dark eyes.

"See anything scary lately?" he asked.

"Not until now." My Japanese was good enough for flirting when I wasn't frightened out of my wits.

He grinned. And invited me out for fried noodles at the grill near the subway station.

I was tempted to say no. After all, he'd laughed at me in my moment of need. But somehow I couldn't refuse him then, or the time after that when he asked me to join him at a *karaoké* box with some friends, or when he invited me to dinner at a Chinese place near Kawaramachi Sanjo. Yes, the attraction was physical. It was hard to resist those swooping, velvet eyes and the lush black hair. His shapely ass and muscular arms called out for some tactile exploration as well, and after a beer or two, I even came to see the charm of that mocking smile.

But Ito did one thing that turned me on more than any of the other guys I'd dated here. He would only speak to me in Japanese. I was used to being the honorable English *sensei*, even in bed, but now I was the one to flounder for the right word while he watched calmly, always the expert, always in control. He even corrected my mistakes – none too gently at times – but I found I enjoyed this linguistic domination, or at least my body did. After an evening struggling through a conversation with Ito, my panties were so wet, I was sure he could smell me.

I was definitely ready to skip the Zen meditation for a little Sumo wrestling on my futon, but even after our third date, Ito merely gave me a curt bow of good night and headed up the stairs to his place. That left me to go home alone, change my damp underwear, and lounge in front of Sony Music TV while I tried to decide whether to masturbate or just fall asleep hungry.

Then came the knock at the door. Deliverymen and proselytizing Mormons usually kept to the daylight hours, and I wasn't expecting any visitors. Still, I dutifully went to the intercom and asked in my most polite Japanese who it was.

"*Boku da yo. Ito.*"

So much for the new pair of dry panties. Just the sound of that low, gruff voice had me gushing. I quickly pulled my cotton bathrobe over my nightshirt and opened the door.

"I forgot something," he said. "May I come in?"

He'd never set foot in my apartment – what could he have forgotten?

I didn't have to wonder for long. In two steps, Ito pushed me up against the wall of the entryway. I was surprised at the power of his lean body. I was trapped, enveloped, his arms and legs wrapped all around me as if he had more than one pair of each. Our gazes locked. His eyes glittered in the shadows, and I would have been trembling if I hadn't been too stunned to move.

But Ito was moving now, his fingers soft and teasing. First he touched my cheek, an oddly tender gesture that sent electric jolts straight to my pussy. His hand slid over my neck and shoulder, snaking under the collar of the robe, pinching my nipple through my shirt. Wherever he touched me, the skin grew warm and slick, as if he were wrapping my flesh in bands of hot, wet silk. His other hand slipped through the robe from below, cupping my ass, probing the crack gently.

I let out a soft moan.

He smiled and wiggled a finger under the elastic of my panties to stroke my swollen pussy lips. I caught my breath as he found my clit. Ito had left the door half open – just the sort of edgy sex game I'd vowed to give up – yet the more he strummed, the more I liked the idea of doing it right there against the wall of my *genkan* for all of Kyoto to see.

"Do you always get this wet so fast?" he asked, holding up a glistening finger.

Before I could argue it was all his fault, he started painting my lips with my own juices, squinting in concentration as if he were applying real makeup, a bright red geisha's pout. Only then did he lean forward and kiss me, our first kiss, tasting of Chinese spices, beer and my own desire.

He pulled away first. "I could tell you needed this all evening. Please accept my apologies for not helping sooner. Until next time, *ne*?" he said and left without even bothering to close the door behind him.

I wasn't sure whether to curse him or laugh, but at least he had settled my plans for the rest of the evening. Masturbate it would be. I stumbled back into the room, rolled onto my futon and hiked my nightshirt up under my arms. Ito was right. I was very wet. My whole body was covered with a thin film of sweat, and my hands skidded over my breasts, palming the nipples, flicking them with my thumbs, sliding farther down to rub my swollen clit. The faint click-clicking sound of aroused pussy filled my ears, and I couldn't resist licking the sticky juice, slowly and submissively, as if I were sucking his fingers instead of my own. Suddenly, my hands did seem thicker and stronger, gliding over my body with a will of their own, not so much to pleasure me, but to remind me that I'd been wrapped up like a package in invisible bonds that pressed gently into my skin, softening me for the feast to come.

Mataserareta. "You kept me waiting in frustration." Just saying the word is torture enough, but when you live in Japan, you come to learn how waiting weaves its way into the fabric of life to the point that they really do need a special word for it. I was used to waiting for Yoshida, that's par for the course when you're boning a married guy, but Ito was a free man, or so he told me. Yet for almost a week after our very promising encounter in my entryway, he simply disappeared.

The wait was definitely frustrating, but I had a feeling he'd be back for more.

I was right.

I'd just returned from my evening class in Otsu, and even before I put my key in the lock, I sensed a presence inside. Heart pounding, I cracked the door and peeked into the dark room. Dark that is except for the glowing tip of a cigarette and a male silhouette outlined against the city lights that glittered through the window beyond.

I snapped on the light. Ito regarded me calmly from my futon, which I left lying open "thousand year style" like the careless housekeeper I was.

"You scared me." My pulse was still racing, but for a different reason now.

"You look pretty when you're scared." He made the Japanese "come here" gesture that looks oddly like an American good-bye.

The proper response, of course, would have been a few choice observations like "You have some fucking nerve ignoring me for a week, then breaking into my apartment like a pervert." But I wasn't quite sure how to say "fucking nerve" in Japanese and my dictionary was buried at the bottom of my book bag. Besides, I was curious to see what his next move would be.

Docile as any well-bred Japanese miss, I sat down beside him. The mattress was warm and I wondered how long he'd been lurking here.

Ito ran his hand down my back, a businesslike gesture. "Is this shirt important to you? Expensive?"

"Not particularly, it's just something I wear for work." I frowned, not quite following the turn of conversation.

He nodded and reached toward the low table next to the bed. I noticed a bottle of *saké* sitting next to one of my Japanese teacups. Ito dipped his fingers in the cup and anointed each breast with a few drops of the chilled liquid. My nipples immediately tightened into points. Farther down, the secret muscles in my belly clenched in sympathy, as if Ito's cold fingers had crept up under my skirt, too.

"Hey, stop, you're going to ruin it," I protested.

A smile playing over his lips, Ito took part of the collar in each hand and pulled. Hard.

I cried out at the sound of tearing cloth, buttons flying.

"I think I already have ruined it. Sorry."

"Fuck you," I shot back in English.

In spite of his claim that his English was poor, Ito seemed to understand perfectly. "Sure, if that's what you want."

Of course, I did.

Lying beneath him, my legs trapped between his, his hard cock pressing against me through his jeans, the fate of one boring white blouse didn't seem so important after all.

But there was still more waiting to endure. Ito stroked and sucked my breasts for what seemed like hours until I was whimpering and arching up against him, the heat of my longing forced inward until my whole body melted, soaking the sheet beneath me with sweat and pussy juice. At last, he moved lower, wrapping his arm under my thighs to hold my legs together while he flicked my clit with the tip of his tongue. I instinctively tried to open my legs, but Ito tightened his hold.

"Don't move. Don't make a sound," he whispered.

I bit back a groan. It wasn't so easy to be still or quiet with that magic tongue sending sizzling jolts of pleasure up my spine. In fact, I suspected I was about to be doing some serious moaning and thrashing very soon.

"Is it okay if I come?" I bleated out.

Ito looked up at me, his lips and chin glistening. "That was a mistake."

I thought I'd used the right words – in Japanese you say "go" instead of "come" – but I wasn't exactly focused on proper grammar. "Did I say it wrong?"

"The problem is you shouldn't have asked at all," Ito said with a tight smile. He sat up and lit another cigarette.

I knew we weren't talking Japanese Culture, because my married lover always liked a warning so he could slip inside in time for the grand finale. Ito was making up his own rules, but I was too horny to submit so easily this time. Besides, he owed me something for that shirt.

I crawled over to him and rested my hand on the obvious tent pole in his jeans. "If I promise to be good now, will you fuck me?"

He stared down at me with narrowed eyes.

"I'll do anything you want," I added.

Ito took a long drag on his cigarette. "All right. Get me the belt of your bathrobe. I'll need those stockings you're wearing and something else – a scarf or another pair of stockings will do."

With my wrists bound over my head and my thighs and ankles lashed together with the panty hose, I was more at his mercy than ever, but I did get a front row seat for a strip show that didn't disappoint. Ito was even tastier naked, with sculpted shoulders; a smooth, golden chest; and an uncut cock jutting out, all hard and ready. If I hadn't been tied up, I couldn't have resisted wrapping my hand around him, licking the swollen head, and taking him deep into my mouth. As I lay there, drooling, it occurred to me oral sex might be all we could manage anyway. How could he fuck me with my legs tied so tightly together?

Ito, on the other hand, had no doubts. He fished a condom from his pocket, straddled me, and pushed his cock down between my thighs. Shifting his hips a bit to get the right position, he slid right inside.

The constriction was definitely a plus. His shaft pressed up against my clit and my cunt was so compressed and swollen, I could feel the knob of his cock stretching me as he thrust in and out through my tingling hole. Ito was a real Mr Octopus, bending to suckle one breast, twisting the other nipple between his fingers. In no time at all, the orgasm he'd chased away came creeping back, a coil of heat glowing and growing in my belly. I wasn't going to ask permission this time. I squeezed my eyes shut and swallowed down my cries as my pleasure exploded, making me strain against the bonds, shooting up through my chest to blow my skull open as wide and black as the midnight sky.

Afterward we lay twined together, the discarded panty hose, belt, and my ripped blouse piled around us.

"I thought you'd forgotten me," I confessed, an easy thing to do now that he was curled around me, his smile much sweeter in his post-come gratitude.

"That's another mistake," he said lazily, stroking my hair. "I think about you all the time. It was hard for me to wait, but I know surprises excite you. And that excites me."

I couldn't help smiling, secretly, into his shoulder.

He was as caught up in this as I was.

Two days later Ito showed up at my door with a gift tied up in a traditional wrapping cloth.

I smiled until I saw what was inside: a coil of golden rope, with the sweet fragrance of new-mown hay. "Thanks, but what do I do with it?"

"Do you know *shibari*?" he asked with the familiar gleam in his eye.

"Is that like those porn pictures where they tie women up so they look like they're caught in a spider's web?" I replied, hoping my saucy tone would hide the fact my pulse was racing.

"I forgot that you're scared of spiders. You shouldn't be. They bring good luck."

"That thing wasn't a spider, it was a tarantula." Since our first meeting, I'd looked up the Japanese name – *jorôgumo* – the prostitute spider, a word that suddenly seemed prophetic.

"Big spiders bring more luck."

I laughed uncomfortably. "I'm not so sure about that."

He lifted his eyebrows. "Let me teach you."

I hesitated. If I really meant to get away from kinky sex, now was the time to draw the line. I couldn't deny, however, that Ito was a good teacher. My Japanese had already improved a lot, and I was curious what else he could teach me about ropes, and worlds where the rules were different, and maybe even big, scary spiders.

Besides, I was so turned on by the idea of him tying me up, I was already creaming in my pants.

And so, just as he commanded, I peeled my clothes off and sat on the futon, my back straight, my legs folded under me in proper Japanese style. With a nod of approval, Ito wrapped the doubled rope around my waist and then pulled the loose ends through the loop to make a belt.

"Lie back and bring your knees to your chest."

As if in a dream, I watched him wrap the rope around my bent leg several times, binding my thigh to my shin. Next he tied it crosswise underneath my bent knee. The bonds were softer than I expected and made a surprisingly pretty picture, too, layers of golden rope criss-crossing over my pale skin.

"Give me your hand."

I reached toward him, my arm trembling faintly in anticipation. He circled more rope around my wrist and secured it to my knee. My right leg and wrist received the same careful treatment, so that in the end I was lying flat on my back, legs spread wide in a fuck-me position. Ito was obviously enjoying this view. Under the heat of his steady gaze, I felt my pussy lips swelling and blushing deep red, and then, to my embarrassment, came a gush of hot juices, trickling down my slit, pooling under my ass.

Ito brushed a finger gently along the slick cleft. "It's better if you close your eyes. Spiders might look ugly, but they feel nice."

I swallowed hard. What had I gotten myself into? But at this point I was literally in no position to refuse. I closed my eyes.

For a moment, there was nothing, just the cool air on my exposed flesh, but then I felt a feathery sensation creeping slowly from the edge of the rope down my thigh. Of course it was just his fingers – a joke – but then the image of the spider's thick brown legs flashed against my eyelids. My stomach tightened. I realized I'd been holding my breath.

The fingers moved lower, teasing the crack of my ass. I'd let lovers touch me there before, but they'd always been quick to put something inside – a finger, a cock. Ito's hand hovered, soft and achingly slow, his fingers tapping and dancing over the moist, exquisitely sensitive skin. I squirmed instinctively, like a little dog happy to please her master, begging for more.

"Have you changed your mind about spiders yet?"

I moaned, the best answer my lips could manage.

As before, the punishment was swift. In the next moment the spider – and the delicious sensation – was gone.

"I do like it. Oh, please, do it again." If he wanted me to beg, I'd do it. I'd do anything to have those fingers back.

"No, I think the spider's hungry now."

I tensed, imagining a bite, but instead I felt a pillowy softness pressing against my asshole. Not fingers this time, it was lips, kissing me gently in that forbidden place. I almost giggled – did spiders kiss ass? – but then came the hot tongue, rolling over my crack like molten silk, darting French-style into the small, lipless mouth. The laugh faded into a sigh. I could feel that tingling heat in my toes, my teeth, my clit. My whole body was dissolving into syrup. In that tiny corner of my brain still capable of thought, I remembered that this is exactly what spiders do – reduce their prey's body to a soup then suck up the sweet juices, leaving only the shell behind.

Maybe it wouldn't be such a bad way to go after all.

It got even better. The spider fingers returned, crawling lightly across my belly, over the mossy hill of my mons to my clit.

"That's really good. Spiders feel nice," I babbled, my limbs twitching helplessly in Ito's golden web. Caught between the tickling fingers and the lapping tongue, I had nowhere to go but up, leaping, twirling, spinning as I climaxed in quivering spasms. My moans were so loud, I'm sure I disturbed a few neighbors this time around, too.

When I opened my eyes, Ito was smiling down at me, just like he had the first day I saw him. He leaned over and touched his lips to mine. Now it was my turn to feast on him, his saliva mixed with a new, faintly earthy flavor.

Yes, I moved to Kyoto to get away from crazy sex. This meant, I imagined, a life of celibacy or at best a tepid rebound relationship: lights out, missionary position only. Fortunately, Ito was waiting here to remind me that if you're open to new things, life in a foreign land can be full of surprises. And some of those surprises are very nice indeed.

Besides, thanks to him, I did see spiders differently after that night. They still got my pulse racing – especially the big ones – but I never tried to harm them again. I'd smile and watch them scuttle to safety, remembering how luck comes in the strangest guises.

Behind the Masque

Sophie Mouette

This was it. Tonight. The biggest job of our short but so far quite illustrious career.

The Lucchese Star. Sixty carats of sapphire, as big as your fist. Makes your mouth water just looking at it. Makes you think of Caribbean seas, the summer you were ten, the eyes of the lover that got away.

Inside my turquoise doeskin gloves, my palms itched. They didn't sweat, not a drop; I wasn't nervous. It was all about the anticipation, baby. The lead-up. The foreplay.

George and I made a good team. I wouldn't go so far as to say he was the brawn and I was the brain, but it shook down kind of like that. He had the most amazing hands – steady, delicate. He knew exactly how, when, and where to touch, to coax out the exact response he wanted. No safe, no security system, no alarm could resist his ministrations. Powerless beneath his touch.

Kind of like a woman.

Oh, yes, George could use those hands to work magic on me. Bring me to helpless, shuddering orgasms long into the night.

Problem was, when we were getting ready for a job, George eschewed sex. Distracted him, he said. Put him off his game. He needed to be focused.

Which left me more than a little on edge, if you know what I mean.

My outfit tonight didn't help that one bit. The custom-made corset fit me like a lover's hands, moulding against my waist, urging my breasts up to pillow enticingly. My hard nipples rubbed against my fine silk underdress just at the line of my corset. Teasing. Taunting.

George might have been the one to cajole the secrets from a coded alarm system, but I was the one who got us in place. He always said I could talk my way into, or out of, anything.

I glanced down at my enticingly displayed décolletage. I could talk the talk, but the girls helped, too.

I can't tell you the number of times I've been pulled over for speeding, only to drive away without a ticket. I can convince the proprietor of a swanky shop that I really did buy this item, but I lost the receipt, and I honestly do deserve a refund. I can charm the fur off a mountain lion, as they say.

Getting George and me invitations to this very swanky, very private reception at The Venetian was child's play.

Ah, The Venetian. An only-in-America fusion of Italian Renaissance decadent beauty, glittering luxury skyscraper and the edgy twenty-four-hour liveliness for which Las Vegas was famous. A huge casino, an in-house wax museum and gondola rides along a faux canal. Talk about gaudy.

But tonight the gaudy was the sort a Venetian doge in his ornate ceremonial robes would have approved. The Venetian also housed the Vegas branch of the world-renowned Guggenheim Museum. Tonight, it played host to a grand Carnival-themed charity ball celebrating the opening of its latest exhibit, "Jewels of Venice". Museum supporters, art lovers and high-society types were crowded into the hotel's largest ballroom, all dressed in top designers' quirky takes on Renaissance dress or some equally elaborate and fanciful getup.

And masks.

Which would make our job – absconding with the Lucchese Star – that much easier.

Faking IDs is so much easier when you don't have to show your whole face. Masks weren't just requested, they were *required* for this soirée. My own was a confection of peacock feathers and pearls, made to match the dress I'd commissioned. Because I had to look the part of the filthy rich patron.

To go along with the masquerade, attendees were asked to pick personas to further "disguise" themselves. We were announced as Count Giovanni Belli and his wife Francesca, and we swept in as if we owned the place. Give yourself a suitably impressive title and the bearing and outfits to go with it, and people will assume you should be on the guest list.

The ballroom looked like it belonged in another century, or possibly in another world. Women in boned and beaded gowns; men in velvet doublets and tights. People dressed as satyrs, nymphs, gods and goddesses, and other fantastic creatures as depicted in Renaissance art. People in ordinary evening dress (all right, *Vogue*'s very expensive idea of ordinary) but they still sported elaborate masks.

A silver-haired woman, tall and elegant in silver-embroidered black velvet with a severe silver mask blanking out her face, led an amazingly costumed anthromorphic leopard on a leash. A couple I'd swear were Brad and Angelina, dressed like Bacchus and Artemis, chatted with a Renaissance lady whose emerald necklace made my fingers itch, even with the Lucchese Star almost in my grasp.

So close. So fucking close.

We'd timed our arrival for half an hour before the viewing, giving us time to mingle and become anonymous, part of the greater crowd. Afterwards, nobody would remember us; we hadn't stood out, looked or sounded different from anyone else there.

The whole purpose of this bash was to celebrate The Venetian Guggenheim's borrowing of the Lucchese Star from the Guggenheim in Venice. (Yeah. Don't think about that too hard.) Everyone here (well, everyone except us, obviously) had donated scads of money to help with the acquisition. As such, tonight we'd get to view it first, before it was put into the museum proper.

They announced the viewing, and we filled our champagne glasses in anticipation. The door (looked like wood, but was lined with steel) opened, and we surged forward. In a polite, societally appropriate kind of way, of course.

I didn't have to restrain my reaction, because everyone gasped and murmured at the sight of the Star. I kept just enough attention on myself (making unremarkable comments to those around me) so that no one would notice that George was stealing glances at the Star's prison of a display case, assessing whether the way it was set up deviated from our research.

All too soon, we were ushered back into the main ballroom. I spared a wistful glance over my shoulder.

Soon. Soon, baby.

I set down my untouched champagne (no mind-altering substances until *after* we were safely away) and nibbled a tidbit that involved Beluga caviar, eyeing one that seemed to combine lobster and Kobe beef carpaccio. Definite perks to this gig.

George seemed cool and collected behind his full-face Harlequin mask, diamonded in rich tones of copper, gold, and an emerald green that brought out the colour of his eyes. Typical. He contained all that sexual energy, internalized it, transformed it into single-minded intent.

Whereas my job was to exude as much sex appeal as humanly possible.

Just before we'd headed to the party, George had sent off the coding that would send dummy images (the ones I'd sweet-talked out of a museum staffer for a magazine article I said I was writing) to the security cameras and disable a few critical systems, just long enough for him to swipe the Star.

My job now was to distract the guard. I admired my abundant cleavage again, stroking the creamy flesh with a fingertip. I shouldn't have a problem with strategic flirting. Unless the male security guard I was expecting had traded shifts with the happily married female ex-Marine. In that case, I'd be faking a seizure and hoping for the best.

I flipped open the pocket watch cunningly disguised as a pendant. It was time.

I touched George on the arm, whispered in his ear as if I were about to head to the ladies' room.

Then I walked right past the ladies' room, headed down the service stairs to the casino level, and up another set that took me up to the far side of the ballroom, into a deserted, blocked-off hallway.

The service entrance to the anteroom where the Lucchese Star was displayed was down that hallway.

A security guard was stationed at the hallway entrance. I made no move to evade him. Instead, I approached him, one hand extended, the other gracefully over my heart, calling attention to my cleavage.

"I'm so sorry," I said, twisting my accent slightly to sound vaguely Southern. Men liked Southern. "I think I've taken a wrong turn?"

"Looks like it, ma'am. This area is off-limits." The guard wasn't the man I'd expected to see. My research into The Venetian's security personnel had prepped me for a fiftyish black man, not a well-built white guy in his mid-thirties.

Damn cute one, too. *Whuf.* Big brown eyes, wavy dark hair and the kind of chest I could all too easily imagine curling up on between rounds one and two of wild monkey sex.

Well, it was entirely possible they'd hired extra staff for this event. This fine hunk would be just as much fun to distract as the one I'd been expecting.

I touched the back of his hand, gently. "Has a man come through here? With a red-headed showgirl type?"

Bingo. I'd picked the right ruse. The mix of concern, sympathy and, face it, curiosity, could only do me good.

He shook his head. "Fraid not." Slight, charming traces of Texas in his voice. "Someone taking those 'what happens in Vegas stays in Vegas' ads too seriously?"

I let my lower lip quiver, just for a second, before I squared my shoulders and composed myself. In a way that clearly implied my composure was all an act to hide my anguish.

"That would suggest the city is the problem." I sighed. "You know, when he keeps it discreet, it's one thing. But to leave me standing there alone – to sneak out of the ballroom and flaunt that he's going off to have his fun . . . It's too dayamn much."

I faked an expression of surprise and embarrassment, knowing that most of it wouldn't show under my mask, but hoping it would be reflected in my eyes.

Eyes that glittered with the threat of spilling tears. "I'm so sorry! I shouldn't be talking about this to a complete stranger."

The big man – the name on his uniform was Joe – shrugged.

"Easier to talk to a stranger sometimes, and you must be mad as a hornet."

I'd been stepping a little closer while we talked, edging Security Joe away from the hallway entrance. I did a quick mental calculation of how much time had passed. George should be at the top of the un-alarmed back stairs, about to step into the hallway at my signal.

Time to step up the distraction level.

"Mad means both angry and crazy." I stepped close enough to smell a combination of healthy man and inexpensive but not unpleasantly spicy cologne. "I feel a bit of both. Humiliated. And yet . . . it's his loss, right? If he can play at the game, why can't I?"

One step closer and I could feel the heat of Joe's body. I touched the peacock-feathered fan dangling from my wrist, triggering the communication to George.

"Ma'am? Are you sure . . ." the Texan politely protested even as he put his arms around me.

"Tonight I'm Francesca," I whispered, and kissed him.

Kissed him more thoroughly than I'd meant to.

I'd planned a little flirting, a little smooching, then dissolving into tears of guilt and jealousy. Most men haven't a clue what to do with a sobbing woman. The security guard would comfort me as best he could, helpless patting on the back and whatnot, and I'd make enough noise long enough for George to relieve the case of the Lucchese Star and get back into the stairway.

Change of plans. Ramp up the smooching instead.

Because despite Joe's protestations, he was getting into the smooching just fine.

His hands tightened on my corseted waist as I parted my lips, flicking my tongue out to touch the corner of his mouth. He pulled me closer, causing my breasts to pillow even more impressively out of the top of my bodice. Polyester may not be sexy, but there was this shocking sense of naughtiness at his uniform brushing against tender flesh that I don't normally expose in public.

All that barely suppressed sexual energy that had built up since we'd started planning this heist bubbled to the surface.

I reached up to stroke the chiselled planes of his face, urging him to deepen the kiss. When his tongue entered my mouth, I couldn't hold back a moan of pure pleasure.

"Francesca," he murmured against my lips. "An exotic name for an exotic lady." He slid his hands up over the curve of my breasts and drew his finger along the line where fabric met flesh. My nipples tightened in response. "But you're not that much of a lady, are you?"

I stiffened, fearing he'd seen through my ruse. But then he was coaxing my breasts free of the corset. First my nipples showed darkly through the semi-sheer silk, but he pulled the top of the chemise away. He brushed his thumbs against the needy buds, and I clutched his arms.

"More like a courtesan," he said. "Brazenly tempting men." He increased the pressure, rolling my nipples between his fingers. A steady, aching pulse started between my legs.

He kept up that maddening, rhythmic pressure while his lips languidly wandered around my neck, my earlobes, my clavicle, the swell of my cleavage. By the time his mouth found one nipple, my hips were moving in time to the rhythm, thrusting forward. He was leaning over me to kiss and lick and suckle, though, so I was humping empty air.

Until he stood and my mound connected with the impressive swelling in his uniform pants.

Oh! *Well* then.

"What have we here?" I murmured. Unable to keep my hands off something like that – a hard cock is almost as enticing as a hot rock, and certainly more fun to play with – I pressed my palm against the bulge.

His hips jerked, and I felt his prick throb even through my gloves. My mouth watered.

Well, what better way to keep a man distracted? With a rustle of silk and brocade, I sank to my knees.

"Oh, sweet Jesus," Joe said as I tugged his pants down. His cock sprang out. Long and slender, with a proud curve and darker mushroom head.

I started to peel off my gloves, but Joe's harsh whispered "No" stopped me.

"Leave them on," he urged, and who was I to argue?

He tasted as earthy as he looked. I took him full in my mouth, slicking him with saliva, and brought my hands up to encircle him while I sucked.

My pussy lips were getting just as slick. I could feel them rubbing together, my clit throbbing between them. As tempting as it was to fight one hand beneath the layers of skirts and fondle myself, I resisted. I *like* giving blowjobs, for one thing. And for another, I had to keep alert for any sounds of George, and make sure I kept Joe from noticing anything other than what I was doing to him.

From Joe's reactions, I was pretty sure he wouldn't have noticed a parade of elephants galumphing down the hall. His hands on my head, he urged me to increase the length of my oral strokes.

"Oh yeah, that's it," he said, his voice rough with desire. "Take me in. Suck me. Play with my balls."

I was more than happy to comply, and moaned my agreement as I did.

"Oh, yeah, you like it when I give directions?" he asked. "Naughty girl. That's it, suck me. Use your hands. The leather feels so good against me. Faster now."

I increased the pressure and speed, feeling his balls contract up towards his body. He was close, and I wanted to bring him off. That feeling of power, of control.

He groaned something unintelligible, and came, twitching. I rocked back onto my heels, savouring his tang, feeling slightly smug about the relaxed, slightly goofy, absolute content look on his face. OK, maybe George wouldn't be thrilled if he found out what I'd done, but it had certainly worked. With that as a distraction, there was no way the guard could have heard any very faint sounds that George might be making.

That George might still be making.

I'd taken my time, both for distraction value and because Joe had a yummy cock and a delightfully dirty mouth.

Where the hell was George? A delicate operation like this one might require more time than we'd anticipated.

Suddenly the corridor seemed tomb-like, so silent (despite all the normal background sounds you get even in a quiet corridor in a busy hotel) that I fancied Joe could hear George breathing in the other room, let alone going through all the meticulous steps needed to snatch the Star.

I could go with Plan A, Part Two: tears, confusion, repentance.

But my slick pussy and throbbing clit had other suggestions for continuing the distraction.

And they sounded like a lot more fun. Never really enjoyed playing out the weeping-woman scenario, though it's killer effective. Ruins the mascara and all that.

I stood up, one graceful motion, swaying only a little in my high heels. (Yes, I do practise things like that. It pays to stay limber, and grace adds to the erotic-distraction factor when I need it.)

Pressed myself against Joe. Might be risking a few lingering drops of come on my brocade gown, but it wasn't as though I'd be wearing this a lot in the future. (Although George had dropped hints that once the job was done, he had some amusing uses in mind for the corset and the nearly sheer split-crotch silk drawers – both historically accurate and practical when you're dealing with sixteen acres of skirt – that went underneath everything.)

Kissed him, letting him taste himself on my lips.

Felt the silk drawers get even damper than they already were.

Moaned "please" into his mouth and didn't have to act to get that tone of sheer, brazen want. I was squirming with need.

"Please what? Tell me what you want, Francesca." His big hands glided over the ample, sensitive mounds of my cleavage, not quite touching my aching, exposed nipples. I arched against him, tried to wiggle my nipples under his hands.

No good. He was onto me. "You have to tell me what you want if you hope to get it."

As he said that, he did pinch one of my nipples – unexpectedly and hard, jolting electricity through my body so once again, all I could manage was "Please".

"Please what?" he repeated, toying with my nipples some more.

This was work. Supposed to be work, anyway. I was supposed to stay focused, even if the job was offering perks beyond amazing hors d'oeuvres. But dammit, my whole body was one giant ache, and I wasn't like George – able to deflect my desire into something else.

I took a deep breath, found my brain just long enough to say, "Please get me off. I don't care how. Just please make me come."

He grinned, a cat who'd found not only cream, but a whole roast chicken and a catnip garden for dessert. Manoeuvred me around so I could lean against the wall – and a good thing too, since my knees were already shaky and I didn't think they'd be getting more stable any time soon. "Lift up your skirts," he ordered, his voice rich and decadent as the best dark chocolate or a fine vintage Bordeaux.

I did, crumpling expensive silk and brocade as if it were cheap cotton. Almost drowning in fabric, I didn't have a good view of what he was doing. But oh, I felt it all right.

His leg roughly pushed mine further apart. Coarse polyester brushed fine silk, taut, wet skin. He ground against me for a few seconds, until I was sure my juices were leaving a stain on his uniform. Then he moved, and his fingers slipped into the slit in my drawers.

"You're soaked," he breathed. "Such a wanton, naughty girl. And so hot."

Fingers circled my clit, sending pleasure spiralling through me. I started making alley-cat sounds under my breath, and my world narrowed its focus to between my legs. Then he got his other hand involved and, sliding two fingers into my dripping pussy, began to pump.

I clutched at Joe's shoulders, held on tight, came like there was no tomorrow and no yesterday either, just a long, mind-melting *now*.

When I could focus again, I could see that Joe was once again standing at attention. Or maybe he was one of those lucky guys who stayed hard even after he came if the situation were interesting enough.

A compliment in either case.

A very distracting compliment. I may have come, but it had been a long, dry few months, and one orgasm, even a toe-curler like that one, was just enough to take the edge off my need. I was still throbbing, still open and ready.

I should save it for George, who'd be relaxed once the job was over, relaxed and full of all the sexual energy he'd been channelling elsewhere for so long.

But that didn't keep me from staring at Joe's renewed erection with the longing of a poor girl staring into Tiffany's display window. It looked hard as gemstones, but a lot warmer . . .

I realized what I was doing, mentally shook myself, opened my mouth to begin the next part of the act (flustered nerves and mild guilt). Before I could say anything, though, Joe took my arm. "Want to be inside you," he said, his voice husky and hypnotic. "There's an electrical closet down the hall. Come on." He tugged at me.

The jewel thief in me sang out gleefully. The only thing better than a distracted guard was an absent one.

The female-in-heat part of me made an inarticulate moan of surrender. I could imagine that cock sliding into me from behind, inch by glorious inch, and while I could imagine more scenic places to do it than an electrical niche – one of the now-empty exhibits, maybe, so I could be surrounded by things I'd like to steal given the chance? – my pussy didn't much care at this point.

But the part of me that did the strategic thinking glitched. On one hand, maybe Joe was just killing time at a job he didn't care about and willing to risk a priceless but anonymous-to-him gem to get some hot sex. (A trait I liked in a man I was duping, especially, as in this case, if it meant I also got the hot sex.)

On the other hand, it seemed almost too convenient, and that made me curious and a little nervous. Not much in our line of work was convenient.

Play the part. I was supposed to have given big bucks to get the Lucchese Star to this country. I'd be at least a little concerned about it. "Aren't you supposed to be guarding . . ." I gestured towards the door.

Joe shrugged. "This place is so wired, alarms will squawk all over the building if an unauthorized person so much as breathes in there. They hired some high-priced security firm on top of what we already have for the casino and they rigged a bunch of stuff – I don't understand half of what they've got set up, but that thing's guarding itself. We're just backup."

"Well, that's a weight off my mind."

And it was. Joe was a slacker – a really hot slacker – relying on a high-tech security system to do his job for him.

Which it would have if I hadn't scrambled half of it and George wasn't dismantling the rest even as Joe and I played. Well, at least Joe would get his hot sex before he got fired without references, poor gorgeous bastard.

He ran his hands over my still bare breasts, sending shudders through my body, making me forget any qualms I had, including the ones involving George coming to find me and hearing strange noises coming out of the closet.

Okay, a little bit of me thought it might serve him right. I was crazy about George, I really was, but a woman can only handle so much chastity – especially when the person she wants to be unchaste with is right there in bed with her, but not interested.

The closet was as unglamorous as you'd imagine: criss-crossed with wires, unventilated, humming with various mechanical noises. It smelled like dust and electricity, and it was barely big enough for the two of us.

And at that point, I didn't care. No time to worry about atmosphere. The only nicety we took the time to bother with was a few rough but sweet kisses, the kind where you try to devour the other as if you'd never get a chance to touch again, which in this case was true.

When he turned me around so I could support myself against the wall, the cold grey-green breaker cabinet I found myself leaning against brought goose bumps to my heated skin.

The good kind of goose bumps that added to my arousal.

I briefly considered flipping a few breakers while Joe was figuring out what to do with my layers of skirt – create some confusion to cover George's retreat, and all that – but then Joe's cock nudged against my heated pussy.

And after its long hunger, my pussy took control of the situation. Just sucked that magnificent cock in, I swear, because

I don't remember any transition between that teasing tap and hot, crazy full-on fucking. Joe's hard cock pistoned inside me, stroking all those long-neglected spots that even the best toy can't hit the way the real thing does. One of his hands cupping my breasts, fingers scissoring and stroking the nipple, the other infiltrating under my skirts to circle my clit through wet silk.

I pushed back, met each hard stroke with a force of my own. No time for subtlety or tenderness. This was an unabashed quickie and I didn't care. Wanted it that way. Wanted to push myself over the edge and take him with me, here surrounded by the drone of the hotel's inner workings.

Besides, we had to be fast. George should be done by now, and Joe was deserting his post. I couldn't speak for him, but the edge of danger just made me hotter, made my inner walls clench around him, made me wild and made him wild along with me.

If I weren't an endorphin junkie, I'd still be creating security systems, not cracking them. I like risky business, and this job was pushing thrill buttons I hadn't even known I had.

Joe's fingers found just the right rhythm on my clit, and his cock pounded into me, and I rolled my hips like a jazz dancer.

And then I thought something must have happened to the electrical system because everything went black, then exploded around us.

I didn't see stars as I came. Not exactly. I saw the Lucchese Star, all sixty spectacular carats of it, cloned fifty times and dancing behind my eyelids.

Strong arms circled me. "That's my good bad Francesca. Feel a little happier now?"

"God, yes."

Another wicked grin from my talented security guard. "Sometimes getting a little yourself is the best revenge."

Oh yeah. I was supposed to be playing a part here, wasn't I?

In a small voice laden with fake confusion, I whispered, "I guess so. It was fun, anyway."

Deep breath. Satiated but somewhat uneasy smile. Sudden concern with smoothing out my skirts and repairing my lipstick, my hands trembling.

We managed to pull ourselves together and get out of the closet and just in time.

"There you are!" George hurried up to us, his hair a little mussed and his Harlequin mask the tiniest bit askew. "I've been looking all over for you. That poor girl – she was feeling sick, so I helped her find the hotel doctor – and when I got back, you were gone."

Nicely played, with hints of both concern and guilt in his voice. Then he narrowed his eyes at Joe. "Who's this?"

"I went looking for you, and got lost, honey," I said meekly. "He was just giving me directions . . . back to the ballroom."

Joe clapped George on the back. The gesture was hard enough to make George stumble forward a step, and Joe caught him. "You've gotta keep a better eye on your lovely lady," he said, sounding all amiable and between-us-boys. "You don't want her to slip away."

"Yeah," George said, staring at him funny. I caught my breath, worried that he'd figured out what we'd done. But all he said was, "Yeah, I'll do that."

We were an hour into the desert, headed towards LA, when my cell phone chimed to let me know I had a text message.

I take it your partner hasn't noticed I lifted his phone. Means he hasn't noticed something else is gone.

I stared at the display for a long time, the glow of it the only light except for our headlights on the flat, straight ribbon of freeway. We had the moon roof open to enjoy the canopy of stars undimmed by light pollution. The crisp desert air poured through, and now it made me shiver.

"What is it?" George finally asked.

"Let me see the Star."

"Fran, we're in the middle of nowhere! I can't just pull over and –"

"Trust me. Get the Star."

With a huff of annoyance, he slowed and pulled over on the shoulder. If a cop came along, we'd claim car troubles.

After we'd left The Venetian, we'd pulled into another parking garage and shucked our costumes for jeans and sweat-shirts. George rummaged in the back seat and found his doublet.

"It's right here," he said, scrunching the fabric to show the lump in the hidden inner pocket.

A car zoomed by, and ours rocked gently.

"I need to see it," I said.

"*Fine,*" George snapped. He dug it out, opened the draw-string bag, and dropped it into his hand. He held it out to me, and, barely able to breathe, I took it.

It was very pretty.

It was very pretty, faceted blue glass. Same size and weight as the Star, but still glass.

The sounds of the night, the rushing of passing cars, faded away. I felt the blood drain from my face.

"Fuck!" George snatched the stone out of my hand and flung it out the moon roof. It disappeared into the sand and scrub somewhere off Interstate 15. He didn't look at me, but I still felt like he knew it was all my fault.

Damn me for an idiot. A horny idiot.

Joe's diction had changed as we talked. Still the slight Texas accent – that might even be real – but he'd gone from all "aw shucks, ma'am" to sounding smoother, better educated, as things got hot and heavy.

Which should have tipped me off that that was his real voice, the one he fell into when his brain wasn't 100 per cent in gear. But I'd been too busy being seduced.

A month later I was on the road again, this time headed south.

I loved George. Plain and simple, I did. And I loved working with him. But a disaster like the loss of the Lucchese Star could ruin even the most solid working relationship.

The personal relationship unravelled with the same effort-lessness. Apparently George lost interest in sex not only when he was planning a heist, but also when he was thwarted in one.

Joe – or whatever his real name was – had texted me again. He'd been impressed, he said, with my creativity, my ability to think on my feet. If I felt like "upgrading", he was willing to negotiate.

When I answered, he gave me the name of a bar in Tijuana. He'd be there for an hour on a particular night, if I cared to show.

I opened the moon roof, enjoying the wind ruffling my hair. The stars weren't as impressive as a fist-sized sapphire, but they were awfully pretty.

It was important, always, to have a Plan B.

Shadow Dancing

Alana Noel Voth

Seven weeks after I'd begun fucking him and only thirty minutes after I'd asked him over for dinner with me and my son, my twenty-six-year-old lover fell off an ATV and broke three vertebrae in his lower back.

He wasn't a big guy – five-foot-six, maybe one-hundred-fifty pounds wet. Broke Back Boy told me later that his father had watched him cut across a gravel road on the ATV from a window, and let his son lie there half an hour before coming to check him. Does a father let his injured son lie on the ground for a reason? I could think of it only as abandonment. Cruel. Like how my son's father left him before he was born.

Broke Back Boy called from a hospital. "I think I might have broken my back, I don't know when I'll call again, I'm scared, this nurse, she said I might have broken my back, fuck I'm scared."

"What?" I said. "What?" I heard him cry. "Where are you?"

"Hospital."

"Who's with you?"

"Dad. Mom."

"Which hospital?"

"Kaiser."

"Which Kaiser?"

"Sunnyside."

"You want me to come? I'll come right now."

"Hex," he said.

"What?"

"Hex," he said again.

They'd pumped him full of morphine. "Honey, I don't understand you."

To my surprise, I started to cry. He was just a boy I fucked. "My ex is here," he said.

What I knew about her: they'd been together four years. They'd broken up three months before I'd begun fucking him. I'd asked why only once. "We fought," he'd said. She was a medical student. His age. Enough about her. She was there. I wasn't.

Longest I stayed with a lover was two years, and by the time he left I was glad he'd left. I was always glad when a lover left because you push a man away with indifference, and you do this to keep an upper hand, so you don't have to endure the pain of abandonment.

Eventually every man leaves you lying there injured.

I met Broke Back Boy when I was thirty-nine, after I'd earned a master's degree and ended up in an office job, a job which reminded me daily that I'd thought I'd become a writing professor, lofty and revered, except after graduate school I hadn't been able to get a decent let alone lofty job teaching because I hadn't published in the *New Yorker*, the *Atlantic Monthly*, or the *Paris Review*. Except I was the sort of person who believed you got what you wanted in life, like Broke Back Boy. I wanted him and wrote accordingly:

Thirty-nine-year-old single mom and former stripper with a master's degree, now working in office, seeks lover, 21–27, cute, literate, and shy.

This boy would become my first lover in five years, and I picked the one I did because his note was short and sweet, and because he was intimidated by me, which would give me the upper hand.

Do you really exist? I'm mid-twenties, and I'm a lineman or a journeyman or just an electrician. Since you have a master's degree you must be smart, which is intimidating and if you were a stripper you must be sexy, also intimidating. Maybe I'll hear from you. If you want, I'll send a picture next time.

First picture he sent had the hex cut out, and her absence made me feel both enflamed and dismissive. I didn't ask about her in letters. We wrote about music, movies, and sexual fantasies. I wanted to tie him up. He wanted me to tie him up. First time we spoke on the phone I felt my body warm with sexually charged euphoria; I laughed giddy laughter. A river thin as thread divides the difference between the tears that roll from your eyes when you're laughing and the tears you experience crying so hard you vomit. I reeled my new lover in like a silver fish, this thin inappropriate boy, this drama in sneakers. No one has ever suited me less.

One month before he broke his back, my lover had to move out of a place he shared with four guys and subsequently moved into an apartment above his parents' garage. A week later he called on his way to Idaho to say his friend had been killed in a bar fight, and he was on his way to the funeral. He didn't cry. He said it was what he'd expected, this violent death for his friend.

Around all this Broke Back Boy called to ask if he called too much. His insecurity made me feel powerful, conveniently detached, and amused. I thought of him only as inspiration, pleasure. This was what I'd been to men my whole life. Yes, Broke Back Boy was selfish; he was reckless too, and in addition to his passion for injuring himself in accidents, Broke Back Boy had a dangerous job manipulating electrical currents with his bare hands. Just waiting to get burned. By the time I'd met him, he had a green card for medical marijuana and ate pain pills like candy – all before he broke his back. He was a pot-head-pill-popping-functioning-junkie and smelled just like one: weed and nicotine and sweat and the cologne he wore, and a wild windy outdoors and hot wires – a heady concoction, the kind a woman about to hit middle age could inhale like cocaine.

One night Broke Back Boy arrived at my apartment after I'd put my son to bed, and took a seat in a chair in my living room like he'd been born there. He'd talked into his phone. I'd stood a few feet away sipping wine and studying the lines of his face, amused and detached, but then I'd inhaled him so many times I became intoxicated by his sweet and sour smell and went down on my hands and knees to crawl across the gray carpet before I knelt between his denim-sheathed thighs; I wedged myself between his thighs and then laid the top half of my body across his lap before pressing my face to his chest.

I became delusional, a girl in daddy's lap. Snug. Happy ever after. With one hand, he'd touched my hair, petted me above my ears, and I'd lifted my head to look in his eyes and saw a boy with a funny smirk on his face.

On 21 December a doctor performed surgery on Broke Back Boy to repair his three broken vertebrae. Later, my boy told me the actor Edward Norton had undergone the same surgery. Experimental, the doctor had told him. No one knew what happened when the cement in his back dissolved, if he'd be paralyzed by the time he was forty. Broke Back Boy told me this after we'd fucked, our bodies like two strings of pasta after an appropriate boiling on the mattress in my bedroom, candles burning, candles that smelled like sugar cookie and cinnamon rolls. Like home. Like a kitchen. And you wouldn't have thought he'd broken his back five weeks before unless like me you'd run three fingers of your right hand across a bruise above his right kidney and then touched each of the tiny incisions around three vertebrae in the small of his back. I stroked his face, his left arm, and then the knobs of his spine.

He smiled and said, "You have a calming touch." His battered body enflamed more than a lover in me. I wanted to fix him. Like a mom when my son fell off his skateboard and cried. I could fix him. Except I never asked Broke Back Boy why. *Why were you going so fast the day I invited you over to dinner?* I didn't want that answer.

New Year's Eve, on the phone, Broke Back Boy asked me, "How many men have you been with?" And I laughed – my reaction at a moment like that. Because this wasn't a question brought on by desire or even curiosity; I heard an accusation. So I laughed. Anything else could bring on madness. Like when you had to claw the sides of your sanity as a gulf opened between you and a man, like the night I told my son's father I was pregnant, and he sat on one end of a couch, arms folded across his chest, fastening his eyes to a wall, and I sat on the other end of the couch, hands shaking in my lap while I fixed my eyes on him. Waiting until finally I couldn't wait anymore because it felt like waiting for death. Like a clam tossed to the beach and laid bare in my half-shell. "Get the fuck out." *I hate you*. You, you don't see my pain.

My irritation that night with Broke Back Boy, however, was turned soft like white bread in brown gravy by alcohol; in other words, I'd had several glasses of wine by midnight on New Year's Eve.

"I can count the number of girls I've been with on two hands."

"Good for you, I guess."

I was older than him, had a history. Experience. Scars. No regrets. I repeat. Scars.

"Why didn't you ask me to come to the hospital?" That was what lovers did, turned the tables on one another. I lay there out of wine now, dangled across the cushions, one limb hanging over the edge of the couch, my eyes turned to a poster of Marilyn Monroe on the wall.

"Because you have other responsibilities," he said, and I heard resentment in his voice, that he resented everything, that I was a mother.

"Yes, I do."

"Besides, the ex was showing up, and I never knew when."

"That's the real reason you didn't ask me."

"I care about her. I don't know what my feelings are for you."

Lovers were good at this, volleying pain back and forth, except you didn't want the hurt to settle in your court. Knock it back, fast.

"Look, it doesn't matter," I said.

"Know how many times I wished it was you instead of her?" His voice had softened, repentant. Very high on dope and pills.

I began to cry, because lovers were good at volleying pain, and I was drunk with it. Fury replaced by wishful thinking. "I miss you."

"I want to see you," he said.

"How?" He was high on pain pills, dope, sleeping pills too.

"I don't know."

Lovers wished for physical proximity to heal all wounds. Yes, sex, so I could consume him like a meal. "I'll come get you," I said.

"Really?"

"Yes."

"I want you to."

"OK."

"You're serious?"

"Yes."

"You'll come get me?"

"Yes." I moved to a standing position and then blinked my eyes at the Christmas lights. *How could I wake my son in the other room and then drive after all this wine?*

"You're serious, baby?"

"I don't know." I retreated to the couch, confused.

"What if you call me tomorrow?"

Silence, like the kind to fall over a jungle when the prey has turned the tables on its hunter, and so the hunter pads away pretending she was never hungry for it. Doesn't care. Fat on denial.

Last time I saw Broke Back Boy, I knew it was the last time. I knew by how he fucked me. He fucked me for over an hour. And the way he did it, the flick of his hips, a particular shove, it all said *there, take that*, and then *there again*. At one point my cunt cried "Uncle."

"You want me to stop?" he asked.

"Yeah, uh-huh." I felt madness getting closer. Really, everyone was close.

Broke Back Boy pulled out, cock still hard. Every glorious inch of it. Shining with remnants of me. My longing. My weeping. Wet kiss in the rain.

He put his hands on my knees; my legs wouldn't stop shaking. "Hey, baby, hey – you OK?"

"No." I fell sideways on the mattress on my bedroom floor then gripped a pillow to my face. Broke Back Boy lay beside me.

"Hey."

I felt the weight of his five-foot-six frame behind me. I turned my face from the pillow to look at him. He was a pale whip of a boy with a down of hair on his ass. His young man's body was old. The hair at the top of his head had already begun to thin. Something caught my eye in the glow from a string of holiday lights and for a moment I mistook a glimpse of his scalp for a halo. His eyebrows slanted in a wicked way. I pressed a finger to one of his sideburns and let that finger ride his cheek peppered by new growth. He had a slim, pale face. I loved it. That face. I saw my future right there in his face.

"Fuck me some more," I said.

He got on me, shoved himself inside and began to thrust. His sweat rained in my bangs and kissed my forehead. My body was coated with Broke Back Boy sweat like one of those potions they sell on TV guaranteed to add luster to your skin. I wanted to languish in it and raked my hands up his back to get sweat under my fingernails. I hugged him just to feel the slide of our skin. The stick. He apologized. "Sorry I'm sweating so much." He stopped fucking me to wipe himself off with his shirt.

I said, "I like it." Fucking sweat on me. He sweat on me some more. And didn't come. So I began to wonder if it was because he was so high on dope and pills he was numb.

"You want to pull out and come in my face?" I asked, testing him.

"Hmm, yeah, would you let me?"

"Yeah."

He pushed a little harder inside me.

"You want to flip me over and fuck me from behind?"

"Yeah."

"You want to fuck me up the ass?"

"Ohh yeah, I do."

"I'll let you."

"You will?"

"Uh-huh, go ahead."

Broke Back Boy was small in stature and wished he were tall and broad enough to overwhelm me, so conscious of his inadequacies he couldn't come. And me, so afraid of one thing, I demanded only one thing from him.

"Fuck me. Don't stop. Fuck me." I felt overwhelmed. "Wait," I said.

Behind every scar is an episode of suffering. In the right light, a soft ethereal glow, no one could see my scars. I looked flawless. But my body, if anyone looked close enough and in enough light, blossomed with scars. Some were the result of cruelty, like the scar on my leg from when the Ferguson boys tossed a lit stick of dynamite at me at the bus stop in eighth grade. "Because your friend's fat, and you're ugly." Others were the result of injury, like the scars from a bike accident in 1982, the one that sent me to the emergency room where my grandmother told a doctor, "Don't you dare shave her head," when he wanted to shave my hair off to clean the gravel from my scalp. I still had gravel in my scalp and scars on my forehead, my elbows, left thigh, my knees.

The rest of my scars, dozens of them, were the result of self-inflicted injuries; I dug at my own skin with my fingernails and then wore long-sleeved shirts to conceal the sores and then scars. Once my sister-in-law noticed my arms in the sunlight and said, "Are you breaking out in hives?" No, scars. I didn't want Broke Back Boy to see them – my vulnerability, the insecurity; things I didn't trust him with; what I'd wished for and didn't get.

"Wait." I rolled him over so I was on top. I rode him while watching us in a mirror, the sliding glass doors behind us. Alice walked right through the looking glass. I fucked in front of mine, lifted my body so I could see the muscles in my thighs straining, my dark bush, the heavy sway of my breasts, the fall of hair in my face. I looked spotless in my reflection, this soft deceiving light. I looked vast and detached.

Broke Back Boy groaned beneath me. He gripped my hips with his hands. He said, "Damn." He said, "I don't want to come, I don't want this to end." He said, "Your pussy feels so good, baby."

"You feel me?" I said.

"I feel you," he said.

Broke Back Boy lifted his head off the mattress. I hit him hard in the face and he gasped. I gasped too.

He widened his eyes at me. "Baby, fuck, why'd you do that?" He dropped his head backwards. "I'm gonna come."

I heard a sound, high-pitched helplessness. Right. He shuddered beneath me. *Come.* Rabbit between my legs, wings of a hawk. I met my eyes in the mirror. Sort of. It started inside before it ricocheted out, like a jumper right through a window.

Secrets in Turkey Bay

Gwen Masters

The engine of the four-wheeler idled quietly between my thighs. The heat from the engine was harsh on my legs. Mud was everywhere – all over the tyres, the engine, even the handlebars. I wiped some of it off and looked at my fingers. My arms were covered with it. My long hair was pulled back in a ponytail and stuck under a baseball cap, and even that cap was caked with dirt. I looked out over the bay as I shook drops of mud off my fingertips.

"That's pretty damn sexy," my boyfriend drawled. Chuck was sitting on the back of his own four-wheeler, which was originally hunter green but was now solid brown. He was covered in mud, same as I was, only his covering looked to be a bit thicker than mine.

I turned to him and grinned. I held up my hands to show him that every finger was covered.

"Better than nail polish," he announced.

"What's nail polish?"

He laughed and winked at me as he gunned his engine. "Race me?"

"Race you where?"

Chuck nodded straight ahead. He wanted to drive right through the center of the major mud puddle, right there through the middle of the marshland bay. I stared at it for a moment, then looked back at him. He raised a mud-covered eyebrow. He looked a bit like a human raccoon. The only clean spots on his face were those circles right around his eyes.

I didn't answer. I just kicked my four-wheeler into gear and hit the gas. My tyres dug in for a moment, then I was rocketing straight ahead, diving into the mud without a second's hesitation. I downshifted again when I hit the edge of the mud, and downshifted one more time before I roared right into it. Chuck was speeding along with me, though I noted with appreciation that he was quite a few feet behind.

The engine howled. Mud flew behind the four-wheeler in a wide, tall arc. Whoops and hollers came from the bank – from people watching and waiting for their turn. Chuck's engine roared and with a quick turn of his wrist he was ahead of me, throwing mud into my face. My four-wheeler bogged down. I geared up, spun tyres and then geared back down. I shot out of the puddle and onto the dry ground, gearing up as I did it, but he was still too far ahead of me.

"Damn you!" I hollered, and thought I heard Chuck laugh.

I cranked the engine wide open and tore across the field, chasing Chuck. By the time he reached the fencerow and swung the four-wheeler around, I was still a good five lengths behind him. And I was covered with mud. He grinned triumphantly at me and revved the engine. His muffler sounded like it was clogged.

His engine died.

I laughed out loud.

"Go ahead and laugh, you little shit," he growled as he tried to start the engine again. It was useless. The engine was flooded. He glared at me and kicked the hell out of the fender. Mud flew off and plopped on the ground.

"But you won," I said with a grin.

"That's not helping," he replied, but he was trying to hide his crooked smile.

I climbed off my four-wheeler. Chuck scooted back on his and made room. I straddled his four-wheeler and faced him. I wiped mud off his face with my fingertips. He kissed my nose.

"Is there mud on my nose?" I asked.

"Actually, you're not that bad."

"I can't say the same for you."

Chuck smiled and pulled a wet rag from the pocket of his mud-soaked jeans. The rag was shockingly white against the dirtiness of everything else. He used it to wipe down my face, and then used it on his own. Motors roared down in the huge mud pit.

"Aren't you smart as can be," I said approvingly. He waved the cloth in the air like a flag.

"If you cannot beat the mud, you must learn how to work around it," he said.

"Apparently."

Chuck grinned at me and this time he kissed me in earnest. His lips were warm and soft against mine. His face was damp. "You're so damn cute," he said.

I smiled up into his green eyes. I reached down to pull up my sweatshirt. Chuck's eyes lit up, then his face fell when he realized I was wearing a tank top underneath it.

"I should have known," he lamented.

"Want to see more?"

"Do you have to ask?"

I stood up on the four-wheeler. Chuck looked up at me with a leering grin. I unbuttoned my jeans and started to shimmy out of them. Men from the opposite bank hollered and laughed. I shook my hips and smoothed the denim down my thighs. I was wearing short-shorts underneath the jeans. Groans of disappointment came from the opposite bank, even though everyone knew I wasn't really going to strip in front of complete strangers.

Chuck shook his head. "You know how to get me going."

I turned the sweatshirt inside out and draped it over the four-wheeler. I sat down on the clean spot. I reached out and unbuttoned Chuck's jeans.

"Whoa," he protested. "What are you doing?"

"Checking to see if I got you going," I murmured as I kissed him. I slipped my fingers inside his jeans. He wasn't all that hard, but after a few strokes he was standing proudly at full attention. The head of his cock peeked out from the opening in his jeans. Chuck looked around to see if anyone was watching, and I cuddled close enough to hide him from any curious onlookers.

"I can't believe you're doing this out here in the middle of all the mud and dirt," he said.

"I can't believe you're letting me," I shot back.

Chuck settled his hands on my waist. He held me lightly as I pulled his jeans down a little more. I could reach every inch of him, and no one else could see. I leaned forward so that our foreheads touched. I wrapped my hand around his cock and started with long, slow strokes. Chuck sighed and his hands tightened on my waist.

"Why do you do things like this?" he whispered.

"Things like what?"

"Things like jacking me off in the middle of Turkey Bay in front of everybody."

"Nobody is looking. Are they?"

Chuck took a deep breath. He was already throbbing in my hand. "No."

"But you wouldn't mind if they did. Would you?"

Chuck's blush was very becoming. I laughed at him and he blushed even harder.

"I do these things because I like pleasing you," I said.

"I'll make it up to you later."

I grinned. Chuck was definitely not the kind of guy who would take pleasure and then not bother to give any in return. "I know you will."

His cock jerked in my hand every time I reached the sensitive spot under the head. I placed my thumb there and rubbed in slow circles. Chuck groaned. He was breathing hard and completely oblivious to everything that was happening down in the pit. His hands on my waist were clenching down tighter and tighter. I kissed him hard as he bucked gently into my hand.

"You're going to make me come," he murmured against my lips.

"Good."

"I don't know what to do," he chuckled. I didn't stop stroking. His whole body was tense. He was right on the verge. I eased the pressure of my hand and kept him right there at the finish line, but didn't let him slip over it.

"You don't know what to do?"

"Where am I going to come?"

I gave him a wicked smile. "Wherever you want."

"But —"

I shut him up with a kiss. He closed his eyes and groaned against my lips. I tightened my hand on his cock and stroked fast and hard. Within seconds Chuck bucked into my hand. He spurted right between us. I covered the head of his cock with my free hand and kept stroking with the other. Chuck clenched his jaw for a long moment, then took a deep breath. His hands eased up on my waist. He chuckled deep in his chest.

"You heathen," he said.

I raised my hand to my lips. Chuck's eyes widened. I took my time in drinking and licking what I found there. He laughed out loud as I licked away the last drops and gave him a seductive wink. Then I reached down and buttoned his pants back up.

Chuck wrapped his arms around me. We both completely forgot that my clothes were clean and his weren't. The cold seep of mud through my tank top made me shriek and pull away.

Chuck laughed and reached behind me. He turned the key and started the engine. It roared on the first try.

"You fixed it," he said in mock surprise. "You handywoman, you."

I cuddled closer to him. I was already covered with mud again, so why not? I kissed the only clean spot on his throat that I could find. He sighed with satisfaction.

"Baby," he said, "your mind is just as dirty as this four-wheeler."

17 Short Films about Hades and Persephone

Elspeth Potter

He filled their bedchamber with narcissus each time Persephone returned, because he knew she found them beautiful. The flowers didn't last long in the underworld, but their aroma lingered. To Hades, the flowers smelled no sweeter than her skin.

His brother Poseidon roared with laughter when Hades told him. Sprawled on his throne of coral, idly fondling the partially-exposed breasts of the Nereid curled in his lap, Poseidon poked at Hades with his trident which, Hades sometimes thought, his brother considered a subsidiary phallus. "Bumbler! You kidnapped the wench with narcissus! They don't like to remember the first time, even Zeus knows that."

Hades did know, but what else was he to choose? There were no flowers in his realm, so he had no idea what other flowers she might like. He had to have *something* to let her know her return was a special occasion, and she scorned his gold and jewels, no matter how intricate the workmanship.

Poseidon's solution was to offer him a Nereid to "take the edge off." Useless libertine. Despite her smiling flash of tiny, pearly teeth and her hand that traveled unerringly below his waist, Hades knew the slender creature in her transparent drapery was afraid of him. He couldn't bear other women's cringes when he sat too near, their flinches from his hands as if they sensed the cold of the grave. He wanted Persephone, if he could only wait for her.

The waiting was the most difficult part.

He wanted her to at least smile upon him, not the sad and terrible smile she gave to beseeching mortals, but the incandescent smile of the young maiden she had been.

Hence the narcissus.

He might not deserve her smiles, but he wanted them all the same.

His sister Demeter always made Hades wish to be elsewhere. Every time he looked at her matronly form, he was reminded that she had once rejected him, going to Zeus' bed instead, and later to that of Poseidon. To her credit, she hadn't struck at Hades with these encounters, but of course Zeus did. At length. He could never resist describing his conquests, stroking his glorious beard the while, as if it were Demeter's fertile flesh. Their union had yielded Persephone.

From Poseidon, there was his usual braggadocio about his stallion rutting. Not only Demeter but woman upon woman – sometimes several at a time – succumbed to Poseidon's carefree laughter and unbridled hands.

Hades was paler and slighter than his brothers, his hair and eyes darker, as if reflecting the darkness of the world below. His nose was long, his lips finely carved, his eyes heavily lidded as if with sleep or eternal contempt; most could not tell which. He did not think himself ugly. Unlike his brothers, his hands were uncalloused, slender and smooth, his chiton always immaculate, his sandals never worn or frayed. He went clean-shaven for the most part, feeling a beard was too profligate, and cropped his thick hair short, though it made futile attempts to escape onto his forehead. True, his body held too much tension for beauty; he knew that; but he was not repugnant.

He could recognize himself in the statues mortals made to represent him, few as those were, and he received worship from mortals, even if that worship consisted only of begging his mercy while banging their heads against the dirt. And he was rich. All the stones and metals below ground belonged to him. He did not understand why women not only refused him but avoided him; not only avoided him but actively ran away.

Of course, had Demeter accepted him in the first place, Persephone might be his own daughter rather than Zeus', and thus could not have been his wife. He supposed he had got the better end of the bargain. He did not know if Persephone agreed.

Persephone should have blamed Zeus for her predicament, not Hades. Zeus fathered her, and Zeus gave her away. Hades only took what he needed.

It began with a pomegranate. She would not linger with him voluntarily, so legality was Hades' only recourse. She had eaten; she had obviously intended to stay. Hades presented the facts thus. Zeus agreed with him, Hades suspected, because he was tired of listening to Demeter's endless plaints about their daughter. If not as romantic as Hades had hoped, at least he had a place from which to begin.

(He never forgot her lips suckling the fruit – scarlet pulp smearing her chin and her defiant eyes when he discovered her.)

Hades did his best for their wedding, belated though it was, and though he could not let Persephone depart his realm to spend the traditional *proaulia* period with her mother, he made certain all of the proper rites and sacrifices were made. He studded the palace's ceilings with diamonds and set them alight with the touch of his hand. He carpeted the floor in plush moss and gave it the colors of his finest jewels, arranged into figures forming the war with the Titans. To accompany the sacrificial feast, he arranged for earthly foods, all the ones he hoped Persephone would like best: figs bursting with sweet nectar, cheese pale and smooth as her skin, honeyed sesame seeds, a rainbow of olives. Then he hardened his nerves and invited his sister Demeter. Luckily, old Hecate took Demeter in charge as soon as she arrived, forestalling a number of possibly ugly arguments.

Begun with song, the wedding continued with processions and the giving of gifts, purifying baths and the sacrifice of Persephone's childhood garments. She presented a lock of her hair to Artemis and helped distribute fresh-baked bread to the guests. Hades endured it all, gazing upon his bride and no other, his trembling fingers tucked in the folds of his chiton. She did not appear afraid. Instead, she seemed to Hades to be more haughty than Hera, taking the guests' homage as her due.

Persephone spent the entire ceremony staring at her mother through her veil. Being a god, Hades could see straight through to her face. Persephone seemed to be angry at Demeter; he could not conceive why.

She would be happy once they were alone again. Surely she would be.

Perhaps it began before the pomegranate, with the narcissus.

True, he did entice her into his realm with the flower's wondrous scent. He'd been surprised and relieved by how easily she'd followed him.

If not Hades, then some other would make Persephone his wife, possibly even one who was not divine. She deserved better. She deserved a god. The King of the Dead was no less than her due.

On their wedding night he brought her to a bedchamber whose walls were streaked with wide veins of gold and silver, catching the lamplight like her eyes. He loved the cool smoothness of stone, but not as much as warm yielding flesh, so much more rare in his realm. He laid her among pillows and plush fleeces, permitting only the faintest plucking of a cithara to tremble in the air. Kneeling before her, he withdrew the pins and flowers from her hair, spreading her topaz tresses between his fingers. All the while, his eyes did not move from her face.

She would not look at him. When he brushed her cheek, gently as a moth's wing, she turned her face away.

He had given her golden fibulae to pin her peplos, and a girdle of calfskin embossed in gold and decorated with freshwater pearls. He carefully unclasped the fibula at her left shoulder. He heard the shaft's drag through embroidered wool as he withdrew it; his fingers closed over the sharp pin, convulsively, before he put it aside. His hands did not tremble as he unhooked the other and folded her garment down over her girdle.

Her breasts held a rosy glow, the nipples dark like the secret flesh of figs. They felt as round and weighty as quinces in his hands, no less perfumed but more yielding. She smelled like fresh bread and very slightly of lanolin, and the relentless odor of narcissus. Her eyes, dark and huge, flicked down to his hands, and back to his face, but she looked away again as soon as she saw him watching.

He had every right to touch her. Hades cupped her breasts and dragged his thumbs over her nipples, feeling the hot rush as they engorged, watching her pulse flutter at the side of her throat. Her skin felt so soft, softer than talc slipping and dissolving under the fingers.

Her nipple tightened in his mouth. He suckled it reverently as his fingers, seemingly unbidden, removed her girdle and pushed aside the folds of her peplos. A faint shiver passed over her skin.

Hades leaned down and kissed her. She knew now to open to him, though she gave him nothing else. Her mouth tasted humid and fluttery, like the wings of a butterfly emerging from its cocoon, and slick, too, like the creatures who lived at the edges of pools underground. He inhaled Persephone's breath and softly tested the plumpness of her lips with his teeth, hoping she would respond in kind.

At last he had to withdraw so he would not fall upon her with his hunger, too great for even ambrosia to satiate. He forced himself to smile and stroke Persephone's soft cheek with the back of his hand. Her lips brushed his fingers as she turned away, but not purposefully.

Frustrated, Hades blew out his breath. "Look at me," he said. "I will not harm you, Persephone."

Then she looked at him, but her dark eyes blazed with anger, not passion.

He flinched. "I only want you to look at me," Hades said, softly.

"I hate you," she said, and looked away, her eyes wide open, fixed on the wall like someone dead.

Well, she would have pleasure anyway. Their wedding night would be perfect. Gritting his teeth, Hades unfastened his finery. His fingers stumbled until, all at once, his bare flesh met hers, and it was as if he embodied phlogiston, ready to burst into flame.

He could smell her musk, almost like the mushrooms mortals ate in worship. He grasped her hips in his hands and lifted her sex to his mouth, for a few moments allowing himself to devour her melliferous petals with his tongue, sucking her tiny stamen between his lips and pressing it between his shrouded teeth. She cried out, a tiny, broken sound, like a soul trapped in Tartarus, and he would have recoiled had her fingers not sunk deeply into his hair. Then he understood, and the next cry from her tore his heart with hope.

Persephone sighed and fell limp. Hades lowered her slight form gently to the cushions and caressed her breast and her face. His hand curled softly around her cheek as he kissed her.

"I hate you," she said.

Persephone spurned topaz and emerald, amethyst and tourmaline. After that rejection, Hades traveled above on foot to bring her armloads of flowers; she threw them in his face.

The first time Persephone left him to go back to her mother, Hades did not accompany her. He had not the slightest desire to see Demeter. The crone Hecate escorted Persephone instead. Hades pretended he was not watching to see if his wife felt sadness at leaving him, or joy.

It would not have been appropriate to send Persephone alone, and to escort her himself might have seemed too . . . possessive. Hecate was a good compromise. She retained privileges in the underworld from some distant time before his own rule had begun; he knew vaguely that she had something to do with mortal childbirth as well, but that was not his concern. Persephone could bear no children after her congress with the King of the Dead.

Hades thought, since gifts proved useless, he could woo Persephone with poetry. That experience did not bear repetition.

For a time, there was comradeship between Hades and his wife. Persephone had known Theseus and Pirithous were coming to abduct her. Hades shared it with her, and revealed his plan for keeping her safe. She laughed with him at the simple cleverness of it. She took to watching the progress of the Heroes through their realm each afternoon, curled against his arm on a couch of cedar spread with wool carpets. For her pleasure, Hades made a wall into a vast window that followed the invaders like Thanatos himself, implacable. Together, they watched the ageing Heroes distract Cerberus with honeyed cakes. Persephone cooed over the creature as if he were a lapdog. Hades had to laugh when she invented her own conversations for the two Heroes:

"Theseus! Oh! I've fallen into this pit! If you pull me out, I will lick your cock for you!"

"Nay! My mighty pillar of manhood shall not be licked by you, but by Hades himself only!"

"Then I, too, shall have only Hades for my bride, because to follow you is my only wish!"

Hades sometimes wished some other misguided fool would attempt to steal his wife, just so they could experience such happy times again, two beings with a single goal.

Persephone never came to him for lovemaking, yet complained when he left her alone.

Her hands on his body were never gentle, but he accepted her roughness as better than no touch at all.

Persephone flaunted the pleasure she found with Adonis, or so it seemed. Hades gritted his teeth and bore it. He would not look. He would not look. He could hear their laughter from her sewing chamber as Persephone stroked Adonis and whispered to him – Hades imagined all sorts of things, probably worse than reality, he told himself; surely Aphrodite, Adonis' chief protector, would not allow Persephone such liberties with her paramour.

All his time underground, however, was fully occupied. Persephone led Adonis about the palace like a pet goat, holding him by the arm or the wrist or the hand, and once by his flowing hair.

She never touched Hades if she could avoid it.

She kissed Adonis in greeting and in parting, and not just a peck on the lips; she kissed his mouth in a leisurely fashion, then trailed her mouth across his cheek and finished with a soft brush of his ear, every time. She made sure Hades saw, and he watched, unblinking. Inwardly, he writhed. That should have been him. He'd meant to be in Adonis' place: the object of her adoration and the source of her pleasure. Except he was not beautiful, not like Adonis, and his smiles chilled even the bravest mortal souls, and his touch somehow repelled innocence.

Adonis had no choice about his visits. For that reason, Hades could not strike him down, much as he desired to do so. He was not Zeus, wielding his power for petty revenges and momentary seductions. Instead, Hades took pleasure in surveying his domain from his chariot; counting his riches; admiring his favorite ornament, the Lapith prince Pirithous sitting in the chair of forgetfulness, his eyes wide and empty. Then he would picture Adonis in that chair, or in the empty one that had captured Theseus: just punishment for men who had tried to take away his wife and lover.

Inevitably, he would return to their bedchamber after his miserly evening meal of olives and bread and lamb, and pretend he was not waiting for her.

Persephone returned to Hades' bed when Adonis left her at last. After his enforced celibacy, abstinence was impossible for Hades. He could easily have fallen on her, taking pleasure while allowing her none, but his pride would not allow that. He could not leave her unsatisfied and have her doubt his prowess.

Persephone's body cooperated savagely in their joining while her words eviscerated. "Adonis," she said, gasping with each thrust, "makes me – forget – words. With – one touch – he –"

But you are mine, not his, Hades thought. Afterwards, as they lay exhausted, he said, "He doesn't love you."

"I know that." She might have been speaking of household accounts. "He cannot love me." She paused. "I cannot love you."

"It doesn't matter. I am your husband. He is a paramour."

"He tastes like honey and flowers. His touch is the sun and the wind."

"He's for the world above. You are for the world below now, as I am. You are its queen. Be content with what you have here."

"I will leave you. Very soon now, husband."

"When you leave our realm, Adonis still will not be yours. He loves Aphrodite. You took him when you could for your own pleasure, but you cannot keep him."

"As you took me."

"To be my Queen."

"I care nothing for being a Queen."

Hades knew she lied but, wiser than he had once been, he said nothing.

More than once Hades thought being without Persephone would immolate him.

"Led by your balls," Poseidon scoffed, but Hades noted that his brother's casual seductions never ended well, if not for him then for someone.

No, Hades knew a faithful marriage was the most prudent course for a ruler, and the most satisfying. And he wanted Persephone. Oh, how he wanted her.

After Adonis was killed, Hades thought to give Persephone a bouquet of the crimson anemones that grew up from his blood, in remembrance of her lover. Then she would also remember their marriage was eternal.

He thought better of it before she arrived, and resolved simply to make her forget that her body had known another.

Hades created windows to the world above, to watch his wife as she went about her daily routine of staining her mouth with grapes and weaving bright woollens and chasing pet piglets in merry abandon and dancing in the sunlight with her maids until they collapsed, laughing. He could not watch for long before his body would quicken, and he had to seek release. The nymph Minthe was enough aroused by Hades' fine quadriga and plume-tailed black horses that she consented to lie with him, provided the horses could watch. Nymphs had strange ways, but Hades was not one to quibble. Poised on the brink of entering Minthe's soft channel, he was brought up short by tender breath on his neck.

"I think not, husband," Persephone murmured in his ear. "Consider what I have given up for you." Curling one hand around his waist, she flicked the fingers of the other into the nymph's startled face.

Crushed mint, he found, made a wonderfully crisp-smelling bed for lovemaking. Persephone bit at his lips and scraped her nails down his back even as her thighs urged him over her; gasps jerked from her mouth as her body skidded in the herbs and damp earth. She threw her head back and cooed in her throat like a dove.

But her eyes were closed.

As Hades wandered the palace corridors, he heard Hecate's cackling mingled with Persephone's sweet laughter. Once, when Hades went to pay his annual respect to the old bastard Cronus, he came upon the two wandering the fields of Elysium, arm in arm, heads bent close in colloquy. The friendship signified, he thought, Persephone's acceptance of her place in their realm.

He wondered if they ever discussed him. He decided it was better not to know what advice Hecate might be dispensing.

Having taken Persephone from her mother's bosom, Hades felt it was only right that she take Hecate as a weird and mysterious substitute.

As his queen, Persephone had the right to contradict Hades' judgement, so he relented and allowed Orpheus to depart the realm of death with Eurydice. However, the singer could not resist looking back, thus sending Eurydice's shade irrevocably back to death.

Later, Persephone watched in pity and grief as Orpheus, numb to his fate, allowed himself to be ripped limb from limb. "I did this," she said. "I thought a love like theirs, at least, should endure. But I should have left well enough alone."

Hades curled his fingers over her shoulders. "None can escape his destiny," he reminded her. "This is none of your fault."

Getting no reaction, he said, "They'll be together again. When Orpheus rejoins his lover, they will be together eternally in Elysium."

"Hecate said to me –"

"Yes?"

"You would not understand."

"I am the queen here, am I not? I am the Queen of the Dead. Mortals look to me when they plead for favors."

"You are, and that is true," Hades said, hands clasped behind his back to restrain himself from embracing her, this day of her return. She looked more regal than he had ever seen her, his pale bride with her long topaz hair held back with a circlet of woven wheatstraw; the smell of sun-warmed stone clung to her skin. She met his gaze without flinching, brows arched, a small smile hinting at the corner of her rosy lips.

She had decorated their bedchamber with colorful hangings showing scenes of sowing and harvest, flowering plants and fruit-bearing trees, but there was a new tripod in the corner as well, surmounted by silver castings of snakes. A coil of rope rested atop the coverlet.

Hades took a step towards her. She held out one palm and said, "Stop."

One eyebrow lifting, Hades obeyed. She seemed less like Persephone and more like someone else. Not Demeter. Demeter bore her responsibilities as Persephone did, but without that sense of leashed power; Artemis had the power, but not the calm control; Athena had wisdom but also violence. And Persephone was far from virgin Hestia, always above and uninvolved.

The knowledge in her eyes, as if she knew his every word before he could utter it – she reminded him of Hecate, as if the old woman had become her true mother.

Yet Persephone was also herself. More like to him than to any of the other Olympians, but beyond that, herself, a power in her own right. "What do you want of me, my queen?" he asked and, impossibly, she smiled at him.

The rope bound his wrists and ankles to the bed posts like Ixion to his flaming wheel. Persephone stood at his feet wearing a milky white peplos, her bare arms flickering with shades of rose and lemon in the lamplight, her hair loosed to fall down her back, a few strands clinging to her breasts. She surveyed his naked body. Whether she was pleased with his appearance or his bindings, Hades did not know.

"Do you want me to touch you?" she asked, her tone cool but her eyes hot. Of course he did, but could not decide what answer she expected. He had been wrong so many times.

Persephone tugged one of the ropes, as if arranging his legs more suitably for display. Hades said, "I always want you to touch me."

"And if I choose not to?"

For a moment he could not speak. "Don't do that," he said, finally.

Persephone walked up and down, gazing at him the while, considering her answer. Hades sighed in relief as her finger touched his chest and drew a line downward, halting just above the navel with a sharp twist of her nail that caught his breath once again. Her nail traced his collarbone; then her fingers slipped into his mouth. "I will let you have this," she said.

Hades nipped her fingertip with frustrated eroticism. He scraped the pad of her finger with his teeth; her lips parted, but she didn't speak. He sucked the length of it.

She withdrew her hand and lifted it to her mouth; with a quiver in his belly he watched her nip the same finger as he had, her tongue curling around her own knuckle; she reached and touched her slippery fingertip to his left nipple. A shock of cold spread across his upper body when she rubbed gently; her hard pinch sent a jolt straight to his phallus.

Persephone's hand soothed his skin. She said, "I liked that." She smiled, slowly.

Hades wished his arms were free. Even one would do. His imagination taunted him with how her skin would brush against the inside of his arm, how her plump breasts would flatten against his chest. The tactile illusion was so distinct, he thought for a moment that he had managed to wrest his arm free of its restraint. He could have done so. But he would not.

Persephone bent and swiftly bit the top of his thigh, startling a jerk from his ankles. She smiled and bit again, and again lower down, teeth and tongue the source of a fiery blush on his skin. She paused and glanced up at him, eyes half-closed, wild and sultry. He gave up attempting to watch and let his head fall back, gasping for breath. She bit him softly above the knee and he sucked in air. More than anything, he wanted her to take him into her body, every fragment of him curling within her skin like a child inside the womb.

He had taken her. Now she took back.

"Close your eyes," Persephone said.

Without sight, he felt as if the very air around him bent towards her, like a worshipper to an idol. Please, he wanted to say. Please. He remembered what his life had been like before her, before the assurance of her touch, no matter if she touched him in hatred.

"Say it."

The word wrenched from his chest. "Please."

"No."

She did not want jewels. She did not want gold. She – "I would – I would set you free," he said in desperation. "Do you want to be free of me, Persephone?"

The bed creaked with her weight. Her knees tightened on his hips as she took the tip of his phallus inside her. His breath escaped him on a moan.

"No," she said. "I am your queen."

Glint

Portia Da Costa

"What the hell *is* that?"

There it goes again . . . that flash of light from the cottage on the headland. Is it what I think it is? Is someone up there spying on us with binoculars?

"Whassup?" grunts Gavin from underneath the towel he's got plonked over his face to keep the sun out of his eyes. I'm surprised he even heard me over the football commentary on the radio. I thought he was totally tuned in to John Motson and the European Cup. I didn't think he was actually paying attention to me at all but it seems he is.

"Nothing . . . I'm not sure . . . I just keep seeing a flash of light or something from that cottage up there."

Suddenly, I'm reluctant to admit my suspicions. They're pretty stupid after all. People stare out to sea with binoculars all the time. There's nothing to say that whoever's in the cottage is looking at us, if, indeed, they are using binoculars. It could just be sunlight glinting off a window pane that's flexing in the heat.

"Right," Gavin mutters, reaching down to idly adjust himself in his trunks while at the same time turning the radio up with his other hand.

Git! He wasn't really listening after all . . .

If Gavin had his way we'd be back at our own cottage and he'd be in front of the telly, watching his precious football instead of just listening to it. Me, I could fancy a bit of steamy, sweaty afternoon nookie – but Gavin, in typical lad mode, seems to be satisfied for the moment with a few beers and the beautiful game.

But it's our first seaside holiday together, and it's the sunniest day since we got here, so I've insisted we hit the beach, football or no football. To give him credit, Gavin accepted this with good grace. I've known blokes who'd go into a full-on sulk if they had to make do with Five Live instead of *Match of the Day*.

Ack, there it goes again! That glint of light . . .

What are you looking at, you horrible perv? There's nothing going on down here for you to lech and wank over . . . would that there were!

I'm not really complaining. There's actually been plenty of sex since we arrived at the cottage, and plenty of orgasms. But it's all been pretty basic stuff, if you know what I mean? Missionary, routine foreplay, the odd bit of oral . . . Satisfying, and almost throat-catchingly tender at moments, but just missing that indefinable something in the thrills department. No adventure. No spice. No Factor X.

Nothing daring and kinky like doing it in public while someone watches through binoculars.

What the hell is the matter with me? Where did that come from?

I ought to be outraged at the thought of somebody spying on me while Gavin and I are making love, but the idea's got into my head now, and I've a feeling it's stuck there. Instead of tilting the parasol so that our distant watcher – or watchers – can't see us, I get up, take hold of it, and twist it around out of the way so it doesn't obstruct their view. And while I'm up here, I lift my arms and do a sort of supermodel thing, pushing my hair back from my face in a way that makes my boobs rise in my bikini top and salute the sun.

Get a load of that, whoever you are, I challenge, running my hands down my neck, and my shoulders and then down the sides of my breasts. Lingeringly and lovingly, as if I really fancy myself . . . It's a shame there isn't more of an audience, actually, but there's only me and Gavin here on the sand this afternoon. This is a more or less private beach for the little cluster of cottages that hug the shallow cliff top and the edge of the band of dunes to the west of it. You can't get down here by road, so there's no passing trade and we've got this pretty expanse of pearly sand all to ourselves.

"What're you doing, love?"

I jump and spin around, and find Gavin has shed the facial towel and is watching me, hands behind the back of his head, and eyes narrowed against the sun. Which is a great pity, because his eyes are one of his finest features – brown as brandy and very deep and dark and sexy.

"Oh, just looking around . . . Getting the lie of the land and all that."

"Okey-dokey then," he observes placidly, not really all that interested after all, "just watch out for the peeping Toms, won't you?" He's suddenly got that look on his face that indicates he's already elsewhere, despite the sight of my skimpy bikini and my rather more than skimpy body. Motty is working up quite a head of steam now, waxing lyrical about a corner awarded and there being plenty of bodies in the box . . . Gavin's eyes close again, and the towel goes back on.

Again . . . git!

I can't really be cross at him for long though.

He's quite a hunk, my Gavin. Tall, big-built, and yet almost pretty despite his size with his sexy boyish face, his snub nose, and his dark, curly hair. When the football's not on, he's actually quite fantastic! Caring. Attentive. Thoughtful. As well as being intelligent, well informed and lots of fun.

Yeah, you up in the cottage . . . take a look at me in my tiny bikini and my fabulous boyfriend with his smashing body and his great big dick inside his swim trunks.

The more I think about this, the hotter I get. And not just from the sun. Kneeling down on the rug, I snag my bottle of Factor 30 and spin off the top. I slop far more than I need into the palms of my hand then begin to smooth it slowly and luxuriantly over my face, my shoulders and my arms.

I close my eyes and imagine the person up in the cottage watching me, eyes wide open. Whoever they are, they're watching with longing as I caress myself or maybe as Gavin wakes up and starts to help me slather on the sun lotion. As he gets bolder, and slips off my bra top, there's a sigh of approval from the watcher.

It's all so real to me that I suddenly realize I'm wet inside my bikini bottoms and my nipples are standing out like little wine corks and rubbing the inside of the bra cups of my top.

"Oh, to hell with it! I'm going topless!"

The towel flies off again. "What about the bloke in the cottage up there?"

The footie is forgotten. Or it's half-time or something. To my surprise, Gavin's switched off the radio.

"Fuck him! If there is a him." I unclip my top and fling it away across our beach rug.

"You'd better get some lotion on those," announces Gavin cheerfully, coming up on his knees and reaching for the sun lotion bottle. "Don't want to burn your gorgeous titties, do we?"

As he straightens again, I notice something else has come up too.

Gavin has big hands, but they're very deft and clever. He's a computer engineer – although not a geeky one – and he handles the tiniest and most fragile components with perfect ease. Much the way his lotion-greased fingers are handling my boobs now. Circling round and round, making sure the Factor 30 coats them thoroughly, thumbs slithering over my nipples again and again, again and again . . .

And still, in my mind, we have an audience. The watcher is getting aroused too, even though I don't know if it's a man or a woman. Maybe it's a couple? I imagine them at their window, passing the field glasses from one to the other. The one who's watching masturbates one-handed while the other one makes do with an unaugmented view and uses both hands to give themselves pleasure.

Gavin is breathing heavily now, really getting into it, squeezing my breasts almost roughly.

And I like it! It makes me feel objectified and slutty, but as hot as hell.

"I think they're done now," I gasp, wanting him, oh God, wanting him to move on to other zones.

"Yeah, right," he gasps, and as I look up into his eyes, they're almost black with lust and gleaming like metal. He grabs up the lotion bottle and pours a great double handful. "Let me do your back . . . and your front . . . turn round a bit."

When I've wriggled out of my bikini pants, his hands assail me, back and front, just as he said. One settles on my bottom, sliding and palpating, and the other inveigles its way into my pussy, fingers going straight for my clit.

This isn't basic. This isn't routine. This is incredible. Gavin kneads and rubs me, his fingers working hard, but just how I want them to, slicking sun lotion in and among my juices, almost working them up into a satin froth. I shake and buck, jerking my hips back and forth, but he never misses a beat, never strays off target. I throw my hands around his neck, leaning against his big, powerful body as he manipulates me, and pressing my thigh against the bulk of his meaty erection. It's swollen so big now that it's poking up out of the top of his trunks, the head slippery and wet with his silky pre-come.

"Oh baby," he purrs vaguely, still paddling at me and rubbing himself against me as his fingers work. "You're so hot . . . It's no wonder people watch you. I bet that bastard up there is wanking himself stupid right now, wishing he was me, down here, touching you."

Oh, oh God, that's it!

I come like a runaway train, my body convulsing, grabbing at empty air until Gavin sticks a finger inside me. It was the thought of the watcher that did it. The idea of hot eyes devouring the sight of us rubbing each other and smearing ourselves against each other in a sticky, sex-mad muddle down here on the sand.

Take a good look, you freak! Or freaks! I call out silently, even as my body goes again, climaxing again on top of my first climax, my fingers gouging deep into the solid muscle of Gavin's broad shoulders.

There's only one thing I want more now than to have some distant perv watching me orgasm with my boyfriend's hands on my pussy and my bottom . . . and that's to have my big, beautiful boyfriend's big, beautiful and very hard dick inside me.

"Oh love, I want to fuck you," groans Gavin, reading my mind.

I whimper as his hands retreat, but then start to murmur encouragements again as he lets me down onto the blanket and almost tears off his trunks. For a moment, he fumbles around in his beach bag, and then he's ripping the foil off a condom – which does make me wonder whether football was all he had on his mind this afternoon after all. He wouldn't have come prepared otherwise, would he?

Naughty Gavin!

And then he's on me and in me, his great gorgeous length hammering me against the hard-packed sand beneath the blanket while my legs wave and kick, out of control. He feels ten times bigger than normal – even though his normal size is pretty fabulous – and I know it's because he likes the idea of being watched just as much as I do.

Is this what you wanted to see, you perverts? The two of us, going at it like knives on a public beach? Well, take a good look! Take a good look and wish you were here with us!

It's too much . . . just too much! I come again, shouting now, howling and writhing and clutching at Gavin, my hands slipping and sliding on his oily back, my ankles hooked around the back of his knees to jam myself against him like a reciprocating engine.

And Gavin's right here with me. He shouts like a bull, goes rigid, then pumps and pumps and pumps at me in an orgasm that seems to go on forever.

I glance towards the cottage, and the sunlight glints again.

Forgiveness

Craig J. Sorensen

Von took a closer look at the label as if eating the pretty image on the box with his eyes. One rickety wheel chattered despite his slow pace down the aisle. A small kneeling woman looked up from a box of boutique orecchiette. She smiled sweetly.

She stood and placed the orecchiette into her nearly empty cart with the jar of gourmet marinara sauce and large wedge of Parmigiano Reggiano. Von smiled back and watched as she passed. At four foot ten she made Von's five foot six positively towering. Though not remarkably pretty, she had a pleasant, carved face and blue irises so pale that they stood out from her whites only by razor bright blue rims. She fixed on the jasmine rice further up the aisle. Von's eyes lingered on the curve of her butt in tight faded blue jeans. He let out a sigh. She swirled her head back and caught him. She gave a broad smile as Von's eyes met hers.

She zipped from aisle to aisle. Von tried to time it so he would pass her again, but she was too quick. Fortunately for Von, she had chosen the slowest checkout girl in the store and was biding her time, her forearms resting on the cart handle eyeing the *National Enquirer* as the ample woman in front of her expended an ammo pouch of coupons. Von took his place in the next checkout stand.

She smiled softly and genuinely. The crow's feet and laugh lines indicated that she was probably a good five years older than Von, perhaps ten. He didn't care. She was perfect.

Almighty perfect.

But Von knew the places to look for the right sort of woman; the grocery store was not among them. He tried to read her face as he unloaded his cart.

Von loaded the trunk of his old Civic. He flinched when a tailgate puffed open behind him. The tiny woman placed her two bags in the back of a beastly black Cadillac Escalade. She nodded softly.

Von smiled and tried to resist the urge to drain his eyes down her.

"Hi, I'm Madeline," she said in a sweet but slightly raspy voice. Madeline. He gave a restrained grin while Beavis and Butthead laughs cascaded through a funneling mind. Von looked down her left arm; one eye took her ring finger and surveyed a rock that could bend an oak branch. Like a lizard, his other eye revisited the shape of her butt. Perfect. He gave out a resigned sigh. Damn. Von never messed with married women.

But she was so perfect.

Her nose softly crinkled as she observed his focus on her ring finger. She held it up and tilted her head. "I paid for it; I figure I still get to enjoy it for a while." Her thumb twirled the ring several times. "Messy divorce. Maybe I should put the diamond in another setting," she concluded.

Von felt like a running back who suddenly found a big gap in the brick wall line. He prepared to make his dash, but he knew there were eighty yards between him and the end zone. Eyes wide, pace steady – don't burn out too early!

Her legs carved out shapely in her jeans. Small unholstered breasts sat high upon her slim chest. Everything would fit just perfectly. He adjusted the front of his jeans. "I'm Von." He displayed his ringless finger casually.

"Von? Interesting name." She compressed the full force of her body against the tailgate of her SUV.

Von closed his trunk. "It's not really my first name. My first name is Helmut, but it's such a bonehead name, I just go by Von." He folded his arms. "So, you're, like, on the rebound?"

"No, the rebound was some time back, just after I caught him cheating. I'm headed the other way up the court now," she said.

Von laughed at the basketball reference given her size. She grinned and winked at him. He might just enjoy her company without the other thing. It had happened like that before.

Von adjusted his oversized jacket and straightened his faux silk power tie. He'd never been to this restaurant before, but he knew it was ritzy. He wasn't a snappy dresser, and despite the formality of his outfit, this day was no exception. But this was where Madeline had wanted to meet him.

The hostess took him to the table. Madeline had already ordered a bottle of exceptional white wine. She deftly poured a glass for him. As he took his seat, he took in Madeline's elegant midnight blue silk evening dress. A shimmering gold wrap over her bare shoulders carried the same leaf pattern as the hand-painted left edge of the dress, in reverse colorings. He felt as out of place as an alley cat in the kitchen that bubbled with tight-lipped nasal French phrases. Von was not a man impressed with finery and elegance, but the setting collapsed like ninety feet of water above him. He opened the menu. No prices. His heart stopped and he nearly spit the wine across the virgin tablecloth. If you have to ask, you can't afford it. Casually he pulled out his wallet under the table and looked in on the lonely presidents within.

"This is my treat, Von. I hope you aren't offended."

Von casually closed the wallet. "Well, uh, if you insist." He choked back the word ma'am. He eased his chair back from the table and rested his elbows on his knees. He watched the eager scurrying of the staff around the proper guests like Marty Stauffer at a busy estuary.

The waitress was a lithe gazelle of a woman with bright red hair caught in a pony tail and cool white skin. Von avoided his compulsions through the appetizer and the better part of the main course, but his eyes finally betrayed him after she came for the dessert order. The waitress' bottom danced beneath a smooth, shiny black skirt. Von's eyes snapped back to Madeline's. Apologetically, he turned his eyes down to the empty table. When he looked back up, Madeline grinned. "Yours is nicer, Madeline."

Her brow arched and she let out a laugh that turned the coolest heads in the restaurant.

Von had never been with a woman like Madeline. He improvised. The two had hit it off famously, but it was best to let things unfold smoothly with any woman whose preferences were not clear yet – especially a woman like this. No bill was asked or offered as she handed her platinum card to the maitre d'. She walked gracefully on gold four-inch heels into the parking lot. He lingered at the door he had opened and watched her butt dance away. Finally he followed her to a jet-black BMW Z4 roadster. She smiled sweetly. "I had a fine time, Von."

Von took her small hand in his. "Me too, Madeline."

"Would you like to join me for a nightcap?"

Von took a deep breath. "I have an early day tomorrow."

"Understandable."

Von leaned in and received a soft kiss that slowly embraced his mouth. Her breath tasted of Sauternes, white chocolate and mint. She rested one palm delicately on his upper arm. The other clutched her jeweled pocketbook. His mouth gaped as she eased away from the kiss. "I hope we'll meet again." She stepped out of her heels and sat in her roadster.

Von nodded. "My treat, next time."

"Of course."

He leaned against his Civic and watched as she revved out of the parking lot.

As at home as Madeline had been in the auspices of her favorite restaurant, so she was at the Steak-n-Ale. She wore faded jeans and a tank-top covered by a flannel shirt tied at her waist. She drank his choice of beer and ate her Delmonico like a logger after a clear cut. She held her own in every topic Von introduced. He let out a Dizzy Gillespie sigh as her rounded butt disappeared toward the restrooms.

He left a nice tip for the efficient, acne-afflicted waiter. The two exited into the parking lot. The smell of diesel fumes and the sound of street-racing churned in the distance as they walked to her roadster.

"Do you have an early day tomorrow?" She took his hand in hers.

"Nope."

"Care to join me for a nightcap?"

"Sure." His heart pounded as she opened the top. The cold late autumn night poured down with the stars. The veins of her hand popped out as she manipulated the gearshift. He gripped the armrest as a man plagued with aviophobia might when charging down the runway. She whipped up a mountain road that hair-pinned beside a clear drop to a river churning silently below.

She pulled into an inconspicuous drive then reached over and patted his hand, which was now glued to the console next to the parking brake. "I hope I didn't scare you too much, but what point is having a BMW Roadster if you don't stretch it out?"

"Indeed." He forced a casual body language. The house loomed big on the hill overlooking the city. Madeline took his hand and led him inside. She pointed to a white leather couch and he relaxed at one end. She brought a delicate mixed drink and he sipped.

She sat on the other end of the couch. "I haven't been out much since my marriage broke up. To be honest, I'm still pretty bitter." She took a drink and licked her lips. "After screwing another woman, he had the audacity to try to squeeze me for support! Bastard. My only regret was that all I could do is make sure he gets nothing from me. Have you ever been married, Von?"

"No, and I probably never will."

"Don't say that. You just haven't found the right woman," she declared.

Von thought to explain. He shrugged.

Each time she stood up, Von followed her – every flex of her muscles. He crossed one leg over as she returned and handed him a fresh drink. This time she sat next to him. He was hard as a girder. He worked up his nerve and kissed her. She opened her small mouth wide. They petted like prom dates until she stood up and took his hand. She smiled sweetly and led him to her bedroom.

*   *   *

It was a rose sunrise that cut through the broad window at the side of the bed. Von turned his head away and let his eyes adjust, then turned back to the lightly snoring form of Madeline. He was finally able to fully appreciate the liquid silver beauty of the sheets that had whistled sweetly into the night with awkward introductions. Now the satin bedspread was entirely off the bed, puddled on the Persian rug. Madeline slept on her stomach, her smiling face toward Von. Her eyes darted in full REM. Her bare back angled to a valley that rose up to the two perfect peaks of her butt covered in the silver top sheet. He gripped the sheet in his toes and slowly pulled them down until only her left calf was covered. She was more perfect than even he had imagined.

And this was something he knew a lot about.

He'd had large ones, tiny ones, bulbous ones and flat ones. He had enjoyed dark ones and pale ones, oriental ones (several nations were represented) and there was this Latin one connected to a feisty woman named Destina. Squirming or demure, fighting or pleading. Every shape and size, and he had found something to enjoy. He honed his skills like a master carpenter. He learned how each type of wood responded to each tool.

The corner of sheet that remained over his groin swelled like a tide of mercury.

"Mmmm." Her eyes were on his groin. She reached down and wrapped his hard-on in the satin and stroked. She removed the sheet and straddled him. The smell of her pussy was fresh as she spread wide and scooped him inside her. But he so wanted just to take a swig – a playful paw. She bobbed above him, her eyes locked sweetly on his. A fine onyx pendant swayed from nipple to nipple. He gripped her legs up to hips and squeezed her butt tightly. She gasped as her head swiveled back. He studied the perfect cut of her pearly teeth. He released one hand from her butt and stretched his fingers wide. He exhaled and bit his lip. He returned to softly stroke her soft butt cheek.

He thought of the moron who had married her, then cheated on her. He knew a lot of women and she was one of a kind. She made love like an angel. Her nipples caressed his rod like virgin silk.

He swayed with her gentle thrusts and watched her cheeks blossom into a silent, shuddering orgasm.

In subsequent dates Madeline paid for the finery, Von paid for the common. One night, when Von had to be in to work early the next day, he followed her back to her place like a caboose on a bungee cord behind a racing train engine. He arrived to find her leaning on her Escalade with a grin.

"Sorry."

He shrugged.

She remained next to the SUV. She looked at it then back to Von. "You know, I just hate this thing." She elbowed the Escalade.

"Oh yeah? Why do you drive it at all?"

"It was my husband's. I guess I feel guilty having it around and not using it, so I take it out from time to time. You know what? You'd be doing me a favor if you took it off my hands."

Von lowered his brow. "I couldn't afford it."

"I don't want anything for it. It's all paid for. It's only got like five thousand miles on it. You could sell it, if you like."

Von shrugged. "Nah, thanks anyway." The oddity of the offer simply rolled off. The pilot flame popped and surged in the back of his mind. It wanted to ignite the starving furnace. There was something he wanted. Though no commitment had been made he also wanted to remain faithful. Still, fantasies could only take him so far.

"I'd really like it if you would take it."

"No, I don't want it. Just sell it!"

"Uh," she started. Her face clenched. She rubbed her hands together and looked at Von, and then the car. "I'd like to give you something," she softly said as her face relaxed.

Von's eyes darted from side to side then eased down her waist. Do I dare ask? He looked up into the laser probe of her stare. No, that's not what she meant. "You give me plenty, Madeline. I don't need anything."

Madeline's facial expression mystified him. He didn't know if she was angry or happy. He felt like he should say something more, but he had nothing to say. "Von, did I tell you about the night I caught him?"

Von did not want to hear, but she wanted to tell. It seemed to be festering. She was a lonely woman; she'd told him that trust had always come hard. So many hangers-on – a life full of money and devoid of honesty. "No, Madeline."

She smoothed her tan linen skirt. "In my own house. He was doing it in my own house. I don't know if she was a hooker or what, but she looked like one to me. I guess it was a good thing that I hate guns, cause if I'd had one, he'd be dead now. The hooker, well," her pupils narrowed to a midday death valley pinhole. Von felt a chill down his spine. She forced out a smile. "I burned the sheets they were on, and replaced the mattress but my stomach still hurts. It's like a bad meal that I can't retch up." She wiped tears from each cheek. She cleared her throat. "I even thought of putting out a job . . . is that what they call it? No – a contract – on him."

Von's eyes widened.

"I could never have done that, though. So it just sits. I don't know how to let it go."

Von got a creepy feeling – suddenly in the eye of a hurricane, its heavy green air comforting but a silent menace. "So channel it." His heart throbbed.

"Into what?"

Von stretched a titillated, but frightened grin. He'd be on the receiving end – giving up control. He was thrilled that it might happen, but frightened that the very suggestion would disgust her. "Have you ever acted?"

"Yeah, in school, why?" she replied.

"You can't do it to him, so find a surrogate."

"What kind of surrogate?" Her face compressed.

Von's heart pounded like a jackhammer. "Someone to punish, let out your frustration on."

"You think it would work?"

"Why not?"

She turned her head slightly to one side but kept her eyes on his. "What do you have in mind?"

There were so many ways to go, and Von knew them all. He'd used a paddle, a switch, a yard stick, even a whip. Bend them over a desk or a table, leaning against a counter, wrists gripped to heels. Clad in leather, cotton, lace and linen. But the best had always been a lava red hand on a ripening bare bottom, draped across an enforcing lap. The classics never go out of style.

Von convincingly played the part of a randy spouse recently caught. He unhitched his jeans and bent over her lap. Madeline's tiny hand stretched wide and clapped across his bottom, and a small shudder of emotion blasted from her like a controlled explosion of live ordinance, then her hand cut loose. Von grimaced. Madeline gasped at the stiffness that grew against her lap. She spanked him harder, as the inner wall of the hurricane struck, a torrent drained from her eyes.

Von's butt burned with champagne sparkles as he stood up and grabbed his pants. "Wait." His rod softened as she left the room and came back with a jar in her hand. She sighed, the dew of tears still in the folds under her crisp jawline and in the ridge of her collarbone. "We're not done." She sat down at the center of the couch, and Von cautiously lay across her lap again. His heart pounded hard again. He smelled rich roses, then he felt the delicious icy cream. She rubbed it deep in his skin and sighed when again he hardened. She encouraged him to sit beside her.

For the first time, Madeline leaned into his lap and took his penis in her mouth. She worked around it like corn on the cob while her hand smoothed his balls. Her silk-clad butt in was in perfect reach. He stroked across one bun, down the valley then back up the other.

She wore no panties.

Von's cock twitched as she took him deep in her mouth. He gripped her butt tightly when she teasingly pulled away. She hitched up her skirt and straddled him. Von fondled her butt as she took him to full depth then pulled back until he felt the cool air on the tip of his rod. "Oh, oh God," he repeated as she increased these long strokes.

He clenched his fists and toes. He exploded deep into her body.

"Forgiven," she whispered into his ear.

★   ★   ★

Neither wanted to back away from the awkward canyon that ensued. They got together several times, but parted ways at the end of each evening. One night Madeline insisted that Von come to her house. Her tail-lights stayed in view for the entire drive. When he got out of his Civic, she was by the Escalade. "I'd really like you to have this."

"Nah."

"I insist."

He shook his head.

She continued to press. His refusals became louder. Finally he blurted out, "I don't want the fucking thing, Madeline!"

She grinned. "I've been a bad girl, haven't I?"

Von's angry brow lifted like a bar bell in a clean and jerk. She turned and swiveled her hips seductively. His eyes fixed on the oriental bright red silk gown that clung to that most perfect bottom. She paused at the door and looked back. She curled her finger toward her blushing face.

Von bit his lip and stepped toward the house.

Stocking Stuffers

T. C. Calligari

Sylvie was curious about Santa. It was the end of the second week, still not quite mid-December, and she was bored. Santa had to be, too; there weren't many kids coming through yet as parents didn't want to build the fever too soon.

Which meant Sylvie needed to create her own fun. She'd volunteered to do her part for charity and the low-income families but being Santa's elf was more tedious than she had imagined.

But Santa; well, he was an enigma. Was he old or young, fat, slim or muscular? Sylvie only ever saw him as Santa; big belly, fleecy white hair and beard, and the crimson suit trimmed in white fur. The elves had complementary outfits; the guys in knee-high black boots, red shorts with suspenders, tight shirts under little red jackets with white fur trim. The girls, Janine and Ashley, besides Sylvie, wore black, high-heel ankle boots, short red skirts trimmed with fur and with suspenders, the same tight shirts and little jackets with a flounce. The elves were there to help put out the wrapped stocking stuffers for each child after their visit with Santa, as well as giving parents something to look at while their kids were waiting.

Sylvie walked back behind the curtains to grab a few more gifts. There was curly-headed Ian kneeling in front of Kevin and pulling down his shorts, nuzzling into the hardening bulge.

Sylvie stopped and rolled her eyes. "Must you do that here?"

Ian turned to look at her, Kevin's cock firmly in his hand. "Jealous, honey?"

She sighed, "Yes."

Kevin laughed and guided Ian's head back to idolizing his growing prick.

"Just keep it down," she muttered. "You don't want to scare anyone who might happen up to see St Nick."

Kevin smiled, his eyes closing as he leaned back. Ian's mouth made a moue and slowly opened as he slid Kevin's cock toward his throat.

Sylvie just had to watch for a bit. The boys had been picked for their physiques and looks and she couldn't help but admire Kevin's muscular thighs as he leaned against the wall, his bald head shining like polished marble. Ian's angelic head of curls slid slowly back and forth, his mouth distended about an amazingly thick penis, moaning in pleasure.

They obviously weren't worried about anyone watching but Sylvie turned away. She was getting too hot. Maybe she could pass that on to Santa, see how bothered he would get. After picking up a few packages wrapped in "boys" gift wrap, she pushed out past the velvet curtain. Santa was just sitting there watching people walk up and down the mall. Nobody was coming up the red carpet at the moment.

Packages for the boys went to Santa's left, and for the girls, to his right. Sylvie crossed in front of him and turned her back, then bent from the waist to put the packages down. She took her time, knowing that in that position the short skirt revealed her white fishnet tights over the white G-string, and consequently her buttocks. Several times she rearranged the packages to make sure Santa couldn't miss the view, and then stood when she heard a child scampering up the ramp. She spun and flounced past Santa, giving him a wink. He stared at her and had to work hard to tear his gaze away to the little boy that fidgeted in front of him.

He did have the most amazing blue eyes. It made sense, since St Nick hailed from an icy realm to the north. Still, what did Santa, or the man beneath, really look like? Was he worth Sylvie working him up? Could she get him to melt? She had asked Ian what Santa looked like but Ian said they usually left before Santa disrobed his belly and beard in the change area.

Tomorrow, she would have to up the ante, to see if Santa would lose his cool.

The next day Sylvie wore black fishnet tights for better contrast to her olive skin, and no underwear. It was only a Tuesday and still slow, so how far could she entice Santa? She had to be careful; it might not end up to be the fun game she wanted.

It turned out in the afternoon, after Sylvie had flounced by Santa a few times, bending down in just the right way to give a glimpse or more of her fishnetted thigh or hip, that they had to pose for a group photo for publicity. Ashley, Ian and Janine were away so it would only be Kevin, Michael and Sylvie. The photographer had arrived just after the busy lunch-hour and started directing them into their places. He wanted a frolic-filled picture so Kevin was asked to lean over Santa's left shoulder, holding a gift aloft. Michael knelt at Santa's feet, staring out at the crowd and Sylvie propped herself across Santa's right knee. Really, she perched because she needed to lean out and forward. Santa's arm helped hold her in place and she realized his hand gripped her thigh.

As the photographer positioned everyone, Sylvie felt Santa's fingers squirm under her thigh. With no underwear, the fish-nets held little barrier and a warm flush started to spread through her limbs. Santa's finger nuzzled through the fishnets, tearing a hole, now delving into the gathering wet of her sex. She didn't dare move for fear of drawing attention but Santa was a sneaky one. He waited till the photographer was directing someone before he burrowed a bit deeper.

"All right, folks, one last one for fun. You," he pointed at Sylvie, "the female elf. Stay where you are but put an arm around Santa's neck, place your cheek beside his and give us a big smile."

As Sylvie made the small adjustment and pressed her cheek to Santa's fuzzy beard, his finger made the last maneuver, tearing the fishnets a bit more and slid inside her. Her whimper was barely audible and she whispered, "Oh, Santa," as the photo-grapher snapped the last shot.

They all stood, except Santa, and Sylvie felt the slow with-drawal of his finger as she stood. She shivered, with the waves of pleasure still moving through her. Santa casually looked over at her and then licked his finger, giving a hearty, "Ho, ho, ho," after.

Sylvie went behind the curtain since Michael would spend the next shift out front with Santa. She grabbed Kevin's arm and asked, "Are you sure you've never seen Santa without the outfit?"

A wicked little smile played over Kevin's face. "Well, he's jovial, has white hair . . ."

She gave him a light smack on his arm. "No, smartass. The guy playing Santa. Any idea what he looks like under the get-up?"

Kevin gave her a look. "Sorry, honey, he's always last into the lockers to change and we're usually gone by the time he removes the mystery. So just what are you checking on your list?"

She shrugged. "Nothing really. Just curious."

"Naughty or nice?" Kevin laughed and went back to get some gifts.

On Wednesday, Sylvie had the late shift until store closing. Ashley and Ian were also in. When she walked out front Santa smiled at her and said, "Well, if it isn't my favorite elf. I have something for you." He held up a small, flat rectangular package.

"What's this?" Sylvie asked.

"Just a little stocking stuffer for being such a good elf. To replace what I damaged."

She raised an eyebrow, then smiled and went behind the curtain to open it. She removed the paper to find a pair of fishnet stockings, black and silky, to replace the tights he'd torn. And it came with a lace garter, much sexier than the tights had been, though they had their mystery. Just imagining wearing the stockings gave Sylvie a little thrill and made her legs tremble with anticipation. Santa couldn't go much farther than he did yesterday and Sylvie was willing to toy with him a bit more.

During her break in the early evening, she changed, getting a little moist at the thought of wearing nothing but the stockings and the short skirt. She had also worn a red satin bustier under her shirt and decided to take the shirt off and stow it in the locker. The top three buttons of the jacket, she left undone, just giving a peak of curving breasts, no more. She couldn't get too risqué.

The rest of the evening passed with enough kids coming through that Sylvie could only give Santa an occasional, tantalizing view. The mall started to clear and they closed down the North Pole booth, putting away the gifts and other items, closing the curtains and turning off the lights. Everyone else had left and Sylvie was about to go to the changing rooms. She sat for a moment on one of the sorting tables, taking a sip from a glass of water, when Santa entered.

Her heart gave a little thump when he stopped and looked at her and walked over. What would he do?

He began to remove his gloves and said, "Ah, there's my elf. Did you enjoy my stocking stuffer?" He moved closer to her and stood right in front, nearly touching Sylvie.

Not feeling quite so bold suddenly, she stopped swinging her legs and said, "Uh, yes, thank you, very nice."

"And are you wearing it?" Before she could reply he moved forward, pushing her knees apart with his body and placing a hand on either side of her thighs, under the skirt. His thumbs ran over her hipbones, and her breath caught. He ran a hand down the outside of one thigh and then up the inside. His other hand came away for a moment.

As his hand moved to the top of her stocking, tickling the flesh there, Sylvie tried to slow down the action. "Why don't you remove that beard and belly?"

He smiled, his icy blue eyes twinkling. "What makes you think they're not real?" And his hand slid farther up between her legs.

Sylvie bit her lip as his fingers brushed over her pubic curls. "No one has hair like that," she gasped.

He moved as close as the table would allow, one hand now burrowing into her cleft. "Ah but you wouldn't want to open your present too soon." He wiggled his hips and pushed her legs farther apart. Sylvie felt she was slipping and set the drink down, reaching out to grab his shoulders, whether to hold him off or pull him close, she wasn't sure. But before she could complete the move, he pulled her to the edge of the table so only her buttocks rested on it. She was only stopped from falling by her legs being around him and his hands on her hips.

Sylvie started to protest when Santa pressed his lips, synthetic beard and all, over hers, and then she felt the heat slide between her labial lips. The hard bulb of his cock slid over her clit, and down, slicking her with desire.

She wrestled with herself. Who was he under the beard and red suit? He could be anyone; the geeky courier guy at the lab where she worked, her mailman, the angry neighbor who lived below her. Sylvie's rational thoughts were losing to the slippery pleasure pushing against her pussy. Wasn't it just a bit more naughty, not knowing the true face of the man about to fuck you? And she had started the whole escapade.

He pushed at the same time as he pulled her forward, a hand around each thigh. Sylvie gasped, then moaned, losing her weak fight with temptation. Her stocking-clad legs went around Santa's suit, belly padding and all. Then he lifted her off the table and slowly embedded his thick, hot cock in her slick cunt. She slid down, her vaginal muscles clamping in spasms of ecstasy, and it was his turn to moan.

Impaled on his cock, Sylvie clung around his neck for a moment, her face buried in the fake white hair. Beneath it, she could smell a muskiness reminiscent of earth and trees. A wild, healthy scent. She groaned into the beard, hoisting herself up on his delicious rod, to slide down again.

It wasn't an easy position but he held her and helped lift her to slide down again. Sylvie trembled as much from the exertion as the heat emanating out from her core. One last ember of reason had her pant out, "Won't we get locked in?" before they succumbed to a piston play of lust and muscle.

Up he hoisted her; down she slid, again and again, the heat of their friction slicking them both with her juices. Sylvie tore at his hair, dislodging hat and wig and beard, but not seeing for the haze of passion and heat blurred her vision in the low light.

They moved in rhythm, up and down, in and out, their breaths gasping as one, their sweat mingling, moans joining as their flesh fit one another perfectly. Sylvie's eyelids fluttered as her heart hammered loudly. Her whole body shivered and clasped his as her orgasm erupted. He convulsed and thrust harder into her and light exploded behind her eyes . . . a thousand shattering snowflakes, sparkling points of pleasure and passion cascading around them, slowly settling, as the vibrations of their bodies slowed.

As her senses returned, Sylvie realized it was the moment of truth. Her face was still buried near his neck but she had torn away the disguise. Slowly, she pulled back and sighed, then opened her eyes. Santa stood before her, or now rather, a man in a Santa suit. He had black hair and those same amazing blue eyes. His chin was slightly pointed and his eyebrows had a nearly elfin upswing at the corners. He smiled at her.

"Well, my little elf, you unwrapped your present a little early."

"Mmmm." She closed her eyes for a moment as he sat her back on the table top, and pulled out of her. "I thought that was you who unwrapped your present first. But we should get going. We'll be locked in for sure now."

He zipped up and then removed the Santa belly, revealing a trim, not overly muscular body. Sylvie liked the look of her present and a flush of relief ran through her. "Oh, we don't have to be worried about that. I'm head of security for the mall. I just volunteered to help out."

She laughed and said, "Me too. The volunteering that is. I work at the lab across the street. This elf's name is Sylvie."

He dropped the padded belly and came up to her and kissed her, "Well, elf Sylvie, I'm Michel, and thank you for such a lovely stocking stuffer. If you play your cards right, there could be a few more early presents before the big day." He helped her off of the table, his warm hands nearly encircling her waist.

Sylvie laughed again, and straightened her clothes. "Oh really? Don't you have a list, and aren't you checking it twice?"

Michel cocked his head to the side. "Most definitely, and you're in both columns. Naughty and nice. So, what say we get changed and I'll buy you a few drinks?

Sylvie nearly wriggled with delight. It was going to be a very good Christmas and Santa had answered all her wishes.

L'Américaine

Maxim Jakubowski

Cornelia took the RER from Roissy-Charles de Gaulle. A taxi would have been easier and more relaxed after the seven-hour plane journey, but she knew she had to remain as anonymous as possible. Cab drivers have a bad habit of remembering tall, lanky blondes, particularly so those who did not wish to engage in needless conversation and reveal whether it was their first time in Paris or was she coming here on holiday?

Because she knew there were countless CCTV cameras sprinkled across the airport and the train terminal, she had quickly changed outfits in a somewhat insalubrious toilet shortly after picking up her suitcase from the luggage carousel, and by the time she walked on to the RER train, she now had a grey scarf obscuring her blonde curls and wore a different outfit altogether from the flight. It was far from foolproof, but at least would serve its purpose in muddying the waters in the eventuality of a later, thorough investigation.

The commuters on the train to Paris looked grey and tired, wage slaves on their mindless journey to work or elsewhere. A couple of teenage Arab kids listening to rap – or was it hip hop – on their iPods glanced at her repeatedly, but her indifference soon got the better of them and she wasn't bothered until the Luxembourg Gardens stop where she got off.

She had booked herself into a small hotel there on the Internet the previous day. She checked herself in under the false name on her spare passport, a Canadian one she'd seldom used before. She took a shower and relaxed before taking the lift to the lobby around lunch hour, and noticed someone new had taken over at the registration desk from the young woman who'd earlier checked her in. She calmly walked back to her room and stuffed some clothes into a tote bag and went down to the lobby again and left the hotel. Fifteen minutes later, she registered at another hotel, near the place de l'Odéon, this time under her real name. This booking she'd made by phone from New York a week or so before. She was now the proud tenant of two separate hotel rooms under two separate names and nationalities. Both rooms were noisy and looked out onto busy streets, but that was Paris, and anyway she wasn't here for a spot of tourism. This was work. She settled in the new room, took a nap, and just before the evening walked out and took a cab to the place de l'Opéra. There was a thin Jiffy bag waiting for her at the American Express Poste Restante. Here, she retrieved the key she had purchased back in Brooklyn Beach from a Russian connection she occasionally used. She then caught another taxi to the Gare du Nord, where she located the left luggage locker which the key opened. The package was anonymous and not too bulky. She picked up a copy of *Libération* and casually wrapped it around the bundle she had just retrieved from the locker and walked down the train station stairs to the Métro and took the Porte d'Orléans line back to Odéon. In the room, she unwrapped the package and weighed the Sig Sauer in her hand. Her favourite gun. Perfect.

The Italian girl had always preferred older men. Some of her friends and other fellow students at La Sapienza, Rome's university, had always kidded her she had something of a father fixation, and indeed her relationship with her gastroenterologist dad was prickly to say the least, seesawing between devotion and simmering anger. At any rate, he also spoiled her badly.

But boys her age seemed so clumsy and uninteresting, coarse, superficial, so sadly predictable, and she found herself recoiling instinctively from their tentative touches all too often. Not that she knew what exactly she wanted herself.

Whenever asked about her plans for the future, she would answer in jest (or maybe not) that she planned to marry an ambassador and have lots of babies. When Peppino – the name she would use for her much older, foreign lover so as to make him difficult for her parents to identify – quizzed her about this, she would add that the ambassador would also be a black man, a big man both in size and personality. Peppino would smile silently in response, betraying his own personal fears and prejudices, only to point out that she'd be wasting so many opportunities by becoming merely a wife. After all, this was a young woman who by the age of twenty-two had a degree in comparative literature, spoke five languages, and would surely make a hell of a journalist or foreign correspondent one day.

Her affair with the man she and her friends affectionately called Peppino had lasted just over a year and he had been the first man she had fucked. To her amazement, he had become not just a lover but her professor of sex; unimaginably tender, crudely transgressive, and it was the first time she had come across a guy who understood her so well that their contact when apart became almost telepathic. However, he was also more than twice her age, lived in another country and happened to be married, which sharpened her longing and her jealousy to breaking point. The affair had proven both beautiful and traumatic, but eventually the enforced separation from Peppino could not be assuaged any longer by telephone calls, frantic emails and mere words. For her sanity, she was obliged to break up with him, even though she loved him. She had a life to live, adventures to experience; he had already lived his life, hadn't he? Now was her time. The decision was a painful one and he naturally took it badly. Not that her state of mind was much better, racked by doubts, heartache and regrets by the thousands as both Peppino and she could not help recalling the days and nights together, the shocking intimacy they had experienced, the pleasure and complicity, the joy and the darkness. Sleepless nights and silent unhappiness followed in her wake and she agreed to visit a girlfriend from her Erasmus months in Lisbon who lived in Paris – ironically, a city he had always wanted to take her to.

It was a wet spring and the thin rain peppered the Latin Quarter pavements with a coating of grey melancholy. Flora had gone to her grandparents' house in the country and left the

Italian girl on her own for a few days. Initially, she had looked forward to the prospect but now felt herself particularly lonely. When she was not busy exploring the city with her friend, memories just kept on flooding back.

She was sitting reading a book by Italo Calvino at the terrace of Les Deux Magots, sipping a coffee, half-watching the world pass by – women who walked elegantly, young men who looked cute but would surely prove dull in real life she thought – when she heard the seductive voice of the bad man over her shoulder.

"That's a quite wonderful book, Mademoiselle," he said. "I envy you the experience of reading it for the first time. Truly."

Giuly looked up at him. He looked older. How could he not be?

Cornelia much preferred ignorance. A job was a job and it was better not to have to know any of the often murky reasons when she was given an assignment.

Had the target stolen from another party, swindled, lied, killed, betrayed? It was not important.

Cornelia knew she had a cold heart. It made her work easier, not that she sought excuses. She would kill both innocent and guilty parties with the same set of mind. It was not hers to reason why.

She had been given a thin dossier on her Paris mark, a half-dozen pages of random information about his haunts and habits and a couple of photographs. A manila folder she had slipped between her folded black cashmere sweaters in her travelling suitcase, to which she had added a few torn-out pages from the financial pages of the *New York Times* and a section on international investment from the *Wall Street Journal* to muddy the waters in the event of an unlikely snap examination of her belongings by customs at either JFK or Roissy. He was a man in his late forties, good-looking in a rugged sort of way which appealed to some women, she knew. Tallish, hair greying at the temples in subdued and elegant manner. She studied one of the photographs, and noted the ice-green eyes, and a steely inner determination behind the crooked smile. A dangerous man. A bad man.

But they all have weaknesses, and it appeared his was women. It usually was. Cornelia sighed. Kept on reading the information sheet she had been provided with, made notes. Finally, she booted up her laptop and went online to hunt down the *clubs échangistes* her prey was known to frequent on a regular basis. They appeared to be located all over the city, but the main ones appeared to be in the Marais and close to the Louvre. She wrote down the particulars of Au Pluriel, Le Château des Lys, Les Chandelles and Chris et Manu, and studied the respective websites. She'd been to a couple of similar "swing" clubs back in the States, both privately and for work reasons. She'd found them somewhat sordid. Maybe the Parisian ones would prove classier, but she had her doubts. Cornelia had no qualms about public sex, let alone exhibitionism – after all she had stripped for a living some years earlier and greatly enjoyed the sensation – but still found that sex was an essentially private communion. But then she'd always had an uneasy relationship and perception of sex, and at a push would confess to decidedly mixed feelings about it.

Would sex in Paris, sex and Paris prove any different, she wondered?

She rose from the bed where she had spread out the pages and photos, switched off the metal grey laptop and walked pensively to the hotel room's small, poky bathroom. She pulled off her T-shirt and slipped off her white cotton panties and looked at herself in the full-length mirror.

And shed a tear.

The bad man had no problem seducing the young Italian woman. He had experience and a deceptive elegance. Anyway, she was on the rebound from her Peppino and a vulnerable prey. Had her first lover not warned her that no man would ever love her, touch her with as much tenderness as he? And had she not known in her heart that he was right? But falling into the arms of the Frenchman was easy, a way of moving on, she reckoned. She knew all he really wanted to do was fuck her, use her and that was good enough for now for Giuly. She was lost and the excesses of sex were as good a way of burying the past and the hurt. This new man would not love her; he was just another adventure along the road. So why not? This was Paris, wasn't it? And spring would soon turn into summer and she just couldn't bear the thought of returning to Rome and resuming her PhD studies and being subsidised by her father.

She rang home and informed her parents she would be staying on in Paris for a few more months. There were protests and fiery arguments, but she was used to manipulating them. She was old enough by now, she told them, to do what she wanted with her life.

"Respect me, and my needs," she said. Not for the first time.

"Do you need money?" her father asked.

"No, I've found a job, helping out in a bookshop," she lied.

The Frenchman – he said he was a businessman, something in export/import – ordered her to move in with him and Giuly accepted. She couldn't stay on at Flora's without revealing her new relationship.

At first, it was nice to sleep at night in bed with another person, a man. Feeling the warmth of the other's body, waking up to a naked body next to her own. And to feel herself filled to the brim when he made love to her. To again experience a man's cock growing inside her as it ploughed her, stretched her. To take a penis, savour its hardening inside her mouth, to hear a man moan above her as he came, shuddered, shouted out obscenities or religious adjectives, and experience the heat waves coursing from cunt to heart to brain. Of course, it reminded her of Peppino. But then again, it was different. No fish face on display at the moment of climax with this new man, just a detached air of satisfaction, almost cruelty as he often took her to the brink and retreated, playing with her senses, enjoying her like an object.

Daytimes, he would often leave her early in the morning and go about his work while Giuly would explore Paris, fancy-free, absorbing the essence of the city in her long, uneven stride. For the first time in ages, she felt like a gypsy again, like the young teenager who would live on the streets of Rome and even enjoy sleepless nights wandering from alleys to coffee shops with a cohort of friends or even alone, drinking in life with no care in the world. In Belleville, she discovered a patisserie with sickly-sweet Middle-Eastern delicacies, near Censier-Daubenton she made an acquaintance with a young dope dealer who furnished her with cheap weed, which she would take care never to smoke at the man's apartment off the quai de Grenelle. As with Peppino, she knew older guys secretly disapproved of her getting high, as if pretending they had never been young themselves. Neither did they appreciate The Clash, she'd found out . . . He would leave her money when he left her behind but she was frugal and never used it all nor asked for more.

And at night, after her aimless, carefree wanderings, he would treat her to fancy restaurants – she'd cooked for him a few times at the flat but he was not too keen on pasta or tomato sauce or seemingly Italian food – and then bring her back to the apartment where he would fuck her. Harder and harder. As she offered no resistance and her passiveness increased, the bad man went further. One night, he tied her hands. Giuly allowed him.

Soon, he was encouraged to test her limits.

She knew it was all going in the wrong direction and she should resist his growing attempts at domination. But the thought of leaving this strange new life in Paris and returning to Rome would feel like an admission of defeat, an acknowledgement that she should not have broken up with Peppino, and broken his heart into a thousand pieces, as she clearly knew she had. Maybe this was a form of penance, a way of punishing herself? She just didn't know any longer. Had she really ever known?

One dark evening, after he'd tied her hands to the bedpost and, somehow, her ankles, he'd taken her by surprise and, despite her mild protests, had resolutely shaven away her thick thatch of wild, curling jet-black pubic hair and left her quite bald, like a child, which not only brought back bittersweet memories of her younger years but also a deep sense of shame at the fact she'd always insisted Peppino should not even trim her.

The next day, the Frenchman used his belt on her arse cheeks and marked her badly.

Sitting watching a film that afternoon in a small art house by the Odéon was painful, as Giuly kept on fidgeting in her seat to find a position that did not remind her of the previous evening's punishment. Her period pains had also begun, as bad as ever; she'd once been told they'd only go away after she'd had her first child.

That night, the bad man wanted to fuck her as usual and she pointed out that her period had begun. He became angry. He would have been quite furious had she actually revealed that she had once allowed Peppino to make love to her on such a day and the blood communion they had shared was still one of her most exquisitely shocking and treasured memories. He brutally stripped her, tied her hands behind her back and pushed her down on the floor, onto her stomach and sharply penetrated her arsehole, spitting onto his cock and her opening for necessary lubrication. She screamed in pain and he gagged her with her own panties and continued relentlessly to invest her. Giuly recalled how she had once assured Peppino as they spooned in bed one night how she would never agree to anal sex with him or anyone. Another promise betrayed, she knew. She grew familiar with the pain. She had never thought it would be so easy to break with her past.

Later, as she lay there motionless, the bad man said: "Next week, I shall continue your education. I'm taking you to a club and I want to watch you being fucked by a stranger, my sweet Italian girl."

Giuly could say nothing. When he left the apartment, he retrieved her set of keys from her handbag and locked her in. They were on the fifth floor and she had no way out. Giuly sighed.

It was a night full of stars and the Seine quivered with a thousand lights.

The taxi had dropped Cornelia around the corner of Les Chandelles. She looked out for a decent-looking café and sat herself at a table overlooking the street, where she would be highly visible to all passers-by. This was one of those rare occasions when she had lipstick on, a scarlet stain across her thin lips. She wore an opaque white silk shirt and was, as ever, braless. Her short black skirt highlighted her endless pale legs.

She'd ruffled her hair, blonde Medusa curls like a forest; and slowly sipped a glass of Sancerre, a paperback edition of John Irving's *A Widow for One Year* sitting broken-spined on the ceramic top next to the wine carafe.

The bait was set. A lonesome American woman on a Friday night in Paris, just some steps away from a notorious *club échangiste*. L'Américaine. She'd found out earlier, through judicious tipping and a hint of further largesse of another nature, from the club's doorman, that her target was planning to attend the club later this evening. The entrance fee for single women was advantageous but she felt she would attract less attention if she were part of a couple. She'd gathered on the grapevine that lone men would often congregate here in search of a partner before moving on to the club.

She'd been told right and within an hour, she'd been twice offered an escort into the premises. She hadn't even needed to uncross her legs and reveal her lack of underwear. The first guy was too sleazy for her liking, and altogether too condescending in the way he spoke to her in the slow, enunciating manner some Frenchmen automatically do with foreigners. She quietly gave him the brush-off. He did not protest unduly. The second candidate was more suitable, a middle-aged businessman with a well-cut suit and half-decent aftershave. He even sent her over a glass of champagne before actually accosting her. Much too old, of course, but then there was something about Paris and older men with younger women. The water, the air, whatever!

They agreed that once inside she would have no obligation to either stay with him or fuck him, at any rate initially. Maybe later, if neither came across someone more suitable. He readily acquiesced. Cornelia knew she was good arm candy, tall and distinctive, a beautiful woman with a style all her own, and an unnervingly visible mix of brains and provocation. She'd worked hard on that aspect of her appearance.

Despite its upmarket reputation, Les Chandelles was much as she expected. Tasteful in a vulgar but chic way; too many muted lights, drapes and parquet flooring, dark corners or *coins câlins* as they were coyly described on the club's website, semi-opulent staircases leading to private rooms and a strange overall smell of sex, cheap perfume and a touch of discreet disinfectant not unlike those American sex-shop cabins or the tawdry rooms set aside for private lap dances in some of the joints she had once navigated through.

She spent some time at the bar with her escort and enjoyed further champagne, and allowed him to show her some of the nooks and crannies of the swing club, which he appeared to be a regular at. Now she knew the lay of the land. She offered to dance with him.

"Not my scene," he churlishly protested.

"It warms me up," she pointed out. He nodded in appreciation.

"Just go ahead," he said. "Maybe we can meet up later, if you want?"

"Yes," Cornelia said.

From the dance floor, she would have a perfect vantage point to observe new arrivals as they passed on their way to more intimate areas of the club. She moved languorously to a Leonard Cohen tune and marked her area between a few embracing couples. She'd always enjoyed dancing, it had made the stripping bearable. Cornelia closed her eyes, carried along by the soft music. Occasionally, a hand would gently tap her on the shoulder, an invitation to join a man, a woman or more often a couple in a more private location, but each time she turned the offer down with an amiable smile. No one insisted, obeying the club's basic protocols.

Among the French songs she had not previously known, Cornelia had already delicately shimmied to recognisable tunes by Luna, Strays Don't Sleep and Nick Cave when she noticed the new couple settling down at the bar.

The girl couldn't have been older than twenty-five with a jungle of thick dark curls falling to her shoulders and a gawky, slightly unfeminine walk. Her back was bare, pale skin on full display emerging from a thin knitted top, and she wore a white skirt that fell all the way to her ankles, through which one could spy her long legs and a round arse just that little bit bigger than she would no doubt have wished to have, an imperfection that actually made her quite stunning. With deep brown eyes and a gypsy-like, wild demeanour, she reminded Cornelia of a child still to fully mature. She wore dark black shoes with heels, which she visibly didn't need, as she was almost as tall as Cornelia. A sad sensuality poured out from every inch of her as she followed her companion's instructions and settled on a high stool at the bar. The man ordered without asking the young girl what she wanted. Her eyes darted across the room, looking at the other patrons of the club, judging them, weighing them. It was evidently her first time here.

Cornelia adjusted her gaze.

The man squiring the exotic young woman was him, her target. The bad man. Her information had proved correct. As she watched the couple, Cornelia blanked out the music.

Less than an hour later, she had made acquaintance with them and suggested to her new friends they could move on to a more private space. Throughout their conversation, the Italian girl had been mostly silent, leaving her older companion to ask all the questions and flirt quite openly and suggestively with the splendid American blonde seemingly in search of local thrills. At first, the man appeared hesitant, as if the visit to Les Chandelles had been planned differently.

"I've never been with a woman before," the Italian girl complained to the man.

"Would you rather I looked for a negro to fuck you here and now with an audience watching?" he said to her.

"No," she whispered.

"So, we all agree," he concluded, getting up and gallantly taking Cornelia's hand. "Anyway, you can do most of the watching as I intend to enjoy the company of our new American friend to its fullest extent. You can watch and learn; I do find you somewhat passive and unimaginative, my dear young Italian gypsy. See how a real woman fucks."

Giuly lowered her eyes and stood up to follow them.

Once they had located an empty room on the next floor, Cornelia briefly excused herself and insisted she had to walk back to the cloakroom to get something from the handbag she had left there as well as picking up some clean towels, which their forthcoming activities would no doubt require.

"Ah, Americans, always keen on hygiene," the bad man said and broadly smiled. "We'll be waiting for you," he added, indicating to his young companion to start undressing.

"I'll leave my clothes too," Cornelia said, turning round. "Don't want to get them crumpled, do we?"

"Perfect," the man said, turning his attention to Giuly's slight, pale, uncovered breasts and sharply twisting her nipples while she was still in the process of slipping out of her long white skirt. There were red marks on her butt cheeks.

When Cornelia returned a few minutes later, the bad man was stripped from the waist down and the Italian girl was sucking him off while his fingers held her hair tight and her head forcibly pressed against his groin, even though his thrusts were making her choke. He turned his own head towards Cornelia, a blonde apparition, now naked and holding a bunch of towels under her left arm.

"Beautiful," he said, and released his pressure on Giuly's head. "Truly regal," he observed, his eyes running up and down Cornelia's body. "I like very much," he added. His attention now centred on her groin. "A tattoo? There? Pretty! What is it?"

Cornelia approached the couple. The man withdrew his cock from the Italian girl's mouth, allowing her to breathe better, and put a proprietary hand on Cornelia's left breast and then squinted, taking a closer look at her depilated pubic area and the small tattoo she sported there.

"A gun? Interesting," he said.

"Sig Sauer," Cornelia said.

There was a brief look of concern on his face, but then he relaxed briefly and nodded towards the American woman, indicating she should replace Giuly and service his still jutting cock. Cornelia quietly asked Giuly to move away from the man so that she might take over her position. The Italian girl stumbled backwards to the bed. Cornelia kneeled. As her mouth approached his groin, she pulled out the gun she had kept hidden under the white towels, placed it upwards against his chin and pressed the trigger.

The silencer muffled most of the sound and Giuly's cry of surprise proved louder than the actual shot which blew the lid of his head off, moving through his mouth and through to his brain in a portion of a second. He fell to the ground, Cornelia cushioning his collapse with her outstretched arm.

"Jesus," Giuly said.

And looked questioningly at Cornelia who now stood with her legs firmly apart, the weapon still in her hand, a naked angel of death.

"He was a bad man," Cornelia said.

"I know," the Italian girl said. "But . . ."

"It was just a job, nothing personal," Cornelia said.

"So . . ."

"Shhhh . . ." said Cornelia. "Get your clothes."

The young Italian girl stood there, as if nailed to the floor, every inch of her body revealed. Cornelia couldn't avoid examining her.

"You're very pretty," she said.

"You too," the other replied, red-faced.

Cornelia folded the gun back inside the towels. "Normally, I would have killed you too," she said. "As a rule, I must leave no witnesses. But I'm not big on killing women. Just dress, go and forget him. I don't know how well you knew him – I suspect it wasn't long. Find a younger man. Live. Be happy. And . . ."

"What?"

"Forget me, forget what I look like. You don't know me, you've never known me."

Giuly nodded her agreement as she pulled the knitted top she had worn earlier over her head, disturbing the thousand thick dark curls. The other woman was in no rush to dress, comfortable in her white nudity. Her body was also pale, but a different sort of pallor. Giuly couldn't quite work out the nature of the difference.

Cornelia watched her hurriedly dress.

"Go back to Rome. This never happened. It's just Paris, Giuly. Another place."

Back in the street, Giuly initially felt disorientated. It had all happened so quickly. She was surprised to see that she wasn't as shocked as she should have been. It was just something that had happened. An adventure. Her first adventure since Peppino. Under her breath, she whispered his real name. The Paris night did not answer.

She checked her bag; she had enough money for a small hotel room for the night. Tomorrow, she would take the train back to Rome.

The Louvre was lit up as she walked towards the Seine, and into a harbour of darkness. At her fourth attempt, Giuly found a cheap hotel on the rue Monsieur le Prince. The room was on the fourth floor and she could barely fit into the lift. Later, she went out and had a crêpe with sugar and Grand Marnier from an all-night kiosk near the junction between the rue de l'Odéon and the boulevard Saint Germain. People were queuing outside the nearby cinemas, people mostly of her own age, no older men here. She walked towards Notre-Dame and wasted time in a bookshop, idly leafing through the new books on display. She would have dearly liked to have a coffee, but no Latin Quarter bookshops also served coffee, unlike her favourite haunt, Feltrinelli's in Rome, where she had spent much of her teenage years. But she knew that if she walked into a café and took a table alone, someone would eventually try a pick-up line and disturb her, and tonight she felt no need for further conversation. So she finally went back to her small room and slept soundly. A night without nightmares or memories.

The man in the Police du Territoire uniform handed her passport back to Cornelia. "I hope you enjoyed your stay, Mademoiselle?"

L'Américaine candidly smiled back at him as she made her way into the departure lounge at the airport. "Absolutely," she said.

Paranoid Polly

Tara Alton

This morning, I woke up to find my boyfriend wanted me to give him oral sex. I wasn't in the mood, so I told him that my sinuses were stuffed up and if I performed such an act, I would no doubt suffocate and die. Perhaps this was a bit melodramatic, but I think the imagery changed his mind. To be honest, I haven't been feeling the same about us lately. Something has been missing in the sex department, and I am worried that it might be me. I have been having other problems, too. Maybe I'm just being paranoid, but I'm starting to think that I'm having a serious run of bad luck.

As I came out of the bedroom, I found more proof about my diminishing luck. My cat had gotten sick on the carpeting right in front of the door, and I had almost stepped in it. It was a lovely beige color with white foam, the puke, not the carpet. After cleaning it up, still warm from the belly of the beast, I changed my mind about having scrambled eggs for breakfast.

At work, I was nearly crushed to death by a frantic elevator button maniac. If I hadn't been carrying my purse and my lunch sack, I would have been a goner. Good thing I wasn't a man, because my balls would have been crushed for sure. As I glared at the psycho nearly responsible for my premature demise, I wondered if I were a man and my balls were crushed, if I could get workmen's compensation. Balls might not be a bad thing to have if some damaged ones got me some paid time off work.

As I came into my office, I noticed there was something odd laying inside one of the donation boxes for the charity drive for the homeless. People had been bringing things like little bottles of shampoo from hotels and dusty cans of vegetables from home. Today, there was something brown and furry. Good grief, it looked as if a giant rat had crawled in there and expired, I thought, and no one had noticed it, but it seemed too big to be a rat. Had someone actually brought in a dead animal to feed those in need? That would be so unhygienic.

Then I realized it looked like the fur from an old mink stole, which I supposed was even worse. I couldn't imagine a homeless person with freshly shampooed hair, eating expired peas while wearing a mink stole.

Part of me wanted to reach inside the box to see what it was, but who reaches inside a charity box? It would be like sticking your hand in a tip jar to see if that really was the latest State Quarter. Therefore, I hurried to my desk before I was late.

For the next two hours, I let the mystery fur thing bother me, until someone else dropped off some more dusty cans and they flipped it over to sit on the top. To my relief, I saw it was a teddy bear, and it was a super cute one at that. I spent the rest of the morning trying to come up with plot to steal it and take it home. Once more, I found myself wishing for some balls.

On my break, I went downstairs to the candy store. I was planning to buy a package of cashews, still clinging to the South Beach shores of weight loss, when my gaze snagged on a snack pack of Zingers, moist little rectangles of cake filled with cream and topped with frosting. I could have sworn I saw the cashier totaling up the calories in her head as she rang me up. Since I was too embarrassed to eat them in public, I dodged into the bathroom and claimed a stall as my dining room. Peeing and eating a Zinger at the same time can be quite satisfying. Now if I did have balls that might be harder to do as I would have to hold my penis and a Zinger at the same time, but since I was a girl both my hands were free.

Before I went back upstairs, I took a gander at the community bulletin board by the smokers' lounge. The belly-dance night-club flyer was still dangling from a tack. I could quite fancy myself being a belly dancer. It would be cool to be able to shake your stuff like that with everyone watching. I still had the shape for it, even with the occasional Zinger folly.

Imagining belly dancing music in my head, I was about ready to give my hips a little shimmy when I spotted a man leaving the smoking lounge. Holy cow. It was the severely height-challenged man who wore a mustache and a full wig who used to work at my company. I think his name was Peter. I had heard that when he was fired, he had been escorted out of the building by security.

It had taken me months to find out exactly why he was fired, but I finally scored the truth from a secretary. He had been looking at porn on his computer. Talk about a voyeur. He couldn't even wait to get home! The first time they caught him, they had given him a written warning. The second time he was called into the conference room to be confronted by our boss, and he became verbally abusive, thus the security escort from the premises.

I never knew someone who actually was canned for looking at porn at work. I wanted to run after him and ask him what websites he had been looking at when they caught him, but I was going to be late from my break.

As I took the elevator back upstairs, I started to wonder why he was back in the building in the first place. Was it for revenge? I tried not to imagine him walking around the office with a gun, looking for supervisors while defenseless secretaries cowered under their desks, praying they had never given him a dirty look.

Once I was situated back at my desk, I couldn't stop looking over my shoulder at the office door every time it was opened, just in case it was him. Adam, my adorable co-worker, who sat next to me, noticed my odd behavior and raised an eyebrow at me. Not to sound like a cliché, but he had the most amazing blue eyes and dimples, worthy of a movie star. His clothes were always immaculate and he knew designer names like the back of his hand. On top of that, he was tall and his build was fantastic. I still hadn't figured out if he was gay or metro-sexual yet, but I had told myself multiple times it didn't matter since I already had a boyfriend. Still, I found myself studying him in great and lengthy detail when I thought he wasn't looking.

I could hardly tell him that I suspected a short man in a wig was going to come kill everyone, so I said the first thing that popped into my head.

"I've got a crush," I said.

He looked surprised at me. Did he think I was confessing my feelings for him?

"On that teddy bear," I said, pointing at the previously identified road kill.

"So, take it home," he said. "No one would care."

"Like I'm going to take a toy away from a child in need," I said.

He smiled at me with his movie-star smile and turned back to his work.

Lunchtime came. Luckily, everyone was still alive. I decided to abandon my packed lunch for a trip to the cafeteria to see if Peter was still lurking around. He wasn't. I bought a small container of hummus and a pitta from the Middle Eastern deli counter and headed to my favorite seat where I opened the container, realizing it was the exact same color as the cat sick this morning.

Tossing it into the trash, I went for another look at the bulletin board near the smokers' lounge. I spotted a sign for a parrot for sale. Who would pay $1,500 for a bird? Not me. Then I noticed a co-worker was actually hawking Mary Kay Cosmetics. Her business cards were the kind you would print off on your computer. She was the last person I would take makeup advice from because you could always see her foundation line at her chin. Didn't Mary Kay teach her anything?

My stomach rumbled. I was still hungry. I turned to have a gander at the vending machines behind me for a snack not the color of cat puke when I heard an odd noise down the hallway.

It sounded as if someone was inhaling a frozen Coke from a party store a mile a minute through a straw. Was someone secretly binging? I had to know.

Tiptoeing on the tile floor, I peered around the corner where there used to be a nook for the smoking lounge microwave, and to my disbelief, I saw that Peter was down on his knees giving Adam a blowjob.

Holy cow! Now I knew for sure what type of porn he had been looking at!

As I stood there staring, I knew I should run away, but I didn't. There was a strange feeling inside me. I wanted to watch. At first, I thought it was because Peter was doing things I had never even considered doing during a blowjob. I thought it was just bobbing your head up and down until the guy came, but he was extremely inventive. He was even acting as if he liked doing it, even using his hands. Maybe I should take notes for the next time I performed oral sex.

Then I thought my reason for not leaving was because I was in shock at how large Adam's dick was. My boyfriend was modest in size, mostly narrow, and it was uncut. Adam's dick on the other hand gave a new meaning to immense: it was a cut, straining love rocket.

Yet despite observing the new blowjob skills and the big dick, I realized I was still standing there for another reason. I was completely turned on by watching them have sex in front of me, and it was the surprise of my lifetime, but then again when had I seen real live people having sex? My boyfriend didn't even like to have the lights on.

Standing there was like having a switch turned on inside me. My girly nether regions were suddenly moist and throbbing. My breath felt tight in my chest, and my hands felt clammy. I really wanted to undo the top button of my blouse so I could breathe.

Suddenly, Adam opened his eyes and looked straight at me. Our eyes locked. I was staring into the depths of those dreamy blue eyes, and I could tell he knew by my expression that I had been there for more than a moment.

Embarrassed beyond belief, I spun around and ran to the bathroom where I locked myself in a stall.

For a long time, I stood there, taking deep breaths and trying to calm myself down, but the images of Adam and Peter kept flashing in my mind. I could not be a voyeur. Voyeurs were supposed to be men named "Tom" who skulked around apartment buildings at night and peered in through windows, not office girls who were named "Polly". Sure, sometimes I liked to replay the sex scenes in R-rated movies when no one else was there, but that was innocent stuff. Didn't everyone do that?

When I finally emerged a good twenty minutes later, I wasn't feeling any better. I was thinking about going home sick. How could I spend the rest of the day sitting next to Adam, knowing every detail of his manhood? How could I sit there with this throbbing between my legs that wouldn't go away?

As I approached my desk, I noticed that Adam was deeply engrossed in his work, but there was still a faint flush on his cheeks. Had he finished with Peter? Thank goodness, he didn't even look my way.

Thinking this could quite possibly be the worst day of my life, I plunked myself down in my chair, ready to phone my supervisor to tell him I was going home sick, when I realized something didn't quite feel right beneath my butt and thighs.

Slowly, I rolled my chair back a few inches, leaned over and lifted my skirt to see a bump where there had never been one before. Had I suddenly gotten my wish to have balls? My hands trembled as I lifted my skirt further to see what had happened. Something brown and furry was between my legs. Good grief. My love muff had exploded from the stress! Then I noticed two black eyes staring back at me and a snout resting against the vicinity of my love button.

I sat bolt upright. Adam had stolen the teddy bear for me and left it on my chair, and I was straddling it as if it was giving me oral sex!

I knew I should have scooted the teddy bear out from beneath me, but my body was still so excited that it didn't care who or what was down there. My thighs clamped together around its stiff snout.

My eyes fluttering shut, I let my mind race back to the days when I used to squeeze a pillow rhythmically between my legs to give myself an orgasm as a teenager. I had destroyed many a pillow that way, but now that I was older, I realized I had control of all sorts of muscles down there.

It was almost like straddling a penis when I was on top of a man, but this was on the outside of my panties. Holding the rest of my body still, I zeroed in all my concentration on squeezing my inner thigh muscles around the snout and I slightly rocked my hips forward. My clit was rubbing against its black yarn nose.

Heat flushed up through my body as I gripped my desk for support. My toes crunched in my pumps as I leaned slightly forward. My hair felt like it was smothering my neck, and that top button on my blouse was really driving me crazy now.

I squeezed as hard as I could, let go, sucked in some air, let it out and shifted my butt. The bear's snout moved a fraction. It was almost a bingo on my clit. Just to the left a little more, I thought, twisting slightly, and I hit the exact spot. That high, screaming orgasm feeling flashed through me as I imagined watching Adam's face as he came. It felt as if my heart stopped.

The moment I unclamped my grip on the mangled bear and returned to earth, I opened my eyes. Reality rushed back at me like a cold splash of water. Holy cow! I had dry-humped a stuffed animal like a horny dog in the middle of my office! I would never live down the shame if anyone saw me.

Hurriedly, I glanced around the room, praying that no one had noticed when I saw that Adam was looking my way.

"Oops," I said as innocently as I could as I pried the bear from beneath me.

Half-wanting to give him a kiss for his cooperation, I shoved my new illicit lover into my tote bag under my desk, feeling the flush of my orgasm on my face and neck.

"Did you just do what I thought you did with that bear?" Adam asked.

I looked at him in horror. He hadn't been engrossed in his work. He had seen the whole thing!

To my disbelief, I watched him reach down between his legs and adjust himself. Why he would he need to do that, I wondered, especially when he just got a blowjob? Could he have gotten hard from watching me get it on with a stuffed bear?

Suddenly, a thought occurred to me.

"Are you bi?" I whispered.

He nodded.

"And what you just did has to be one of the hottest things I've ever seen," he said.

"You liked watching me?" I asked.

He nodded enthusiastically.

Suddenly, I felt another massive throb downstairs. This never happened. After an orgasm, I usually cooled off like the arctic winter. Was I getting horny again just from thinking about him watching me?

Another massive pang hit my clit. It wanted more. It was as if this new world of possibilities was opening up for me. Maybe it wasn't my fault in the sex department with my boyfriend. Maybe I wasn't having such massive bad luck, and it was a good thing that my cat got sick so I didn't want my lunch and I caught my co-worker getting a blowjob.

I scooted closer to my desk, trying to wrap my mind around the fact that I wasn't only a "Paranoid Polly", but a "Peeping Polly" as well.

My foot knocked over my tote bag and the teddy bear fell out. I reached down to stuff him back in when I heard Adam clear his throat.

"I don't think you should be taking our new little stuffed friend home so soon," he said.

The Erotica Writer's Husband

J. D. Munro

The erotica writer's husband bangs open the front door and stomps outside. Barefoot, with his fly half-open, he'd interrupted his current activity when he heard barks and feline screeches.

His wife's cat, puffed up to dramatic size, hisses from the safety of the yellow window box. Marigolds splash against bristling black fur. Fastening the buttons of his 501s, the sex author's spouse scans the yard for the offending dog, but the husband's eyes meet the neighbor's instead.

"Sorry!" The neighbor snaps a leash onto the collar of his now slash-nosed and cowering mutt. He notes the open-flied jeans of the erotica writer's husband. "Oh *hoh*, your wife must be home. I bet you spend a lot of time with your pants down, being married to a porn writer and all. Doing *research*."

"Uh huh. Well. Gotta get back. She's waiting."

"Don't let me keep you!"

The sex author's spouse waves and carries the angry cat inside. The cat rakes his wrist in one final protest and leaps free. But instead of returning to the slick and sprawled wife his neighbor imagines, pen tucked behind her ear to take notes as she commands him to enact tawdry scenarios, he returns to the john to finish his interrupted piss.

His buddies and neighbors, jealous of a man married to a scribbler of lewd tales, imagine his rampant and orgiastic sex life. His wife is obsessed with sex manuals and adult websites, they think, not home décor catalogues like theirs.

In fact, as husband to a smutty authoress, he suspects that he's getting less than they are. He doesn't know whether to dissuade them from their faulty beliefs in order to gain their sympathy or to continue to bask in the glow of their misplaced admiration. After all, they think he'd been stud muffin enough to capture a lusty wench in matrimony, whereas they had landed frumpy *fraus* more interested in dozing than dildos. There were worse things a guy's friends could assume. They'd given him unsolicited and unearned respect, rarely seen by a monogamous, suburban man with no aptitude for sports. How empty would their lives be if they no longer had his prowess to worship? Who was he to disappoint them by correcting their misapprehension?

As he contemplates the remote control or a nap, the erotica writer herself cracks open her study door. Her laser printer huffs in the background, expending more energy over sex than husband and wife have in the past month. "Everything okay?" she asks.

"Just Dufus Rufus chasing Frizbeehead again. She scratched me." He holds out his clawed arm.

"Better sterilize that. Antiseptic's in the bathroom cabinet. Oh, mind doing the dishes? I've got this deadline."

"Sure, hon. Listen, can we talk, I –"

"Damn, now I've forgotten that perfect word. Shit, I spent the last half-hour with a thesaurus and now . . . stupid dog. Somebody needs to put him out of our misery." She scoops the cat up and closes the door.

He wishes she would spend a half-hour with her finger in something other than a book.

That evening he suggests that they might spend some time together, since it's the weekend, but she encourages him to go and watch the game with his pals. "Go out and have some fun. Becky's giving me her feedback on that story I've been working on."

"The slaves in the ice castle one? In Greenland?"

"Not Greenland. A hidden fjord in Svalbard. No, I couldn't figure out how the characters could stay warm enough to be turned on. I got cold just thinking about it. Now they're on a boat. Only the Master goes ashore, but that gives the favorite slave time to secretly practice his violin. But of course someone hears him playing the *Paganini Caprice No. 24* and finds him, and then he has to decide whether he wants to stay willingly."

"Still working the gay market? I thought you'd had it with all that spunk." He knows better than anyone that both the dentist and doctor have documented her strong gag reflex, which precludes certain bedroom activities.

"Pays better, and you said yourself the truck transmission's about to go. Anyway, the slave's going to have a *guiche*, so I need to do some research before Becky gets here."

"I know how to make quiche."

"A *guiche*. Not quiche. A piercing *down there*."

"Ouch."

"Anyway, then I'm hitting the hay early so I can get up to do my edits. Mind sleeping on the couch when you get home so you don't wake me up?"

"How about we roll in the hay instead of hitting it?"

"Funny man. I married you for your sense of humor."

He receives an ovation when he arrives at the bar. His friends clear a stool for him.

"Have a beer!" Dean cries. "You must be exhausted!"

"Drink up!" Doug says. "Replenish those fluids!"

"Do a shot, man," Dave advises. "You can't spare the time for a pint! Gotta get back to the little wife!"

They check their watches. "How long you need to regenerate, man? We'll let you know when time's up."

His cell phone rings. "It's my wife. I better pick up."

"Time for dessert!" They all jeer. "Second helpings!"

"Mind picking up some buttermilk on your way home?" his wife asks. "I'm making bread tomorrow."

"Sure, hon." He wishes she would knead something other than flour. The only thing rising in his house is dough. They could milk his meat, instead. Beat his eggs. Eat her jelly roll. Toss his nuts. Warm her bread basket. Hot cross his buns. Maybe make baby batter and put a bun in the oven.

"So, what'd she want? Come on, you can tell us."

"Lovin' in her oven."

They whoop and slap him on the back. His Hefeweizen splashes his shirt.

"Come on, spill the beans, man. You never tell us anything."

He swipes at his soggy shirt, imagining:

He bangs the front door open and stomps inside, adjusting his wide load. His wife pauses with her lipstick-stained teacup halfway to her lips. "You're home early, honey," she says tremulously from her jasmine steam cloud.

"Jig's up," he growls. "Be my whore, or I'll divulge your pen name to the neighbors."

Her hand goes up to the red-rimmed "O" of her lips. She sets down the cup in its saucer with a small clink and drops to her knees. "Of course, whatever you want, honey." She lifts her moose-with-puffball-nose nightshirt to reveal a red lace teddy with nipple cutouts.

"Hello?" Dean snaps in his ear. "Yo, dick brain?"

"Earth to Stud Man," Doug says. "You gonna give us some dirt, or what?"

"Yeah, your mind's definitely in the gutter." Dave orders another round. "Should've seen the look on your face."

"Well, you know, it's private. Husband and wife."

"Yeah, and the thirty thousand people who read her stories!"

He can't blame his wife for his current status as a begrudging icon of virility. She would have kept her kinky stories a secret, but he blurted out the news to the world when the *Penthouse* check arrived. He hadn't considered the ramifications. Well, maybe he had, just a little. He was not without pride at his own magnanimity in allowing her to be who she was. That he didn't hold his wife's rampant public perversions in check, but allowed them to march unfettered across magazine racks far and wide, was a testament to his part in Steinem's new race of unthreatened Man. What other husband would be so secure in his manhood that he would be permissive – nay, *encouraging* – of his wife's transgressive acts, particularly when they did not involve his own penis? Involved a whole parade of phantom penises, in point of fact.

Ironically, from what he's heard, his neighborhood has an above average *times-per-week* compared to most suburban outposts, owing to the fervor of imagination the erotica writer and her husband inspire.

Does he want them to know the truth, or does he want to continue to stand tall among them as the man who is getting the most nookie? The rare beast who has to keep up with his wife's ravenous appetite? The stallion who snagged a nymphomaniac? The man who has the pleasure of acting out every filthy scenario she devises? He has more sexual intrigue than the guys on covers of romance novels. He's not mowing the lawn like the rest of these poor schmucks; he's munching her bush.

"It's fiction," he finally ventures to his bar mates in response. "You don't have to commit murder to write a mystery."

They snort and pump their hips suggestively. A woman down the bar looks at them in disgust and carries her Pinot Grigio to a distant table.

Dean notes his scratched wrists. "Whoa! She got a little carried away, huh?"

"So what *is* the little lady up to tonight?" Doug asks.

"She's got a friend coming over."

"You dog!" Dave wipes his beer moustache. "A threesome!"

He bangs the front door open and stomps inside. His wife and her friend pause with their lipstick-stained teacups halfway to their lips. "Jig's up," he growls. "Be my sluts, or I'll delete your American Idols *off the TiVo."*

Her hand goes up to the red-rimmed "O" of her lips. She sets down the cup in its saucer with a small clink and drops to her knees. "Of course, whatever you want, honey. You, too, right, Becky?" His wife lifts her World Peas sweatshirt to reveal a black leather teddy with nipple cutouts. But Becky, being small, quick, and lithe, has already crawled halfway across the floor, on a mission to get his cock into her mouth before his wife can. Her breasts fall out of her cardigan as she makes like a Slinky toward him. "I've been hungry for you to ask me! All of my sinful stories are just flimsy cover-ups for the real fantasies I'm having about you! Come to mama, my divine sausage, and gimme the works."

"It's a dirty job, but somebody's gotta do it."

When he leaves a while later, whistles and catcalls follow him out the door into the rainy night.

He pulls into the driveway of 613 Cedar Lane and surveys the dark house. He takes his shoes off on the front porch and carries them inside, careful in his socked feet to make no noise on the wood floor. She's a light sleeper, and the smallest creak that jars her from REM will disrupt her circadian rhythm for weeks.

He hears a small voice calling to him, and he cracks open the bedroom door. His wife sits propped up in the bed, in a dim circle of light from her bed lamp, Sudoku book and pencil in hand. A teacup and saucer perch on the comforter beside her.

"Glad you're home," she yawns. "You saved me from myself. I was about to cheat. How pathetic."

"What're you doing still up? Thought you had to get back to work at the crack of dawn."

"Couldn't sleep. Missed you." She pats the bed beside her.

"Hold on a sec." He holds up the buttermilk. "Lemme put this away first."

"Nuke this for me while you're up?" She holds out the teacup.

He punches in twenty-two seconds on the microwave. There's not a lot he feels he can do for her, other than the occasional oil change or too-tight jar lid. But if she's comfy on the couch and in the middle of a book, she can, without a word, hold out her half-finished tea to him on his way past. He's got it down to a science and punches in numbers on the timer depending on how empty the cup is. She likes her tea hot, but not too hot.

He hands her the warmed cup and stretches out beside her. She wrinkles her nose while she sips.

"Too hot?" Impossible.

"No. It's just that it's chamomile."

"I thought you hated chamomile."

"I do. It's so horsy-smelling. I feel like I'm in chewing cud. In a barn. In Kentucky. But it's supposed to be good for you. Helps with dewy skin or better eyesight or memory or something. I'm old and fat. I need all the help I can get. Can't hurt. Think I should cover my gray?"

Uh oh, bad writing day, he can tell. "What gray?"

"I don't believe you, but thanks, hon. What'd you and the boys talk about tonight?"

"That crabbing show. They filmed the last episode at the same bar we were at."

"That *Deadliest Crabs* one?"

"No, I had those once, and it's nothing you'd care to film." She laughs. "What else?"

"Just the game and stuff."

She rolls her eyes. "You boys have no imagination."

He bangs the front door open and stomps inside. Naked, his wife sits backwards on his favorite armchair, her breasts pressed to the chair back. Her legs are spread each side, and the crack of her ass holds communion with the seat. Tattoos of naked women cover her back. "Oh, honey," she looks at him over her shoulder. "Look what I got done today. I was out shopping for pumps, you know with the arch support like I need? Which reminds me, I need to take my glucosamine later. Anyway, I just felt like something a little more fun, y'know? Some good ole retail therapy. The grind's really getting to me lately. I started with stilettos, and wound up with ink, and a nipple and a guiche *piercing, too. I just figured, why not go the whole nine yards? Come see." She swivels around and slouches low in the chair, hooking her legs up over the arms to give him a full display. "Slather some ointment on me, and then fuck me up the ass, hard as you can, 'kay? And tomorrow we'll get you something fun, too. Maybe a cock ring. Although," she muses, "it might be tough to find one big enough for you. Maybe a special order?"*

"You don't think so, huh?"

She snaps the book shut. "Try me."

"What've you got on under that nightie?" Tonight it's the daisy-print flannel. The nursing one she bought by mistake, with lots of convenient buttons that she starts to undo.

"Guess, Mr Cocky Brainstorm."

"Nothing."

"Bingo."

"My favorite."

"What'd you boys *really* talk about? Were they at it again? All with anal sex on their mind but too afraid to ask about it? Like it makes them pansies or something?"

She still wants to talk. He's in no hurry. It's one of those things all those sex movies fail to mention: the small talk. He shifts closer toward her. He knows what this is, these superficial questions of hers. To someone else it might seem like idle chitchat, meaningless dithering going nowhere. But he recognizes it for what it is: foreplay. Getting reacquainted again after the daily separations of a humdrum life. A casual reconnection before the more intimate one that he knows is around the next bend. Step on the gas and try to cut a corner and it's all over before it started. She'll cut the engine.

"They think I'm having a threesome."

She looks around the room. "There's always the cat."

"That's not the pussy I had in mind."

"No?"

His hand creeps up under her nightie, finds her inner thigh, and he lets it rest there, just shy of his ultimate target. Her hand simultaneously finds his fly, and she starts undoing the buttons with one hand. All that typing has at least helped keep her fingers strong.

"I was thinking," he says, his hands just brushing the tips of her pubic hair. "Maybe I'll write a story."

"Oh, sure, everyone thinks it's easy. But try coming up with new ideas all the time."

"Yeah," he says, his finger finding the bullseye, "that must be tough."

Sparklewheel

Kris Saknussemm

Night time. Warm. Humid. A vast, mostly uninhabited fairground with weird giant clown heads leering out of the darkness of closed attractions . . . statues of goofy characters off in the distance of dead rides looking sinister now . . . abandoned booths . . . broken lights sparking . . . silhouettes of people, not clear enough to be certain of their intent.

We arrive at a ride that is still running. It's like a huge roulette wheel, which can ratchet itself up the central axis as it whirls. The man running it has a white redneck face but the body of a black bodybuilder. No one is in any of the car-containers near us – the few people there are all on the other side of the circle and we can't see them.

The ride begins and the spinning starts to get really intense, the feeling heightened as we lift higher off the ground, seeing both more of the fair and less, with the shadows and the shut-down sections. You take notice of the rhythm of the rising and revolving and say, "It's like a sex machine." I say, "Yes, and like a time machine."

Then we start to get really hot . . . touching each other . . . kissing . . . and then we think what it would be like to fuck while on the wheel, flying around this haunted fairground. You've got this flimsy mint julep dress on with no panties and I'm wearing microfiber cargo pants. You're wet and ready. It's easy for me to pull it out and slide into you. You can ride me while we speed higher and harder around and around.

No one can see because we're up too far from the ground and moving too fast. You rise and squat – and pump, feeling my whole cock inside you, thickening even more with the texture and the pressure. At first you ride me, just like a merry-go-round, me playing with your tits. The texture is perfect. Squishy, but not soaking. Tight like a mare's grasp . . . so that I can feel the walls of you suck in around the head and shaft like a deep muscular mouth. I start bucking up inside you to meet your grind, pulling your skimpy cotton dress up so your ass is fully exposed to the warm wind blowing past, and I can peel the cheeks back, getting the whole meat of you in my hands . . . from your moist puckered asshole to your quivering flanks that I slap with my hands as the pressure starts to rise and you shove in against my chest to rub the shaft against your clit.

I ease a finger into your ass, which is dripping and loose now . . . your breasts free of the dress and my mouth moving between the nipples, which look bigger to you than you've ever seen them, hard and wet and pointing out . . . almost wanting to be bitten off.

The ride seems to accelerate in time with our hunger . . . like a mania we've infected the machine with . . . and just as we're both about to come . . . there's a massive wrenching sound and a blast of what looks like neon starlight . . . then steel and live wires go whipping past our heads and the limbs of someone on the other side of the wheel fly by and we feel this rush of dizziness as the whole ride snaps from the axis and tilts madly, hurling us into the air, still fucking.

We only become disentangled when we land . . . in this lagoon-like marsh on the other side of the fairground. We can see the faint reflection of the few ride lights off the underbelly of low clouds, but it seems like a million years ago. There are shouts and sirens, but they get muffled and more distant very quickly. We've fallen into a kind of swamp. Half-submerged holiday cabins and mired bulldozers covered in lichen and moss lurk all around us. There are gas flares and burbling pockets of bubbles rising. Inner tubes float . . . and a big fiberglass ice-cream cone that looks like it was shot at by a rifle. Then you feel something brush against your leg and you let out one of your squeaks. Maybe it was a mud turtle. Maybe it was something else. There are clearly other things in the water than just algae-coated shopping carts and stolen road signs. We both start to panic a little, wondering what we've fallen into.

Then we see it misting into view – like a mirage – until the iron and timber emerge. It's like a houseboat . . . or rather . . . it's like a farmhouse built on top of a rusted barge or channel dredge. We swim for it . . . the flaking ladder on the near side. You climb up first, your dress ripped down the back, and when you reach the top, your butt is right in my face. For a moment, I forget everything else that's going on. I want only to fuck you in the ass, right there on the deck of the barge. Then an owl swoops down with a plump, sopping water rat in its talons, and I remember what's just happened. We don't know where we are. We might've fallen into toxic sludge. And who in the hell lives in this floating house? Are we really alive still?

There are a couple of foggy lights on and some music playing. Something sappy and lost in time, like a Jackie Gleason record. Music to pour a martini and get the girl into bed by back in the 1950s. We're freaked. We're wet . . . we appear to be unhurt . . . but we need help. So we go inside. No knock. The screen door is open.

There are more mosquitoes inside than out, but at first it's kind of a strangely cheerful scene – reassuring compared to what we were expecting. My dick is still hard from the image of your ass arched up before me when we climbed onboard, but we can't be fooling around right at the moment.

The room we've entered is a homey old farmhouse kitchen with awful green and yellow painted cupboards and cheesy knick-knacks everywhere – a refrigerator armored in souvenir magnets . . . what looks like a frozen dinner now steaming on the table, as if whoever lives there was just about to sit down and eat. We call out but no one answers. We wait but no one comes. So we peek into the next room.

There's a candle in a screened lantern burning, but it's enough to light up the walls and we see them all staring down at us. Animal heads. Hundreds of them. From deer and wildcats to pigs, donkeys, even mice. They've all been expertly mounted, but crammed together. The candle casts a glow down the hall to the rest of the house, and we see there are more animal heads – fish, snakes and birds. Cats. Dogs. Horses. We shit ourselves. The whole place is a grisly taxidermy museum, but oddly innocent and farmlike. The contrast really gives us the shudders. And still no one answers. No sound in the place. Just the swamp noises outside . . . the burbling of the water, the hiss of escaping gas . . . and the jut and bump of the barge rubbing against sunken or drifting bits of debris.

After a moment of fussing and arguing about what to do, we decide to check the whole place out. I take the candle and we do a room-to-room. Every chamber is exactly what you'd expect a quaint old farmhouse to look like – except for the stuffed animals. Frogs, rabbits, even a couple of eerie clown heads from the fairground. Plastic thankfully.

But in what is sort of like the parlor where a television sits, there's a table laid out with a miniature trailer park on it. The detail is remarkable. Perfect little Winnebagos and older enclosures. Tents. Toy cars and itsy-bitsy people, like expensive mold-cast figurines . . . willow trees made of strips of cardboard and torn flannel. Everything is exactly proportioned . . . and there's a curious sense of order to the layout . . . all the people and vehicles positioned around this gleaming silver miniature Airstream trailer. And then, at the same time, we realize . . .

The miniature trailer park is laid out like a kind of board game.

Just then, we hear a sound outside that brings us to full alert.

The sound . . . is actually two sounds. One is disturbingly near at hand – but impossible to place. It seems to be an extension of our inner turmoil, as if the hypersensitive channels of intimacy and anxiety between us have escaped and are now animating the bizarre houseboat. The other sound is clearer and more immediately compelling. A rush of water . . . as if the barge has cut loose from the sludge and gurglings of the swamp . . . the reed tussocks and the carcasses of metal . . . and is now in some swifter flow . . . heading toward we know not what. We bolt outside to the deck, bumping into each other, dropping the candle in the caged lantern in our hurry.

The sight outside is mind-stopping. The barge has indeed wandered out of the lagoon and is quickly slipping into a genuine bay.

Before us are two things. Closer at hand is a ferry boat, like the Staten Island ferry, only the size of a very large cruise ship. Every single window is lit and blinking fiber optic cords festoon the sides so it almost looks alive. The odd thing is that people keep leaping off the top deck, which is a long way down to the water on a boat that size. They fling themselves off like they're drunk or stupefied, splashing and whinnying. Fragments of clothing follow them down . . . old-fashioned hat racks . . . newspapers and magazines . . . and money. It's as if whole cotton bales of currency have been torn apart and flung over the side. The bills waft down in the lights like leaves on fire . . . all over the harbor . . . some blowing past us as the barge lurches, gushing into the stream of the bay.

The second and even more imposing thing we see is a city with spotlights slicing back and forth – and skyrockets that may either be fireworks or bombs spurting overhead.

Part of it is like Laughlin, Nevada, crowded up against a palisade of cliffs . . . but with colossal faces carved in the rocks . . . billboards collapsing down the embankment . . . the signs of campfires and shelters in the clefts. The part overlooking the water looks more like Louisville or Memphis, an American river city, but with hallucinatory Asian and Middle Eastern influences. Like Damascus on the Mekong. It's hard to be certain of anything because the city is literally falling down as we look at it. Enormous demolition equipment is attacking it, like dinosaurs smashing a model village. We can see looming cranes and wrecking balls swinging, lit by anti-aircraft lights. There are men with luminous green hard hats all over the wharf area . . . with gauze face masks . . . and people with lunch boxes for heads or parking meters. It's a like a City of Idiots . . . completely demented. Except for one huge pillar of scaffolding. Within this framework, thousands upon thousands of people hang, scurry or climb like spider monkeys . . . all wearing signal orange jumpsuits and headlamps. There are so many they give shape to the structure, making it a skyscraper – but writhing with instability and change. Every so often one of the scalers plummets – but their place is instantly taken. More and more swarm from below, driving the others higher, until the building has a true and sustaining shape even when some of the individuals fall.

Only when we have gawked at this scene for a few moments . . . trying to take it all in . . . make sense of it somehow . . . do we realize that the lantern we'd left behind in the farmhouse has set the place ablaze. The windows and door frames crackle with the heat, shattered glass from the panes raining down over the deck, flames whooshing out. We're heading into a collision course with the giant ferry of lights and jumpers and snowing money . . . on a barge with a burning farmhouse roaring . . . approaching a city gone insane.

Somehow, the whole frightening pandemonium of the situation charges us. We wanted trouble and bright lights – and we've got it. In spades. Our best option looks like jumping ship before we smash into the ferry – the barge might well survive in sections – but we recognize that we might get eaten up by the screw propeller or flounder to drowning in the wake. Plus, we're feeling a little flush in the luck department remembering the roulette wheel ride. Then two things happen.

Out of the wildfire farmhouse charge these people with animal heads – they must've been behind the walls – imprisoned or secretly watching us – we'll never know, because they stampede off the barge into the bay, the flames flaring out when they hit the water. The whole structure explodes as they do, and almost sends us into the drink with the repercussion. Then we hear a voice from down on the water. We think it's one of the animal head people who's okay and now calling for help. But it's not. They're gone – too badly burned.

It's a big fat guy in a life raft. Only he doesn't have hands. Arms, but no hands, and so he can't row very well. He's in even greater danger than we are of being crushed by the ferry because he's just in a little inflatable. But if we were in it and were rowing, we could get to land. So we jump. No words between us . . . nothing. Except . . .

At the last second, you turn around and run back into the farmhouse, with timbers crumbling down and flames pouring out. I think, this is it. She's cracked. She's dead. Charred. Gone.

And then you reappear. You're clutching the Airstream from the trailer park board game. Your dress is on fire. And you run right past me, grabbing my hand as you go . . . and we leap into the bay as the farmhouse really blows . . . lumber, melting fridge magnets and scorched animal heads hailing down behind us.

We hit the water about fifteen feet from the life raft and swim toward the fat man, who's waving his stumps at us. You're closer. You make the raft. Then you do something I'm secretly really grateful for, but shocked to see. The moment you're settled in the spongy little yellow boat – that looks so very small up against the nearing ferry, you let go of the Airstream, pick up one of the oars and smack him in the side of the head, knocking him over the edge. I scramble in and pick up the other oar, with him nearby in the water, still conscious and beginning to flail. When he gets close enough, I nail him over the head as hard as I can. You started it and I have to finish it – and I instinctively understand your point. We don't know him. We don't owe him. There's ash and destruction all around, we may already be dead and in some inferno. We have only ourselves.

Then I start to row like holy hell. But I'm a very good rower. Have been since a kid. We slip out of the ferry path just as it hits the barge, the iron and steel of it doing more damage to the ferry hull than vice versa. But the incinerated farmhouse slides off the back into the harbor taking all the animal heads and miniature people secrets with it . . . extinguished in a last fire swirl of disintegrating studs and a monstrous belch of steam. The ferry plows on, passengers still chucking themselves off, the lights still twinkling, a wicked gash to fore from the barge impact spraying water and ruptured wood over our heads. But we're too busy tumbling in the waves and trying to stay in the raft.

We row toward the city. There are fires up and down the shore. Some seem to be consciously lit bonfires of furniture and drift-wood – or smaller cooking fires. Others are the smoldering bodies of cars and machines. We don't have much choice but to try to land. The raft is too small to risk crossing the harbor, and we have no idea where we're going. There are people outside the rings of fire along the quay and the spit of rocks and sand – all of this below a wall of broken cement and razor wire beneath the city. Some people are surf fishing, oblivious to the chaos around them. Others seem to be engaged in what looks like a paintball game. Farther down, in the shadows from the spitfires and the lights of the self-destructing city, it looks like uglier things are happening. Rapes, dismemberments, unknown rituals.

Back behind us, people begin shoving cars off the ferry as water surges into the damaged hull. We can't tell if they're desperately lightening the load to keep from going down – or enjoying the vandalism – because they cheer whenever a car goes over and splashes into the black bay, the ferry still churning forward even as it takes on water.

We have to turn our attention back to bringing the raft in while avoiding the rocks and stuff along the shore. There are oil cans and plastic bottles everywhere in the dirty foam. Other things look sharper and more dangerous. But we come in on the waves from the ferry and drag the inflatable up toward these granite seawall reinforcements. I carry the miniature Airstream under my arm like a breadbox.

Once we're up below the glare of the city on the other side of the wall, we see that we've pulled in right in front of two Slavic-looking men. One is sitting by a stick fire with a sheep on a leash, as someone might with a dog. The other has a row of great clam shells laid out on the sand, which seems to percolate with a squishy kind of residue as we step across it. If the shells were smaller, he'd look like a street vendor of knock-off jewelry. As it is, they look more like shelters. They're big enough for people to sleep in.

"Good thing you made it," the Clam Man says and blows a huge jet of snot.

We're not at all sure about that. There's something distinctly creepy about both of them, and as we look around, it's clear they live here. They've got a larger raft with an outboard motor on the back, cooking utensils and whole lot of what looks like recently stolen electrical goods, all hooked up to a diesel generator covered in grime. But at least they're not cutting people's limbs off. Yet.

I start to ask a question, but then I realize I don't know which one to ask first. The Clam Man cuts in before I can speak.

"There's a rain comin' . . . better take cover in a shell. First night's free."

The idea of climbing into one of the giant clam shells doesn't do much for either of us. Rain seems to be the least of our problems.

Then a series of fireworks explode overhead and we feel the first drops of the storm. Heavy, burning drops. It's like the magnesium of the rocket flares have mingled with the moisture from the sky. Down the beach and over the rocks we see the silhouettes of people scrambling for cover. It's not ordinary rain. It's an acid rain. Two big drops smoke on your arms and I can smell the flesh sizzle.

The man with the sheep leads the animal into a shelter that looks like a huge mailbox, and then he and the Clam Man start pulling on these Haz-Mat suits. Our skin is starting to burn. You leap into one of the shells and the lid comes down behind you suddenly and clicks like a lock. I get a bad feeling – worse than the rain – which very suspiciously seems to stop.

"What happened to the rain?" I ask.

"Oh, it comes and goes," the Clam Man says . . . with a rather nasty smile.

"Then let her out," I say.

"Sure," he says. "Just give me what you've got in your hand there, and I'll open it up. Otherwise, you'll need more than a jackhammer to get that thing open."

There's a smashing sound out on the water – wood and metal giving way – the ferry is really starting to submerge.

"You'll have time to think about it," the Clam Man says, and pulls out a shining little harpoon gun about the size of a sawn-off shotgun. He points it at me while the Sheep Man drags their boat down to the water, then he backs toward it and they shove off, heading out toward the ferry, where people are still throwing things off and jumping – some of the bodies occasionally landing on the cars that haven't sunk with a sickening sound of broken bones and choking.

I figure giving up the miniature trailer is no big deal . . . but something makes me resist. The metal has stayed cool in my grasp and feels strangely satisfying, reassuring. Valuable. But if

I give him the trailer when they get back, how do I know he'll open the shell? The Clam Man doesn't look like the kind to honor his end of any bargain. I don't know what to do – but after kicking the shell a few times and bashing it with a rock, I'm pretty sure he was right about how hard it would be to open by force. I don't even know if you can breathe inside. I start to freak out, pacing the gooey tar sand. Then I hear a voice. A woman's voice. But not yours.

It's coming from under a pile of kelp by the Sheep Man's dwindling fire. A woman crawls out, seaweed still clinging to her skin. She's naked other than the damp strands and is very beautiful, but I can see she has some open sores over her body, as if she's buried herself in the seaweed for skin relief. She tells me the men have gone out to salvage from the ferry. They're sort of pirate-scavengers. I have a little time to open the shell. But there's only one way to do it.

I have to piss all over it – and then ejaculate on it. At first I don't believe her, but what choice do I have? So I urinate all over the clam shell – and to my surprise and relief it starts to hiss and corrode, softening. "Quick!" she says. "You have to come on it too."

Great, I think. I had to have a piss – I was actually dying for one. But I'm not sure I can just get it up right there . . . not with people getting hacked up and a whole city falling down in flames on the other side of the wall. Then she removes some of the seaweed to show me her breasts. They're large and full, gorgeously shaped. Even with a couple of patches of sores, they're something to see. I start to think that maybe she means for me to fuck her and then shoot over the shell. But when she pulls back the seaweed from around her waist and thighs, I see her vagina is a mass of festering sores and chancres . . . a bacteria stain surrounding a gaping wound that she's attached leeches to in order to eat at some of the blight. Beneath the leeches, tiny white, worms wriggle out of the necrotic flesh. I want to vomit – she covers herself again.

Then she approaches, kneels down on the springy sand and takes my cock out of my pants, still wet from the bay. Her mouth is exquisitely formed, with thick, sensual lips . . . and soon I feel them sucking me, licking and breathing on me. She runs her tongue over the head, following the contour of the glans . . . defining its helmet shape. Then she sucks the whole head in, taking two . . . and three inches of the cock into her warm wet mouth without moving her neck. More of it goes down her throat. She seems to be slowly inhaling it. I harden with the suction and the sight of her taking me. Deeper. Seen now from this angle, her sores aren't visible. She's beautiful, early thirties maybe, with scarlet hair, and big firm tits she brushes against my balls, as she lifts her head, taking my cock higher as the erection strengthens.

Meanwhile the clam shell is fuming and loosening. Dissolving. I'm wondering if you're still alive. If you can see or hear – or know what's happening. What you're thinking. What you would think.

The Seaweed Woman increases the speed of her sucking, working her soft full lips back and forth over the head, then licking the tip of the shaft. Faster. Her head is bobbing hard now, her breast jiggling rhythmically. I start to wonder what the men will do to her when they get back and find out she's helped us. Me. I feel a tenderness toward her . . . mixed with raw lust. Suddenly even her festering sores seem erotic. I can feel I'm going to shoot. I get ready to pull back – to pull out of her mouth and jerk over the shell. But as my cock slips out of her mouth, which I'm reluctant to leave, I have to admit – a part of me wants to come down her throat, or to spurt over her breasts – she gasps and says, "No, I must have it! I need it for my sores. It will heal me."

I'm just about to blow. I have to make a decision. She's thrown me off completely.

"I can't!" I tell her. "I have to get the shell open."

"She's already dead," the woman says.

Something in her eyes tells me she's lying. I push her away and rush to the shell and give myself a final vigorous stroking, slurping out a gush of hot semen that shines silver in the light. The gobs hit the slowly decomposing shell and a chemical reaction starts, spreading over the surface like a phosphorescent shadow. Soon the whole clam shell is pulsing and then liquefying. I turn back to the woman who's fallen on the sand, breathless. I squeeze my cock and drip a last little pearl of cum down on her spread legs. The pus-filled infection seems to spasm and the blind white worms waver and retract. The droplet has eased some of the putrefaction. I drape some of the seaweed up over her like a blanket and her breathing quiets as she seems to black out. Just then an explosion rocks the ferry and it slips deeper into the water. It can't stay afloat much longer.

Turning back to the shell, I see you alive – squirming in a mess of what looks like tapioca afterbirth. It's wet and sticky and you're hysterical with it clinging to you – but it doesn't seem to be hurting your skin. A minute later I have you out and am leading you down to the water to wash you off.

The water isn't all that pleasant but it's better than the muck of the shell, and you're so relieved to be out of there you don't care. But now you're naked and we have to get away before the scavengers come back. I'm not sure what to do.

Then I walk you back to the remains of the shell where I've left the Airstream. The woman in the seaweed stirs as we pass. "The Sheep will give her some clothes," she mumbles.

"Who's that?" you ask.

"A friend," I say.

It doesn't even occur to me to question how or why the sheep will give us some clothes for you. I go to the big mailbox enclosure and find that inside it's actually as large as a hangar at a country airfield. There are hundreds of Vietnamese people working old sewing machines and looms in narrow rows. One of them, a youngish man who looks like he's the foreman, gets up from a bowl of clear soup and pulls some clothes out of a big pile of what I imagine are discards or defective goods. The outfit has a sweet smell of lanolin, the smell of babies and farm fields in spring time. He gives me a lambswool vest with a leather exterior . . . and these chaps things . . . pants cut out at the ass . . . with a pair of lambswool-lined moccasins.

I hand them to you and you grumble about running around showing your ass, but I point out that we don't have much time . . . and you start to think that they're sort of cool. So you suit up and I grab the Airstream and we book out of there, leaving the Seaweed Woman either hiding more completely in the kelp, or having fled – I can't say which, and the raft with the men is coming back overloaded with things we can't see clearly.

It takes us a while to negotiate the rocks and find a crack in the seawall big enough to scrape through. There are constant fireworks or incendiaries . . . the clang of torn metal . . . the jar and quake of buildings being torn down . . . sirens . . . and mob sounds . . . but we keep moving . . . the borderland between the city and the waterline ends up being quite a bit more complicated than it appeared from below . . . with all sorts of hideous injured people hunkered down between the pylons and the boulders – and the sewage conduits. Catatonics. Corpses. I'm amazed how the sight of your bare ass cheers me as we flee. Everything else has been stripped away inside. Only primal thoughts remain. A good thing, as it keeps me on edge.

When we finally reach the city proper, we find ourselves on an old cobblestone street like in Lower Manhattan. An enormous flag billows up on a pole. It's a $100 bill. There's a stretch of park filled with statues covered in white tarpaulins and canvas sheets . . . and a group of people who appear to be worshipping a fallen electrical tower they've propped up against an old brick building with marble pillars out the front. Bulldozers with halogen lights power through a wall down the street . . . manholes steam and water mains erupt . . . people in wheelchairs either stranded in the shower or there to bathe, we can't say.

A man rushes by in a trenchcoat carrying a fishbowl. He yells "The Run is on, look out! Look out!"

He trips on a cobblestone and drops the bowl, which shatters, releasing some brightly colored tropical fish. But there's no time to save the fish because mechanical thunder reverberates off the remaining buildings. A herd of MX riders sweeps out of an alley, helmeted and shining in plastic and steel. They're revving their bikes, chasing down a pack of middle-aged men in their underwear . . . with javelins raised . . . or the ceremonial swords the picadors use at bullfights. It's like the running of the bulls in Pamplona. They chase and hound – and then hurl their barbs – either nailing or running over the older men as they charge in panic, trying to get away. Some do and are greeted with bouquets of roses or lopped-off pigs' heads. Others are skewered, crushed, or run down till their hearts burst. We slip into a side alley, away from the turmoil.

A carriage appears . . . like the kind that should be drawn by horses. Instead it's pulled by people, men and women, naked and with heavy leather blinkers on.

After the motorcycle insanity, we think we can handle this slower moving group and yell "Halt!" They do.

Perched on top of the carriage, in the driving whip position is a rotting corpse in a tuxedo.

"Where are you going?" we ask.

The blinkered man in the lead says, "Wherever Mr Hugo wants."

We look at each other. Somehow they haven't cottoned on to the fact that Mr Hugo est mort. He gone. Wid de flies. Surely they can smell him. But apparently they don't. They're just wandering around in circles.

"Mr Hugo isn't feeling well," I say. "He wants you to take us some place. He wants you to take us to . . ."

And then I'm stumped. I have no idea where we should go – or where might be safe.

"The zoo!" you yell suddenly – having looked up at the cliff and seen a rotting billboard showing a woman in a mix of park ranger/white lab coat gear holding a bunch of parrots in her oversized hand. The fading caption says . . . "THE ZOO IS FOR YOO . . . All the questions of a lifetime . . . all the fun of a blind cherry pull."

I go along with this notion. The zoo might at least provide some shelter. Maybe. They're usually open, park-like places with more vegetation. So we hop up next to Mr Hugo, where the odor of decay is so much more unmistakable . . . but our blinkered, harnessed friends don't take any notice. They seem happy to have a destination to reach.

Except for another gang of motorcycle riders who have lassoed some young girls in bikinis and are applying white-hot branding irons to their stripped asses, we don't see anyone else along the way – other than shadows of people running and the lights of tractors down distant streets. To our surprise, one of the motorcycle wranglers whips off a metalflake blue helmet and shakes out a big mane of auburn hair. It's a hot Goth Asian woman who gives us a haughty smile that has a hint of fangs.

The zoo turns out to be a ghastly derelict place filled with barred pits and enclosures with fake animals made of Styrofoam and peeling plaster. The only illumination comes from grim orange security lights scattered about on caged poles. The only true building is a dark glass pavilion in the shape of a hexagon. Facing it, across a lawn of garbage, is a yard filled with shacks and burrows – surrounded by a very tall steel fence with brutal spikes on top and covered over by a mesh of netting that looks like it's made of heavy-gauge fishing line, the sort they sometimes use on high-speed rotaries to decapitate animals in abattoirs instead of blades. Behind the bars are hundreds of dirty children . . . dump kids, ferals, kids dressed up like dolls – looking woeful and vicious in the sodium orange. They chant when they see us and the Airstream . . . "Knick-knack Paddywhack . . . Knick-knack Paddywhack . . ."

We don't know whether to feel sorry for these filthy orphans or afraid. Are they rounded up here by their own strategy – for protection – or are they the prisoners we suspect them to be? And of whom?

The answer isn't long in coming because some of them start to have seizures. Others start chanting, "Zookeeper . . . Zookeeper . . . Zookeeper!"

They point and gesture frantically . . . and over a rise we see approaching headlights.

The Zookeeper, who is obviously a source of profound fear for the children appears on a John Deere ride-on lawn mower, out of the dark of the supposed savannah, which is really a wasteland of fiberglass lions, chickenwire antelope and mangled giraffes made of retaining rods for concrete walls. The figure wears a white jumpsuit with black-green mirrored headgear, like night-vision goggles – and we aren't sure what this means for us – until the mower gets nearer.

To our amazement we see that not only is the Zookeeper

female, she looks exactly like Yoko Ono when she gets up close. And she has a tranquilizer dart rifle slung over her shoulder. "ZOOKEEPER! ZOOKEEPER!" the kids grunt, twirling around and having these mini epileptic fits. Others moan out some other word, which sounds like Goober.

"Good, I see you've brought me a present," the Zookeeper says, ignoring the wild kids and pointing with the rifle to the Airstream. "Give it to me now, and you can stay in the hippo pond. It's got the freshest water."

"We're not staying with any fucking hippos," you say.

"Perhaps you'd like to feed the children then," the Zookeeper says with a nasty crease in her lips.

"Why don't you feed them – if you're the zookeeper?" you ask.

"That's just what I mean," the Zookeeper laughs . . . and we realize that she intends to feed us to the children, who look hungry and savage and deranged enough to rip us apart.

"We're not going to give you anything," I say. There are, after all, two of us, and the kids appear to be secured within the pen.

"Maybe you'll feel different when you see the Gooper," she answers and blows on this silver whistle.

The mention of that name and the high-pitched tweet of the whistle drive the feral children berserk. They're like birds in a net.

And then we see why. Out from the other side of the zoo, up closer to the cliffs, comes this towering, lumbering form. He's about twenty feet high, a kind of ogre, but oozy and dripping . . . leaving pieces of himself as he moves. His body is like some kind of resinous glob made up of bandages and honeycomb – chambers of bee pollen that split open and spill behind when he walks – or mud daubers' funnels that crack and powderize. His head is like a huge paper wasp's nest – yellowjackets and white-faced hornets flitting in and out. He can't in fact keep a single expression in place for more than a few seconds, because his face is whatever the insects make it out to be at any given moment. The children chant "Gooper! Gooper!" as he nears, crying and shitting in their pants. Wherever he steps he leaves a squash of something like maple syrup or honey . . . American mustard

. . . and treacle. Objects he's absorbed into his mass squish out, followed by a cloud of bees and flies.

Up close there's a disgusting odor to him of molasses and the disinfectants used in public toilets. He's dripping and weeping himself all over, his face forming and reforming with the wasps' excitement.

"Now," says the Zookeeper. "If you won't give me my present, then you'll give it to the Gooper."

I slip you the Airstream in preparation for telling you to run while I distract the monster. We know the thing can't move very fast.

A blob of yeasty-stinking brown sugar-gunk plops off at my feet . . . and I feel your hands take the Airstream . . . sliding over the smooth metal coating. As you do, there's a click in the top and the roof opens like a box. This surprises us both enough for us to look away from the Gooper and the pen of drooling children.

From out of the Airstream you extract a remarkable implement. It's like a crystalline tuning fork . . . but more organically shaped . . . like a large wishbone made of some super-fine blown glass. It's hypnotic to behold . . . and has the same effect on the Zookeeper, the Gooper and the children. Suddenly, the protective feelings we've had about the Airstream, which seemed sort of irrational and silly before, are now all vividly justified. The slightest glint of the object, the feel of it to the hand – it's unquestionably precious. And it seems to have an inner life to it, changing weight and reflectivity with our touch.

The Gooper eyes the wishbone, the wasps swarming to maintain his face. He makes a sound like a clogged garbage disposal and stretches out a thick resinous hand as the beeswax and dishtowels flowing inside his mass flop and slurp out in a mess of golden gelatin. He wants it – whether to eat or play with, who knows? The awfulness of it makes you drop the bone. I pick it up. It has a luminous sheen to it now – like something almost radioactive. And then when I hold it up – and I can't think of anything else to do – partly to taunt the giant – partly to try to ward it off – the wishbone catches the reflection of one of the sodium lights beside the children's pen.

A kind of prismatic effect erupts all around us – like a kaleido-scopic grenade going off. And then the shards of light stream together like iron filings to a magnet . . . focusing down into a beam like a laser, shooting out from the bone. When I raise the bone a little higher the ray strikes the Gooper's head and sets it on fire – the nest exploding in a ball of red flame. A sticky slab of body drops off and sends the creature toppling into the steel spikes of the children's yard, impaling the thing . . . so that it smushes down and begins to melt. Furious hornets fill the air like shrapnel or flecks of hot ash. The children start smearing their hands and faces into the transparent yellow-brown bulk of burning, soft-ening jelly . . . and within seconds the Gooper is a puddle of caramelized honey and kitchen utensils – like some school cafe-teria flooded with diabetic urine and Jell-o.

The Zookeeper is beside herself, and levels her rifle at us, sputtering and seething with rage. The light beam from the bone has disappeared and I can't seem to catch the reflection of the yard light again. I can almost hear the thud of the dart that will strike me. Or you. We're both done for . . . unless . . .

You reach out for the bone . . . whether you think I've suddenly frozen or not, I don't know . . . but in reaching for it, one of the stems seems to ting. It's a clear, bell-like, bird-like sound – just like the tines of the tuning fork it partially resembles. Hearing the sound, you strike it more forcefully with a finger and the resulting sound is now like a crystal chandelier vaporizing.

The Zookeeper drops the gun and clutches her ears. The children begin to wail like ambulances. The air reverberates in all directions. And we hear and feel it bouncing back off the darkened glass walls of the hexagram pavilion. Then . . . ka-smash!

All the windows of the building blast out or in . . . we can't tell . . . because fragments fly everywhere like knives . . . and from inside the pavilion swoop hundred and hundreds of shrieking bats. They storm outward in a black smoke of flap-ping wings. Some hit us in the head – some claw or bite as they whisk past – but while we duck and swing at them, waving the wishbone between us . . . they cover the Zookeeper completely

– like sheets of black newspaper glued to her goggled head. The white suit quickly disappears beneath them. The claws clasp on. She is simply a clump of leathery wings and feasting teeth, rolling and thrashing helplessly beneath them.

Some stray fliers the children snatch out of the air, gnawing into their wings while they're still alive. Others catch them by wing or claw and beat them on the ground before biting off their heads. Other children aren't so adept and are hit in the face, blood from the cuts leaking down their faces as they charge in panic around the pen.

Without a word we hop on the ride-on mower and I gun it over the rise. As we pass the sad, trash-strewn enclosures, lights come on and some taped message about the animals that are supposed to be on display comes on . . . a generic cheerful female voice talking about habitats and places of origin. Some bats and hornets trail after us, but we leave them behind when we pass through a stand of artificial trees made out of some stiff synthetic fiber like welcome mats. The landscape opens up again into some kind of war memorial with a bronze Sherman tank the size of a chapel.

We finally reach a wide boulevard of fluted iron streetlamps and burned-out cars. Park benches have been dragged into the middle like barricades. Down the way we see the spit and glitter of welder's sparks and some kids doing tricks on skateboards. We abandon the mower. Then we hear someone shout . . . "Rags! Rags!"

It's an old-time rag merchant's street wagon, but not pulled by a horse. The beast of burden is a huge and deeply wrinkled gray Neapolitan mastiff, at least ten and maybe twelve hands high, the biggest dog we've ever seen by a long shot. It looks half-asleep in its heavy harness – or maybe deaf from the shouting.

Seated on the wagon is a bearded, red-faced man with a silk hat that rises and then slants crookedly and then back again, like an improvised stovepipe. He looks wasted and worn – and beside him sits a sleek black monkey that looks as well groomed as the man looks disheveled and sick, wearing a little white robe, like a kind of priest. The man sees us, and sees how close we are and still he belts out loudly, "Rags! Rags!"

"Why would we want rags?" you ask. "Especially now."

"You can't go from rags to riches without rags, can you?" the man answers.

We don't know what to say to that . . . and then the man seems to slump . . . not like someone who's passed out or had a stroke – like a machine that's stopped working. I look at you and see that you've held up the wishbone, and I wonder if that's what's caused the effect. Then it dawns on us both . . . the man is some kind of machine. A toy . . . or a tool. The owner of the wagon, or the master, is really the monkey – who seems to grasp our recognition.

"You're quicker than most, yet dumber than some," the monkey says, with sort of a wheezy little laugh. "What'll it be, rags or remnants? Shreds or patches?"

"We want to know where this place is and what we should do?" you ask.

"This place is here," the monkey says with another wheezy laugh, as if he's made a good joke.

"But what should we do?" you ask again . . . this time with some real frustration and despair in your voice. "We want to get out of here. Now!"

Maybe something of the desperation in your tone gets through to the monkey – or maybe it's because you've waved the wishbone at him – but he changes his expression quite dramatically, becoming more doglike and more human at the same time. Then he reaches over to the man, who now seems propped like a piece of furniture next to him. The monkey snatches off the man's eccentric hat and puts it on his own head. "Some questions require a hat," he says.

He sits there with the tall zigzag hat on for what seems to us like a very long time – so that we begin to wonder if he might not be some kind of machine too. But at last he comes out of his trance and makes an announcement.

"You two ask what you should do . . . as if I knew. So, here is what I have to say. To get away . . . maybe . . . you should try to stay."

The idea of a talking monkey wearing a big silk hat we just let go by. We've seen so many extraordinary and distressing things we're not easily flummoxed anymore. But the actual advice, which we weren't really expecting to get, takes us both aback.

The monkey seems very pleased with his recommendation and restores the hat to the man-machine's head. When he does, the man instantly snaps into animation again and bellows, "Rags! Rags!" at full volume.

The enormous gray mastiff comes alert again too and the cart pulls off, with no more comment or any kind of goodbye from the monkey. After a while, the echo of the man's voice and the clatter of the wheels fade away down the avenue – and we're left wondering what the hell the monkey meant . . . and what this whole nightmare world means. Why, how – and when can we leave?

Which eventually gets us back to mulling over what the monkey advised us to do. To get away, try to stay.

Beyond the rhyme there does seem to be at least some element of reason to this remark. Try to find something you've lost, stop looking for it. Try to remember something you've forgotten, think of something else. The contra nature of the counsel strikes us both as maybe somehow being on the right track.

But if we were to try to stay, where would we take shelter?

"We have to get out of this shithole war zone," you say. "It's an insane asylum let loose in a bombing range."

"We need a vantage point," I say.

So we start scanning the palisades . . . the crackpot sheds clutching onto the cliff face . . . what look like old mining tunnels with sulfur yellow lights glimmering out. Then . . . way above the billboards and the little encampments . . . we spot a plateau and some kind of kiosk. We have to wait until the spotlights that criss-cross the sky sliver past and reveal more detail . . . but when they do . . . we see cables running over the void between the cliff . . . and another canyon wall we can't make out. There's some kind of cable car that runs over the city. And the car, which is stranded out about a quarter of the way on the wire from the plateau looks just like an Airstream trailer.

There's no escaping the similarity. It has to mean something, and so, not knowing what else to do, we set out with the wishbone, heading toward and up the cliffs, to try to reach the cable car.

We walk for about two miles without seeing anyone directly, except for an old phone booth crammed full of yelping people, some of whom have clearly disjointed limbs or injured themselves in trying to fit. We sprint past not wanting to get involved – and not knowing if they're there by choice, seeking refuge – or if it's some kind of contest. Or have they been stuffed in there against their wills? A couple of the inside faces pressed up against the spider-webbed glass are unmistakably the faces of dead people.

Once we reach the base of the palisades, the prospect of actually making the plateau safely seems daunting. The cliffs are folded in and steep, with countless crevices and hiding places . . . and who knows how many hostile, paranoid, or just plain evil people – or creatures – waiting to ambush us. I'm worried about you trying to climb in moccasins. I'm feeling exhausted. The whole project seems fruitless – especially starting in the dark. And the luminous quality of the wishbone appears to register this discouragement because it sputters and pulses. Dimming.

And then, just as we're beginning to really pant and puff, slipping and starting rockfalls – and wondering when we're going to get picked off by some sniper shot, or one of us will tumble off into nowhere screaming – you start laughing hysterically. I think, shit, she's lost it. Now what are we going to do? You're laughing so hard now you let out a little teapot fart – like a note on a kid's toy horn – and that gets me laughing. We've been through so much. We may well be dead. It's all so hopeless. Your little toot acts as a pressure release and all the emotion just empties out. It's like another kind of sex. Complete, unrestrained breakdown. But together.

Only when we've laughed ourselves sick, am I able to understand that you've been pointing at something off in the dark for a couple of minutes. When this finally sinks in, I look – and look again. And I'll be damned if I don't at last see what got you snorting and breaking wind. It's an escalator system build right into the cliff. Neat and flowing like a waterfall of gridded metal. All our exertions were unnecessary. The whole system is sheltered by a tall shaft of cage . . . and while that means an ominous ride up . . . with no way out if we're waylaid . . . it's nonetheless a way up. And a fast one as it turns out – although our hearts pound the whole way . . . wondering if someone or something is waiting for us – hoping for just something like our arrival.

"If the thing suddenly stops," I say. "We try to smash through the barrier and go over the side. We don't want to be cornered and taken alive."

As terrible as that sounds, it gives us both a jolt of energy to be in such a situation. We feel more alive because of it. The dread, the anticipation – it's like an amphetamine and an aphrodisiac. I want to go first, in case there's trouble up ahead of us. But you insist on riding on the higher step. "I want you to see my ass the whole way," you say. "It's a primal thing. I need your animal. And I promise not to let another one go."

That gets us both giggling again. Our morale has lifted . . . and as we ascend we start to feel stronger. More together. More decisive. We're taking some active step now, not just wandering. The fear is still strong. Rich like the smell of sweat or meat. But it's sharpened us not cowed us now. If this is all a drug we're on, the bewildered lunatic phase is behind us. This is clear – bright and etched with our concentration.

The vigilant, combat-ready but optimistic mood seems to carry us upward at least as much as the moving stairs . . . and gives us the illusion of a shield around us. The wishbone tuning fork starts to shine more intently again.

Switchback level by chainlink landing we climb and reach the plateau without incident or sight of anyone else. Once at the top, you slip off and squat for an enormous pee, while below the fireworks thud, the juggernaut of demolition equipment rolls and crowds of masked and maimed people pound and flee like fools for slaughter.

The plateau is a lonely, barren place. The kiosk is boarded-up and riddled with bullet holes. No sign of any equipment or controls inside – no way to call the cable car back. The trash and bones of old fires lie scattered everywhere. Bras, condoms, shell casings, syringes and pieces of busted Japanese toys. But the cable to the Airstream-looking car seems strong and hangs with a reassuring level of tension. In the occasional flash of the spotlights from below we see a line of seagulls perched along it. They look spectral in the gloom, but maybe benign. Spirits of opportunity.

Counting the gulls, it looks like about 200 yards out into the abyss . . . about the same distance you might feel you could safely swim drunk on a hot summer night to some little island in a river. For the first time since we fell out of the roulette coaster in that other lifetime, I feel strangely confident and relaxed. And then you peer out over the edge and say, "I can't do it. I can't do heights. Not like this. We'll have to stay here."

I immediately feel my own fear rise. It's a thousand feet down at least. What was I thinking? There's no way. It's suicide. Just as insane as those wounded shadows stampeding in the ruins. Better to hole up in the bird-infested kiosk and wait for the people with the guns and the needles to show up. Maybe they won't know we're here. Maybe we can even join their tribe – whatever it is they are. The wishbone light stutters.

But then one of the arc lamps below sweeps over the car suspended out on the cable. It really does look exactly like the miniature Airstream, only full-sized. We were dead right about that from down below. We can't have come this far . . . through so much . . . for this not to mean something. What other hope do we have? What other clue? Somehow, we've been drawn to the cable car. We were meant to find it – to reach it.

"We have to get out there," I say. "And I'm not strong enough to carry you. How can we do it? We have to try."

You've never looked so pale . . . so white you seem like a stray piece of spotlight that's come to life. As white as one of the gulls. But you answer very clearly. "I want you inside me as we go. If I have something else to think about, I can do it. And if we're going to fall, then I want us to fall that way."

You turn and give your butt a wiggle, and then peel back the chaps in front to show me your pussy. Frankly. So innocent, and yet so lewd.

It's like the first time I ever had a chance to stare openly and unashamedly at a real naked girl. Someone whose skin I could taste. Not a centerfold on some tree fort wall or some "playmate" in a magazine dragged out from beneath a bed to jack-off to . . . but a real flesh female, close enough to catch her scent . . . to know that there is a scent to women, and that no one is exactly like the other. The terror and the wonder of it . . . understanding that this is where we all come from . . . and yet seeing past the mother-phobia and lost womb security – always switchbacking like the escalator – to some crude but pure desire . . . a thinking past the thinking . . . an acceptance of the base wants as the basis of all.

And soon, we are entwined. Converged. Slow and meditative. Slipping and sliding forward in the dark like caterpillars. We go fist-hold by pump along the thick braid of the cable, the lubricated metal smell getting us hotter, as you wrap your long legs around my waist, feeling me, barely moving inside you, but pushing, squirming forward . . . not just fucking you . . . but fucking myself into you . . . fucking us both along this slender strand of twined steel, as the seagulls squawk and take flight.

The windswept ashes of the plateau seem miles and years behind us . . . we don't remember the moment of giving way and letting go of the rock wall, kicking out into the dark air. All we are is a creature wrinkling itself along in a line . . . the squish and plunge of it leveraging us closer. Closer. Closer.

It's funny, because there are so many times, as a male, when you long to fuck. To enter. To thrust. It's been a wonderful blowjob, thanks very much – the sixty-nine has gotten me wired and wet and hard . . . the gentleness, the delicacy and time-taking, the snuggling and nuzzling – all these pleasures have their engorging moment, their special, needful appeal. But then suddenly all you want to do is to plunge and stab. To butt and ram. To own and occupy. You've moved past wanting pussy. You now crave cunt. You want to shove past the consensual . . . to the elemental. To feel cunt walls pushed apart by the strength of your hard-on. To command and control the rhythm of the drive. To spray . . . like a fire hose on fire. Like starlight in a small, overheated room. To yell and pound – and pulverize. Smash out the windows and let the rain in. Fuck everything. You want only to groan and bellow like the animal you have to hide from being so much of the time. So many hours of every day. So many minutes of such a short life. You want for just one blood-warm second, the freedom of all evolutionary time – the right to violate. And then, for that violence, for that base-of-the-spine predatory hunting party impulse to somehow be assimilated back into normality. For your revelation of the Creature within you, to have been embraced by the other's Monster . . . for the cunt's Hydra-Gorgon-Venus flytrap greedy sucking fertile vacancy to understand. Oh, to let the Creatures really loose in the company of another demon. How they throb and glisten when they have a chance. How their craving, once sated, gives back light and heat – and will. More hunger for life.

But there are other times, when one longs to be mouth-centric. To suck and pluck at slickening pussy lips. To tease the meaty little bud of clit, the female penis. And nipples . . . the ultimate psychosexual crisis point, firing the brain across the lobes, across the years. To not only tongue a tender, succulent female asshole – but to devour it. To feast on where your woman shits . . . to submit . . . to serve – and to consume. To give way absolutely to the oral child within. To taste. To desecrate oneself with the smear of enjoyment. To give and bite. To be humiliated and to reign supreme, literally eating your lover like a conquering cannibal. To go down and not worry about what comes up or where it leads.

And this was where I found myself now.

The inability to realize my oral fixation . . . the slow screw-piston enjambment of cock into vagina as a means of transport . . . the only means of sexual contact . . . this heightened my connection. And yours. Your nipples burned with want for my mouth. My fattened rod stuck up to the cervix inside you – you felt your clit tingle with the imaginary urgings of my tongue – your ass exposed to the wind and the darkness, you felt what it would be like to have my lips covering it in a rude, cheek-parted kiss. But there was nothing we could do, except wiggle and gyrate together. And not look down.

We reach the car and the simultaneous climax is like nothing we've ever felt before. Like we've burst open and spurt out all our organs. The second we grab onto the roof of the car, the shockwaves hit us . . . the vibration of longing and fulfillment radiating through us . . . turning into an almost electric current. We've done what we set out to do.

But almost immediately, the mood turns sour and anxious. We climb in and collapse onto the floor of the car, which is empty but for a silver railing around the side and an operator's console. Our muscles ache beyond description. We're suddenly famished and thinking we may well just pass out from hunger and fade to black in our sleep. We don't have any supplies. We don't have any water even! What did we expect to find up here? Just because it looked like the Airstream? How did we think we could live on nothing but wind and sex?

The gulls return, curious or antagonized. They flock and peck at the windows. You nestle into me, the wishbone between us . . . as we await the end . . . both of us believing it will be like some doomed polar explorers' mission we've read about . . . tragically but peacefully slipping off into a terminal daze while the wind howls outside the nylon tent – the pelting snowflakes turning into pestering, screeching gulls.

One of the ghostly white birds strikes the window with a crack of broken neck and falls out of sight. Maybe, once the pangs and cramps of hunger have passed – the delirium that will come with thirst – we'll be free. Forever free and dead.

Things go silent immediately outside as we dangle in the enlarged Airstream over the phantom city. Only distant sounds of detonation and dismay . . . a flicker every once in a while of harsh quartz light from below. Our thoughts give way to fatigue and surrender.

However, just as this resignation fantasy is beginning to really take hold, we hear the cry of the gulls again. They're flying about once more, but not attacking the windows of the car this time. No!

Just as the ravens nourished Elijah in the wilderness, the gulls have returned to us with food – perhaps from some looted supermarket. Torn strips of wilted lettuce and not quite molding fruit. Cans of beans and steak and onions. Bags of peas and lentils. Jerky. Chocolate! Muesli bars and breakfast cereal. Smoked ham, tinned tuna . . . protein . . . survival fat and vitamins. Everything they bring and deposit on the roof I retrieve . . . and we consume . . . not even tasting the flavors, just accepting the nutrition, the chance to keep going. Every single morsel is a banquet. Every mouthful a miracle.

We savor and gorge on the food as we wanted to orally

indulge in each other's bodies before. We realize that we may have a means of staying alive for a while longer.

"This could be the solution," we say aloud – at precisely the same time.

And the moment we say this – an old man appears in the car.

"Where did you come from?" we cry again in unison.

"Whenever you pick up two words and rub them together like sticks," he shrugs. "I'm the Old Man. I won't stay long. I'm always here."

He really is old. And dirty. Like a scarecrow left out in a field of cow corn too long. But he smells good. Like lanolin . . . and an oven-warm Cornish pasty in a paper bag.

"What should we do?" I ask.

"You keep asking that," he says, raising a hand that seems too big for his thin body. "Why don't you try driving the cable car? You've got the handle."

"Is that what this is?" you ask, holding up the wishbone.

It seems to have changed shape again, and now appears to be more of a human-designed device. Industrial, although beautifully crafted.

"Why don't you try it?" he says – and points to a slot in the car's console that now, when we think of it, does indeed look like it was meant to accommodate such a shape.

"How do we know we can believe you?" I ask.

He smiles. "You mean, how do you know you can trust me? Tell me, who gave you the handle?"

"Was it your house with the animal heads?" you squeak.

"What are you talking about?" he replies. "I don't need a house. I'm the Old Man. I meant that however you came by the handle is how you can trust me."

"But where does the cable car go?" we howl at the same time.

"How would I know that?" He shakes his head. "You've got the handle."

"We're safe up here," I say.

"We don't know where the car goes," you add.

A skyrocket booms nearby and the aftershock sets the car rocking.

"Safe," the Old Man repeats.

We see people tightrope-walking on the wires. They have headlamps on. At first there is only a couple. Then more appear. Some are wiggling along precariously or going hand over hand. Others move nimbly like rodents, closing in on the car.

"Suit yourselves," the Old Man nods. "I'm off now."

"Wait!" we cry. "You're not just going to jump!"

"No . . . I'm not," he answers, as if we're stupid. And that's certainly the way we feel.

"But what will happen . . . where are we and how do we get out?" I want to know.

"The question you should ask yourselves is how you came by the handle."

"The wires just go off into the dark," you say.

"Darkness is all there ever is until you attend to the right questions," he answers – and then disappears right in front of us.

Shit, we think.

Some of the headlamp people shimmying along the cable are nearing the car. Gulls circle around them. Balloons float up from the city below. Silver foil, bubblegum pink and satiny red Valentine hearts. One of the climbers is about to leap for the roof of the car. We don't know what they want – or what to do. It doesn't seem like a good idea to just wait there like sitting ducks. Besides, how many people can the cable support? It seems like now or never. Once again.

So, together we slot the wishbone into the metal sleeve the Old Man indicated – and like a lever we pull it. We expect the car to lurch forward – but instead, there's a rush of wind and gulls and paper. The bottom of the car has dropped open! The floor is gone and we're left clinging on to the sides . . . all of the remains of the groceries blowing down over the water and the city. "Fuckersnattle!" you scream. "Fuckersnattle!"

The Old Man appears again in mid-air.

"You tricked us!" you shout.

"I did not," he says, looking calm despite the draft blowing up under his dirty old coat. "I didn't say how the car runs."

"What do we do now?" we yell together. "Fall to our death?"

He frowns at us, like we're upstart kids. "I don't think you're much good at falling. Why don't you try finding. You seem to have some knack for that. Just take the handle."

He vanishes again, and we can no longer hang on . . . we can't . . . there's no choice . . . so we tug at the wishbone, just as a couple of people land on the roof of the car. We wrench it free and let go of the sides of the car, holding the wishbone between us . . . hollering at first in horror . . . but also high on the finality of our decision. The release.

And it doesn't feel like falling.

After a second . . . or another million years . . . the nausea of letting go is gone and we feel this pitch of pleasure and power. Just like we did back on the ride at the fairground. It doesn't make any sense – it makes less sense than anything else that's happened to us since the fairground – since as long as we can remember. And yet, it feels totally natural. Like something we were made to do and have done before. We'd just forgotten.

If we're falling, why doesn't the ground start rushing up beneath us? Why doesn't the collapsing city of tractors and spotlights and psychotic crowds get closer? If anything, the lights and the noise seem to recede. We feel this fantastic buoyancy, as if our bodies were opening up to engulf the night. It makes us laugh, like the coming-on buzz of some intense drug. Tears stream out of our eyes with the thrill of it.

People start leaping off the wires and clasping on to us like skydivers in a routine. We aren't afraid. More appear – pouring out of the cliff face and down the cable from both sides. They fling themselves off and into formation – joined by gulls and bats and balloons – and still more people who slide down the wire on chains and then let go.

Together we form this undulating circle. The people's lights flash. The ever widening wheel we make turns, spinning around us and the wishbone that glows at the center. I look out at the spokes of the sparklewheel – the limbs and the wings and the fabric all meshed together. All the lives rippling their lights, with more people leaping, building and growing the spinning machine. Crystal. Feather. Blood and bone.

And still it doesn't feel like falling. It feels like a new kind of travel. A new kind of home.